LOUISE BATES

Pauline Gray Investigates

A Pauline Gray Mysteries Omnibus

First published by StarDance Press 2023

Though Canton, NY, is a real place, the people and events taking place in this story are entirely fictional. The author has attempted to be as accurate as possible within the bounds of fiction as regards places and businesses, but the names, characters, and incidents portrayed are works of her own imagination, and any resemblance to actual persons, living or dead, or events, is entirely coincidental.

First edition

ISBN: 979-8-9858009-2-0

This book was professionally typeset on Reedsy.
Find out more at reedsy.com

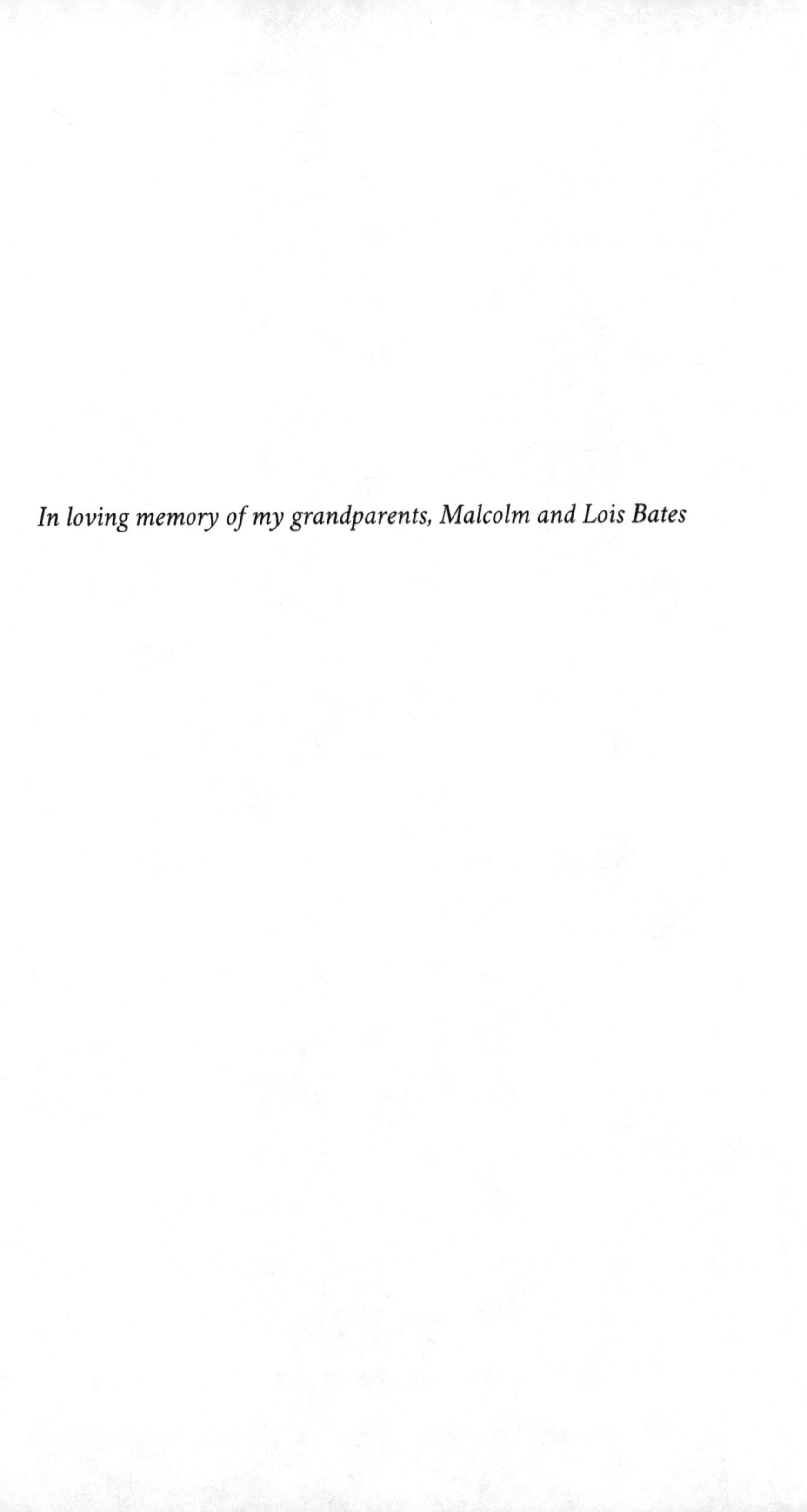

In loving memory of my grandparents, Malcolm and Lois Bates

Contents

III   SECRETS OF THE PAST

I

CANDLES IN THE DARK

*The light shines in the darkness, and the darkness has not
overcome it.*
-John 1:5 (NIV)

A Friend in Need

A patchwork quilt of orange, red, gold, and brown covered the ground in preparation for its winter's nap. Pauline Gray couldn't help but scuffle her boots through the welter of leaves on the sidewalk as though she were a schoolgirl again instead of an independent woman of twenty-eight who had finished delivering her latest interest piece to the new post office. The "crunch-crunch" under her feet brought a smile of pure delight to her usually pensive face, as did the vault of piercingly blue sky above her head. A whiff of smoke from someone burning a leaf pile drifted past her nose, causing it to twitch in enjoyment.

Autumn was the finest time of year in northern New York state, there was no question about that. Even the economic troubles shaking the entire nation in the year 1933 couldn't spoil the charm of an October day in the foothills of the Adirondack mountains.

Pauline buried her hands in the pockets of her plaid wool skirt and paced on, mulling over the opening paragraph of her next novel. She wished she could set in here, in the village of Canton, but she doubted her readers would believe romance and adventure could be found in a small rural town. She herself doubted it. Canton was as placid and peaceful a place as she'd ever known, not a hotbed of excitement. She wouldn't have it any other way.

That aura of calm around the town was the main reason she had stayed here after being graduated from St. Lawrence University and starting her column for the semi-local *Watertown Daily Times*. The town had accepted her as an eccentric spinster and over time began to boast of her as one of their intellectual lights. She kept her other writing career a tightly-bound secret.

Pauline would never dare show her face at the college again if her former professors and classmates discovered she wrote cheap adventure novels on the side.

She wasn't ashamed of them on her own account, or so she told herself. They gave enjoyment to hundreds of people and helped pay her share of the rent and grocery bill. It just wasn't—exactly—what people had expected of the brilliant, fiercely ambitious student when she had graduated from St. Lawrence near the top of her class six years ago. Rather than face their disappointment or scorn, she kept that part of her life private.

The air was so invigorating and the sun so pleasant on her crimson beret that Pauline abandoned her original plan to write for a few hours at the university library and turned her steps toward the park instead. She strolled down the path leading to the fountain in the park's center, dreamily thinking of nothing in particular. Her steps checked when she saw Ruby Ferris sitting on one of the benches bordering the path, her reddened eyes and nose showing signs of recent tears.

For a moment, Pauline considered turning back. She liked Ruby well enough, but she didn't want this glorious day spoiled by anyone's grief.

Then she set her lips and quickened her pace to reach Ruby sooner. Shame! Ruby had enough troubles to make anyone weep: a widow with a young son, her husband killed four years ago in an accident at the nearby grist mill. She never burdened her friends or neighbors with her troubles, quietly persevering and making ends meet. She worked as a cook in one of the local restaurants during the day while her son was in school and took in sewing to do at night.

For her to be seen distraught in public, something must be terribly wrong. Pauline could not be so selfish as to shy away from sharing, and perhaps thereby lightening, her load.

"Good afternoon, Ruby," Pauline said in her clear, cool voice, coming to a stop before the bench. Rather than look down upon the other woman, she sat beside her.

Ruby glanced up, eyes blinking rapidly, unable to meet Pauline's gaze. She had been a pretty woman a few years ago, with long, shining black hair and strong features inherited from her Iroquois grandmother. Sorrow and hard work had dulled the luster in her once-bright brown eyes and had engraved lines across her face. Pauline felt another pang of pity.

"Oh … Pauline," Ruby said. She straightened her back and attempted a smile. "I'm so sorry, I didn't even see you. How are you today?"

She clearly did not want to talk about her troubles. Pauline's distaste for interfering or being interfered with struggled against her compassion, and lost.

"I am well, but you seem unhappy," she said, gentling her voice as she would for a skittish horse or unhappy child. "Is it anything I can help with?"

Ruby's lips trembled, but she shook her head. "I don't want to burden you."

"It isn't a burden if I ask for it," Pauline said, nudging Ruby's arm companionably with her elbow. "Truly, I don't mean to pry, but if you want someone to listen, my ears are at your service."

For a moment, it seemed Ruby would speak. Then, as a couple strolled arm-in-arm past them, with a small child darting around them shrieking with delight, she changed her mind.

"You are very kind, but I'll be fine. I'd best be off. Almost time to pick Jeremy up from school."

She rose to her feet and walked away swiftly, her shoes tap-tapping against the sidewalk in a staccato accompaniment to the nervous clenching and unclenching of her hands.

Pauline frowned after her retreating back, then stood up decisively. Perhaps she was meddling in an unwarranted fashion, but she didn't think so. Folks looked out for each other in small towns. Right now, Ruby needed a shoulder to lean on, even if it wasn't Pauline's.

Leaving the park to the young family, Pauline made her way toward the Town Hall. She mounted the smooth stone steps and slipped through the big front doors just as a wave of town councilors, reporters, and policemen left the building.

The massive stone Town Hall building held much more than records and civil servants. It also was home to the local branch of the *Watertown Daily Times*; a newsstand; a gift shop; and most relevant to Pauline's current needs, the village police.

She was in luck. Her quarry was behind the main rush of policemen finishing their shift, though already wearing a warm coat and wool scarf, hat in hand. Lieutenant James Richardson's warm blue eyes fell on her and crinkled as he smiled.

"Hello, Pauline!" he greeted her with a wave of his hat. "What brings you here?"

"Looking for you," she responded, the relative emptiness of the hallway allowing her to speak freely.

She and James were friends, nothing more, but seeking a man out could ruin a single woman's reputation. Not to mention it would earn James unending teasing from his colleagues.

His eyebrows went up. "Trouble? Or do you need my expert opinion on an article?"

She shook her head and motioned to the door. They stepped back out into the mellow October sunshine.

"Sarah vetted my most recent article," she said, naming the woman with whom she shared an apartment. "I'm here about Ruby."

James stopped. He spun around to look Pauline full in the face. "Ruby Ferris? What do you know about that business?"

Pauline stepped back. That was not the reaction she'd anticipated. "What business? I came to tell you she seemed troubled but wouldn't tell me why. I hoped you could sound her out and perhaps help her with whatever it was."

Everyone knew James and Ruby were seeing each other; the village confidently expected news of their engagement any day. It was a good thing all the way around, everyone agreed. James needed a wife to stop him breaking hearts, and Ruby and her young Jeremy needed a man.

Pauline hated that phrase: "needing a man," as though any man was needed regardless of character or personality, but she agreed that James and Ruby were well-suited to each other, and Jeremy would do well with a kind, honest father.

Now, under James' piercing stare, she flushed, wondering if he thought her too presumptuous. "I wouldn't normally interfere, but Ruby is usually so self-contained, and she seemed so miserable, and I couldn't walk away without doing something to help," she said, tripping over her words.

James' expression softened and he started walking again. "I'm not upset with you, Pauline. I'm thankful Ruby has such caring friends. Unlike some!" His mouth closed with a snap.

Exasperation stirred in Pauline's chest, replacing the uncertainty of but a moment before. "Then do you mind explaining yourself?"

He walked a few paces without saying anything, his hand creeping up to rub his clean-shaven, square chin. Pauline was not a small woman, but she almost had to trot to keep up with his strides. Finally, he spoke.

"Maybe I'm betraying her confidence by telling you this, but I believe you can keep it to yourself. A few weeks ago, Ruby started getting letters. Anonymous letters."

"Oh my," said Pauline. That sounded ominous.

"They stated, in varying forms, that her husband's death was not an accident, but murder. They didn't accuse anyone in particular, but the writer 'thought you ought to know,' or so she said."

"How cruel!" Pauline cried. Hadn't Ruby enough to endure without having that sort of thing thrown at her? "No wonder she's so upset." A thought occurred to her. "You said 'she.' Do you know the writer?"

James shook his head and shrugged. "I'm assuming a woman because anonymous letters usually are," he said. He caught her ironic look. "It's a proven fact," he defended himself.

Pauline sighed. "I suppose so. Are you looking into it for her?"

"Unofficially. It's not a police matter, since the letter writer hasn't threatened her or done anything illegal. I've already checked fingerprints, handwriting, stamps, all that, but so far nothing has given me a clue into her identity. I don't mind telling you I'm about at my wits' end."

Pauline rubbed the bridge of her nose. "It seems so senseless," she said. "Why say something like that? They're not trying to get money out of her, she's a harmless creature so no one would want to injure her specifically … James. You don't think it's true?"

"No!" he said. "Darn it, Pauline. This is the danger of anonymous letters, you see? They start people wondering, and muttering, and the next thing you know, accusations are flying and people get hurt. Don't even think it."

"Sorry," she apologized, but even his impassioned words couldn't stop her from wondering, mainly because she could imagine no other reason for someone to write something of the sort to poor Ruby.

"If it was true, this person would have come to the proper authorities," James said, sounding stuffy. "Anonymous letter writers are only in it for themselves. They get some sort of sick satisfaction out of causing pain to other people." He stopped and cast a glance at her, checking to see if he'd offended her sensibilities. Pauline's calm face reassured him. "My main concern is what this is doing to Ruby's nerves, and what happens if the letter-writer decides to move on to somebody else. If she—or he—isn't satisfied with one victim, we could have an epidemic on our hands. For all we know, it could already be happening. Anyone could be getting letters and be too ashamed to admit it."

"What can I do to help?" Pauline asked.

"You don't want to get involved in this," he protested, but weakly.

"Ruby is my friend, as are you," she said. "You already said the police can't take the case, and you don't know what else to do. You need help, and I am available." She smiled. "People expect me to do odd things anyway. You'd be amazed what a writer can get away with. Come now, James, give me a task or I shall start snooping around on my own, and who knows what sort of a mess I'll make of things then?"

"You don't play fair," he grumbled.

"That's because I'm not playing," she said, smiling sweetly.

He capitulated. "Talk to people. Chat, you know? Don't go asking any obvious questions, just get a feel for things. Oh, and here."

He dug a scrap of paper out of his pocket and handed it over. "This is a handwriting sample. See if you can match it to anyone. Ask them to write you out a recipe or something. But be careful, Pauline!"

"I will," Pauline said, glancing at the paper.

It read: *thot you shud no your husbant dint dye on axident.* Pauline grimaced, feeling as though she had touched something slimy and decaying. She tucked the paper into her bag, resisting the urge to scrub her hand against her skirt. Briefly, she regretted getting involved in this at all. So ugly!

Uglier still to know about it and do nothing.

"I'll let you know once I've found something," she promised James. He smiled wanly. "Once, not if, eh? I like your optimism."

It was spoken more bravely than Pauline felt, but she was determined to succeed, no matter how difficult the task. The sooner this letter-writer was found, the sooner Canton could return to its tranquil existence, the one that soothed her often-turbulent spirit so well.

For all that Pauline preferred an orderly, calm life, she found herself restless and anxious more often than not. It had been especially bad during high school, the normal emotional turmoil of adolescence made worse by inner storms that would sweep across her soul on a frequent basis, leaving her shaken and distressed for days afterward.

The day she arrived on campus to start up life as a student at St. Lawrence University, she felt those storms settle. The great oaks and maples stretching their branches above the green lawns of the college and town, the brick and stone buildings exuding a sense of stability, the people all knowing each other and caring about one another, all combined to make this place a haven. She decided then and there that city life had been responsible for much of her inner turmoil, and the months and years to follow only seemed to confirm that diagnosis.

Her remaining restlessness and anxiety she dispersed through her writing, her novels providing the best outlet for that.

James tipped his hat to her and went on his way toward The Tick-Tock, one of the best restaurants in town, famous for their spaghetti and homemade meatballs and their Lobster Night, when they served lobsters fresh from the Maine coast.

Pauline was tempted to follow him—her cooking was nothing to write home about—but nobly resisted the urge. Even with the supplement from her novels, money was always tight these days, and the rent was due soon.

Dinner of Herbs

Pauline shared an apartment on the outskirts of town with her friend Sarah Jones. A black woman in a mostly-white region, Sarah frequently faced enormous prejudice. Even Pauline, though she hated to remember it, had been hesitant to room with her when Sarah had first answered her advertisement for an apartment-mate.

"Oh," she had said when Sarah entered the front hall. "You're—oh."

"I'm a nurse, yes," Sarah had stated with a glint in her eye. She had removed her cap and cuffs, transforming from a practical nurse to a sweet-faced young woman with a wary twist to a mouth built for laughter. "I work at the hospital in Potsdam, just finished my shift. I hope that doesn't bother you?"

"Oh no," Pauline had stammered, too embarrassed to confess the real source of her shock. "I have no problem with, er, nurses. As long as you don't expect me to listen to your cases over the dinner table," she had surprised herself by adding.

Sarah had thrown back her head and laughed, a free, merry peal that echoed throughout the small apartment. "Fair enough! I think I can live with a newspaper columnist as well, so long as you promise never to put me in one of your columns."

From that unorthodox start, their friendship had grown into something solid and satisfying to both of them. Pauline still came up against her ingrained prejudices at times, but Sarah never hesitated to tell her when she was doing so, and Pauline worked to overcome her assumptions.

For her part, Sarah had days where she raged against "small towns and small minds," but she did her best to not hold Pauline responsible for the faults of others.

Though Sarah had not been to university, she had one of the keenest minds Pauline had ever encountered (another prejudice to overcome: thinking only those within the ivory walls of scholarship knew how to think and reason), and the two enjoyed discussing everything from current events to poetry and even modern art. Sarah was one of the few people in the world Pauline trusted with her novel-writing secret, and her analytical skills had improved many a story and unraveled many a knot in Pauline's plots.

James hadn't given her specific permission to share Ruby's story with Sarah, but Pauline trusted her friend. With any luck, Sarah might have some insight into the problem.

Sarah was already in the kitchen of their second-story apartment by the time Pauline mounted the steps and entered, hanging her hat in the small foyer and walking through to see what her friend was concocting for dinner.

"Tomato soup, I'm afraid," Sarah said, indicating the pot she was stirring. "Pay-day isn't for another few days, and the rent—"

"I know," said Pauline, suppressing a sigh.

She could be eating well at her parents' house, or even—ghastly thought—presiding over a dinner table of her own with a husband and baby, had she followed her mother's wishes and returned to Albany after finishing her degree.

Yes, and be a miserable knotted mass of frustrated ambition and suppressed interests. What did the Scriptures say?

"Better a dinner of herbs with a friend than the fatted calf with hatred therein," she said aloud. "Or something like that."

Sarah turned from the stove, her brow wrinkling. "Isn't the fatted calf from the Prodigal Son story?"

Pauline waved such minor details away. "The idea is the same."

She moved to the counter and opened the breadbox. "One slice or two?" she asked about the Wonder bread therein.

Sarah requested one, and turned off the flame under the soup as Pauline got out plates and bowls and buttered the bread.

Over their simple meal, Pauline told Sarah of her encounter with Ruby, followed by James' shocking revelation. Sarah sniffed.

"Anonymous letters! I've experienced a few of those in my time. Cowards, that's all the people who write those are, somebody who had nothing better to do than spew hate at others but doesn't have the courage to do it publicly."

"Why would anyone send you an anonymous letter?" Pauline exclaimed. She couldn't imagine her friend living anything but a blameless life.

Sarah raised her eyebrows. "People who don't like the color of my skin or the fact that they have to see me, or that I work in a job that involves me interacting with the likes of them."

Pauline flushed, ashamed both of the naivety of her question and the blind prejudice of people who shared her own skin color.

"My advice to Ruby would be to ignore the letters," Sarah concluded.

"These are different, though," Pauline said, staring into her bowl of soup. "These are aimed at uncovering a secret, not saying nasty things about Ruby."

"You think there's something to them," Sarah said, watching her with a knowing eye.

Pauline raised a hand and tilted it back and forth. "James said I ought not to entertain the notion, but—well. Either way, we need to find out who's behind it. Where would be the best place to find out if a woman has been scheming or acting strangely lately?"

"Ladies Aid," Sarah said promptly. "Missionary Circle. Choir practice. Sunday School. Sewing Circle."

"Enough!" Pauline said, catching her breath on a laugh. "Why are you so much more knowledgeable about gossip than I?"

"Because you are too busy writing or researching most of the time to pay attention to such things," Sarah said with a smile. "And when you are looking out for gossip, it's for your newspaper column and you can ask people directly. You don't have a sneaky mind."

Pauline wasn't sure whether this was criticism or praise. She dismissed it to focus on Sarah's suggestions.

"I am not a member of any of those groups," she said, tapping the edge of the bowl with her spoon. "By the time I join and people are familiar enough with me to talk freely, weeks or months could have passed. I need something more immediate."

Sarah reached across the small round table and gripped Pauline's wrist to stop her tapping. Pauline started, unaware she had been doing so.

"The Episcopal Ladies Sewing Circle meets tomorrow, doesn't it? All you have to do is telephone Mrs. Hansen this evening and tell her you'd like to attend. She might think it odd, but nobody would raise an eyebrow at it. At most, they'd feel smug that at last you are starting to see the value in their groups and gatherings."

Pauline narrowed her eyes. "The Sewing Circle, really? After how they treated you?"

She had agreed to go once last year, when Sarah wanted to join but didn't feel comfortable attending on her own. Though nobody had demanded outright Sarah leave, the cold shoulders, the snubs, the whispering behind hands, had left Pauline in a rage, vowing never to attend another meeting so long as she lived.

Sarah had taken the rejection more philosophically, finding other societal outcasts and forming a private Sewing Club with them instead.

Sarah's smile turned mischievous. "Think of it this way. With your sewing abilities, it'll probably be more punishment for them to have you there than not. They'll be so focused on your mangled seams that they won't even notice if your questions are odd!"

Pauline couldn't help but laugh. It was undeniable that while Sarah could transform an old dress into a completely new garment overnight, Pauline could not so much as stitch a smooth buttonhole.

"I do appreciate domestic skills," she said ruefully. "I just can't seem to cultivate any of them."

"It's decided, then," Sarah said. She looked down at the rim of orange circling the inside of her empty bowl. "Perhaps you can tuck some snacks into your bag to bring home, as well."

Sewing and Gossip

Sarah had the early shift at the hospital next day, so she was out of the apartment by the time Pauline was up and about. Though Pauline longed to be one of those people who rose blithely with the sun each day, without the impetus of an early class or an outside job to propel her, she rarely managed to crack her eyes open before eight o'clock.

After eating a spartan breakfast of a boiled egg, one slice of toast, and the much-needed cup of coffee to accompany it, Pauline did her share of tidying: she washed the few dishes left from the morning meal, ran the carpet sweeper over the floors, and dusted the furniture and bookshelves. These chores out of the way, she sat down at her typewriter to get in some editing before leaving for the Sewing Circle.

It was no good. She couldn't concentrate on the perils and triumphs of her dashing heroine Emma, who in this chapter was supposed to be trekking through the desert in search of her kidnapped niece and nephew, and instead kept getting herself mired in a swamp of grammatical errors and plot holes.

Rather than focusing on the task at hand, Pauline found herself staring out the window into the branches of the flaming maple tree growing close by their building and pondering the mysterious anonymous letters.

She could accept James' dictum that there were people out there in the world who would send anonymous letters for the thrill of it. She could even accept that there were such people in this village, distasteful as the notion was. She relied on Canton to be kinder and gentler than Albany or any large city, but she knew there were hate-filled and loathsome people here as well as there. She couldn't imagine any of her neighbors, friends, or acquaintances doing such a thing, but everyone had a private life, secrets they wouldn't share with anyone.

Look at her! She held her novel-writing tightly to her chest. Surely others had joys and sorrows they refused to reveal as well.

Much as she hated to think there was somebody—someone she might know, might even see today at the Sewing Circle—who took pleasure in bringing misery to Ruby, she still couldn't understand why they would use Bob's death. There had to be more recent rumors one could concoct. Was it that Bob's death was the cruelest thing they could think of? But sending her nasty notes about Jeremy, or her relationship with James, or … well, Pauline could think of a hundred small, spiteful things one could say if one truly wanted nothing more than to spread vitriol.

Granted, not every person had her imagination, but even so. Pauline leaned back as best she could in her upright wooden chair, eyes still absently fixed on a stout grey squirrel rummaging for seeds in the maple tree, and tried to remember what she could about Bob's death.

Four years ago, Pauline had been two years out of college, struggling to make ends meet. She hadn't secured her job as a newspaper columnist then, getting by with the occasional feature or "domestic" article. Her novel writing had begun around then, stirred on by desperation and the feeling that "anyone can write this kind of trash."

She had met Bob and Ruby at the big Episcopal church they all attended, but she hadn't known either of them well when he died. The details of his accident were hazy. All she could remember for certain was that he had fallen into the Grasse River from the third-story window of the grist mill, hit his head on a submerged rock, and drowned before help could arrive.

Tragic—and Mr. Wharton, the mill owner, had been chastised for not having proper safety railings and window bars in place to prevent such things—but there had been no hint of foul play. Bob was a courteous, well-spoken, gentle man; Pauline couldn't imagine anyone wanting to kill him.

Unless—suppose he had known something dreadful about somebody, so that person killed him to keep it a secret. Or maybe there was a man who had always been in love with Ruby, and he killed Bob out of jealousy. Or maybe it was a childhood squabble that had festered for years, leading a person to kill out of sheer hatred. Or—

Pauline snorted softly and got to her feet. She had been reading too many of her own works. People might kill for those sorts of reasons in lurid adventure novels, but not in sensible, everyday life.

She checked her appearance in the mirror over the mantel to make sure her dark hair was smooth and tidy in its low bun before putting on her jacket and hat to walk to the church. The Sewing Circle met in one of the basement rooms to avoid putting undue strain on anyone's hospitality. In these economically challenged times, it was a bit much to ask someone to host twelve to twenty women in her home once a month, eating up her food and dirtying her furniture and floors.

This way, a few different ladies could each bring food to share with the group and others could help sweep and tidy after they finished, and nobody had to bear the brunt of the cost and effort alone. It did mean for a less homey atmosphere, but alas, times changed and people changed with them.

The basement of the stone church was chilly as always, and Pauline shivered inside her plain brown broadcloth suit. She wished she could have worn her thick, hand-knitted sweater from Aunt Mildred, but for an occasion such as this, looking proper was more important than warmth. There was only so much she could get away with as an eccentric young writer.

She would have to wait until she was an eccentric *elderly* writer for the rest of it.

Turning a corner after the last flight of uncarpeted stairs, she entered the large, well-lit room filled with ladies and sewing material of all types and descriptions. Pauline's heart sank as a perfumed and powdered Lucy Westin rushed up to her, gushing about her latest "piece" in the *Times* and pressing a frilly white baby dress on her—

"So sweet, you know, so dainty and delicate for some neglected little love."

Here Miss Westin stopped and sighed, her blue eyes rounded and mournful.

Pauline smiled politely. "Actually, I'd prefer something with plain stitching," she said.

She caught the flash of malice in Miss Westin's face, a sense of satisfaction as Mrs. Hansen hustled Pauline away and handed her a plain woolen blanket to be hemmed. Why?

Understanding came a moment later. Miss Westin had wanted to point out Pauline's inadequacy with a needle, and felt she had succeeded by making Pauline admit fancy stitchery was beyond her. That it hadn't bothered Pauline in the slightest did not matter in the least to her.

Such pettiness! Pauline nodded in genuine gratitude to Mrs. Hansen and settled in between two stout matrons, senses alert to the first chance to turn the tide of gossip toward anonymous letters, Ruby Ferris, or mysterious deaths.

At first, the chat was solely about who was seeing whom, who was about to give birth, and whose husbands had recently lost their jobs. Pauline was nearly ready to scream with frustration before at last one woman commented,

"Such a pity about Ellis Crawford. Only forty years old, and dead of pneumonia. Doesn't seem right."

They all sighed in agreement. Pauline let the conversation linger on Ellis, his family, and their prospects now before casually inserting a comment of her own.

"We don't get too many deaths of that sort—I mean, men of that age—around here, thankfully. Why I think the last one was ..." She pretended to think about it. "Bob Ferris, wasn't it?"

That sparked a lively debate as to how many people had died in between Bob and Ellis, before Pauline was able to speak again.

"Of course, they aren't exactly alike. Poor Mr. Crawford died of illness, while Bob's death was sudden and shocking. Some might even call it mysterious."

Mrs. Hansen sniffed. "Nothing mysterious about that. Mr. Wharton was not keeping the mill in good condition, and Bob paid the price." A pinched look settled on her plump face. "It seems Mr. Wharton is getting his comeuppance now, though. Have you heard that the mill might close? Not enough work to keep them in business."

Exclamations arose around the room. It seemed none of the ladies had heard that particular rumor.

"That's horrible," said one of the matrons beside Pauline. "What will his workers do?"

"Same as everyone else who has been laid off in the last few years—the best they can," said Mrs. Hansen.

"I am sorry for them, but not for Andrew Wharton," said another woman. "He's been a mean, tight-fisted boss form the beginning. It serves him right to go under now."

Pauline made a mental note. Andrew Wharton was unlikely to be the letter-writer, but could he have been a murderer? What if he and Bob had gotten into a fight? Perhaps he'd threatened to cut Bob's wages, or even talked about letting him go, and Bob had lost his temper (for even the gentlest of men might turn ugly at such a prospect) and swung at him. Wharton had defended himself and knocked Bob out the window. A passer-by could have seen it and ...

But here Pauline's imagination failed her. Why this hypothetical person would not have reported it to the police was beyond her. Could somebody have seen Wharton from the road below, anyway?

Or wait! Maybe it was another worker who witnessed it from inside the mill, and he was afraid of losing his own job if he ratted on the boss, so he kept quiet. Only now he was in danger of losing his job because of the mill closure, so he had nothing left to lose. He felt too guilty to tell the police after all this time, so he wrote to Ruby in hopes that the police would investigate the case and discover the truth without him having to be involved.

A neat case. Pauline was proud of it. She determined to present it to James at the first opportunity.

The circle broke for coffee and snacks, Pauline smiling as she remembered Sarah's charge to bring some home. She'd do her best, but only if she could sneak them into her bag without anyone noticing.

This was not that moment, as Lucy Westin oozed up to her.

"What made you say that about Bob's death being mysterious, Miss Gray?" she asked.

Pauline assumed a careless air. "Oh, I don't know. I suppose it's my newspaper training, always looking for a story. Nobody saw him fall, did they?"

Miss Westin's eyes rounded. "Do you think he was *pushed*? Or that he jumped, like those bankers we read about in the city papers?"

Pauline felt a frisson of alarm. She hadn't meant to start this sort of speculation!

"Goodness, when you say it like that it does sound nonsensical," she laughed. "Of course Bob wouldn't jump. Nor can I imagine anyone wanting to push him. I'm not sure what sort of mystery I was imagining, but now we're talking about it, I realize it had to have been an accident."

Miss Westin looked unusually thoughtful. "I don't know, I'm sure. There were those who said he regretted marrying Ruby. His older sister Iris kept house for him before he and Ruby married, and stayed with them a few months after until she moved out to the boarding house. She and Ruby hated each other. They fought constantly, until Bob was fed up with the both of them and paid Iris's board at Mrs. Johnson's just to keep them apart."

"A man doesn't kill himself over his wife and sister squabbling, especially years later," Pauline said.

She made another mental note all the same. Could Iris be the one writing to Ruby, one final way of hurting the sister-in-law she loathed? Perhaps she, in some twisted way, blamed Ruby for Bob's death and wanted to make her suffer for it.

Another theory to bring to James's attention, though it was ugly enough she almost wished she hadn't thought of it. Thinking about that sort of malice made her stomach twist and her muscles clench.

"I suppose not," Miss Westin said. "Not that you or I have any experience in such matters!" Her laugh rang shrilly in Pauline's ears.

It was common knowledge that Lucy Westin hated her single status as much as Pauline enjoyed hers. Pauline pitied her, but she couldn't like her. It had nothing to do with Miss Westin's desperation for a husband and everything to do with her insincerity. You never could trust her; she said sweet things to your face but always with a hidden sting in them.

Pauline almost wished they could pin the letters on her, but she doubted even Miss Westin would go that far to spread a nasty rumor. She preferred face-to-face gossip.

"Certainly Iris Ferris has gotten all the more sour since her brother's death. There really seems to be only one person who didn't regret his passing," Miss Westin mused now.

Pauline sharpened her ears. "Oh?"

She knew better than to trust Miss Westin, but however false her claim, it might give Pauline a clue in the right direction.

"Oh well, I shouldn't gossip about such things. Only everyone knows that John Kitteredge has been in love with Ruby Ferris since they were in grade school together."

"Yet he and Ruby aren't together now," Pauline pointed out.

Lucy Westin shrugged. "I suppose James Richardson got there first." She raised her eyebrows.

To respond with the insistence that she and James were only friends would fuel the fire of Miss Westin's insinuations. "James and Ruby are so well suited to each other," Pauline said cheerfully instead.

Miss Westin sighed and moved on to other victims, leaving Pauline inclined to dismiss her words, but holding John Kitteredge in reserve in case there should be a shred of truth in them.

She resolved to find out if he really had been in love with Ruby and if he was the kind of man to kill out of passion.

She loudly praised the quality of the homemade goodies to Mrs. Hansen, saying how much she wished she could bake half so well as all the ladies there. As she had hoped, this spurred an instant offer of recipes, all to be written as soon as the ladies returned home and delivered at the next Sewing Circle. It didn't give Pauline handwriting samples for comparison right now, but it was a promising start.

The group resumed their sewing after that, and the meeting ended without any more revelations. Pauline felt it had not been a waste, especially as Mrs. Hansen took her aside afterward and pressed a platter of cookies and muffins on her.

"To take back and share with Miss Jones," she said. "I, er, do wish she could join us on these occasions."

A nicely ambiguous statement, conveying as much the impression that Sarah couldn't come because of her work schedule as because of society's prejudices. Pauline would have preferred an outright apology for the treatment Sarah received, but at least Mrs. Hansen was making an effort.

Leaving the church building with plate in hand, Pauline sifted through everything she had heard, forming two columns in her mind to write out as soon as she got home. One column was labeled "murderer," and in it were Andrew Wharton and John Kitteredge.

The other column was "letter-writer," and consisted of Iris Ferris and an unknown mill worker.

Mulling things over, Pauline didn't notice the man approaching until he nearly ran her over. They both stopped, startled by the near-collision.

"Oh!" Pauline straightened her hat. "I'm so sorry, I didn't even see you coming."

"My fault," he said. The man in question was short and burly, with well-muscled arms and broad shoulders, brown hair and eyes, and a well-defined chin. He looked vaguely familiar, but Pauline couldn't quite place him. "Did I hurt you?"

"Not at all," she assured him. She gave up her attempt to recognize him and asked outright, "Do I know you? I'm so sorry, I'm terrible at remembering faces."

He managed a smile, which lightened his face considerably. She hadn't realized how dour he looked until that smile briefly lit his features.

"Dan Harwood. We've seen each other a few places, but I don't think we've ever been introduced. I know who you are, though: you're P. Gray, the woman newspaper writer."

Pauline admitted her identity. Then she placed Mr. Harwood.

No wonder she hadn't recognized him: the last time she'd seen him was at Bob Ferris's funeral four years previously. Perhaps he would have a clue as to what had happened that day at the mill!

She was racking her brains trying to figure out a subtle way to ask him when he spoke again.

"Are you working on a story right now? Is that what distracted you?"

"I—yes," she said on the impulse of the moment. "I'm thinking of a piece on local businesses. I want to write something about the grist mill. You work there, don't you, Mr. Harwood? I don't suppose you could give me a quote?"

It was a pathetic way to introduce the topic of Bob's death, but it was the best she could do spur of the moment.

His face darkened. "The mill! Not much point in including that in your piece, unless you want to talk about businesses that shut down and put all their employees out of work after years and years of faithful service."

"Oh dear," said Pauline inadequately. Clearly the rumor about the mill closing wasn't unsubstantiated gossip. No wonder Mr. Harwood was so upset he nearly ran her down. "I'm so sorry."

He made a visible effort to calm down. "Not your fault. Sorry, Miss Gray." He attempted another smile, this one less successful than the first. "Have a nice day. Good luck on your story."

He stepped around her, leaving Pauline to make her way back to the apartment without any other untoward encounters. She dropped off the snacks with a note stating: *Mrs. H's attempt at an apology to you,* and turned right around and left again, wishing she still had her old bicycle.

Walking all over the village kept her in good trim, no doubt, but it was wearing on shoe leather.

Murder!

auline chose to come the back way into town rather than walking past the churches and the park, and the allure of the Canton Free Library. Many a day had she come out of browsing through the library stacks to blink in the bright sunshine and take her book (or books) to sit under a tree in the park and finish reading. No such joys today, alas.

She came out onto Main Street higher up than that dangerous turn to the library, heading once more for the Town Hall. James Richardson intercepted her before she arrived.

"Pauline! What are you doing?"

Pauline had never seen James look so distressed. His usually crisply curling hair was untidy and mussed beneath his uniform cap; his eyes were restless and his face shadowed.

"Coming to see you," she said, surprised both by his appearance and his tone. "I have some theories about those letters."

He exhaled loudly. "Too late."

"What?" Indignation rose in Pauline's breast. Had she wasted an entire morning at the Sewing Circle for nothing? "You caught the culprit?"

James's face turned grim. "Someone did."

Pauline's stomach lurched, though she hardly knew why. "What?" she said again.

James took her arm and led her closer to the buildings lining the street so pedestrians could get past them. He lowered his voice. "Do you know Jemima Root?"

Pauline frowned in concentration. The name didn't bring a face to mind. "Possibly, but if so, not well."

"It doesn't matter. She's one of the old maids who proliferate all small villages. Too nosy for her own good, a little spiteful, probably bitter about never getting married."

Despite the situation, Pauline leveled him with a gimlet stare. "*Really*, James."

"Sorry. I shouldn't say things like that about her now, God knows."

"You mean …?"

"She was murdered this morning."

The words were blunt, unforgiving. Pauline rested her hand on the warm brick of the shop front as the world spun around her. A familiar cloud of stomach-clenching black nausea rose in her stomach.

"I found some unfinished letters when I examined the scene," James went on, his voice harsh and guttural. "They were addressed to Ruby, same handwriting and everything. She's—she was—the letter writer. And either she wrote a letter to someone who took it very badly, or what she wrote was the truth and Bob's murderer finished her off as well."

Pauline had a hold of herself now, forcing the anxiety into a box in the back of her mind until she could write her way through it later.

Murder was an ugly thing, but she was a scholar, and she would not let emotions get in the way of facing facts.

"In that case, I have a few suspects for you," she said.

"No," James said.

Pauline blinked her dark brown eyes at him a few times. "I beg your pardon?"

"This is beyond a Poison Pen. This is murder, Pauline. It's far too dangerous for you to be mixed up in. I with I'd never told you about the letters in the first place!"

"What if I had evidence in the case? Would you tell me to run along home and not trouble over it because it might be dangerous?"

"This isn't evidence. It's speculation."

Outrage swelled in Pauline. She rose to her full height, as opposed to the scholarly slouch she normally adopted, a side-effect of too much time spent hunched over a desk. "You don't want to hear my suspects and deductions? Even if my 'speculation' could help you catch the murderer? Even if all I do is tell you my observations and then walk away?"

James shook his head. "I know you, Pauline. You can't walk away from your own curiosity. You'd tell me, and when I expressed doubt you'd be determined to prove yourself, so you'd keep digging and ferreting around, and the next thing you know I'd have your dead body on my hands as well."

There were several fallacies in that statement, from the assumption that he would disbelieve her to the idea that the murderer would find her even if she was on the wrong trail, but Pauline wouldn't pick apart his logic now.

"What makes you think I'll be any more docile if you refuse to listen to me at all? Aren't I far more likely to dig around and get into trouble to prove myself right if you won't listen to me?"

James groaned. "A curse on all strong-minded women!" he said, looking up at the cloudless sky. He lowered his gaze to Pauline's stubborn face. "Very well. But not here, and not now."

"Do you want me to come make a statement?" she asked tartly.

He didn't appear amused. "I'll stop by this evening after I get off duty and listen to your theories then. If you promise me that will be an end to it!"

"I can't promise I won't keep thinking about it," she said. "But theoretical speculation only. I won't go around looking for trouble, I promise."

She wanted to see justice done, but she wasn't a trained investigator, and as much as she loathed James's over-protective and outdated attitude toward women, he had a point. She was not physically equipped to physically confront a murderer—not, she added to herself, because she was a woman, but because she lived far too sedentary a lifestyle. Sitting and thinking was much more her style.

"I'll take what I can get," he said grimly. "See you this evening."

Left alone on the busy street, Pauline strove to order her thoughts.

Murder—in Canton. This was no long-past "perhaps" as with Bob's death, or far-off violence one read about in the papers. This was real, and present, and the fact that she could not picture the dead woman's face made it all the more horrible. She ought to have known her. They were neighbors. She ought to be able to mourn her.

Ahead of her, Sarah exited Newberry's with a small woven bag over one arm, dressed in a pretty flowered frock now her nursing shift was done. Glad for the distraction, Pauline called her name and hurried forward to join her.

"We needed more soap, and ..." the other woman's voice trailed off as she took in Pauline's face. "Good heavens. What happened?"

In a low voice, Pauline told her the news. Sarah's lips tightened.

"I see," she said.

"James is coming over this evening so we can talk through my list of suspects and theories," Pauline said.

"Good," said Sarah, setting a faster pace back toward the apartment on Pleasant Street. "Because this isn't fun anymore. Murder isn't a game, after all."

Interference—or Not?

James stretched out his long legs before the fireplace, swirling his tumbler of whiskey thoughtfully. He seemed to take up twice as much space in their small living room than he really did, simply by virtue of being a man. Neither Sarah nor Pauline was in the habit of bringing young men home.

James seemed comfortable enough there, slouched in the best armchair, staring into the flickering red and gold flames. Pauline was curled up on the hearthrug, with Sarah occupying the other armchair.

Pauline also had whiskey; Sarah didn't care for the taste and therefore nursed a glass of orange juice.

"I shouldn't be indulging, you know," James said at last, taking another sip. "Not as a law enforcement officer."

"I'm not selling it or buying it," Pauline said, her voice a tad prim. "I inherited it from my grandfather. And you're not here as a police officer, you're here as a friend."

"True," James conceded. He sat up a little straighter with a grin. "Still, best to destroy the evidence, eh?" He swallowed the last of what was in his glass and set it down on the side table with a clink. "Let's hear what you have to say about the Root case."

Pauline tore her mind away from Prohibition. She wasn't a hard drinker by any stretch of the imagination, but from her mother's father she had learned to appreciate fine wines and other liquors. Word was that President Roosevelt was going to overturn Prohibition as early as this winter. The sooner the better, said Pauline. Grandfather's stock was dwindling, and she was tired of having to hide her enjoyment of the occasional glass from her more respectable neighbors.

Without looking at James for fear of seeing derision at her deductions and suppositions, she laid out for him the reasons for her two suspects in the case of Bob's death. She finished up by saying she had at first wondered if Iris Ferris was the Poison Pen, writing to Ruby out of empty spite, but that theory was shattered in light of Jemima Root's authorship.

A brief silence hung over the room as she finished. Sarah stood up and switched on a few more lamps to dispel the gloom. In the homey yellow light spilling from beneath their fringed shades, James stirred himself to speak.

"I'd be drummed out of the force if I suggested we investigate Andrew Wharton. He's one of the richest men in St. Lawrence County! Not that that means much, compared with New York City," he added in a bitter aside, the lament common to every rural dweller forced to live in the shadow of that shining metropolis. "And John Kitteredge … it's weak, Pauline. He never made any move to pursue Ruby after Bob's death, and he's certainly never shown any enmity toward me."

"Perhaps he was horrified by what he did to Bob and couldn't follow through on it," Sarah suggested in her soft voice.

James shook his head. "In my experience—well, this is my first murder, but from what I've learned in training and from older officers, if a man works himself up to commit murder, he's not going to shy away from taking advantage of it afterward."

Pauline leaned forward, locking her arms around her updrawn knees. "But what if it was an impulse of the moment? Giving way to the overpowering emotion of jealousy, only to be horror-stricken the moment it's done? He might not even have meant it as murder—if Bob hadn't hit his head he might well have survived that fall."

James laughed. "What a description! You should be writing novels, not just newspaper features."

She was glad the fire made an excuse for her cheeks to grow hot.

"So you really think Kitteredge did it?"

"I don't know," she said frankly. "I think Wharton is more likely, but when I really stop and think about it, it seems ridiculous that it could have been anything but an accident. It seems ridiculous that Jemima Root could have been murdered, too, yet here we are."

"It is hard to picture a murderer in our little community," James agreed. "The chief is of the opinion the letters were the result of her being a repressed spinster—I know it's awful, Pauline, you needn't snort at me like that—rather than truth, and he's looking for other recipients, one of whom might have killed her for her insinuations. He wouldn't consider Bob's death as a possible murder."

"Shouldn't the police want to look at every possibility, as well as every suspect?" Sarah asked. "Instead of avoiding Andrew Wharton, avoiding the possibility of two murders, avoiding anything too unpleasant that isn't right under your nose and demanding attention?"

"It's not entirely the chief's fault," James said. "He wants to solve it quickly, before the city newspapers get a hold of it and the state police decide we can't handle it ourselves. If I brought him hard evidence, he'd investigate even Andrew Wharton. He does have a point: it is far more likely Miss Root sent out letters to many people and someone attacked her for it. The only reason I'm pursuing the possibility of Bob being murdered and Miss Root's death covering it up is because I am the lowest man on this case. Everyone else is investigating the more plausible lines; this out-there notion is all that's left for me. Besides, if someone *did* kill Bob, I owe it to Ruby to find out."

The firelight flickering over the amber whiskey left in the bottom of her tumbler started a new train of thought for Pauline. She unwound her arms from around her knees and sat up straighter. "What if it wasn't personal?"

"What do you mean?"

"We're assuming someone killed Bob because of who he was, but what if he was simply in the wrong place at the wrong time? What if he saw or heard something he wasn't supposed to?"

James groaned. "Then it could be anyone who did it!"

"No, because it would still have to be someone who had access to the third floor of the mill," Pauline said. "And I wasn't thinking in vague terms. James, are there any smugglers in Canton?"

She'd startled him. He froze in his chair, eyes wide.

"James?"

He relaxed again. "Sorry. I—you took me aback. Before Miss Root's murder, our biggest focus in the forces across the county has been on clearing out a smugglers' ring that's been operating in this area for the last five years or so. We know they're based in the Thousand Islands. The whiskey they bring across the St. Lawrence River from Canada goes to New York City, but there's a transfer station in one of the small towns hereabouts, we don't know which one. It's one of the reasons the chief wants this murder solved quickly, so we can get back to the smuggling problem."

"I hardly think smuggling is more important than a murderer," said Pauline.

"Not more important, no, but you have to understand, we're part of a joint operation between village police departments and the state troopers, and it's been going on for a long time. The chief feels we'd be letting down all the other people involved if we dropped out for a more localized issue."

"But what if they are connected?" Sarah asked. "Pauline, you think Bob might have seen a smuggler in action and been killed to prevent him talking to the police?"

"Not likely—they don't tend toward violence—but more plausible than Wharton," said James. "If one of Bob's fellow workers was a smuggler on the side, and Bob saw or heard something some night along the banks of the St. Lawrence or coming into town … yes, I could see a man panicking and killing him to keep that from coming to light. Most folk around here look the other way when it comes to smuggling, but Bob was an upstanding citizen. He might not have been willing to let it be."

Or perhaps, Pauline speculated, Bob didn't care, but the smuggler offered him a bribe to keep quiet, and Bob was so furious at the implied stain on his honor that he swore he would go to the police that very day, and so the man had to kill him.

But who would it be? Who amidst the mill employees might be smuggling on the side? Pauline didn't know of anyone in town whose style of living was higher than his income allowed.

Sarah tapped her fingers against the arm of her chair. "The other person I think we should keep in mind is Iris Ferris. We now know she wasn't the Poison Pen, but how angry was she at her brother for marrying Ruby and robbing her of her position and home? What if she pushed him?"

"She didn't work at the mill," Pauline objected.

"Besides, she loved Bob," James said. "It was Ruby she hated. And it's not as though they kicked her out or left her penniless. She was no longer Bob's chief confidante and housekeeper, but they would have let her keep living with them. It was her own choice to move to the boarding house and take a job."

Pauline and Sarah's eyes met above James's head. No man could ever truly understand the thwarted fury of a woman who had her entire value taken away in one fell swoop by another woman. Who would want to live on charity in the house where she had once ruled?

No, if it weren't for the fact that Iris would have no reason to be at the mill when Bob was killed, Pauline would consider her a likely subject.

"She might have brought him lunch or something," Sarah persisted.

Pauline snapped her fingers. "That's it! Then he could have thoughtlessly told her that Ruby had already packed him one, and she, consumed by jealousy and bitterness, pushed him with all her strength, not intending death but helpless to stop it once he fell out the open window and landed on that rock. In a moment of weakness she confessed her crime to Jemima Root, who became determined to see justice done and so wrote to Ruby. When Iris found out she had to kill again, not out of anger this time, but for her own safety."

James's laughter broke the hush that filled the room after Pauline finished. "I'll say it again, you ought to be writing for the talkies! You could call it, oh, I don't know, *The Perils of Pauline*?" He winked.

"Ha ha," Pauline said flatly.

Sarah hurried to speak. "You bring up a good point we haven't considered yet. How *did* Miss Root find out about Bob's murder? Where did she get her information?"

James stood up and stretched, his fair hair nearly brushing the ceiling. "I'll look into our suspects as discreetly as possible and try to find out if Miss Root was anywhere near the mill that day to see something incriminating or if, as Pauline so colorfully speculated, someone confessed to her and then regretted it afterward. I'll also look into any possible links between the mill and the smuggling ring. Pauline, Miss Jones, if your speculations lead to any other theories, I'm happy to hear them. But remember your promise, Pauline—no active investigating!"

Pauline rose to her feet as well, brushing down her skirt as she stood. "I remember," she said.

She preferred the emotional distance provided by treating this as an intellectual exercise, which immediately led her to suspect her own motives in agreeing so promptly. Was it fair to isolate herself so from the matter? And how much further could she pursue her investigation without talking to people?

Did casual chit-chat, such as this morning at the Sewing Circle, count as "active investigation?" She should have made James clarify, but he had already put on his hat and coat and bid them goodnight.

Pauline closed the door on the frosty, starlit night, and returned to her seat by the fire.

Sarah picked up the skirt she'd been hemming before James's arrival and said, "You know, you are a newspaper writer. What was that line you fed Mr. Harwood this morning?"

"You mean about me working on a story about local businesses?"

Sarah nodded. "You could always arrange an interview with Mr. Wharton about the mill; maybe even talk to some of the other employees. You could even put an angle on it about the need to support local businesses so they stay open and continue to provide jobs for our towns."

Pauline was tempted. "I promised James I wouldn't interfere."

"If you keep yourself strictly to newspaper questions, I hardly see that as interfering," Sarah said, a demure smile playing about her mouth. "Your speculations as a result of those questions is entirely your own affair."

It felt like splitting hairs. On the other hand, that was exactly the sort of story the *Times* appreciated from her, and the promotion of a local business, especially one that employed so many people in the county, was a good thing in this troubled time.

If James catechized her for it later, she could truthfully tell him it was a legitimate story inspired by their investigation, not an excuse.

Her conscience was still mildly troubled, but she decided she was being squeamish and selfish, and silenced it.

"Do you suppose it is too late to call Mr. Wharton and ask for an interview tomorrow at the mill?" she asked.

Sarah's smile turned vulpine. "Not at all."

The Mill

At precisely 10:00 the next morning, Pauline presented herself at the front entrance to the Wharton Grist Mill. Rather than spend her entire morning walking the six miles from Canton to the mill, Pauline had borrowed a bicycle from a St. Lawrence University student, telling herself once again she really needed to buy a new one for herself with her next royalty check

She had given away the rusty, rickety old thing she had used while a student herself as soon as she'd signed her first book contract. She'd felt it beneath her dignity to get around on such an ancient contraption. With a few more years under her belt now, she wished she had not been so eagerly imprudent.

Still, Jean-Paul wouldn't have passed his freshman English classes without her tutoring last year, so he owed her a favor. Loaning her his bicycle for the day hardly put a dent in that, especially as he'd painted it bright red, making it (and its rider) dreadfully conspicuous.

Pauline had enjoyed the ride, the sharp air making her cheeks tingle and filling her lungs with life, the pageant of the trees on either side of the road dazzling her eyes every time she looked, the sound of Canada geese honking overhead as they flew south striking an adventurous chord in her soul. As she drew closer to the mill, she could see and hear the Grasse River burbling placidly away on her left. Some of the dark emotions that had been troubling her ever since learning about the anonymous letters eased out under the influence of that ride.

Pauline's family occasionally wrote asking when she was going to tire of her "rusticating lifestyle" and return to "real life" in Albany. *Never*, she told them. Days like this only confirmed her resolve. Whatever troubles might plague this town, it was still the place where she felt the most at home.

Dan Harwood met her at the entrance to the mill and told her Mr. Wharton was awaiting her in his office. Following him through the old stone building, weaving her careful way around the various pulleys, wooden shafts, stones, and sacks, coughing a little at all the dust in the air, glancing at the blank, empty faces of the workers, shivering at a chill in the air that had nothing to do with the actual temperature of the place, Pauline searched for something polite to say to Mr. Harwood.

He saved her the difficulty. "Miss Gray, would you—do you mind—could you not say anything to Mr. Wharton about seeing me yesterday?"

"Certainly," Pauline began in surprise.

He hurried into further explanation, eyes glancing around the building as he spoke. "I was supposed to be picking up supplies at the train station, you see, but Mr. Wharton had just announced about the mill shutting down and I was upset, and I had to walk around town to cool off enough to return to work. Mr. Wharton, he wouldn't understand, and if he fires me for shirking tasks I'll be out of a job that much sooner, and have that much of a harder time finding some other work."

A pang of pity smote Pauline's heart. How awful to feel so trapped and desperate for even a few more days of work. She didn't know much about Dan, but she knew there was an old Mrs. Harwood and at least three younger siblings.

What kind of a world were they living in, where a hard-working, honest man couldn't even be guaranteed the opportunity to feed his mother and younger siblings? She felt almost ashamed of her own relative ease. She was not wealthy, but her two writing jobs brought in enough income for her to never fear losing her home. Even if Sarah married or moved on, Pauline would simply have to move to a smaller and less comfortable apartment; she wouldn't have to sleep on the streets. She might not eat caviar and *fois gras*, but she had three meals a day, filling if not fancy.

Pauline's voice was often called brusque by people who did not care for her, so she consciously modulated it to a gentler tone to respond. "Of course, Mr. Harwood. I won't tell a soul. I see nothing wrong in needing to clear one's head after such distressing news, and if Mr. Wharton does, he shan't hear about it from me."

The tension in those broad shoulders eased slightly. "Thank you, Miss Gray."

By now, they had arrived at the small inner office belonging to Mr. Wharton. Dan knocked, and that smooth tenor Pauline had heard over the telephone last night rang out.

"What is it?"

"Miss Gray from the *Times*, Mr. Wharton," Dan called back.

The door opened and there he stood, the mill owner himself in all his sleekly polished glory. Pauline couldn't help but compare his aura of well-being and comfort to the dull hopelessness of his employees.

"Ah, Miss Gray!" he boomed, taking both her hands in his. Another count against him—had she been a male reporter, he would have shaken her hand. "So pleased you could come. Thank you Harwood, that will be all," he added in an abrupt aside.

Dan ducked his head, mumbled something, and left them. Mr. Wharton drew Pauline into his bright, well-lit office, closing the door behind her.

"I apologize for that. Harwood needs someone on him at all times or he's useless. My regular foreman is not in today. Harwood is filling in for him, but he's rough around the edges." He flashed a smile. "This is all off the record, of course."

"Of course," Pauline said, burying her dislike of him under a layer of professionalism.

He seated himself behind his massive oak desk, so tidy on its surface Pauline suspected it was never actually used, and waved her to a chair opposite. Pauline drew her skirts around her, sat down, and pulled her notepad and pencil out of her handbag.

"Tell me, Mr. Wharton, how long has this grist mill been operating?"

The interview was underway.

Pauline was surprised to hear the mill was not a family business; Mr. Wharton had bought it from its previous owner twenty years ago and had striven to increase its output and efficiency after that owner had let it fall into disrepair. It was a larger operation than many small-town mills, one reason why its closure was so devastating to the town.

She had to grudgingly admit he was not perhaps as bad as she wanted him to be when he spoke of all the modern improvements he had brought in, how he had wired it for electricity a few years ago and the efforts he had made to improve working conditions and pay rate.

"It was a risk, but it would have paid off were it not for that wretched stock market crash and everything that's followed," he said, dropping his air of bonhomie and showing her a glimpse of the shrewd businessman underneath. "It would have better for everyone—the employees, the town, the customers …"

"And yourself?" Pauline suggested sweetly.

He laughed and leaned back in his chair, toying with a fountain pen. "Naturally! I am a businessman, not a philanthropist." He sighed, looking around the bookshelves living the office walls and the one small window showing the rushing waters of the Grasse outside. "And now it will all go away."

"Is there any way the mill can be saved?" Pauline asked. Despite his practiced patter, her sympathy was still more for the employees than their boss.

He shook his balding head. "We went through a bad patch a few years ago where things were touch and go. I don't need to tell you how hard it is to keep a thriving business in rural areas in this day and age, I'm sure."

"No," she agreed. "That's one of the reasons I'm doing this feature, in hopes of bringing attention to the plight of rural towns and small businesses." The phrase rolled glibly off her tongue due to having practiced it on her way over. She'd thought it might come in handy.

"I had to lay off about a third of my workers and cut back on operations, but we survived and I dared to hope we were through the worst of it. I had even started thinking of re-hiring some of my old employees. Now, though …" He shook his head. "If there's a way out, I can't see it."

Pauline frowned and closed her notepad. This was not something she could put in the article, but her insatiable curiosity prompted her to ask,

"What about a business partner? Or give your employees a share in the business, make them more invested in it?" She motioned vaguely in the direction of the door. "Your foreman, perhaps, or Mr. Harwood?"

"Not a bad thought, Miss Gray. You clearly have some experience in these matters. Learned from your father, perhaps?" He raised his eyebrows, but she did not respond to the invitation. Her family was no one's business.

After a moment, he continued. "Unfortunately, workers like Harwood never make good bosses. They can't see beyond their immediate needs. As for my foreman … well, Kitteredge is a decent fellow, but he doesn't have the passion for this place I'd need in a partner. If Bob Ferris hadn't died, now, he would have made a good partner. I had originally planned on making him my foreman when the old one retired, in fact, but then there was that ghastly accident. Harwood was the only employee with the seniority, and Kitteredge the only one with the abilities. I gave him the position and Harwood a raise, but neither of them have proved much use."

He rubbed his face with a pink silk handkerchief. "What a time that was! The accident happened the same month I was having to shrink the staff and cut back on our operations. I had people accusing me of criminal negligence, former employees threatening to burn my house, people talking of boycotting the mill, a potential investigation by the state police, everything." He gave her a weary smile, tucking the hanky back into his pocket. "Seems a mite unfair to have weathered all that only to lose it now, doesn't it?"

Pauline had no time for pity. He had given her the perfect opportunity to talk about Bob. "Oh yes, then," she said, nodding. "I, of course, mostly remember how wretched it was for Ruby Ferris and their young son."

Perhaps it was unfair of her to assume the solemn expression that immediately covered his face was false.

"Ah yes," he said. "Such a tragedy, for a young wife to lose her husband and a boy his father." He sighed gustily. "Your readers might be interested to know that I too was raised without a father, Miss Gray. Yet look how I succeeded! Young Ferris may very well thrive as I have, driven by a sorrowful childhood to make something good of his adult life."

This mill wasn't such a success, the nasty part of Pauline's mind said, but she restrained herself. She would not be petty! She couldn't help but ask, however,

"And what will you do when the mill shuts down, Mr. Wharton? I'm sure my readers will want to know."

"Ah." He blotted his face with the handkerchief again. "I could, of course, retire. I have enough put away safely to be able to live comfortably the rest of my days. But ..." Did he actually look embarrassed? "I don't know that I would ever feel right with my conscience, living well while my former employees were all struggling. I can't go into any details, my dear, but I can tell you I am looking into the possibility of opening a new business in the county, one which would hopefully give work to all the mill workers and more. I may lose the shirt off my back, but by gum, what a challenge!"

He jutted his head forward, showing her in a flash the real man who lived and breathed business under the surface geniality.

Pauline still couldn't like him, not least for that patronizing "my dear," but she was developing a reluctant respect for him.

"Perhaps in time you could take on and train Jeremy Ferris," she suggested.

His eyes brightened. "Now there's an idea! I'd like to do something for the lad and his mother. She wouldn't take any money from me at the time, you know. It wasn't charity, I wanted to show my respect and regret for Ferris, but I had to admire her stance." He paused. "It wasn't guilt, either. I accepted the fine because the mill was my responsibility, but that window was *safe*. I'd swear it."

"How do you think Bob fell, then?" she asked.

He shrugged. "A question I've asked myself many a time. If you ever get an answer, I'd like to hear it."

There it was—as close to proof that Bob was murdered as they were going to get. Pauline was no closer to finding the murderer, though she was inclined to write Mr. Wharton off after this conversation, but at least she was now certain they weren't chasing a will o'the wisp.

Wharton stood up. "And now, would you like a tour of the mill, Miss Gray?"

She agreed, thinking it would both be good in the article and might give her a hint as to how someone might have pushed Bob out the window without anyone else noticing, save mysteriously for Jemima Root.

She didn't understand much of the terms Wharton used as he extolled the superiority of their rollers versus conventional millstones, the ingenious way their elevator system worked, and the "middlings purifiers" that separated the dust, bran, middlings, and flour from each other, but she nodded and took notes while surreptitiously scanning the interior of the building.

Beneath the main floor was the old water turbine that had provided the energy for the mill until Wharton converted it to electricity. With all the grain elevators, pulley systems, and machines around, Pauline saw how easily a man could fall—or be pushed—from a third-floor window into the river without anyone noticing until too late. The dust floating in the air made it hard to make out details even on the floor she was on, much less the others.

"And this will interest you, Miss Gray," Wharton boomed, motioning to a stack of filled flour sacks waiting to be delivered. "We get our sacks specially printed with this pattern so that women can make frocks from it that look as fresh and pretty as anything in a big-city department store! I had thought of having a write-in competition, where people sent us designs and we chose our favorite to print on our next run, but … alas. It doesn't seem likely there will be need to purchase any more. After the batch we have in stock is used up, we will be done."

Pauline found the large red poppies with vivid green leaves against a stark white background a little garish for her taste, but she made an admiring noise and jotted down a note. That was the sort of detail her female readers would appreciate.

"It's very bright," she said in what she hoped was an admiring voice, running her hand over one of the sacks that was set a little apart from the others.

Her fingers came away damp and sticky. She frowned, but before she could say anything about it to Wharton, he had moved on to something else. Pauline wiped her hand on her handkerchief and shrugged the incident off.

The tour ended, Wharton personally escorted her out the front door.

"Thank you for your time, Mr. Wharton," Pauline said.

"My dear, it was a pleasure! I look forward to reading your little piece in the *Times*. Who knows, perhaps it will attract investors when I embark on my new venture."

Tamping down irritation—her "little piece" indeed—Pauline shook his hand and walked the short distance to where she'd left Jean-Paul's bicycle leaning against the stone wall lining the riverbank. As she rounded the corner, she was surprised to see an older woman standing next to it.

Pauline quickened her pace, wondering if there was a problem.

"Excuse me!" she called, just as the woman lifted her head and looked toward her.

"You there!" the woman called.

Pauline stopped. It took her a moment to recognize Iris Ferris in the gaunt, lined face of the lady before her. She had aged nearly twenty years in the four since her brother's passing.

"Oh," said Pauline, picking her way carefully down the leaf-strewn slope. "Hello, Miss Ferris."

Iris blinked a few times before recognition dawned on her own face. "Pauline Gray, the newspaper woman," she said, putting a wealth of scorn into her words.

Taken aback, Pauline forgot to be cautious and skidded forward on the slippery dead leaves, barely catching herself on a slim birch growing near the water's edge.

Iris laughed. "You want to be careful you don't bring about another accident here," she sneered. "Bash your head on the wall, or tumble right over it into the river. Can you swim, Miss Gray?"

Pauline regained her breath and her composure. She wondered if Miss Ferris was quite sane.

"As a matter of face, I can," she said.

She took the bicycle's handlebars and wheeled it toward the road. Iris trailed after her.

"Is that contraption yours?" she snapped.

Pauline considered her answer. Technically it wasn't, but she was the one responsible for it at the moment. "Yes," she said.

"It's a hazard," Iris said. "If someone were to injure themselves on account of it, you would be responsible, not the mill."

"What sort of injury could it cause, against the wall as it was?" Pauline inquired, eyebrows raised.

"Never mind," snapped Iris. "Bad things happen around this mill. You don't need to add to it."

Skepticism crept into Pauline's voice. "Bad things? You mean a curse?"

Iris's faded blue eyes flashed. "You can laugh, but you don't know! You weren't here the day my brother—when he—I was here! I know!"

Pauline had been wondering how quickly she could get away. Now she stopped.

"You were here the day your brother died?"

Iris's gaze slid away. "I was out for a walk," she mumbled. "No law against walking. I like the river."

Pauline steeled herself to rest a hand on Iris's arm in an appearance of sympathy. "Did you see your brother?" she asked, once again gentling her voice. "That must have been terrible."

"No—no!" the other woman cried, shaking free. "I saw nothing, but I felt it. I felt the evil here. There is a curse about this place! Jemima

Root, she could have told you."

"What?" Despite herself, Pauline's voice rose sharply.

Iris nodded, seeming satisfied to have gotten a reaction at last. "You've heard about her death, then? I told you there was a curse. She was here that day, too. I didn't see her, but she saw him. She saw my brother fall! And now look what's happened to her."

"Jemima Root was killed by a human, not a curse," Pauline said. In a distant part of her mind, she noted her hands were shaking. This was the first proof they had to connect Miss Root to Bob's death.

Of course, if Iris Ferris was the murderer, Pauline was in terrible danger right now.

Iris stepped closer. "You think you're so smart, Miss Newspaper Writer, looking down at the rest of us, wheeling around on your ridiculous bicycle without a care in the world. You're no better than I! You're just another spinster. One day you too will look around and realize you're all alone, with nobody to care if you live or die. You, me, Jemima … we're all the same."

Pauline stepped backward. Were the stone walls too thick for anyone inside if she screamed? Would it do her any good to mention that people knew she was here?

"I'm afraid I really must be going now," she said inanely. "Goodbye, Miss Ferris."

With that, she hurled herself onto the bicycle with more force than elegance and pedaled away for dear life. She glanced back just once.

Iris Ferris was still standing beside the road, staring after her with a look of intense hatred on her face.

Fear and Madness

Still shaken by her encounter with Iris Ferris, Pauline couldn't face the idea of going back to an empty apartment for a lonely lunch. Pedaling into Canton, she stopped at the Sugar Bowl Restaurant to indulge in coffee and a bowl of soup. To her surprise, she met James at the counter.

"I think we should raise Iris Ferris to the top of our suspect list," she said without preamble.

"What? Why?"

"I was at the mill this morning—" she began.

His face turned an alarming shade of red. "Pauline, you promised!"

She steered him to a booth to sit before he choked. "I went out there to interview Mr. Wharton for the paper, that's all," she said, a touch more defiantly than she intended. "All this talk about the mill closing and people being out of work made me realize that attention needs to be drawn to our local businesses, to support and promote them. Since the grist mill was so prominent in my mind, I pursued that one first." She made a point of glancing around the bustling restaurant interior. "I'm thinking of making this my next article."

James raised an eyebrow. "Really."

Pauline folded her hands and rested them on the table top. "Yes."

"And the reason you told me this in such detail is …?"

"I don't want you to misjudge me," she said primly.

"If your conscience was absolutely clear on the matter, you wouldn't care what I or anyone else thought," he said.

She refused to let herself blush. "At any rate, I didn't bring up Bob, but Mr. Wharton did, and I don't think was the one behind the death."

"Does he have an alibi?"

"Not that I could ascertain," Pauline said. "I didn't want to ask outright."

"Thank goodness for that," James said.

He broke off to accept his coffee and wrapped sandwich from Suzy, the petite red-headed waitress.

"Your soup will be right out, honey," Suzy told Pauline while setting a mug in front of her.

"Soup and coffee? It's not that cold," James commented.

Pauline shivered. "You wouldn't say that if you'd seen Iris Ferris."

At his urging, she told him the entire story. By the end, he still seemed skeptical.

"So she's crazy. It's well known that spinsters …" He faltered at Pauline's steely glare, and coughed. "It doesn't prove anything. It doesn't even absolutely prove that Jemima Root's death is connected with Bob's."

"But Miss Ferris said Miss Root saw Bob die!"

"She also said the mill was cursed and your bicycle was going to kill someone," he said dryly.

He had a point.

"I agree that *if* Jemima Root saw something that could identify Bob's murderer, that person had a good reason to silence her. But why now, instead of four years ago? And why would she be quiet all this time and only now start writing to Ruby?"

"Guilt," Pauline suggested. "If it was Miss Ferris, then Miss Root wouldn't want to turn her in because they were friends. But she couldn't keep quiet forever, her conscience kept nagging at her, and she had to write to Ruby about it. Then she felt guilty about betraying her friend, confessed to Miss Ferris, and Miss Ferris killed her." She leaned back. "And if you tell me I should be writing dramatic fiction, I shall throw this cup of coffee at your head."

He laughed. "Sorry. I suppose that sort of comment is galling to a serious writer like yourself, isn't it?"

Ouch. That one stung.

"You make it sound plausible, but the most reasonable explanation is still that some tramp broke into Miss Root's house to look for food and money, lost his head and killed her before escaping, and is probably heading for Canada right now. The letters are most likely coincidence." He shrugged. "That's the chief's theory, and he's probably right. There's a reason he's the chief and I'm a lowly lieutenant."

"For all you talk about me sounding like a blood-and-thunder writer, I know one thing," Pauline snapped. "I don't believe in coincidences except as convenient plot devices!"

He smiled good-humoredly at her, drained his coffee, tucked his still-wrapped sandwich into his coat pocket, and left her to her cooling soup and temper.

Silly to get so irritated by his comment. She *was* a serious writer, after all. Not the novels, nor even the features. Oh, but she had dreams. More than dreams, she had plans!

Once she had enough savings built up in her bank account, she could take a break from her adventure novels and start serious research into a biography. Or a history. Or—well, she hadn't quite settled on the topic yet. She didn't have anything close to a thesis in place. But she knew it was there, the real work, waiting for her.

The newspaper column and novels were merely a way of getting by. Everyone had to start somewhere. They were good practice for when she was ready to get down to her real work.

A mocking voice in the back of her mind told her these were all very fine excuses, but who was she arguing against, James or herself?

Pauline finished her meal and left the restaurant in a distinctly sour mood. The laughing, chattering, bright-eyed college students filling the building and spilling over onto the sidewalk didn't help improve it. Soon enough, she thought darkly as she wound her way through the crowd, soon enough they'd be graduated and facing real life, and then they'd know.

What, exactly, they'd know, she couldn't say, but it would be something along the lines of how life never worked out the way you expected it to, and all those other cliches she had thought so foolish when she was eighteen.

She tripped and almost fell flat on her face when she reached the sidewalk and saw Jean-Paul's bicycle. Both its tires had been slashed, and somebody had dumped a bucket of black paint over the seat and frame, leaving the bucket dangling defiantly from the handlebars. It had to have been recently done—as she recovered and approached it to prod gingerly at the mess, her finger came away coated in wet black paint.

How was she going to explain this to Jean-Paul, was her first thought. How someone had done this in the middle of town without anyone noticing was her second. Her third, most chilling, was: someone wanted to scare her.

James's warnings to her came back in full force. They made more sense now.

"I told you the mill was cursed."

Pauline looked over sharply. Iris Ferris stood beside her, eyes glinting in satisfaction as she looked at the ruin of Jean-Paul's bicycle.

Fear vanished in a burst of sickening anger.

"You—you did this!" Pauline cried.

Miss Ferris did not deny it. "And if I did, what more do you think I might do to you?" she said, her voice soft and slippery.

Pauline's anger ebbed, leaving behind nausea and a terror that precluded rational thought. Iris Ferris was mad—unquestionably so—she had most likely murdered two people and had destroyed Jean-Paul's bicycle in the middle of town during the busiest part of the day. What was to stop her from trying to hurt or even kill Pauline herself?

As if in answer to her thoughts, the wind picked up, pushing clouds over the face of the sun to darken the day. Dry leaves whirled around Pauline's feet, rustling past and catching at her stockings with their rough edges. The crowds on Main had vanished, everyone inside a building where it was warm and light and safe. Across the street a lone black dog tied in front of the drugstore howled for its master.

Pauline took one, two, three steps back from the bicycle and the madwoman beside it. Where was James when she needed him?

Iris Ferris laughed.

Pauline's nerve broke, and she ran.

Had she kept her head even a little, she could have gone around the corner and run the back way to the little apartment on Pleasant Street. Instead, she found herself crossing the road, narrowly missing being run over by a large green car driven by a portly man who shook his fist out the window and shouted something about "fool women" after her.

Past the library, so often a place of sanctuary but not a haven today, not when Iris Ferris could follow her in there. Past the houses lining the street and the side roads that would lead to secluded areas where anything—absolutely anything—could happen.

Pauline did not look behind her. She didn't want to know if Iris Ferris was following. She didn't want to know if her fears had any base in reality. She wasn't running away from Iris, not really. She was running away from the ugliness of the attack on the bicycle, from the violence that had erupted into her peaceful world, from her own horror and terror.

Of their own accord, her feet turned onto the long drive leading into the heart of St. Lawrence University. Under the overarching boughs of the trees lining the drive, with students and professors crossing the leaf-covered lawns, arms full of books and papers, chatting about their classes and interests, her heart slowed to a normal beat, and her feet slowed likewise.

When all other havens were lost, this one remained.

Pauline felt thoroughly ashamed of her panic. How could she have lost her self-control like that? She, who prided herself on her rationality, who shied away from strong emotions as messy and vaguely distasteful, to throw her poise and her calm detachment out the window without even a good reason.

Yes, it was horrid to have Jean-Paul's bicycle vandalized like that. Yes, Iris Ferris had shown alarming behavior. Yes, news of a murderer loose in Canton had people on edge. It was no excuse for giving way like that.

Pauline found her steps had led her to Gunnison Chapel, the Gothic-styled limestone building that served as the center of worship for St. Lawrence students. She hadn't spent much time there as a student, but it was familiar enough.

She slipped through the heavy front doors into the empty nave. Sitting in a back pew, she tilted her head back to look up at the vaulted ceiling, buttressed by old ships' timbers from Maine.

Pauline wasn't much for organized religion. She attended the Episcopal Church regularly, but she found the emotionalism of devout worship uncomfortable. All the same, she released the last of her fears and tension in a long breath as the quiet peace of the place seeped into her spirit.

Glancing down at her ungloved hands, she frowned at the black paint still marring her right forefinger. She pulled out her handkerchief to scrub at the stain and became aware of a strong odor of spirits filling the air.

Pauline sniffed, looking around. There was nothing in the building to cause that odor, not even communion wine. She looked at the handkerchief and brought it closer to her nose.

Ugh. No question but that was it.

Why should her handkerchief smell like a distillery?

Mind flashing back to the morning, Pauline remembered brushing her hand against something wet and sticky on a flour sack, and using her handkerchief to wipe it off. The bag must have been soaked in alcohol. The flour inside would be ruined—

Her brain caught up with a jerk. Flour? No! It was alcohol that must have been inside that bag, bottles of Canadian whiskey smuggled across the river and hidden inside an innocuous, brightly-patterned sack to be sent on to New York City. One bottle must have broken and its contents leaked through.

Entirely by accident, Pauline had stumbled upon the smuggling ring at the mill.

But who was behind it? Andrew Wharton, the owner? Mr. Kitteredge, the foreman? Surely not Dan Harwood, or he wouldn't be so distressed over the potential loss of his job. Or—would he? With the mill closing, the smugglers would have to find a new way to hide their illicit goods for transport.

Or was it someone else entirely?

And where did Bob Ferris and his sister fit into all this?

It was with a calmed heart but a head full of new questions that Pauline rose and at last left the chapel. As she walked down the path leading off campus back toward town, the bells in the copper tower rang out their 5:00 peal.

It was time to go home.

The journey back to Pleasant Street seemed longer than usual.

Pauline was tired and wrung-out after her emotional experience earlier. Her thoughts dwelled longingly on home, a cozy fire in the living room, conversation with Sarah, a simple meal.

Therefore it was with an unpleasant shock jolting through her body that she saw Iris Ferris waiting for her on her very doorstep.

"Miss Gray," the woman said. There was no trace of madness about her now. "I need to speak with you."

Pauline glanced up. Shining through the curtains of the second-story window was lamplight. Sarah was home. Even if Miss Ferris wanted to harm her, she could not prevail against the two of them.

"In that case," Pauline said, "you'd better come in."

The Plot Thickens

Iris Ferris's first words, once inside and ensconced in the armchair James had sat in the previous night, were unexpected. "I wish to apologize for my behavior this morning, and again this afternoon. I realized after you left so precipitously that I must have given the impression I meant you ill. I assure you, I had nothing to do with the damage to your bicycle, and I am sorry for the … wild manner in which I spoke. I was not entirely myself."

Pauline's suspicions deepened. Was this a woman trying to cover her tracks? Who else could have damaged the bicycle, if not Miss Ferris? Who else knew Pauline was riding it?

Sarah interrupted. "Miss Ferris, please don't think me rude if I ask when the last time was you ate."

The older woman hesitated. "Why—last night, I suppose. Sometime yesterday, at any rate."

"That will never do! No wonder you say you were not yourself. Wait right here. Pauline, I insist, no more questions or conversations until Miss Ferris has some food in her."

"No, really, I often skip meals," Iris protested, but to no avail.

"All the more reason to eat now," Sarah overrode her. "That is an unhealthy habit, if you will allow me to be blunt."

Miss Ferris sank back into her chair, and Pauline shrugged, offered a small smile, and built the fire while Sarah whisked out to the kitchen.

Pauline ought to have gone with her—she didn't want to make Sarah wait on her guest—but neither did she feel comfortable leaving Miss Ferris alone.

"Chicken broth and a slice of white bread for now. Nothing too heavy until we see how this sits on the stomach," Sarah said, coming back in a few minutes with a tray holding a bowl of steaming bouillon, a plate with buttered bread, and a tall glass of milk.

She set it on the small table beside the armchair and stood over Iris Ferris until the woman had consumed at least half of everything on the tray. Then, and only then, did Sarah agree to sit down and allow the conversation to proceed.

"I found out about Jemima Root this morning when I met the milkman on the front steps of Mrs. Griffith's," naming the owner of the boarding house where she lived. "I was shaken."

"Did you know her well?" Pauline asked, cautiously sympathetic.

Miss Ferris drank the last of her milk before answering. She set the glass down and stared into the flames flickering in the fireplace. "Jemima Root was the closest thing I have to a friend in this town," she said. "She had gotten odd these last few years, but so have I. We were schoolgirls together, she a few years ahead of I, but we were still close. We both dreamed of going past grade school, but our families couldn't afford university for either of us and felt high school was a waste of time. No man wanted to marry either of us: we were too sharp-tongued, too independent, not pretty enough. So we grew into spinsterhood together, cheated of our dreams and our families' hopes alike."

Pauline couldn't hold back a flinch. Were it not for her grandfather's emotional and financial support of her education before his death, she could be well on her way to a similar fate.

"When I heard she was dead—not only dead, but murdered, it shook me. I couldn't face going back in to breakfast with Mrs. Griffith's prying questions and the nosiness of my fellow boarders." Miss Ferris's lip curled in disgust.

"I went for a walk and found myself at my sister-in-law's house—what used to be mine."

Despite herself, Pauline leaned forward, her whole being caught up in the story. She tried to hold back, reminding herself that Iris Ferris was still her strongest suspect for the murder, but she couldn't help but believe the older woman's tale as it unfolded. If it was fiction, it was woven better than anything Pauline could write.

"The older I get the harder it is to hold onto hate," Miss Ferris said. "With the loss of my only friend, I wanted to reconcile with what family I had left." Her face worked against some strong emotion.

Without a word, Sarah rose and took the bowl back into the kitchen for more broth. Returning, she set it before Miss Ferris and settled back into her chair, nodding for the other to continue.

"Ruby wouldn't have anything to do with me. I knew she disliked me, but I'd never thought her spiteful! She wouldn't even unlock the door. Told me to go away through the keyhole."

"Ah," said Pauline, wondering how much to reveal.

"I left and kept walking, eventually finding myself at the mill—that wretched place which took my brother's life. Jemima saw him fall, though she would never tell me more about it than that, saying it was too distressing. Her death brought back the memories of his, on top of Ruby shutting me out of her and Jeremy's lives, and then I saw you—" She drew in a long, shaken breath.

"I think I understand," Pauline said.

But Miss Ferris wasn't finished.

"I don't remember much about my walk back to town, except that I saw your bicycle with its tires ruined and the black paint, and somehow it seemed to me a fitting punishment for … something." She raised a thin hand and let it fall again. "I don't know now why

I felt you deserved punishment, but I did. I didn't wreck your cycle, though, Miss Gray, and I'm only sorry I didn't see who did."

Sarah let out a brief exclamation. "Your bicycle? Pauline, what happened?"

Pauline explained, her mind working furiously. Miss Ferris's tale made sense. If it was true, she was neither the murderer nor the one who ruined Jean-Paul's bicycle—which, she reminded herself, she needed to fetch and have fixed before giving it back to him. Pauline had already ruled out Andrew Wharton.

That left John Kitteredge or an unknown mill worker and smuggler for the suspect list.

Before she could rule Miss Ferris out entirely, she would make one more test.

"Did you know that Jemima Root had been writing to your sister-in-law to say that Bob was murdered?"

Iris Ferris dropped her soup bowl onto the floor, where it shattered into a thousand pieces, leaving shards of white porcelain in a pool of golden broth. Face white as paper, she slumped to one side in the chair, eyes fluttering back in her head.

Pauline sprang to her feet with no idea of what to do next.

"Really, Pauline!" Sarah exclaimed, a wealth of exasperation in her voice.

"Did I kill her?" Pauline asked, barely restraining herself from wringing her hands.

"Nonsense," Sarah said. "She's fainted. You clean up the mess, I'll bring her to."

Pauline meekly retreated to the kitchen for rags and the brush and dustpan.

Within a short time, Sarah had restored Iris to consciousness and Pauline had cleaned up the broken bowl and spilled soup. Following directions, Pauline made a cup of tea heavily laced with sugar and brought it for Miss Ferris to sip. Only once some color had come back to her cheeks did Sarah allow Pauline to apologize.

"I am so sorry, Miss Ferris," she said quietly, shame for having suspected her of murder as well as for the shock she had given her weighing her words down. "I should never have said that."

"Is it true? Jemima believed my brother was murdered?"

Pauline rubbed her thumb nervously against the side of her forefinger. What to say?

"Tell her," Sarah said, holding Miss Ferris's wrist to check her pulse. "She'll only fret more unless you do."

"The letters were anonymous, but the police discovered that she was the author after—after her death."

"Why wouldn't she tell me? She must have seen it happen! Why haven't the police arrested anyone for his death? Is that why Ruby wouldn't let me in?"

"You believe her?" Sarah asked.

Miss Ferris seemed fully restored to life now. She waved an impatient hand. "Of course, Miss Jones. Jemima Root was not given to fancies. She was there that day. She must have seen it and been too afraid to tell anyone. Perhaps the killer threatened her."

That hadn't occurred to Pauline.

"But eventually she must have been no longer able to keep silent, so she did the only thing she could think of." She hit her open palm with her other fist. "Oh, if only she had come to me about it! She might still be alive."

"Or you could be dead, too," Sarah said cynically.

She must no longer have been worried about her patient's condition for that sort of comment to slip out.

Miss Ferris raised her chin haughtily. "I only wish the murderer had come for me, Miss Jones. I would have made him wish he'd never been born."

Pauline could well believe it.

"I think Ruby kept the door locked on you out of fear," she said now, turning the subject. "Lieutenant Richardson knows about the entire matter, and I believe he warned Ruby against letting anyone into the house until the murderer has been caught."

Miss Ferris sniffed. "Even her sister-in-law?"

There was an awkward silence.

"Ah. I see. I have been a suspect as well. Against my own brother? And my closest friend? No, no, I understand. Embittered by his marriage, I killed my brother, and of course a woman like me couldn't have a true friend." She broke into a rusty laugh. "No wonder you ran away from me earlier! Tell me, Miss Gray, am I still a suspect?"

Iris Ferris rose to her feet, her eyes flashing. Pauline stood as well. Though Miss Ferris was taller, Pauline carried herself with a natural dignity that bore up well against the other's height and indignation.

"I cannot speak for the police, Miss Ferris, but for myself, I no longer suspect you of any wrongdoing whatsoever."

"Neither do I," Sarah added.

Miss Ferris's shoulders slumped a little. "Thank you," she said. She sighed a little. "And to think I simply came here to assure you I had no idea how your bicycle was vandalized."

"I still don't understand how a thing like that could happen in the middle of the day on Main Street," Sarah said, shaking her head.

"Quick enough work to stab tires with a penknife and overturn a bucket of paint before walking on," Pauline said. "I just want to know why. It isn't as though I've learned anything helpful. No one should feel the need to threaten me."

"Perhaps you saw or heard something that seems irrelevant to you, but to the murderer it seems of great importance," Sarah said. She frowned. "Oh, that's all muddled up. You know what I mean."

"Yes, I think I do," Pauline said. She thought again of the whiskey-saturated flour sack. Had someone noticed her drying her hand after touching it? Was the bicycle a warning to leave well enough alone?

She would tell Sarah about the incident after Miss Ferris left. Even with her new trust in Bob's sister's innocence, she wasn't ready to share everything yet.

"You could always ask John Kitteredge if he saw anything," Miss Ferris said. "I noticed him standing nearby as I came up to the restaurant."

John Kitteredge? But he hadn't even been at the mill that morning. He couldn't have seen anything to raise his suspicions, even if he was a smuggler or (possibly and) a murderer.

Pauline pushed her hair back from her face. "I can't think about it anymore," she said, her voice trembling with exhaustion. "It's been a long day."

"And I am taking up too much of your evening," Miss Ferris said at once. "I'll leave you two now. Keep me informed about any progress with the case."

The light in her eyes showed it was a demand rather than a request.

It wasn't until after Pauline was in bed and drifting off to sleep that the most obvious question of all came to her:

Why had Jemima Root been at the mill the day of Bob's death?

Pursuing the Leads

"You're up early." Sarah glanced up from the morning paper as Pauline stumbled into their tiny mint-green kitchen, heading straight for the coffee tin.

"Dreams," Pauline said briefly.

She plugged in the stainless steel percolator and spooned in the coffee. While she waited for it to brew, she stared out the small window above the sink, mind playing back over the dreams of running in the dark, chased by faceless men and women, people who both needed her help and meant her harm.

It had not been a restful night.

"Are you going to tell Lieutenant Richardson about the whiskey today?" Sarah asked, rising from the table to rinse her sticky oatmeal bowl. Pauline had told her about the flour sack incident and shown her the handkerchief after Miss Ferris left the previous evening, and Sarah had agreed it was their best clue yet.

Pauline sighed. She took a bowl of her own down from the cupboard and spooned oatmeal from the pot into it. Sitting down, she swirled maple syrup into the bowl, tracking the swirls and loops the amber liquid made over the oats. "I haven't decided."

Sarah turned from the sink, hands on her hips. "Haven't decided? What is there to decide?"

"The police seem more interested in stopping this smuggling ring than they do in solving the murders," Pauline said. "James is the only one who really cares. All the rest look at Miss Root as nothing but a lonely old spinster given to writing crazed anonymous letters, most likely murdered by a passing tramp, not much of a loss to anyone. If I tell James about the whiskey, it will take his attention away from the murders as well, leaving no one who will care enough to get to the heart of the matter."

"But if the smugglers are the ones who committed the murders, telling the police will solve both cases at once. Besides, it's your duty. Who are you to decide what information the police should have and which they shouldn't?"

Pauline pushed the oatmeal away, stomach twisting. She got up and poured herself a cup of the now-bubbling coffee, hoping that would settle her enough to be able to eat her breakfast. "What's the good of having a brain and a conscience if I don't use them? Deciding what information the police need and what will only get in the way is part of the responsibility I took on when I involved myself in this matter."

"That sounds dangerously close to arrogance," Sarah said bluntly.

"Anything else seems like cowardice to me," Pauline responded.

"Is it cowardice to recognize that someone vandalized your bicycle as an attempt to frighten you? That alone should tell you these people are dangerous. Even if it they don't have anything to do with the murders, you need to turn them in for the community's sake."

"And if turning them in means the case is closed on Jemima Root and never even opened for Bob Ferris? Is my own safety really worth that?"

Sarah shook her head. "I have to run or I'll be late to work. Think about it some more, please? You're not God; it's not up to you to make all things right. Sometimes you have to humble yourself enough to know you can't see everything, and to accept your limitations."

Her words rang in Pauline's ears even after she left.

Was she being arrogant in her hesitation? Was she taking too much authority onto her shoulders? It did seem as though deciding what information to share and what to withhold was a foolish action.

And yet … she couldn't shake the thought that blindly handing everything over to James without sifting through it first was the act of someone who wanted the thrill of the chase without the burden of responsibility.

Though her stomach was still in knots, she forced herself to eat her breakfast so that it would not go to waste. As she scrubbed out the oatmeal pot afterward, she made her decision.

She would tell James—but she would gather more information herself first.

The first step would be recovering Jean-Paul's bicycle and finding John Kitteredge to ask if he saw anything. If he was the guilty party, Pauline could be putting herself in danger, but she couldn't see any way around it.

Whether it was arrogance or not, she couldn't walk away from this now.

She finished the dishes and left to go back into town to fetch Jean-Paul's bicycle from its spot in front of the Sugar Bowl. There, she found a older police officer looking at the bicycle and writing down some notes.

"Oh!" Pauline said, coming to a halt. "Good morning."

"Is this your machine, miss?" the officer said, looking over at her with an expression that strove for severity.

"No—yes—that is, I was using it when this happened, but it doesn't belong to me. I borrowed it from a friend."

"Ah," said the officer, making a note. "Then you were aware of this occurrence and yet you didn't report it or take care of it?" When Pauline hesitated, unsure of the best way to answer, he continued.

"Leaving a bicycle in this condition out in the street like this makes the entire town look bad, miss. It's a violation of propriety, that's what it is. It's an offense to people's eyes. It's—"

"I was going to report it today," Pauline interrupted, feeling a pang at this statement. She *would* have … probably. Once she was certain it was her duty. And once she was certain it wouldn't make James order her off the case entirely. "I was too upset by it yesterday, when it happened."

A fatuous smile appeared on the officer's face. "Ah. Ladies' sensibilities. I understand, miss."

Pauline wanted to smack the smile off his face, but at the moment his assumptions were working in her favor, so she restrained herself.

"Any idea who might have done it?" the officer asked.

"Naturally not," Pauline said.

"Hmm … your friend the owner, miss, would she happen to be a student?"

"He, and yes, he is."

The officer snapped his notepad closed and tucked it back into his pocket. "Ah-ha. As I suspected. A student prank. It's a distinctive contraption, and a fellow student most likely saw it and, not realizing you were using it, decided to play a trick on this student. Happens all the time."

Pauline found this theory highly unlikely. However, if it meant she could put off talking to James until after she'd spoken with John Kitteredge, so much the better.

"What we'll do now, miss, is I'll take the bicycle back to the station with me and we'll contact the owner and let him know what happened. If you'll give me his name?"

"Yes, of course. Jean-Paul Allain, at St. Lawrence University. And do let him know that I will of course pay for repairs if you cannot find the individual responsible for the damage, since the bicycle was in my care when it happened."

"Very kind and proper of you, miss, to be sure. Miss, ah …?"

"Gray. Pauline Gray."

Enlightenment spread across the officer's face. "That's right, the newspaper lady! Using it in pursuit of a story?"

"Something like that."

He grinned at her. "Now, I don't suppose it would be a disgruntled interview-ee, upset about an article, would it?"

Pauline forced a laugh that sounded weak to her own ears. "Ahahaha. No. I doubt it."

The officer chuckled, tipped his hat, and wheeled the bicycle away.

"Next time don't wait to inform the authorities, Miss Gray!" he called over his shoulder.

Coming on the heels of her disagreement with Sarah as it did, it sounded like an ominous prophecy.

Pauline closed her eyes briefly before proceeding down the street, her heels clicking on the sidewalk with determination.

She had to do this her way. Though the whole world might stand against her, though in the end she might prove to be an utter fool for disregarding everyone's advice, even if it was hubris propelling her forward, her path was set.

She noted with absent surprise that her stomach had not twisted itself into knots and her throat hadn't closed from rising, formless panic. Either her attack of nerves yesterday had drained her enough that she didn't have the energy to be anxious today, or her determination to pursue justice on her own terms had steadied her for the first time since she got involved in this case.

She preferred to think it the latter.

It occurred to her as she walked that she didn't know exactly where she was going. Was John Kitteredge at the mill today? If so, how would she get there? How would she justify her return there to Mr. Wharton?

If she were exceptionally lucky, today would be the day Kitteredge was either delivering goods or picking up supplies from the train station and she could accost him there—but as she'd told James, she didn't believe in coincidences except as sloppy writing techniques.

Still, it did no harm to walk in the direction of the station and see. The station manager would know when people from the mill were supposed to be there for deliveries and the like. It was better than aimlessly wandering around town hoping for something to happen.

To the train station she accordingly went, nodding greetings at the people she passed, occasionally stopping to exchange courtesies. She smiled warmly at the small boy and only slightly-larger girl, brother and sister by their similar ears and chins, staggering out of the public library with arms full of books, arguing shrilly over who was going to read the new Doctor Dolittle book first.

It was another glorious September day, with the sun shining down warmly in a brilliantly cerulean sky and a crisp breeze swirling the leaves in people's lawns. Pauline spotted many people out raking, laughing and exchanging jokes with their neighbors, and more than once caught a heavenly whiff of fresh bread or apple pie baking through someone's open kitchen window.

Even though the country was in a Depression and a murder had happened in their own village, the people of Canton were resilient as always, refusing to let their troubles weigh them down and spoil their enjoyment of life. It was one of the things Pauline loved about living here.

"Oh yes, John will be here within the hour," the station master said when she reached the small brick building that served the town's train needs. "Yesterday was the day he came to pick up supplies, today is the day he drops off the flour to go down to Albany and New York City and them other big cities."

Pauline wondered why Dan Harwood had been at the station two days ago, then, if today and yesterday were the regular days for the mill's freight. A special order, must be. Or else something to do with the smugglers? Was she led astray by his apparent lack of wealth? Perhaps he was more upset about the mill's closure because it would curtail the smuggling operation than he was about being out of regular work.

Maybe Kitteredge was a red herring, only distracting her from what she needed to see.

She couldn't know for sure without talking to the man. She told the station master she was there to get further information on her piece for the *Times*, and he nodded and pointed her to a low wooden bench she could sit on to wait.

"Or you could—but no, I don't suppose that would be appropriate."

"What's that?" she asked, ears pricked.

"Oh, it's just that Miss Root, the one who was murdered. Her house is only a five minute walk from here. I thought at first that you might want to take a look, you being a reporter and all, but I don't suppose that's the sort of story you cover, what with you being a lady."

Pauline's curiosity rose, and she stood with it. "As a matter of fact, I believe the editors of the paper would appreciate a report from someone on hand. Give it a personal touch," she added, seeing his horrified expression. "Talk about the woman's gardens or something. Show that she was a real person who should be mourned, not just another number, like in the cities."

His expression cleared. He plainly was still doubtful about the propriety of the matter, but was not as shocked and horrified as if she had set herself up as a hard-boiled reporter going after a sensational scoop.

"Right you are, miss. The house is that way," he said, pointing down a side street. "Little place, painted yellow, two apple trees in front. Can't miss it. I'll give you an interview, if you like," he added, puffing his chest out. "The police have already talked to me. Seems they think the murderer must have gotten away by the train, wanted to know if I could tell them who got on and off that morning. I told them no one! No trains stopped at all that morning, there was a problem further down the line and so everything was delayed until the afternoon. They weren't too pleased with that, I must say, but it wasn't my fault."

"Quite so," said Pauline, mostly to stem the flood of eloquence. She nodded her thanks to him and walked in the direction he'd indicated.

This in no way fit with her promise to James—this was active investigation with a vengeance—but she couldn't hold back now.

Besides, she felt in a way she owed it to the dead Jemima Root to learn a little more about her. If Pauline was going to take up the banner of justice on her behalf, it was only right she know something about the way she lived, the things she cared for, what went in to making her the person she was.

To be a voice for the voiceless involved knowing who those people were as individuals, not just a silent mass.

Apple Trees and Whiskey Bottles

Jemima Root had lived in a small yellow cottage with white trim and shutters and a tidy garden along the porch. As the station master had promised, two apple trees stood in front, one on either side of her closed front door, their boughs hanging low with ripe, unpicked fruit.

"Seems a shame to let them go to waste, doesn't it?" sighed a voice beside her. Pauline started and looked over.

A woman in a house dress and apron leaned on the fence between Miss Root's house and the house next door. She nodded at the trees.

"The apples, I mean. It would be disrespectful to pick them, I know, but it somehow seems worse to let them hang there until they rot. Poor Jemima. She was so proud of those trees. Called them her 'orchard' and gave away baskets of the apples to all her friends and neighbors."

Pauline swallowed. "She sounds like a lovely person."

The neighbor laughed. "She does, doesn't she? It's funny, though. She was as sharp-tongued and sour-faced as they come, and nobody thought much of her when she was alive. Only now we remember all the good things she did without anyone noticing, all the kind acts hidden behind her sharp words." She sniffed and dabbed her eyes with the apron edge. "It's actually not that funny, come to think of it."

Pauline stood awkwardly, unsure of what to say next. The neighbor saved her the trouble.

"Edna Wright. You're Miss Gray, the newspaper lady, aren't you?"

Once again Pauline marveled at how many people knew her by sight without her having any idea who they were in return. "Yes, that's right."

Ms. Wright scowled. "I wouldn't talk to most reporters, vultures they are, but you, well … you're almost like one of us. You'll treat her respectfully, won't you?"

"I will," Pauline said, though she felt a pang of guilt at deceiving this woman.

Though she was not, in fact, writing a piece on Jemima Root, seeking her murderer was the most respectful thing Pauline could think of to do for her. It wasn't what this woman meant, but it would have to do.

"Were you here the day it happened?" she asked now. The police would have already questioned all the neighbors, of course, but it never hurt to ask again. There was a chance someone might have remembered something, or that they would speak more freely to Pauline than they would to a policeman.

The woman shook her head. "Oh no. I wish I was, I might have been able to help! I was visiting my sister who lives in Potsdam. She just had her sixth, and I promised I would stop by and help out, bring them some food …" She trailed off. "Not that it matters. The point is I wasn't here. The first I learned of it was when I got home that evening and found the police here and everything all in an uproar." She shivered. "I made sure to lock our doors that night, you can believe me! Even if it was just a passing tramp, I won't take any chances."

"Indeed not," Pauline murmured.

Ms. Wright waved at the house on the other side of Miss Root's. "Now Betty there, she was home. She might be able to tell you something. She's not the one who found Jemima, though. That was Rick Tracy, across the road. He dropped by with some crab-apple jelly from his wife, walked into the kitchen and found her lying there on the floor, head bashed in." Her color changed and she swallowed hard.

Pauline felt queasy herself. James had carefully *not* given her any details of how Miss Root had been killed. She had, perhaps, been annoyed at his over-protectiveness, but now she found herself grateful he had spared her sensibilities. Even in her novels she tended to shy away from detailed descriptions of violence.

"How dreadful," she managed.

"Screamed like a small girl, he did," said Ms. Wright, regaining her composure and speaking with a hint of smugness.

"I will speak with both of them," said Pauline. "Thank you."

Betty, possessor of a dark red house tucked back among the oak trees and a taciturn disposition, could not or would not give Pauline any more information than the first neighbor did. She seemed to consider the entire affair vulgar, and Pauline a ghoul for showing interest in it. Mr. and Mrs. Tracy, across the road, were more forthcoming.

"Oh, it was dreadful," gasped Mrs. Tracy, bouncing her whimpering baby on her shoulder. "He's teething," she said in an aside, and then continued with the story. "Jemima has—had—always been kind to us, sending us food when this little one was born, teaching our eldest—Rachel, she's at school now—to read when the school teachers had all but given up on her, even bringing us chicken soup this summer when I fell ill. So when I made crab apple jelly last week, it seemed the least I could do to send a jar to her."

"Yes," said Pauline, hoping Mrs. Tracy would get to the point soon.

Whether she would have or no, her husband, a gaunt, grim man sitting in the corner of the kitchen took up the tale instead.

"And when I got there, she was dead. On the floor, head crushed, the poker from her own fireplace beside her, papers and ink scattered all over the kitchen table. I've never seen anything like it. Hope I never do again."

Papers and ink … "As though she had been in the middle of writing something?"

Mr. Tracy nodded. "Yep."

"Jemima was very intelligent, Miss Gray," Mrs. Tracy hurried into speech again. "Always reading or writing something. Though lately she'd been more secretive about her writings … she'd hide them under the newspaper or something like that whenever anyone stopped by. I assumed she was trying to write a book or the like and didn't want anyone to know." She sighed. "I guess we'll never know now. Her nephew, when he came to collect all her things, burned all her papers. I saw the bonfire in the backyard myself. Seems a shame, but maybe that's how Jemima wanted it."

Pauline barely heard this, her mind wrestling with the question of why an intelligent woman, always reading and writing, one who could teach a child to read when the schoolmarm had given up on her, would have written such illegible letters.

Ah. To disguise her identity, of course. Poorly-spelled, grammatically incorrect letters would hide an educated woman's brain quite well, even a self-educated woman.

Pauline had a flash of insight into the dead woman: denied her chance at high school or college, starving for knowledge, doing her best to gain that knowledge on her own and use it for the good of others, enduring the reputation of oddity, frustrated in her dreams and nearly friendless but still striving to improve her life and the lives of her neighbors … Pauline was pierced with sorrow that she'd never met Jemima Root and that she'd never have the chance to do so.

A murderer destroyed not only the person he or she killed, but a part of all the people that individual had touched or might have touched. For someone like little Rachel Tracy, she lost a teacher and friend who might have helped her achieve the dreams Jemima Root had been denied. For Mrs. and Mrs. Tracy and the rest of the neighbors, it was a friend in need. For Iris Ferris, it was her only friend. And for Pauline, it was a woman who might have enriched her life greatly.

Pauline was more determined than ever to bring this murderer to justice, not only for the sake of the victims, but for the community who was so injured by this deed in ways many of them might never realize.

"Thank you for your time," she told the Tracys, checking her watch to see that it was nearly time for the train to come in. "I'm afraid I must be off."

"I'm glad to think there's someone out there who cares enough about ordinary people like Jemima—like us—to see to it her name isn't forgotten in some corner of the obituaries," Mrs. Tracy said.

Pauline experienced a moment of guilt over that—this was now the second time she had used her journalism as a cover to gain information without much intention of following through on a story, and the dishonesty of her actions combined with the trust of others ate away at her.

She vowed that as soon as she had finished this case, she *would* write up something about Jemima Root, a tribute to a woman overlooked in life and barely noticed in death, and she would insist her editor publish it.

For now, she must hurry back to the train station.

The station master met her return with a nod.

"You're just in time, miss. The train's come in and Kitteredge is here supervising the loading. Ho, John! Here's the lady wanting to see you I mentioned earlier."

A tall, broad-shouldered, square-jawed man looked over from where he was hoisting a bag of flour onto his shoulder from the wagon bed preparatory to placing it in the freight car.

To the best of Pauline's knowledge, she'd never seen him before. Yet upon setting eyes on her, John Kitteredge turned white, dropped the flour sack with a dull thud, and turned tail and fled.

The station master's jaw dropped. He pushed back his cap to scratch at his grizzled hair. "Well now … what do you suppose that was about?"

Pauline ached to chase after Kitteredge, but she held herself back. For one, his legs were longer and he could easily outrun her. For another, if he were the murderer, as seemed increasingly likely, it would be extreme folly to present herself to him as another victim. Here in the train station, surrounded by witnesses, she was safe. On a quiet back street somewhere, not as much.

"Did you tell him who exactly it was looking for him?"

"No, just that someone had dropped by to see him and would be back before he left. Why?"

So his sudden panic was on recognizing her specifically. How did he know her by sight, when she could have passed him on the street without giving him a second look? Granted, more people knew who she was than she did them, as Edna Wright had proven earlier, but it still seemed odd.

And what did he have to fear from her, that her very presence should cause him to flee?

"Sir," Pauline said to the station master. "Do you have a telephone here?"

"Sure do," he answered, still staring after Kitteredge's vanishing figure. "But I can't let you use it. Station business only."

Pauline released a breath, aware that she had made her decision about the smuggling after all. This wasn't what she had wanted, but it was the only option left. Sarah would be pleased, at least. Pauline was not.

"I need you to call Lieutenant James Richardson of the Canton Police Department and tell him to come down here at once to receive evidence of smuggling."

The station master jerked his attention back to her. "Smuggling! On *my* trains?"

"I'm afraid so," Pauline said.

"Do you have proof?"

She nodded at the fallen flour sack, now discolored on one side from liquid seeping out of its contents. "There's your proof. Unless you know of another reason why flour would leak? There's whiskey in that sack, sir."

The station master swore, blushed and apologized, and darted for the telephone.

Pauline, sick at heart and with aching feet, sat down on the wooden bench to await James's arrival.

The Final Clue

It didn't take long to explain the situation to James and the bright young Officer Wallace accompanying him. They tore open the flour sacks as soon as they grasped the facts, revealing whiskey bottles nestled inside the soft flour in six of them.

"Well!" said James. "This settles it. Wallace, you get back to the station and tell the chief. We need to bring Kitteredge in for questioning, and we'll need a warrant to search the mill."

"D'you suppose Mr. Wharton is in on it too, Lieutenant?" Officer Wallace breathed, looking in awe at the bottles filled with liquid amber.

"That's one of the things we need to find out," James answered. He made a shooing motion with his hands, and the freckled, red-headed young policeman finally tore himself away to ride his bicycle back to the Town Hall to mobilize the forces.

"Well done, sir," James said to the station master. "You've answered the question that's been plaguing us for ages, how the smugglers were transporting the whiskey from the river to the cities. They must hide it in the grain to get it to the mill, and then in the sacks to transport it to the city. By gum, there must be an entire network of people involved! Now that we've uncovered the center of the web, though, the rest will fall into place."

The station master looked pleased, but wouldn't take another's praise. "Thank you, Lieutenant, but it's really Miss Gray here you have to thank. She was on Kitteredge's trail even before he got here, and she's the one who noticed the whiskey leaking after he ran away. It's a pity he knew you were on to him, Miss Gray, or we might have caught him in the act, but I'm sure these fine officers will catch him before long. He won't be leaving town on one of my trains, that's for certain."

James's eyes narrowed as Pauline assumed a demure expression. "Really. How providential, Miss Gray. Tell me, how did you suspect John Kitteredge of smuggling?"

"I never reveal my sources," Pauline said firmly.

James took her arm in a courteous yet unbreakable grip and hustled her to the end of the platform away from the station master and all the idle bystanders.

"Pauline, what on earth are you up to?"

"None of your business," she snapped, recognizing the illogic of the statement even as she spoke it. What was smuggling and murder if not James's business? And what would she know about any of this had he not involved her in it to begin with?

Her palms tingled and her breath shortened in her chest, a sure sign that her nerves were acting up again. Pauline concentrated on breathing in and out as slowly and steadily as she could, waiting for her racing heart to slow to normal before speaking again.

"I thought we had a deal," James said. "You promised you would stay out of active investigation. First you go out to the mill, now you come here to confront Kitteredge—how is any of this keeping quiet and safe?"

"The mill was for a story," Pauline said. "The rest of it ..." There were no more excuses. She would have to tell James all.

She told him how her hand had come away wet from a flour sack, and how only later had she recognized the smell as alcohol, and only after that had made the smuggling connection. Rather than tell of her struggle with her conscience over whether or not to tell him anything about the matter, she merely stated that she wanted further proof before talking to him about it, and thought it worth investigating if it had any connections to the murders on her own.

"And yes, I realize that I broke my promise to you in doing that," she said. "I am sorry."

"I should hope so," he said, anger still evident in the tight line of his mouth and hard light in his eyes.

"I've also realized that you were wrong in making such a request of me," she continued. "Or rather, not you, but that I was wrong in agreeing to it. When it comes to justice and truth-seeking, I cannot hide behind my sex or my profession. If there's something I can do, I must do it."

"Even if it puts you in danger?" James pressed.

"Even then," she said.

Her stomach stopped twisting. Apparently uncertainty, more than danger or distress, brought about her crises of nerves. Uncertainty about herself, uncertainty about the world, uncertainty about the right thing to do. Once there was something she could do, no matter how unpleasant, her strength returned.

Perhaps it wasn't living in the country at all that had saved her, but rather finding a community where she belonged, where she could both give something of value and receive goodness from others in return. These murders had upset the balance, and if she could help restore it, she would.

Whatever it took.

James's face eased back into its more regular expression of good humor. "I'm not happy about it, but I suppose I can understand. I'm still going to nag at you to be careful, and to not do stupid things like put yourself deliberately in danger without telling anyone, just for a clue."

"Believe it or not, I appreciate that," she said. "And I will do my best to comply, particularly with that last point."

He laughed. "All right. Thank you for your help here. Are you going to be offended if I now ask you to go home and let us take care of things?"

"Do you think Kitteredge is the murderer as well as a smuggler?" she asked.

James sighed, his eyes drifting in the direction of Jemima Root's house. "I don't know. There's a good chance of it, but … I suppose that's one of the things we'll have to ask him when we catch him. At this point, I don't even know if he's the head of the ring or merely a pawn."

Pauline thought back over her interview with Andrew Wharton. "For what it's worth, I doubt Mr. Wharton knows anything about it. I don't like the man, you understand, but he seems too shrewd a businessman, not to mention too proud of building the mill up by his own wits and hard work, to engage in something like smuggling."

"Your opinion means a lot to me. Whether the chief agrees is another matter," James said. "We'll see what turns up when we search the mill."

"And James—" Pauline didn't quite lower herself to grab him by the coat lapel, but he must have sensed her urgency for he stopped in the middle of stepping away and instead turned back to her.

"Yes?"

"You won't—don't let them use this as a distraction from Jemima Root and Bob. They deserve more than to be a footnote in a successful smuggling case."

He nodded once, soberly.

It was the best Pauline could do.

She left the station to make her way back home, mind turning over the events of the morning. She couldn't help but feel there was something she'd missed, some small, personal detail she'd overlooked in the excitement of the larger picture. What was it?

The matter nagged at her the entire way back to the apartment, where she firmly set it aside in order to put in some solid work. She'd been neglecting her writing these last few days, too busy chasing after clues and criminals.

She had to write the story on the mill to send to her editor, along with a note that she intended to make this a series. She had to finish the edits on *Emma Daring: Danger in the Wild West* in order to get that in to her publishers in time. And she supposed she really ought to think about preparing supper for a change; it might be nice to have something other than soup out of a can with sliced bread on the side.

Pauline tossed her hat and coat on the side table and sat down at her desk, clearing her mind of all distractions for at least this space of time.

Some three hours later, she pushed her wooden chair back across the floorboards until its back feet caught as usual on the edge of the rag rug. With a sense of satisfaction, Pauline stood up and stretched her arms as high above her head as they could go, bending from one side to the other before reaching down to touch her toes. She repeated this a few times until she was able to fully disengage her brain from the distant place it went when she wrote and return it to the real world.

She neatly replaced the chair in front of the desk, put the cover back on the typewriter, straightened the rug, hung up her hat and coat, and sighed deeply.

This might not be the kind of scholarly work she had expected to do when she finished college, but it was satisfying in its own right. It had been rather clever, the trick she had used to allow Emma to rescue her niece and nephew—

Nephew.

That was it! That was the niggling detail she'd been trying to remember. Mrs. Tracy had said something about Miss Root's nephew coming and burning all her papers.

Who was he?

Supper would have to wait. Pauline was on the trail of another clue. It might prove a dead end, but she had to follow it through just in case.

Hat and coat back on, she exited the apartment and hurried down the steps, orienting herself in her mind to the location of Mrs. Griffith's boarding house. Iris Ferris was clearly the person to ask about Jemima Root's family.

The air had more of a chill than it had had that morning. Pauline couldn't help but smile at the houses lining the streets, fancying them huddling together against the coming cold. Winter would be here soon enough. Boys and girls trick-or-treating on Halloween night in a month could be wearing snow boots and heavy coats over their costumes; it had happened before.

In the meantime, she enjoyed these days of it being cold enough to wake one up, but warm enough to be able to step outside without ten extra layers. Many of the trees had shed their leaves, leaving bare branches to stretch against the sky and provide a contrast with the brilliant reds and golds still defiantly hanging on neighboring branches.

It was a scene to rejoice an artist's eye. Pauline had no skill with pen or pencil in that way, but perhaps Sarah would take advantage of the sunshine when she finished her shift at the hospital. They had one or two of her sketches hanging on their walls already; the young nurse had a talent for art that never ceased to amaze Pauline.

Mrs. Griffith was out doing the daily marketing when Pauline arrived at the boarding house, so she was able to meet Iris Ferris in the parlor without having to worry about anyone eavesdropping on their business.

"Miss Ferris, who was Miss Root's nephew?" she asked without preamble.

Miss Ferris didn't bat an eyelash at the abrupt question.

"Dan Harwood. His mother is—was—Jemima's younger sister."

Pauline stared at the ugly flowered wallpaper on the parlor walls as her mind began putting pieces together.

So that was why Miss Root had been at the mill the day of Bob's death. She was coming to visit her nephew.

Her nephew who was facing demotion or even losing his job while Bob Ferris was going to get a promotion.

Her nephew who got a raise once Bob was no longer there, who might have expected to get the promotion due to his seniority.

Her nephew who was in the village the day Jemima Root was killed.

Her nephew who had asked Pauline to not tell anyone she had seen him that day, and who claimed to be picking up supplies at the station on a day no train stopped.

Her nephew whom Miss Root might very well have felt impelled to protect even if she saw him doing something dreadful.

Like murdering a man.

Pauline stopped herself, appalled.

Dan Harwood? No, no. Not someone she felt pity for, someone she almost liked. He had a mother and three siblings depending on him for their livelihood.

Why couldn't it be John Kitteredge, a man she'd never met, a man who most likely destroyed Jean-Paul's bicycle as a warning to her after one of his fellow smugglers at the mill warned him she'd seemed too interested in the flour sacks, a man whom the police were already after?

For a moment, Pauline was tempted to leave the matter, to walk away. Let the police charge Kitteredge with the murders as well as the smuggling. Let Dan go free.

Her entire being, soul and body alike, cringed away from that. How could she live, knowing she had hidden the truth? How could there be justice for the dead? Ruby and Jeremy deserved better—Iris Ferris deserved better—little Rachel Tracy and all those other lives touched in one way or another by the dead people deserved better.

Bob and Jemima themselves deserved better. Pauline couldn't give them back their lives, but she could give them truth. It was all she had.

She stood up.

"I need to see James."

"Right," said Iris Ferris, watching her with keen, if faded, blue eyes. "I'm coming with you."

Light in the Darkness

Pauline managed to convince Miss Ferris to wait for her inside the Town Hall until Pauline had found James. As one who had been influential in uncovering the smuggling operation as well as a journalist, Pauline's interest in the case was easily explained. Iris Ferris, on the other hand, was an anomaly, and Pauline was afraid the officers wouldn't speak as freely in front of her.

She left Miss Ferris browsing through the paperback novels at the newsstand, noting with ironic amusement that the older woman had picked up the latest Emma Daring book and was leafing through that in an attempt to look busy.

Meanwhile, Pauline made her way to the police headquarters, tucked away in the back of the building. She was in luck—Officer Wallace was on duty at the front desk.

"Hello, Miss Gray!" he said, nearly bouncing up from his seat before settling down with an attempt at dignity. "That was some excitement this morning, wasn't it?"

"Yes, it was," Pauline agreed. "I need to see Lieutenant Richardson; is he in?"

"I'm afraid you just missed him; he left five minutes ago."

"I see," said Pauline. She wondered if she could persuade Wallace to tell her where James had gone. Probably not.

In the end, it wouldn't matter if she waited until this evening to tell James about Dan Harwood. A few more hours wouldn't hurt.

"I'll speak with him later, then," she said, starting to turn away.

"If you're here for more information about the smuggling operation, I can't tell you much, but I can tell you that Lieutenant Richardson is off making an arrest right now! And ..." Officer Wallace leaned over the wide mahogany desk, eyes glittering as he hissed, "We now believe the smuggling is connected to the murder of Jemima Root!"

That stopped Pauline in her tracks. "What?"

Officer Wallace sat back down. "Oh," he said, suddenly reticent. "I probably shouldn't have even said that much."

Pauline covered her emotions with a mask of polite interest. "Not to worry, I won't give any information to my editor until someone here has given me permission. Since you have told me this much, you can't leave me in suspense now. Who ... who is being arrested?"

"Well, you already know the warrant is out for Kitteredge's arrest. But it seems ... I shouldn't tell you this, but I guess it can't hurt ... it seems Andrew Wharton was behind the whole thing! Can you beat it?"

"What?" Pauline said, annoyed to hear her voice squeak. Really, she thought she had better self-control than this.

How had this happened? She had specifically told James she thought Wharton was innocent, and he'd—well no, he hadn't agreed, but he had at least listened and respected her opinion.

Or had he? Had he only been humoring her? She hated to think that of him.

"The chief told Lieutenant Richardson that since he was the one to crack the case, he could be the one to make the arrest. The lieutenant didn't even want to! He's a swell guy, but that's carrying modesty a little too far, if you ask me."

Now she understood. James was carrying out orders against his own judgment. This way, if there was a mistake, the chief could push the blame onto James's shoulders. He was a scapegoat.

She couldn't let that happen. She had to get out to the mill and stop James before it was too late.

"Thank you, Officer," she said to the young Wallace, and left before he could stop to think of asking why she'd come by in the first place.

At the newsstand, Miss Ferris dropped the book she was holding and rushed to meet her.

"Well?" the older woman demanded.

"I need to get to the mill," Pauline said. "I don't suppose you have an automobile?"

Miss Ferris sniffed. "Do I look like I inherited wealth from *my* grandparents?"

Pauline ignored this. Her grandparents hadn't been all that wealthy, but she had grown used to the assumption she was living off her family's money—how else could she afford to exist on her meager salary from the newspaper?

"James is about to arrest the wrong man, and I have to stop him before it's too late," Pauline said.

Nobody had ever accused Iris Ferris of being dense. "Right," she said, taking the lead out of the building. "We need to find Mrs. Hansen."

"What—why?" Pauline didn't want to drag anyone else into this.

"She has a car we can borrow. I'll drive; you explain as we go."

Pauline protested, but Miss Ferris ignored everything she said. Finally, Pauline capitulated. She'd always considered herself to have an iron will, but she looked positively flimsy compared to Iris Ferris.

To her surprise, the Episcopalian minister's wife did indeed let them take her car without any questions, requesting only that they fill the tank with gasoline before returning it.

In a shorter time than Pauline would have believed possible, they were whizzing along the road out of Canton toward the Wharton

Grist Mill.

"Yes, she keeps the auto solely for the use of other people," Miss Ferris said in response to Pauline's bewilderment. "She says there's always somebody who need to get someplace off the bus route, or too far for a bicycle, or who doesn't have a horse."

Pauline had to adjust her mental image of Mrs. Hansen as a woman who was kind-hearted but weak in the face of society's expectations to a person who did the best she could for other people within the bounds of her role. They couldn't all be zealots.

"Now, tell me!" Miss Ferris demanded.

Pauline wrenched her mind away from philosophical musings and explained the chain of events and her reasoning thereof that had led her to this place.

She barely finished when Miss Ferris pulled to a stop in front of the mill, right behind the black car with the police insignia on its side.

Pauline didn't hesitate. She wrenched open the door and leapt out. Most of the mill workers were gathered out front in small knots, muttering to each other and eyeing the doorway speculatively. Pauline approached the nearest.

"Where is Lieutenant Richardson?"

The man nodded at the door. "Inside with the boss. Why?"

She didn't answer. With Miss Ferris hard on her heels, she ran inside, heading for Andrew Wharton's inner office. She darted around the abandoned equipment and half-filled bags with single-minded purpose, not noticing when she lost the older woman.

She did notice when an arm of steel encircled her neck, dragging her to a choking, sputtering stop.

"I knew you suspected me, but I thought I'd thrown you off my scent," panted Dan Harwood's voice in her ear. "I can't let you betray me now, not when I'm finally safe."

"*Glugg*," said Pauline, prying at his arm with her fingers.

It was no good. She was a relatively strong woman, but she couldn't loosen that rock-solid grip. A mill worker far outweighed a writer in strength and fitness.

She twisted and turned, trying to slip away, scrambling to stomp his feet, but she couldn't stop him from inexorably dragging her back, down the steps to the lowest level of the mill, down where the water glistened under the no longer in use water turbine.

"I don't want to kill you," he said, and sounded like he genuinely meant it.

He was going to, though. He would hit her over the head and throw her in the water, and she would drown just like Bob. Everyone would say, "Oh, another tragic accident," and Dan Harwood would get away with three murders.

He didn't know about Iris Ferris, though. He didn't know that Pauline had already told everything to another person. Even if he killed her, he wouldn't be safe.

If only he would let her speak so she could tell him!

Pauline had a moment's hope that Miss Ferris might have seen Dan grab her, but as the moments passed and the other woman did not appear, that hope vanished. If they'd stayed on the main level there was a chance, but down here, no one could find them.

"I never wanted to kill anyone," Dan continued. Spots danced in front of Pauline's eyes as his grip tightened yet further.

He wouldn't knock her on the head, she realized. He would simply choke her until she lost consciousness and then let her slip into permanent oblivion in the dark waters beneath the mill.

"I needed that promotion Ferris was getting," he went on. "We needed that money! And then old Wharton went and gave it to Kitteredge instead. Serves him right, getting arrested for this murder. It is his fault, if he weren't so tight-fisted he wouldn't have driven me to that extreme. I didn't mean Bob to die! Just be out of commission for a little while, so I could take his place. It was sheer bad luck he hit his head on that rock.

"Then Aunt Jemima had to see it, and see me looking out the window after him. The old woman should have held her tongue—I was her nephew! Instead she went and wrote all those letters to Ruby, dragging it all up. It was only a matter of time before she told the police everything. I had to kill her when I stopped by that morning and saw the letter she was writing to Ruby. It was the only way!

"I knew, the moment you showed up at the mill, that you were on my trail. That's why I telephoned Kitteredge that you were onto his smuggling scheme. I figured he could scare you off, and even if you figured out he was the one who vandalized your bicycle, you'd pin the murder on him instead. After all, I'd known about the smuggling he'd been doing under Wharton's nose for years without splitting on him, and he never even offered me a cut. Why shouldn't he take the fall for me? It ought to have worked perfectly. Why'd you have to come back?"

Pauline couldn't speak—she couldn't breathe—she was going to die right there and her death wouldn't do anyone any good at all.

She was a moment from despair when there was a resounding *CLANGGGGGGG* from behind her and Dan Harwood's arm fell away.

Pauline fell forward on her hands and knees, retching and gasping for air. She barely heard the startled shouts from above, nor took any notice of James and another officer thundering down the steps to come to her aid.

Seared into her brain, even in the dim, uncertain light, was the image of Iris Ferris standing over Dan Harwood's prone body, a corrugated metal roller from an old separator held high in her hand, looking for all the world like a Valkyrie of the north.

"Never mind about Andrew Wharton," she said in a ringing voice. "This is the man who killed my brother and Jemima Root, and who tried to kill Miss Gray as well. I heard his entire confession."

James knelt down beside Pauline, checking her neck for damage. "What did I tell you about not rushing stupidly into danger?"

She managed a weak smile. "At least I brought Miss Ferris with me."

It was all rather anticlimactic after that. James and the other officer released Wharton, cleared now of both the murder charge and the smuggling charge thanks to Dan's statement. They arrested Dan once he came around. He didn't even try to deny the charges, instead continuing to blame his actions on everyone but himself.

His most vitriolic hate was directed toward Pauline.

After he was dragged into the police car and taken back to town, Miss Ferris helped Pauline into Mrs. Hansen's automobile.

"Shall I take you to the hospital?" she asked, looking at Pauline.

Already bruises were darkening around Pauline's throat.

"No," Pauline croaked. "Sarah will be back by now. I just want to go home."

"Very well." Miss Ferris cleared her throat as she pressed the starter. "I suppose I should apologize. I saw that man lurking in wait for you, and I dropped back so as to catch him in the act. I ought to have come to your rescue at once, but it occurred to me that if I could hear him confess, it would make the case much stronger against him than your train of logic. I didn't anticipate him damaging you quite so much."

"It will pass," Pauline said. "I'm only thankful you were there at all. You saved my life."

Miss Ferris was still unsmiling, but Pauline detected a treacherous shimmer in her eyes as she answered.

"You deduced who killed my brother and my friend. Even though it didn't affect your life. Even though you didn't have to. Your life wouldn't have needed saving if you hadn't pursued the truth so vehemently. Thank you."

"You're welcome," Pauline said awkwardly.

It wouldn't bring back the dead. It wouldn't magically heal the hurt done to those left behind. Ruby and Iris would still need to come to terms with their relationship. Jeremy was still going to have to grow up without a father. The community would feel the gap left behind by Jemima's death.

But hopefully, with truth revealed and justice done, they could all begin to heal in a way they couldn't before, and their path forward would be made a little easier.

Despite her bruises and the shock starting to rack her body with shivers, despite the fact that she was sure to have nightmares for the next month of that moment under the mill when she was sure she was going to die, Pauline was satisfied.

She was sorry for Dan's family, but she couldn't regret her actions. This was her place of peace. Not in a bucolic country village that only, perhaps, existed in city folk's imaginations. Not even in her scholarly accomplishments.

Rather, she found her strength and her sense of purpose in pursuing justice for the oppressed and in remaining faithful to the truth no matter how ugly. This was her way of lighting a candle against the dark.

At the end of the day, it was enough.

II

DIAMONDS TO DUST

Ashes to ashes, dust to dust ...
-Book of Common Prayer

All that glisters is not gold ...
-William Shakespeare

A Peculiar Legacy

Pauline Gray would rather have spent this March morning working on her newest Emma Daring manuscript, but the telephone call from Ruby Richardson, asking if she could meet with Arabella Warren, had intrigued her. She was just putting the final scoop of coffee in the percolator when the knock came at the door.

On her way though the living room to answer the knock, out of habit Pauline checked her desk. Yes, she had hidden the novel pages under the stack of books and inserted the half-typed page for her newspaper column in the typewriter instead. Nothing there to indicate that Miss Gray, newspaper columnist and St. Lawrence University graduate, wrote adventure novels on the side.

"Oh, hello," the woman at the door said in a gasp.

Pauline wondered what right the woman had to sound so surprised. If you knock at a person's door, you ought to expect them to answer.

Then again, Pauline thought, looking at the narrow steps that wound up the outside of the building to her second-floor apartment, perhaps the woman was merely breathless from the climb. Pauline did it so frequently she often forgot how strenuous the stairs could be if one wasn't accustomed to them.

"Hello," she answered, her voice revealing none of her thoughts.

Its very calmness seemed to reassure the woman, who blinked her large, pale blue eyes several times and gave a little sigh, seemingly of relief.

"Are you—you are Pauline Gray, the newspaper woman, aren't you?"

"Yes," Pauline said. "Are you Arabella Warren?"

"Yes—oh good, Mrs. Richardson told you about me. She said she had, but I—well, there. You already know all about it."

In truth, Pauline did not. Had Ruby not mentioned a problem, she would have supposed Miss Warren wanted her to run a piece in her column on something or other—a social function she was organizing, or a grandfather turning 100, something of that sort. Pauline did get those sort of requests from time to time. Occasionally her editors at the *Watertown Daily Times* even let her write them.

"Won't you come in and tell me about it?" she said now. "Mrs. Richardson only said that something odd had happened to you, and she recommended you bring it to me. I haven't heard any details."

"Yes, it is odd," Miss Warren said, following Pauline inside the apartment and then standing irresolutely in the tiny entryway. "I don't know what to make of it, and I didn't know who to go to. It's not a police matter, so Mrs. Richardson told me when I asked her about it, nothing so serious."

Ruby was married to James Richardson, a lieutenant with the Canton Police Department.

"I haven't got a husband or brother or anyone to advise me, either," Miss Warren continued. "I don't dare go to the lawyers, they talk so much and use so many fancy words I can't understand them half the time—though it was a lawyer who brought the news to me, and he seemed like a nice enough fellow. But then Mrs. Richardson said, well, why not try that nice Miss Gray, she has those newspaper contacts and she has a knack for figuring tricky puzzles out, so well, here I am."

Pauline found herself tempted to do some blinking of her own. She was half inclined to send the woman on her way to save herself the bother of trying to unravel why she was here, much less whatever puzzle she had that needed solving, but Ruby had trusted her with Miss Warren's dilemma and she hated to let her friend down.

Besides, her interest was piqued.

"The coffee should be just about ready," she said. "Do let me take your things, and we can discuss this matter while we share a cup."

Miss Warren sighed again. "That is kind of you, Miss Gray. I'm that flummoxed I don't know what to do with myself. And it's a chilly morning to be walking across town, no doubt about it. A cup of coffee would be just the ticket."

Pauline took her hat, an unadorned grey felt with a deep crown and narrow brim, a style fashionable a few years back but not much in vogue this past winter. It was exquisitely neat and clean, indicating the wearer cared more for the quality of her wardrobe than the style.

The gloves Miss Warren handed her next confirmed this. The cotton lisle material and plain design were not particularly fashionable, but where they had worn through at one or two of the fingers Miss Warren had darned them so neatly as to be almost invisible. Pauline, whose darns always came out bunchy and looking worse than the original hole, felt a flash of admiration as she set hat and gloves on the carved walnut table in the hall and moved toward the kitchen.

She had expected Miss Warren to remain in the living room, as a proper guest, but to her mild alarm the woman followed her into the kitchen and sat right down at the square wooden two-person table. Pauline spared a moment to thank heavens she had washed the breakfast dishes and swept the linoleum floor before Ruby had telephoned. While she valued a clean environment as much as anyone, when deadlines loomed the housework did not always get discharged as promptly as she would prefer.

The floors weren't perhaps as gleaming as a diligent housewife would have had them, the counters not as spotless, but it was reasonably clean for an apartment shared by two working women, and Pauline put the matter out of her mind.

"Do you take milk or sugar, Miss Warren?"

"Oh—milk, if you have it. My father was a dairy farmer, you know, so we always had milk and cream around, no matter how short we were on anything else, and I grew up used to putting milk in everything. Not sugar so much, though, no, sugar was more of a treat. We used maple syrup generally for sweetening, but I don't take it in my coffee, good coffee is fine without any sweetener at all, don't you think? Even if I did prefer it, I would feel downright wicked wasting sugar in coffee when I think of how many people don't have enough food to keep from starving, poor things. It's a terrible world sometimes, Miss Gray."

Pauline pulled the milk bottle out of the tiny ice box without bothering to answer. Thus far Miss Warren was proving a fine contradiction: finicky in her dress and inconsequential in her speech; a woman of conscience but little gumption.

Her age appeared to be around forty; there was no grey in the blonde hair that frizzed about her round face, defying her attempts at smoothing it into finger waves, but she had laugh lines emanating from her faded blue eyes and an overall air of having lived through a good portion of her life already.

She removed her coat to reveal a light pink cotton dress which was, as Pauline half-expected, neat and tidy but a few years out of date; her low-heeled sensible shoes completed the pattern. In appearance, if not in speech, this was a competent, practical woman.

Pauline could think of no higher compliment to bestow on her fellow man—or woman.

"There," she said, handing a filled cup across the table to Miss Warren and sitting down across from her with her own cup. "I'm sorry I have nothing else to offer you, I am a terrible baker. Perhaps an apple …?"

Miss Warren took a sip of her coffee. "No no, no thank you. I do so hate to ask people to feed me when we're all struggling to make ends meet. If I want food, I can prepare it for myself. No, this is fine. Thank you, Miss Gray. I suppose you want to hear what I've come about?"

"If you are ready to tell me," Pauline said with a smile.

The older woman drew in a steadying breath, drank some more coffee, then set the thick white cup down and interlaced her fingers around it.

"It's not a bad thing, not by any means. I ought, I suppose, to simply accept it and be happy. I mean, a diamond necklace …! But it's so odd, and I can't help feeling nervous that there's some mistake, and well, I don't want to get mixed up in anything improper. You understand, I'm sure."

"I'm afraid not quite," Pauline said. "Perhaps if you went back to the beginning?"

"Of course. Well, I don't know where the beginning is exactly. If I did, I wouldn't be so muddled, would I? I suppose I should start with the lawyer. That's where it began for me, you see."

"Yes, the lawyer," Pauline said, gratefully seizing on this one concrete tidbit. "You mentioned him before. He brought you some news?"

"Yes, about the will."

"A will?"

"Yes, Mr. Van Camp's will. He left me something, you see."

"That was kind," Pauline said, feeling her way forward tentatively. "Did you know him well?"

Arabella Warren sat upright, pushing her hair back from her face. "No!" she said explosively. "I have no idea who the man is! I've never even heard his name before the lawyer showed up at my door this morning. According to Mr. Ramsey—that's the lawyer—Horace Van

Camp was a wealthy man living in Clayton who died two weeks ago, but I don't know him from Adam."

Clayton was a small village on the St. Lawrence River, about fifty miles from Canton. It was part of the famed "Thousand Islands" region, that area of the river dotted with countless small islands that was considered one of the most beautiful areas in the state.

"Then why …"

"Why should he leave me a diamond necklace in his will? That's what I want you to find out!"

Pauline sipped her coffee to cover her confusion. "I beg your pardon?" she said after she swallowed.

"Miss Gray, that lawyer man showed up on my doorstep to tell me someone I've never heard of died and left me a diamond necklace in his will, and I haven't the faintest idea why. Not that I wouldn't like a diamond necklace—who wouldn't?—but I don't want to accept something I shouldn't. What if he meant another Arabella Warren? Or what if there's some deeper mischief afoot? I don't like it—it makes me nervous—and I want to know more before I accept the necklace."

"Well," Pauline began.

"And that's why I came to you," Miss Warren carried on. Her knuckles were white around the coffee cup. Clearly the situation was more of a strain on her than Pauline would have expected.

Most people would be delighted with a mysterious bequest. They might puzzle over it a bit, but ultimately they would accept it and let the story become part of family lore.

Not Miss Warren.

"I asked Mrs. Richardson if her husband could look into it for me, and she said no, it wasn't a police matter, and that's when she said I should ask you. So here I am."

"What exactly are you asking of me?" Pauline said, searching for clarity.

"I want you to find out more about Mr. Horace Van Camp, who he was, who else he left things to in his will, and how he heard of me in the first place, not to mention why he would leave me a valuable necklace. I want you to come with me to the lawyer's tomorrow to get the necklace—he's holding it in his office for me to claim—so you can make sure it's all straightforward and aboveboard. I don't care if you make a story out of it for your paper, I just want to know the truth. Will you help me?"

Pauline considered it.

This woman seemed to have a keen mind under her rambling conversation, and judging by her attire, a love for order and neatness. A disorderly and puzzling affair such as this would affect her pleasure in the bequest and bother her every time she wore the necklace if it didn't clear up.

Pauline would have been the same in her place. She made up her mind.

"Miss Warren," she said. "I will."

Preliminary Investigations

After Miss Warren left, Pauline allowed herself the luxury of a second cup of coffee and sat back down at the table with it. A pleasant tingle filled her fingers and toes, the allurement of the unknown, a fresh puzzle of be solved.

Last fall she had gotten involved in a murder mystery. It hadn't been enjoyable, exactly, and at some parts had been both appalling and terrifying, but the thrill of discovery combined with the knowledge that she was helping find justice for those unable to seek it for themselves had given her a sense of purpose and a deep-rooted contentment that she had missed in the months since.

On the face of it, this little mystery of Miss Warren's didn't seem as important as murder, but it was an exercise for her wits as well as a chance to help a neighbor in need. Pauline would not scorn either of those things.

She propped her chin on her hand and stared out the kitchen window at the bare treetops just starting to show hints of red at the tips of their branches. Why *would* a man leave a diamond necklace to a woman he'd never met? If Pauline were writing this in a novel, what would the reason be?

Clearly, because Arabella Warren was either his long-lost daughter or sister, depending on his age.

Pauline laughed and shook her head, then picked up her cup and finished her coffee. Alas, real life was rarely as uncomplicated or melodramatic as her adventure stories. Far more likely was Miss Warren's prosaic fear that he had meant to leave it to another Arabella Warren and it had come to this one by mistake.

Or perhaps he had been an acquaintance of her father or mother and wanted to leave their daughter a remembrance in his will. Perhaps he had heard of her or met her without her being aware of it and decided she was worthy of a diamond necklace. Perhaps she shared a name with a woman he had loved in his youth, and he wished to commemorate the lady.

She caught herself. There she was getting romantic again! Too much novel writing and not enough sound scholarship of late, that was her problem.

She wasn't going to get any answers sitting here thinking up less and less likely scenarios, and if she drank any more coffee she'd float away. The next step was to find out more about Mr. Horace Van Camp, and about Miss Arabella Warren herself.

Pauline washed the cups and spoons and dumped the coffee grounds out of the percolator into a bowl. Later she would take the bowl downstairs to her landlady, who used coffee grounds as a fertilizer for her prized roses.

The kitchen tidy enough to assuage her conscience, she pulled on a warm sweater, a pretty green cardigan knit for her by her favorite aunt for a Christmas gift. It had come with a matching beret, with Pauline now set at a jaunty angle atop her smooth dark hair. From habit, she tucked a notepad and freshly sharpened pencil into her handbag, and set out.

Emma Daring and her adventures would have to wait. Real life had become more exciting than the adventure novels Pauline wrote in secret to supplement her newspaper salary.

The March air was brisk but not unpleasant. The farmers insisted more snow was on the way, but today, with the sun shining and the pussy willows beckoning from the sides of the road, spring's promise was everywhere.

Pauline was thankful. Goodness knew that anyone who chose to live in northern New York state had no business complaining about long winters, but all the same, endless snow and bitter cold from November to February wore on her spirits more than a little. The benefits of living in this beautiful small village far outweighed the disadvantages, but it was sometimes hard to remember them when one was up to one's ears in snow and unable to poke a nose outside for fear it would freeze off.

Her goal was the Opera Theatre, not for tickets to see the next grand show to come their way, but to visit the town clerk's office on the first floor of the building. If anyone would be able to give Pauline information about the Warren family as well as Horace Van Camp, it was Susan Hao.

The petite Chinese-American woman looked up from her spotless desk and smiled welcomingly as Pauline entered her office.

"What can I do for you today?" Susan asked cheerfully.

Susan was about fifteen years older than Pauline, the granddaughter of immigrants who had originally settled in New York City's Chinatown but had chosen to exchange city life for the country when Susan's father was a small boy. Despite the age difference, the two women knew each other well from all the times Pauline came to the office looking up information for a story.

"What can you tell me about Horace Van Camp?" Pauline said.

Susan nodded. "The man who died recently? You'd do better asking about him in the Thousand Islands region, but I can at least tell you what everyone knows."

What "everyone knew," apparently, was that Mr. Van Camp was a former resident of New York City who had retired to live permanently at his summer house on the St. Lawrence River about ten years ago. What his business had been, no one was quite sure, but he was rumored to be fabulously wealthy, with a small but dazzling collection of rare art and jewelry. He had been unmarried and had no children, and had died peacefully in his home of old age two weeks ago.

"I see," said Pauline.

"Are you doing his obituary for the *Watertown Daily Times*?" Susan asked.

"Not exactly," Pauline hedged.

It wasn't that she didn't trust Susan to be discreet, but she didn't feel comfortable sharing all of Arabella's story with any outsider just yet. It would make getting the information she needed that much trickier, but Pauline believed firmly in the right of every person to privacy.

It was, perhaps, an odd stance for a journalist to take, but Pauline could no more abandon it than she could her scholarly love of finding reasonable answers to difficult problems.

"Was he connected to anyone here in Canton or the general region, do you know?" she asked instead. "What led him to the Thousand Islands?"

Susan waved a slim hand. "Oh, plenty of rich people have summer homes along the river. It was especially popular thirty or forty years ago. The wealthy from New York City, Chicago, Pittsburgh, and elsewhere all liked to come play at a 'rustic' lifestyle. Not so much now, of course, with the economy the way it is."

Pauline's grandparents had a summer cabin in the Adirondack mountains. She had loved visiting there when she was a little girl, and it had contributed to her desire to attend college and then live in this area. She had never been to the Thousand Islands, though, and hadn't realized it held the same appeal.

"I never heard of Mr. Van Camp having any particular connection with anyone in this area," Susan continued. She paused a moment, then said, "If you're wondering why he would leave Arabella Warren a diamond necklace, I can't help you. It's a mystery to me as much as anyone." Her deep brown eyes twinkled with amusement.

Pauline smiled wryly, acknowledging the point. Try keeping a secret in a small town! It was the price one paid for the close-knit community.

It was a wonder that no one had yet discovered Pauline's identity as the author of the popular Emma Daring novels. She could only put it down to the fact that she was not yet considered entirely "of" the town. A welcome outsider, but an outsider nonetheless. She hoped that by the time she'd lived here fifty years, she would be considered a proper local, but she had her doubts.

She also hoped that by the time fifty years had passed, she would be finished with journalism and Emma's adventures alike and have moved on to the scholarly work that was her true passion. She sometimes had her doubts about that, as well.

"Miss Warren asked me to look into the matter," she told Susan, now that secrecy was no longer necessary.

"The lawyer asked at the post office for her address while I was there buying stamps this morning," Susan said. "He said she'd been left a legacy."

Pauline was horrified at this garrulousness. Her grandfather would never have approved. "He announced in public what the legacy was? How shockingly inappropriate!"

"Oh no," Susan assured her. "He only said a legacy. May Oates was in the post office at the same time, so she went right to her sister Minnie's house, next door to Arabella's. They kept watch out Minnie's kitchen window, and as soon as the lawyer left May went over to ask Arabella what had been left her, and Arabella was so shocked she told her. May told Minnie, who told Lucy Westin when they were both out doing their marketing, who told—"

"The entire town," Pauline said. "And what is the town's opinion?"

"Oh, that there is some scandal behind it, naturally, especially as soon as we heard Arabella went to see Ruby Richardson and then on to visit you. Where would be the excitement in something tame and ordinary?"

"Where, indeed," Pauline murmured. "Susan, what can you tell me about the Warren family? I am trying to find out if there's something in Miss Warren's parents' past that connects them to Mr. Van Camp."

"The Warrens have lived in Canton for ages," Susan said. "Long before my grandparents moved here, the Warren dairy farm was a byword. Arabella was her parents' only child, and when her father died one of her uncles took over the farm. Arabella moved to a small house in town, apparently quite happily. I can't think of anything that would connect the family to Mr. Van Camp, unless it had something to do with cows."

Without knowing what Mr. Van Camp's business had been, there was no way to be certain. Still, it didn't seem likely that he would leave Miss Warren something so valuable if he had only been a business associate—and surely her parents would have told her about him.

Unless they considered business matters above a woman's ability to understand. The leaving of the farm to an uncle indicated as much—but there, Pauline was speculating ahead of her facts. For all she knew, Miss Warren had asked her uncle to take over the farm. It was just as likely that she didn't care for farming as it was that her parents despised a woman's brain.

Pauline had to be careful to not always assume the worst of people.

"I'm glad he left her the necklace, whatever the reason," Susan said now. "I think it's high time something good came Arabella's way. She doesn't complain ever, but I think she's lonely. She was always scatter-brained when we were children, but it's gotten worse since her parents' death. Maybe the necklace will give her a new interest in life. If nothing else, I'm glad you're helping her. She needs people to care."

Pauline was humbled by Susan's words, and left the office vowing to do her best, both in solving the puzzle and in supporting Arabella Warren. She wasn't particularly good with people—she much preferred books and facts—but she would do what she could.

A quick stop by the Richardson house was next on her agenda. She hadn't seen Ruby since she and James returned from their honeymoon a month ago. Pauline looked over at the wide front porch, where Ruby was shaking out a carpet. Marriage suited her friend: she carried herself straighter, head higher, had rosy color in her cheeks, and a sparkle in her eyes that hadn't been there since her first husband died.

"Pauline! Lovely to see you," Ruby called, giving the carpet one final shake. "Do come in."

Seated at the kitchen table with a cup of coffee in her hands before she could blink, Pauline had a sudden insight into the trust Miss Warren had shown her by coming into the kitchen that morning. Guests sat in the living room. Friends sat around the kitchen table.

She had to swallow against the unexpected tightness in her throat.

"I thought I might see you today, after sending Miss Warren your way. I hope I didn't presume by referring her to you?" Ruby looked momentarily anxious.

"Not at all," Pauline assured her. "I am happy to take on the puzzle for her. I think it will prove a satisfactory challenge."

Ruby settled back with the smile back on her face. "Good."

Pauline asked her friend the same questions about the Warren family she had asked Susan, and received much the same reply.

"The height of respectability, the Warrens. And kind-hearted people, every one of them. You never heard a harsh word from any of their mouths, not to each other nor to anyone else. Mrs. Warren was always the first to help her neighbors if they were in trouble, and Mr. Warren used to hire tramps no one else would give the time of day to, in order to give them a helping hand. They were good people, and their daughter is the same."

"So perhaps the necklace really is a recognition of a kind deed done once to Mr. Van Camp," Pauline mused.

"Maybe, but … I can't see Miss Warren not knowing about such a deed if that's the case. They were a close-knit family."

Unless they hadn't known who it was they were doing the good deed for. Wealthy men were often eccentric. What if Mr. Van Camp had been hiking cross-country and they took him for a tramp, and he never bothered to correct them? What if he'd waited all the years afterward to repay their kindness?

It was far-fetched, but more likely than the other scenarios Pauline's imagination had concocted.

"Hopefully the lawyer will have more information tomorrow," she said.

In the Lawyer's Office

It was about a two-hour drive from Canton to Clayton by automobile; the train would have been more comfortable but taken longer. On a winter's day with nothing else to do, Pauline would quite enjoy a leisurely train ride and a chance to work out her latest plot. Today, with a specific task and a reason to reach the end destination, she was thankful Miss Warren owned her own automobile. With the sharp wind blowing that morning, Pauline was even more thankful for the closed top and—luxury indeed—electric heater.

Miss Warren was a good driver, able to concentrate on the road as well as maintain a seemingly endless stream of chatter. Thankfully she required little in response, leaving Pauline free to pursue her own thoughts while she watched the muddy fields eventually turn to river slipping by.

Even aside from Ruby's glowing endorsement of the family, Pauline had a difficult time connecting Miss Warren with scandal. She seemed not only the epitome of respectability, but she practically radiated goodness, as well. If there was scandal connected to the legacy, Pauline was certain it did not personally involve Miss Warren. A distant relative, perhaps, but not the lady herself.

People's appearances were no true indicator of their character—more words of wisdom from her lawyer grandfather before his death—but even so, she couldn't shake the conviction that Miss Warren was as upright and moral as she seemed, and as Ruby had claimed.

Pauline could sense some of the loneliness Ruby had spoken of as well. It was in the woman's garrulous nature, as though she was starved for conversation. It was also in a certain wistful quality to her smile, an indefinable something in her demeanor. Whatever it was, Pauline couldn't help but pity her, diamond necklace inheritance or not.

Gradually the river on one side and trees on the other gave way to houses and other buildings as they passed through Alexandria Bay and then came into Clayton. Pauline scarcely had time to admire the smart white houses with their air of brisk prosperity and green lawns running down to the water's edge before Miss Warren turned a corner and they were downtown, with brick and cobblestone buildings rising on either side.

"Here we are!" Miss Warren said, pulling expertly into a parking space between a delivery van and horse-drawn wagon on the side of Riverside Drive. A long row of offices sat parallel to the river: the one closest to the automobile discreetly displayed a sign reading "Law Offices of Ramsey and Ramsey" above its front door.

Pauline exited the vehicle thankfully. Two hours of endless chatter combined with the stuffiness from the heater had left her with the start of a headache. The fresh river air permeating the village did much to brighten her spirits and lessen the throbbing at her temples. She was thankful; often headaches were the precursor to worse difficulties.

In her younger days, Pauline had been particularly prone to what her mother referred to as "melancholia," and her father called "female vapors." Pauline didn't think either of those two descriptions were entirely fair, but there was no arguing with one's parents.

It had always felt to Pauline more as though her body and mind were under attack at such times. Sometimes caused by uncomfortable situations, sometimes for no reason at all, she would find herself in the grip of a fierce headache, followed by stomach cramps, shortness of breath, nausea, and trembling hands. The only cure she'd ever found for such attacks was to quietly rest in a dark room.

Thankfully, her move away from the noise and bustle of Albany, first to the restful campus of St. Lawrence University, where academics had given her life a new sense of order and purpose, and then to her apartment in the village of Canton after her graduation, had helped decrease her affliction significantly.

The moods, or attacks, or whatever they were, still came on occasion, but far less frequently, and when they did come, she was finding better ways to combat them.

She would not have welcomed having to deal with one in a lawyer's office, however, so she was relieved to have her headache disperse in the bitingly cold March air.

Gulls wheeled overhead, crying out in their raucous voices. Skiffs, canoes, and other boats Pauline could not identify bobbed in the water just off the docks, their owners ready to say goodbye to winter's ice punts. The streets were scrupulously tidy, the shops all scrubbed free of winter's grime; she even saw one or two enterprising business owners preparing to give their clapboard fronts a fresh coat of paint to welcome the spring. Overall there was an air of energy and good cheer pervading the little town of Clayton, giving it a wide-awake and hearty feel.

Mr. Ramsey's office was spruce and welcoming, as well. Its cheerful yellow exterior harmonized nicely with the white, green, and blue colors of the other buildings along the row. Inside it was an almost blinding white, and scrupulously neat.

The secretary, a woman who managed to so wholly efface herself as to be almost invisible, greeted them in low, well-bred tones and murmured that Mr. Ramsey would see them in a few minutes.

Arabella Warren fell unusually silent the moment they walked through the door. She perched on one of the uncomfortable chairs waiting rooms always seemed to have, biting her lower lip and twisting her gloves in her hands. It did not take any spectacular act of deduction to gather that this odd business with the necklace was deeply troubling.

Pauline wished she could comfort her, but the colorless receptionist, for all her discretion, made it oddly impossible to speak freely. Her non-presence acted as a smothering blanket. Pauline would have preferred someone with more personality—she might have been able to speak then.

It was with great relief she saw the inner door open. Mr. Ramsey himself came through to greet them, dismissing a younger man Pauline presumed to be his clerk as he did.

"Hello and welcome, welcome!" he cried, tripping over his own feet as he approached them. He ignored this, shaking hands with each lady with every appearance of glee.

His receptionist's suffocating presence had no effect on *him*, apparently. "Miss Warren, so glad you could come today. And you brought a friend, how nice. A friend, surely? Not a sister—it would be too unfair for the gods to put two such beauties in one family."

Pauline felt instantly tired, and her headache returned. How she loathed this kind of raillery. Old Mr. Gray, her grandfather, had been the solemn, quietly reassuring type of lawyer. Pauline far preferred that to the unctuous inanities offered by Mr. Ramsey.

"Miss Gray," Miss Warren introduced her without any more explanation, for which Pauline was thankful.

She didn't want to tip her hand too soon. If Mr. Ramsey thought she was a reporter after a story, she'd never get any information out of him.

He shook their hands a second time and stood back to allow them to precede him into the inner office.

"George, you may take your lunch break now," he told the clerk. "Eleanor—" to the secretary— "see to it no one disturbs us."

In the office, thankfully, the painful white of the walls in the reception area was replaced by a softer beige, the uncomfortable seats by old leather chairs, and the overall air of an antiseptic operating theater by the smell of pipe tobacco and old books. It was almost too dim to see anything, aside from the reading lamp on the clerk's desk, but that only added to the mellow atmosphere.

The throbbing in Pauline's head receded once again in this familiar setting, and the tension lines in Miss Warren's face smoothed themselves out.

Mr. Ramsey stumbled on his way to his seat, caught himself, and settled in behind the broad oak desk, flushing a little as he did.

"Ah, excuse me. Terribly clumsy these days. That is—yes. So. Here for your inheritance, Miss Warren? Excellent, excellent. Mr. Van Camp, God rest his soul, would be so pleased to see it going into your worthy hands."

"Before I accept it, Mr. Ramsey …" Miss Warren began. "Oh dear, this is difficult. I just want to know why, you see. It's all so confusing, and I'm afraid I don't feel entirely comfortable taking the necklace until I understand. It is such a valuable gift, isn't it, and it wouldn't be right to accept it if there was some mistake."

"Mistake?" Mr. Ramsey said, bewilderment crossing his broad, genial face.

Pauline deemed it time to step in. "What Miss Warren means, sir, is that she would like to know why Mr. Van Camp left her such a generous bequest."

"You mean you don't know?"

Miss Warren shook her head. "That's why I want you to tell me," she said, quite simply for her.

"But, my dear lady, I'm afraid I haven't the foggiest notion."

"You don't?" the two ladies said in unison.

Mr. Ramsey shook his head. "Not in the slightest."

This was a twist.

"You see," Mr. Ramsey went on, "I had never met Mr. Van Camp until a few months ago, when he rang me up and asked me to come to his house. I took my clerk and we made out the will according to the list he handed us with his bequests and legacies. No explanation was given of any of them."

"How many people?" Pauline interrupted. If the lawyer was going to be indiscreet, she would take advantage of it.

"Oh, a dozen, Miss Gray! A full dozen! Aside from the usual dispersion of house and money to various people and charities, there were a dozen personal bequests. Jewelry to eleven of them, as with Miss Warren here, and Mr. Van Camp's three Moillon paintings—surely you've heard of her? The Baroque painter woman?—to the twelfth. That's how Mr. Van Camp wanted it, so that's how George and I wrote it. And you really don't know why he chose you, Miss Warren? Remarkable, remarkable."

"No, and I—" Miss Warren began, when there was an interruption.

Even in the quiet closeness of the inner office Pauline heard the front door crash open and the receptionist raise her voice for once. The words were unintelligible, but the purport was made clear a moment later when the door to Mr. Ramsey's sanctum was flung open.

"I told you, you can't go in there, he's in a meeting!" the receptionist insisted.

"I don't care if he's with the President of the United States!" roared back the interloper over his shoulder.

He turned and faced the three startled individuals squarely.

"I ought to apologize for interrupting you, but I'm afraid I'm not particularly sorry," he said abruptly. He was quite a young man, a boy really, no older than seventeen, dressed in clothes that were clean but well-worn. He carried himself with the assurance of an older man, but the softness in his cheeks and jaw gave him away.

"I am Jonathan Van Camp, and I understand you are the lawyer responsible for giving my great-uncle's property to strangers?"

Arabella Warren gasped audibly. The young Van Camp glanced in her direction briefly before turning his attention back to the unfortunate Mr. Ramsey, who began to bluster.

"Now look here, young fellow, I am in the midst of a private meeting with these ladies, and you have no business coming in here and making these sorts of accusations! I ought to have you arrested for slander. I most certainly did not 'give away' your uncle's property. I made out his will according to his specifications, and I am one of his executors, but I bear no responsibility for the contents of it. Now then!"

Jonathan Van Camp stood his ground. "Uncle Horace told me over and over since we met that he was going to leave his baubles—the jewelry and paintings—to me, along with a trust to replace my allowance. Now he's dead and I'm cut out of the will entirely, why?"

"You had better ask yourself that," Mr. Ramsey said. "Perhaps your great-uncle thought your manners left something to be desired."

Pauline rose to her feet. Her detective instincts tingled. "Perhaps young Mr. Van Camp would be willing to go for a walk with me while you and Miss Warren conclude your business here," she said.

"Why would I do that?" the boy asked rudely.

Pauline faced him. She hadn't wanted to announce herself in this manner, but she saw no other choice. "Because Miss Warren has requested I investigate this business of the will."

While Jonathan Van Camp hesitated, Mr. Ramsey turned as red as a turkey's wattle, his eyes taking on a glassy sheen.

"A private detective? A lady detective! Now look here, this is highly inappropriate. Miss Warren, I can assure you that everything is aboveboard and perfectly legal here. You have no right bringing a detective—much less a *lady* detective—into the matter."

Pauline's respect for Miss Warren went up a notch as that lady came to her feet as well. "Mr. Ramsey, you have no business speaking so. You yourself admitted you know nothing about why the bequests were made the way they were, and if I want to be certain I am not cheating some poor soul out of his proper inheritance—morally, if not legally—that is my affair."

Pauline hadn't thought it possible for her to speak so clearly and coherently. It had an impressive effect on Mr. Ramsey as well as Jonathan Van Camp. The young man's face eased and something approaching a smile softened his mouth.

"I—you—most improper—no respect—most irregular—I have always conducted—that is—no one has ever accused—" the older man sputtered.

"I would be happy to take a walk with you," Jonathan now told Pauline. "I think a detective, especially a lady detective, is exactly what is needed in this case."

Jonathan

"Now," Pauline said once they were on the street. "Let me take a look at you."

He was tall and lanky, with the over-large hands and feet of adolescence. His blue eyes were cold and shadowed and there were faint lines of bitterness around his mouth, but Pauline thought she could see the seeds of a good-hearted man inside the angry boy.

"You and your great-uncle were close?" she said.

He shrugged, withdrawn and silent now the fire of his anger had burned out.

"Where are your parents?" Pauline tried.

"Gone," he muttered.

"Do you truly suspect Mr. Ramsey of attempting to cheat you out of your inheritance?" she persisted.

Another shrug.

Pauline threw her hands into the air. "How am I supposed to help you if you won't even talk to me? Goodness knows you were voluble enough in the lawyer's office. I thought you *wanted* a detective involved in this business."

"I do, but ..." he trailed off.

Pauline didn't have much experience with boys. Her male cousins were all older than she was, and her few childhood friends had all been girls. She had made friends with both sexes in college, but Jonathan

Van Camp was a bit younger than they all had been.

One thing that did seem to be a universal with boys and men alike was their appetite. The hotel dining rooms were out of the question, with Jonathan's shabby clothes. An ice cream soda at Ellis's drugstore would be the obvious choice, but it was hardly conducive to private conversation.

The establishment down the road from where Arabella had parked might be just the thing.

"Let's get a cup of coffee and a bite to eat," Pauline said, turning her steps toward the Hub Cafe (Ladies Lunchroom and Ice Cream Parlor Upstairs). "Perhaps we'll find some common ground for conversation then."

As with any growing boy, Jonathan's eyes brightened at the mention of food, and he regained a measure of zest as he walked beside her, courteously offering his arm to help her over any rough spots on the sidewalk and shortening his stride to match hers.

The pretty waitress with a pink bow in her hair that matched her rosy cheeks seated them at once at a corner table on the second floor, and brought them coffee and a plate of muffins with admirable promptness. In between devouring muffins and the enormous piece of apple pie the waitress brought after seeing how quickly he moved through the muffins, Jonathan finally unbent enough to tell Pauline his story.

His father had been the only child of Horace Van Camp's only brother.

"Dad died when I was a baby. Mother married again a year or so later, and we moved to Pennsylvania. She died about four years ago."

Pauline listened without comment as the story continued, the tragedy made all the more stark by the simple, straightforward way Jonathan told it.

"After Mother's funeral, my stepfather told me I was old enough to get by on my own, that he had enough to do to feed my half-sisters and himself."

Thirteen years old and on his own, Jonathan managed to track down his father's people. He introduced himself to his great-uncle without knowing how wealthy he was, but wouldn't take charity from the man once he did learn of it.

"It was one thing to ask Dad's uncle for a place to live and food to eat in exchange for work when I thought maybe he was a farmer or something," he explained, wiping his mouth on a spotlessly clean napkin. "But not like that. It—it just didn't feel right."

Despite his inability to articulate his reasons, Pauline understood, and admired him for them. Despite his difficult upbringing, this boy had fine moral principles. Her mother, poor choice in second husband aside, had clearly done well by her son.

Horace Van Camp seemed to agree. He insisted on giving Jonathan a small allowance, helped helped him find a job and secure a room at the Bouchard guest house, and had him out for dinner every Sunday.

"He *said* he would provide for me in his will," Jonathan said. "He *promised*. He said an inheritance was different from charity, and he didn't want his collections to pass out of Van Camp hands. He'd promised the house to a hospital, and was going to put most of the money toward charitable organizations, but family was important, he said. The jewelry and the paintings should stay with kin, because they were personal. He didn't want them divided among strangers. He specifically said so."

Jonathan had been doing some work out of town for the past couple of weeks, and had returned to his landlady's information that his great-uncle was dead and the will had already been read. The house and grounds had been given to a hospital, as the old man had wanted; the money donated to local charities likewise. Against his stated purpose, however, nothing had been left to Jonathan, and the jewels and paintings were split between twelve individuals.

"If he'd been angry with me or if I'd done something to offend him, he would have told me, he wouldn't have changed his will secretly," Jonathan said, picking at the crumbs left on his plate. "He didn't brood, he blew up and then calmed down."

Like his great-nephew, apparently.

"Do you really think Mr. Ramsey is responsible?" Pauline asked.

Jonathan rubbed his fingers together, avoiding her eye as he looked around the small cafe.

"No," he finally admitted. "I suppose not. It's not like the will was changed to benefit him, and I don't know why anyone would do something like that. I was just … angry."

"The problem at hand is," Pauline said, thinking it through, "why did Mr. Van Camp change his mind right before his death to cut his only relative out of his will and instead leave his most beloved possessions to strangers? Once we find the answer to that, we will hopefully know why he chose those twelve people, and Arabella's conscience will be at rest, and you will have peace of mind. It is quite the puzzle, I must say."

On the surface, the easiest answer seemed to be that while Jonathan was out of town, Mr. Van Camp had learned something to the boy's discredit and in a blind rage made up a new will to ensure he didn't receive anything.

But what could that be? Could Jonathan Van Camp be a fraud? What if he wasn't really the old man's great-nephew?

That didn't make sense—surely someone as canny in business as Horace Van Camp would have thoroughly inspected the boy's credentials when he first arrived. And it was an awfully long time for a con artist to wait for a payoff, four years which could have stretched on even longer, had Mr. Van Camp's health permitted.

Plus, that still didn't answer the question of why Arabella and the other eleven had been chosen instead of Jonathan. If Mr. Van Camp didn't know them at all, how did he get their names? How did he learn of their existence? Why, in heaven's name, leave a diamond necklace to a perfect stranger?

No, the simplest answer didn't seem to be an answer at all. Well then, moving along.

What if Mr. Ramsey *had* altered the will? That was the next simplest idea. However, Jonathan was correct when he pointed out that the lawyer didn't benefit from this new will, and why should he want to cut Jonathan out in favor of strangers? It would have been more in his interest to ingratiate himself with the new heir.

So much for Mr. Ramsey as a villain. Who, then?

"Jonathan, did your uncle have any staff at the house?"

"A sort of butler-valet fellow and a gardener. Why?"

"Were they left anything?"

He shrugged, looking startled. "I don't know. That lawyer man would."

Pauline frowned. Now that Mr. Ramsey was annoyed with her involvement in this matter, he was much less likely to volunteer information.

"Do you think that's important?"

"If they were left out of the will as well, then your uncle wasn't angry at you," Pauline said, working her way through her thoughts as she spoke. "It would have been something else that made him alter it. If he left them in but cut you out …"

"Then it was spite." He slumped down in his chair. "Swell."

Pauline stood and gathered her handbag and gloves. "Do you know where to find them?"

"I suppose." Jonathan stood up as well, curious and wary but still a gentleman.

"If the lawyer won't tell us, perhaps they will. I'll leave a note on

Miss Warren's auto so she won't think you've abducted me, and then we shall go find these two."

She chose not to hear his muttered comment about the abduction working the other way 'round.

Back out in the fresh air, Jonathan told Pauline that the gardener, Jasper Randolph, lived in a small cottage in Clayton. Mr. Gagne, the butler-valet, was still living at the Van Camp residence, a mile outside the village.

"At least, that's what my landlady says."

Pauline, mindful of the changeable March weather, decided they would visit the gardener first and let Miss Warren drive them to the estate when her business with the lawyer was concluded.

Jasper Randolph's house was neat and tidy, a small white clapboard cottage a short distance from the river, with immaculately tended gardens both in front and in back. Nothing was growing yet, of course, not even the crocuses, but Pauline could see where he had been stirring the dirt and starting his pruning. She would have thought it early even for that, but perhaps it was warmer here by the mighty St. Lawrence than in Canton.

Mr. Randolph's house, unfortunately, was locked up tight, with a sign on the front door saying, "No Milk Until Further Notice."

"Not simply gone for the day, then," Pauline said, turning away from the closed door.

"Now what?" Jonathan said, shoulders slumping.

If there was one thing Pauline had learned from her profession, it was perseverance. She led Jonathan to the house next door and knocked.

The door was opened by a pleasant-faced older woman with snow-white hair, dark skin, and shaky hands. "May I help you?" she said in a soft voice with a distinct southern accent.

"We are looking for Mr. Randolph," Pauline said. "Can you tell us when he'll return?"

"Oh, not for a long time, miss, I'm sorry to have to tell you. He's gone off to New Mexico."

"New Mexico!" Pauline said.

The woman nodded, a smile creasing her cheeks. "Oh, it was so exciting. Jasper, he was so saddened by poor Mr. Van Camp, his employer, dying, and he didn't know if he'd be able to get another job. He's a fine gardener, Jasper is, but he's almost as old as me—we were children together down in Virginia, him and me and my husband, and we all came north together and settled down here, and here Jasper and I still are, even though my husband's gone now. But not everyone is willing to hire someone Jasper's age, don't you see, so he was worried."

"Mm," Pauline said encouragingly, while at her elbow Jonathan stifled a yawn and couldn't keep his eyes from wandering toward the river.

"Then, two days ago, he knocked on my door beaming. 'Emmy,' he said—that's my name, Emmy Tuttle—'Emmy, I'm off to New Mexico!' And I said, just as you did, miss, 'New Mexico!' He laughed and said that even though he hadn't been able to leave him anything in the will because he was one of the witnesses, Mr. Van Camp had arranged a reward for his faithful service after all by setting in motion a trip to New Mexico for him to take after he died."

It took Pauline a few moments to untangle Mrs. Tuttle's pronouns. "Mr. Van Camp couldn't leave Mr. Randolph anything in Mr. Van Camp's will because Mr. Randolph had been one of the witnesses to the will, so instead Mr. Van Camp arranged for a trip for Mr. Randolph after Mr. Van Camp died?"

"Yes, that's what I said, miss. That nice young man from the lawyer's office came out to tell him so, and wasn't Jasper tickled pink! 'That stuffy Mr. Gagne didn't get a holiday, for all he thought he was so much better than me,' he told me. 'Both witnesses, we were, and only I get the trip. They say virtue is its own reward, but it's nice to see something more solid!' That was just his way of speaking, you understand."

Pauline assured her she did.

"So, Jasper's going to be gone at least a month, but he said he might not come back at all if New Mexico is really as beautiful and warm as everyone says it is. We feel the cold in our bones these days, we do, but I love it here and wouldn't move back south if you paid me, even if I am sorry to see Jasper leave. This is where Mr. Tuttle is buried, and this is where I plan to be buried, right next to him—though not for a good many more years, the good Lord willing. I'm sorry I can't be more help, miss."

"You've been a considerable help," Pauline assured her. "Thank you so much, Mrs. Tuttle. Come along, Jonathan."

She mulled this new information as they walked back to the road.

"That was interesting," she said.

"Jasper left, what does it matter?" he returned, kicking a stone out of the road.

Pauline case a severe eye at him. "In a case like this, everything matters."

At the Van Camp Estate

rabella Warren was waiting for them by the auto, as was Mr. Ramsey. Beside Pauline, Jonathan sucked in an audible breath through his teeth. She didn't have time to inquire the reason before he extended his stride, outpacing her in seconds, and approached the lawyer with his head high and his fists clenched.

"I apologize for my behavior earlier, sir," he said, in a tone that stopped just short of imperious and did not indicate any sort of genuine sorrow. "I ought not to have made such accusations."

Mr. Ramsey smiled, then frowned. "Not at all, not at all! That is to say—it was terribly rude, young fellow, but there, I'm sure you were upset—not that I can excuse those sort of statements! Some people in my position would sue you for slander, not that I would go to such lengths, but all the same … But there, we can let bygones be bygones, I am sure. After all, to expect an inheritance and receive nothing is a terrible blow, terrible. Dreadful how forgetful these old men can be. Why, George—that is, I—had to ask him once or twice to clarify something he had written in the draft of the will, and would you believe it, he couldn't even remember writing it in the first place! Well, there it is, and it is indeed hard lines on you, young man, so we'll let this little incident slide. In fact, if you are in need of financial assistance in any way, I'm sure I can—"

"No, thank you." Jonathan's voice was curt as he pulled his hand free from the lawyer's half-hearted shake.

Geniality fully restored now, Mr. Ramsey ignored this and turned to Pauline. "Miss Gray, I really do believe I owe you an apology myself. Miss Warren explained that you aren't really a private detective, merely a friend with—now, how did you put it, Miss Warren?—a good head for puzzles, that's right. Under the circumstances, I can understand how Miss Warren might want someone to help clarify the situation. It is a puzzle to be sure, but the answer is merely the peculiarities of older folk. All the same, I think I reacted a mite hastily back in the office."

Pauline favored him with a gracious, if cool, smile. "Not at all, sir."

Mr. Ramsey smiled fatuously. "Excellent, excellent. Should have known such a lovely young lady as yourself, with such an excellent taste in clothing, couldn't truly be a private detective. Such a pretty shade of yellow, your blouse—looks just like a daffodil."

Pauline was puzzled by this effusion—not only were such personal comments inappropriate in a lawyer, her blouse was white.

She looked again at his beaming face and deduced that he considered the best way to restore relations with a female was to compliment her clothing, regardless of how inaccurate his statement.

Having settled that, she looked at Miss Warren, deliberately using formal language to move away from this false intimacy. "Has your business been transacted satisfactorily?"

Miss Warren opened her handbag and peeked in, then looked up with a flustered expression, closing it again hastily. "Yes," she said. "That is—yes. I think I'd best get right home and take this to the bank. I don't feel quite comfortable carrying it. Dear me, I don't wish to seem ungrateful, but I'm still so puzzled by it all. You say he was peculiar and forgetful, Mr. Ramsey, but I'm sure I don't see how either peculiarity or forgetfulness can make you leave something to a stranger. And I still don't know how he even learned my name! It seems downright spooky, if you ask me. Oh dear, but yes, Miss Gray, I am ready to leave."

"Excellent. Do you mind going back by way of the Van Camp estate? Jonathan would like to show us where his great-uncle lived."

"I would?" the young man began, when Pauline discreetly kicked his ankle. "Oh, that. I mean, yes, I would."

Pauline didn't care to let Mr. Ramsey know she was still investigating the matter, but nor was she inclined to let it go now. Arabella Warren was right: no amount of forgetfulness or peculiarity could incline someone to leave gifts to individuals he had never heard of.

Through the open office door, Pauline saw George-the-clerk (she couldn't remember his surname, if indeed Mr. Ramsey had bothered to introduce them at all) stand up from his desk. "Sir, Mr. Ramsey, do you recall that letter from the hospital?"

"Oh yes, oh yes," said Mr. Ramsey, fingers twitching. "I'm sorry, Miss Warren, Miss Gray, but we had a letter from the hospital, the one Mr. Van Camp left the estate to, asking that we be sure not to allow trespassers or sight-seers on the property. It is theirs now, you know, and we must respect their wishes."

Miss Warren frowned. "Surely they would not object to their benefactor's great-nephew taking one final look at the place. I hardly think he counts as general public."

"Alas, dear lady, the law is the law, and we must follow the letter of it rather than the spirit, however much we might wish otherwise. Besides, you must get that necklace to your bank right away! The longer it is in your personal possession, the more danger you are in."

"I must say I don't understand at all why one would want a diamond necklace if one is never to be allowed to wear it, but must always keep it in the bank," said Miss Warren with a frown. "But oh well, there seems to be far too much about all this that I don't understand, and nobody asked my opinion on any of it! If they had, I could have given them an earful, let me tell you."

"Exactly so, Miss Warren," said Pauline. "Good day, Mr. Ramsey. Come along, Jonathan."

Miss Warren had opened the driver's side door of the auto when Pauline remembered that they needed one more thing from the lawyer before they could leave.

"Oh, Miss Warren, you were going to ask Mr. Ramsey for a list of the other heirs, weren't you? So that you could see if any of you had anything in common that might have caused Mr. Van Camp to choose you all?"

Miss Warren blinked a few times before picking up her cue. "Yes—yes, of course. Would that be acceptable, Mr. Ramsey?"

"Naturally, my dear lady," Mr. Ramsey said. "George, jot down a list for Miss Warren."

"Sir, are you certain? You are always saying it isn't appropriate to divulge that sort of information."

"George, my boy, I admire your caution, but in this case, I think we can make an exception. After all, in an ordinary state of things, all the heirs would have gathered together to hear the will read, and would therefore each know what the others had inherited. In this case, I think it entirely appropriate to give Miss Warren a list, especially if it sets her mind at ease."

George pulled a sour face but did as he was bid, bringing out a handwritten list a few minutes later. He handed it to Mr. Ramsey, who didn't bother looking at it before passing it along to Miss Warren.

"I hope it sheds some light on the matter for you, Miss Warren, so that your conscience may rest and you can fully enjoy your magnificent inheritance. Good day, Miss Gray, young man."

Miss Warren handed the list to Pauline "to take care of on the ride," and at last they were on their way.

"Thank you for the ride, Miss Warren, but I don't actually need it,"

Jonathan said once they had pulled away from the curb. "My boarding house is only over on Union Street."

"We are going to your great-uncle's estate, Jonathan." Pauline spoke with quiet firmness.

"Oh dear," said Miss Warren, one hand fluttering loose from the wheel. "But the lawyer said—"

"Even if the hospital does want strangers kept away from what is theirs, we are not visiting the property. We are visiting Mr. Van Camp's butler, who is still acting as caretaker."

"Oh." Miss Warren considered this. "I suppose that makes sense. But why do we want to speak with him?"

Pauline explained. "Despite Mr. Ramsey's anecdote, I doubt Mr. Van Camp was forgetful enough to accidentally leave his personal manservant out of his will. I want to see if he left Mr. Gagne anything. If he was, I might believe Jonathan was simply forgotten. If not, there would seem to be a different answer to this riddle, one that still eludes us."

"Is his name on that list?" Miss Warren asked.

Pauline glanced down at it. "No, but that only means he did not inherit some of the jewelry or paintings. He still could have received a monetary legacy."

"But that Mrs. Tuttle said Jasper said Great-Uncle Horace couldn't leave either of them anything because they were both witnesses, and only Jasper got rewarded for it," Jonathan contributed from the back.

"True, but there must be more to the story than that," Pauline said. "Besides, a good journalist—or investigator—never believes third-hand information. We must always track it down to its source."

Miss Warren wanted to know who Jasper and Mrs. Tuttle were, and that explanation lasted the rest of the drive to the estate.

"I must say I don't care for any of this," Miss Warren said as she maneuvered the auto up the long, winding drive to the Van Camp residence. "I do wish—I know I should be thankful, but I do wish that Mr. Van Camp hadn't left me anything at all. I don't need a diamond necklace, and when am I ever going to wear one? Look here, young man—you said in the lawyer's office that your uncle promised to leave the jewelry and such to you. Why don't I just give you the necklace? That feels much more fair."

There was a startled sound from the back seat. Then, Jonathan spoke up slowly.

"That—that is awfully good of you, Miss Warren. But I don't think I can accept. If Great-Uncle Horace really did leave me out of the will on purpose, then it would feel like cheating for me to accept your necklace. Besides, you don't even know me!" His voice turned incredulous on that last point.

"I suppose you're right," Miss Warren said. "But if we find there was a mistake, this necklace is yours whether you want it or not, young man."

Jonathan said nothing, perhaps too stunned by this generosity of spirit to reply. Pauline was touched as well. She couldn't think of many people who would respond so to this sort of situation. It made her even more determined to discover the truth behind the puzzle.

"Besides," Miss Warren continue, "It is far too grand for me, and for Canton. I mean really, Miss Gray, can you see me going to church or doing the marketing wearing diamonds?"

The image was so incongruous Pauline had to laugh. A gruff chuckle from the back seat indicated Jonathan was tickled by it as well. Miss Warren's cheeks flushed and her eyes showed her pleasure at having amused her companions so.

The drive crested a hill, and the Van Camp estate opened before their eyes. Miss Warren put on the brake. "Oh my," she said softly.

Pauline had to agree.

The house itself was unpretentious, if large, built of grey stone and standing solidly in the middle of a sprawling lawn. It was the vista behind it that drew one's eye and took one's breath.

The greening land rolled away behind the hill the house was built on, fields and trees alike receding down to end at the magnificent St. Lawrence River. The silver waters, undulating swiftly past, were dotted with some of the thousand islands that gave the region its name. Far off on the distant horizon lay the misty borders of Canada.

Pauline could see why someone would want to retire to this place.

Jonathan scrambled out of the backseat first, opening the door for Miss Warren without thinking.

"I'm glad he gave this place to the hospital," he said abruptly, offering his hand to the older woman absently. "That, at least, is what he had promised, even if he forgot or changed his mind about everything else."

"You don't want to have all this," Pauline waved an encompassing hand, "for your own?"

"It would be too much for me," Jonathan said, scorn edging his tone. "Could you see me living here all on my own?" A reminiscent smile played around his finely-drawn mouth. "I asked Great-Uncle Horace that when he asked me the same question, and he just about killed himself laughing. We agreed the hospital was better. All I want is a small place, something no one can take from me. A little bit of land all my own, to call home." He closed his mouth with a snap.

"Let's see if Mr. Gagne is home to visitors, shall we?" Pauline said.

They pressed the doorbell and thumped the lion's-head knocker, but no response came to either.

"Oh well, he must be out," Miss Warren said.

Jonathan frowned. "But his auto is still here, look." He pointed to the small shed Pauline had overlooked earlier in her amazement at the view. The black nose of an automobile poked out from the front.

"He has his own auto?"

"Great-Uncle Horace hated them," Jonathan said, laughter crossing his face and making him look like the boy he was. "So Gagne bought his own and used it whenever they needed to drive anywhere, Great-Uncle moaning and complaining the entire time."

"Well then, perhaps he's gone for a walk," Miss Warren suggested. "I know I should, if I lived in this place, even as the hired help. I should walk all over it, every day, just to marvel at its beauty."

"Gagne isn't much for walking," said Jonathan, his tone doubtful.

"Let us spread out and see what we can discover," Pauline said. "Perhaps he needed to tend something on the grounds."

The gathering shadows cleared from Jonathan's face. "Sure."

The three scattered, Miss Warren going to the left of the house, Jonathan to the right, and Pauline straight behind. Her companions' voices echoed in her ears as they began calling for Mr. Gagne. She added her own voice to the mix as she entered the woods and outside noise became muffled.

"Mr. Gagne? Mr. Gagne, are you here?"

She kept to the path that wove its way through the trees, until a splash of color to her left caught her eye. She turned, trying to make it out in the green gloom. There, a bit of red on the ground near that fallen log …

Pauline stepped off the path to inspect it more closely. It was probably nothing but a maple leaf left over from autumn, but her curiosity was piqued. Most fallen leaves had faded and turned into ground cover after the winter.

She was nearly on top of him before her brain caught up with what her eyes were seeing.

It was no fallen log at all, and no maple leaf.

The body of a man lay prone upon the ground, blood from a head wound staining the earth.

Pauline swallowed something between a gasp and a scream. She forced herself to step close enough to bend down and check his wrist for a pulse.

The coldness of his skin sent chills down her own spine. There was no pulse, and as she looked more closely she saw that the blood on and around his head had dried. The red, which she had initially taken for fresh blood, was in fact a handkerchief left carelessly beside the fallen man.

It seemed she had found Mr. Gagne, but he would never answer her questions now.

Suspects and Theories

"Well, you have been making a day of it. On the trail of a new story?"

The question died on Sarah's lips as she took in Pauline's state as the other entered the apartment. "What on earth is the matter?"

Pauline glanced at herself in the mirror over the mantelpiece. Pale at all times, her skin was practically translucent now, and the shadows under her hazel eyes made it appear she hadn't slept in a week.

In short, she looked ghastly.

"I found a dead body in Clayton," she said, wearily dropping onto her favorite seat on the hearthrug before the cozy fire.

"What, another?" was Sarah's response, more exasperated than sympathetic.

"I didn't 'find' the last one, and the police have declared this one an accident," Pauline said, irritation bringing some of her usual crispness back to her voice.

Sarah, a nurse to her core, said, "Let me bring you a tray for your supper, and then you can tell me the entire story. Something hints that you don't necessarily agree with the police's opinion."

Under Sarah's professional eye, Pauline had a plate of beef stroganoff, a slice of bread, and a glass of milk right there in front of the fire, and found herself revived enough to tell her friend about the day.

Sarah took up her sewing, most likely transforming a simple frock into something stunning and glamorous, as usual, while she listened.

As Pauline finished her story, Sarah shook her head.

"I don't like any of it. Too convenient: the gardener gone and the butler dead? The lawyer must be behind it. Daddy always said to never trust a lawyer."

"But there's no motive," Pauline protested, arguing against her own suspicions as much as Sarah's. "Even Jonathan admits that. The lawyer doesn't get anything from the will, any more than Jonathan himself. So why would he forge a will and remove the witnesses—Jasper Randolph at considerable expense to himself, no less—if he didn't even benefit from it?"

"What other options are there?" Sarah persisted.

Pauline wiped her hands on a napkin and set the tray aside to tick the possibilities off on her fingers. "One: the police are right and Mr. Gagne's death was an accident, and Horace Van Camp decided for reasons unknown to disinherit his great-nephew and select twelve unknown persons to receive his collections instead, despite previous insistence that they should remain with family."

Sarah's snort showed how unlikely she thought that option.

"Two: Jonathan Van Camp was so angry at his great-uncle that he went to the estate in a rage before coming to the lawyer's office, got into a fight with the butler, and killed him."

Sarah interrupted indignantly. "What a horrible suspicion to have of that poor boy!"

"That's what the police initially suspected before they settled on an accident," Pauline said. "I don't like it, but we have to consider it."

"Did he try to prevent you from visiting the estate at all?"

"No."

Sarah stabbed the needle triumphantly into the next stitch. "There you have it. Surely if he had killed the man, he wouldn't have wanted all of you going there and wandering around to find the body."

It was an excellent point, one Pauline hadn't yet considered. She was thankful to Sarah for bringing it up. "The third option is a mysterious person who persuaded Mr. Van Camp to change the will, and then got Mr. Randolph out of the country and killed Mr. Gagne to keep them from telling anyone about it."

"About what? Do be more specific."

Pauline shrugged. "That's part of the mystery. The way the will was changed? The reason for it? Our mysterious individual—Mr. or Miss X, let's say, though it sounds ridiculously melodramatic—must have been there in person when Mr. Van Camp changed the will, and he or she doesn't want anyone to know."

Sarah considered this, mulling over all the options over before nodding decisively. "As much as I still want to blame the lawyer, your mysterious Mr. X does seem most likely. One of the twelve persons inheriting under the new will?"

"That was my thought," Pauline said. "And the other eleven are a blind."

"But goodness! What could one bequest be worth that this person would be willing to give away the rest?"

"If we could determine that, we would be one step closer to discovering Mr. X," Pauline said.

"Are we leaving Arabella Warren off the suspect list?"

"I think we must," Pauline said. "Not only do I doubt she has the character to plot, scheme, and murder, I do not see why she would bring me in on the matter if she had a hand in it. Perhaps she is a cunning actress and has a deeper purpose than we can divine—"

"But it's not likely," Sarah finished. "I agree. So what is our next step?"

"I thought you disapproved of me getting mixed up in this affair?"

Pauline asked.

Sarah folded her strong brown hands together over her knee, letting her sewing slip. "I disapprove of you wandering in here looking like the ghost of yourself. However," her black eyes flashed, "I disapprove even more of murder and robbery, especially of those too poor or innocent to help themselves."

Pauline reflected, not for the first time, how lucky she had been the day Sarah had answered her newspaper ad for a roommate. Some in this small, rural village might raise eyebrows at their situation: two working women, one black and one white, both defying convention in their career choices—Sarah as a hospital nurse in a mostly-white community; Pauline as a newspaper columnist and dedicated scholar—but their friendship enriched both their lives.

Pauline knew someday Sarah would marry and move to a home of her own; the other girl was not as content in her singleness as Pauline was.

Until that day came, Pauline would continue to be thankful.

She pulled out the list the reluctant George had given Miss Warren earlier. "Miss Warren didn't recognize any of these names, so I think the next step is to contact each of them to learn if they knew Mr. Van Camp or each other, or if they have anything in common. I hope there will be something about one of them that will shed some light on whether he or she is our mysterious X."

"Surely we can eliminate some of them even before that point," Sarah said. "What is included on the list?"

Pauline handed the piece of creamy stationery over to her. "Names, ages, addresses."

"Arden Jamison, age eighty-seven, Adams, NY," Sarah read out. She stopped and raised her eyebrows. "Eighty-seven? I believe we can cross him off. One cannot imagine an octogenarian plotting murder for gain, never mind having the strength to murder a younger man."

Pauline acknowledged the point with a wave of her hand. "Oh," she said, stopping her wave halfway through. "I think I've heard of him. Yes, that's right. He dug up an ancient helmet they think might be Roman in his backyard, and the anthropologists are wild about it. I remember because the *Jefferson County Journal* scooped us on it, and our editors were furious."

"A Roman helmet in New York State? Surely not," Sarah said, diverted from the main point.

"Hence why anthropologists are wild about it," Pauline said.

Sarah shook her head. She picked up a pencil and drew a line through Arden Jamison's name. "Maria Thompson, five, Sacketts Harbor. Five?"

"Very well, cross out Maria Thompson—though I suppose her parents could be responsible."

"Honestly, Pauline. That is far-fetched even for one of your novels."

Sarah was the only person outside of Pauline's publishers who knew of her novels. A secret of that sort was difficult to keep from the person with whom one lived. Luckily for Pauline, Sarah was utterly trustworthy.

"Maria is off the list, then," Pauline agreed.

Richard Bracken and Caroline Swanson were also taken off the list due to old age, leaving them with Jane Casper, thirty-three, Cape Vincent; Denis O'Leary, forty, Watertown; Alan Caruthers, twenty-one, Carthage; Bertha Nelson, fifty-nine, Potsdam; Brian Nettleton, nineteen, Clayton; David Anderson, twenty-nine, Clayton; and Miller Horton, thirty-one, Toronto.

"Good grief," Sarah said. "Where on earth did Mr. Van Camp or Mr. X pick up on such a disparate group?"

"I have a feeling if we could answer that question, we'd have our finger on the entire problem," Pauline said.

"How will we begin to approach them?"

"Oh, that's simple enough. We tell them we are running a story in the *Times* on the unusual legacies of Mr. Van Camp. My editor might even approve the story, who knows? Shall we split the list?"

"We can't possibly interview them all even if we split the list," Sarah said. "Unless you are planning a trip to Toronto?"

"Some will have to be done via letter or telephone," Pauline said. "But we can do some of them here."

"I can stop by and query the one in Potsdam tomorrow after my shift at the hospital ends. I'll already be halfway there," Sarah said. The Canton-Potsdam Hospital, where she worked, was located squarely between the two towns.

"I want to check in on Jonathan anyway, so I can interview Miss Casper, Mr. Nettleton, and Mr. Anderson," Pauline said, running her finger down the list.

"That leaves Denis O'Leary, Alan Caruthers, and Miller Horton," Sarah said, taking the list from Pauline to look at it herself. "I will write to the first two, and you can write to Mr. Horton."

"Excellent," Pauline said. "Thank you."

Sarah set the list on the side table and began to sew again. Her dark eyes were troubled. "You say you will try to write the story we are using as an excuse?"

Pauline understood her difficulty. It seemed wrong to use half-lies and outright deceptions in order to reach truth. It was something she had wrestled with in her conscience even when she told the lawyer that they wished to pay their respects to Mr. Gagne when they really went to gain a greater understanding of Mr. Van Camp's will, or letting Mr. Ramsey initially believe she was Miss Warren's friend rather than that she was accompanying her to seek out the reasons behind her bequest.

Was it ever right to use deception in order to provoke honesty? Logic said yes, but her heart said no.

"I will do my best," was all she could promise to Sarah.

Her friend nodded. "And—you don't feel this is—at all—meddling? Is it really our place to go about hunting down a murderer? I realize we can't leave it to the police when they are convinced the death was accidental, but it still feels—over-officious, I suppose."

Here, Pauline was on surer ground. She had spent considerable time pondering this matter after her previous case. "So long as we aren't meddling purely for our own enjoyment, say out of a desire to manipulate people, I have no qualms. If we have the ability and the inclination to bring about justice for those who can't receive it any other way, it cannot be wrong to act." Honesty compelled her to add, "I do, admittedly, get a great deal of satisfaction out of unraveling a puzzle, but that isn't my only motivation."

Sarah laughed, set aside her sewing for good, and pulled the writing materials out of their drawer in Pauline's desk. "There's no rule that says you can't enjoy yourself even while doing something good for others. If I didn't get satisfaction out of nursing, I wouldn't have been able to make it my career, no matter how many people I was able to help."

On that note, they set to writing their letters, comparing them for clarity, addressing them, and setting them aside to give to the postman in the morning. That finished, Pauline took her turn at washing the dishes, as Sarah had prepared dinner, while Sarah finished her sewing.

An ordinary evening, the perfect antidote to the troubling events that had marred the day. Pauline even dared hope she would be able to sleep without being plagued by nightmares of finding Mr. Gagne's body.

She did: her sleep was deep and untroubled and she woke the next morning ready to face anything. Sarah had breakfasted and left already for her shift, leaving behind a note saying she wouldn't forget to look up Bertha Nelson after work.

Pauline scraped what was left of the oatmeal Sarah had prepared into a bowl, adding cream and maple syrup to make it more palatable to her taste buds, and sliced an apple to accompany it. She looked longingly at the coffee can, but after hearing the grounds rattle inside when she shook it, she sighed and pulled down the jar of chicory instead. She far preferred the real thing, but at least chicory was a reasonable substitute, and far better for the pocketbook.

She generally enjoyed reading the newspaper with her morning coffee, a habit picked up from summers spent with her grandparents when she was a girl. Her grandfather had taken several papers, and would read excerpts aloud to Pauline and her grandmother in between sips of his coffee.

This morning's paper delivery was late—the *Watertown Daily Times* had a new paperboy, and efficiency was not his watchword—so Pauline picked through the pile of read papers by the fireplace to find something else, finally settling on an old copy of the *North Country Advance* that she had somehow missed when it first came out. Even old news was better than nothing.

A photograph of an intricate patchwork quilt caught her eye first; quilting being one of the many skills she admired without being able to master. The accompanying story told of how the quilt's creator, a Mrs. Bertha Nelson, had sold the magnificent work to the governor of New York after he had seen it displayed at the State Fair last summer.

Bertha Nelson … that was one of the people on the list from the lawyer's office. Pauline was musing on the nature of coincidences when she was interrupted by a knock on the door.

9:00 in the morning was early for visitors, with most people either at their jobs or getting housework done and out of the way for the day. Pauline put the paper down, set her dishes in the sink, and answered the knock.

It was Arabella Warren.

"I am so sorry to disturb you this early, Miss Gray," she burst into speech. "But I'm driving back to Clayton today, to visit that poor lad Jonathan Van Camp and make sure the police haven't bullied him further or decided after all that he is responsible for that poor Mr. Gagne's death, or anything like that. I know, it's dreadful to keep using gasoline like this, but I can't just sit at home and do nothing. I also want to know more about Mr. Gagne, if he has any family and what's being done about his funeral, because it seems to me we who inherited from Mr. Van Camp have a moral obligation if not a legal one to see to it he has one, a funeral, that is. I thought perhaps you would care to come with me, but if not I'll take myself off with apologies for disturbing you."

Pauline had intended to wash the dishes and sweep and dust, and then take the 10:30 train from Canton to Clayton, but this was far better. She relinquished her housework without regret.

"Let me leave a note for my friend and then I will be right with you," she said.

Sarah—gone with A.W. to Thousand Islands for the day. Unsure when we'll return. For heaven's sake don't enable my slothfulness by doing my chores—I'll tend them when I get back. Good luck with Miss Nelson.

"Here is your paper, by the way," Miss Warren said, handing her the *Times*. "It was at the foot of the stairs as I came up. Your paper boy must be dreadfully sloppy."

Pauline agreed and thanked her with a nod while taking the paper.

Miss Warren sighed. "My father, God rest his soul, always said it was inappropriate for a lady to have her name in the paper for anything besides her birth, marriage, and death. Well, my name was in the *Times* last month because I was foolish enough to answer a reporter's questions about my opinion on the end of Prohibition, and I suppose it will be again if someone gets a hold of this story. Oh—not you, Miss Gray. I know you won't print anything without permission. I trust you, naturally. You're not just a reporter."

"Thank you," Pauline said, putting on hat and gloves and making sure her bag held a fresh notebook and enough sharpened pencils. "But I must warn you that I am planning on using a story for my column as an excuse to ask questions of the other heirs, in order to hopefully find a connection between you all that would tell us why Mr. Van Camp chose you. However, I will not use anyone's name without permission, including yours."

The air felt even more springlike today than yesterday; Pauline even saw the green spikes of some early crocuses out on various lawns as they flashed past in Miss Warren's auto. Perhaps more snow *was* coming, as the farmers insisted, but today held the promise of daffodils and sun rather than snow and clouds.

"I do feel sorry for that Van Camp boy, I tell you, and I wish he would let me give him the diamond necklace. I don't think I'd ever feel right about owning it, knowing it had been promised to him, especially after all he's been through."

Pauline had, after obtaining Jonathan's permission, shared his story with Miss Warren on the drive home the prior evening. It seemed to have been preying on the other woman's mind ever since.

"But then," Miss Warren mused, "if Mr. Van Camp changed his mind, would it be right for me to go against it? He might have found out something dreadful about Jonathan, but I must say he seems like a nice boy to me. Oh, a bit rude, of course, but I've never met a boy that age who isn't rude occasionally, and he has more reason than most, and he could be polite enough when he put his mind to it. Helped me out of the auto, remember, and that's more than many would do. It makes me feel downright ill, thinking about him having to make his way in the world like he has, without ever a bit of kindness or affection shown him, and no family besides a few half-sisters he hasn't seen since he was twelve. A boy belongs in a family, not in a boarding house! I tell you I almost offered to bring him right home with us yesterday after the police finally let us go. It didn't seem right to leave him there at the door like a stray cat."

"Indeed," Pauline agreed.

"And I tell you something else, I do not agree with Mr. Ramsey. Oh—you weren't there for this part, you and Jonathan had left the office by then. He said that Jonathan reminded him of his clerk's brother, who caused the family so much trouble that Mr. Ramsey finally paid for him to go to Canada to spare the family any more disgrace. He thought he had done a fine and noble act, you could tell from how he spoke, but with the clerk right there! The poor man—the clerk, not Mr. Ramsey—just shriveled right into himself. Well, Mr. Ramsey plumed himself so much for his actions I could barely get a word in edgewise, but I spoke up all right when he started running down young Jonathan and making all sorts of unfounded accusations against him."

Pauline had tried to follow all this, but the endless flow of conversation left her dazed. "Mmm," was all she dared reply.

"I told him outright he had no business saying such things about that poor boy and making such accusations when he didn't know a thing about it, and I was there on business, not to listen to gossip! He changed his tune then, right sharp, got in a fine huff and said he never gossiped, and finally his secretary—you remember that Miss Peck?—had to intervene and calm him down, and that's when he finally gave me the necklace. He, I say, when really she was the one who opened the safe and removed the necklace, treating him like the petulant child he was acting. And I must say, Miss Gray, I was a tiny bit disappointed in the necklace. Oh, it's beautiful all right—I meant to show it to you yesterday, but we were all so distracted by that poor Mr. Gagne's death, it didn't seem right—but somehow, I always thought there would be something more magical about a diamond necklace.

This just looks like bits of glass. That's another reason I wouldn't mind giving it to Jonathan. It doesn't seem all that special. But there, he already said he wouldn't accept it, and I'm sure I don't know how to convince him to take it, he's that proud. What do you think?"

Thus adjured, Pauline had to force her mind back along the tortuous trail of Miss Warren's thoughts to find the original point.

"I don't know," she said, and braced herself for another spate of volubility.

It was going to be a long drive.

Complications

Jane Casper of Cape Vincent, NY, was only thirty-three, but discontentment had shaped her life such that she looked and sounded twenty years older. Her only satisfaction in life came from her award-winning cabbages, which, she informed Pauline, had won the blue ribbon at various fairs so many times the *Cape Vincent Times* had done a piece on it last month.

"And I consider that far more important than some inheritance which has nothing to do with me in the first place," she said. "That old Van Camp only left it to me because of my late brother."

Pauline pricked up her ears. "Really? Mr. Van Camp was acquainted with Mr. Casper?"

"What? No, of course not. The likes of him don't mingle with folk like us. I doubt that man ever set eyes on Elwin in his life."

"Then why ..."

"I'm telling you, aren't I? Listen: my brother Elwin Casper was a very important man here in Cape Vincent."

Pauline longed to ask what award-winning vegetables he had grown, but she bit her tongue.

"He owned the general store, and everyone shopped there, and they came to ask his advice about everything in their lives even when they didn't need to buy anything. None of them ever paid any attention to *me*, mind you. But what can you expect?"

"But you said Mr. Van Camp never met your brother. How then would your brother have given him advice …?"

"That ain't what I'm saying at all! Clearly, Van Camp had heard of my brother being one of Cape Vincent's most prominent citizens, and since he had died, decided to instead leave his nearest relative—that's me—a token of appreciation for all he'd done for the town."

Pauline blinked at this convoluted logic. "That's …"

"After all, why else would the man leave me something? I've certainly never met him. Barely even heard anything about him, only as that rich New Yorker who bought a place in Alex Bay. And this bracelet: great big thing with gaudy green stones all over it. Emeralds, the lawyer man called it, but I doubt it. Just big green pieces of glass, if you ask me. Nobody would leave me a real emerald bracelet, not for my brother's sake or anything."

"Maybe he heard of your cabbages and wanted you to have a proper award for them," Pauline said, and made her escape to the next house on the list.

Brian Nettleton was the eldest of five children, working as a farmer alongside his father, and utterly bewildered by the legacy of a small but lovely diamond ring.

"I'm walking out with a girl, but we ain't anywhere near getting hitched," he said. "What'm I supposed to do with this here ring?"

Pauline asked if he'd known Mr. Van Camp at all, and he returned the answer she was coming to expect: not even if he had passed him on the street.

The third person on her list, David Anderson, was not at home. His tired-eyed wife, answering Pauline's knock with a baby on her hip and a toddler clinging to her skirt, sighed when Pauline explained her purpose and asked when he was likely to return.

"If I knew the answer to that, I'd be a happy woman. He spent the winter working up the river at a logging camp, came home a few weeks ago and left just a few days ago to look for more work downstate."

A faint memory of something Pauline had recently read stirred. "One of the nine local men who brought back their fallen comrade?"

One of Pauline's colleagues had covered that story, along with reporters from half a dozen other papers in the area. Many local men went up to Canada or to Maine as loggers during the winter, a way of earning enough money for their families to survive the long, cold, snowy season.

But logging was dangerous work, and tragedy had struck for one of them. He came home in a coffin, accompanied by an honor guard of sorts of his fellow local lumberjacks. The papers had played it up tremendously.

Mrs. Anderson passed a weary hand over her eyes. "Yes. Oh, how I wish he didn't have to do that sort of work! I spend every winter scared he won't come home, and then what'll me and the little ones do? When the clerk from that lawyer fellow came and told us that Mr. Van Camp had left David a pair of sapphire earrings, I was sure it was the answer to all our troubles. I told David we ought to sell the things and put the money right in the bank, but he said it had to be a mistake. The clerk insisted there was no mistake, but David took the earrings with him downstate to have them appraised by a jeweler. He says if they are cheap imitations we'll keep them, but if they're valuable then they were supposed to be left to some other David Anderson, so either way we won't see any money from them."

"I'll stop by in a few days to see if he had returned," Pauline said, cursing the inadequacy of words to convey her heartache at her own helplessness in the face of Mrs. Anderson's struggle.

Never knowing from day to day if your husband was alive, or if you were going to have enough money for the next day's groceries. Raising your children practically on your own because your husband had to be gone so often just to be able to make enough money to keep a roof over your heads. Always hoping for something better, but unable to trust it when it comes.

She found herself fiercely hoping that for this family, at least, there had been no mistake or underhanded dealings, and that this could be a turning point for them.

It had been a singularly unprofitable day for her. She had spent the entire morning interviewing people, and had gotten no further along in understanding why Mr. Van Camp had made out his will the way he did, or who Mr. X was, or if there even *was* a Mr. X.

Neither Jane Casper nor Brian Nettleton nor Mrs. David Anderson knew of each other or had ever met Mr. Van Camp. The closest connection was Mrs. Anderson knowing of Miss Casper's award-winning cabbages, as her mother complained every year of losing the blue ribbon to the sour spinster. Nor were any of them familiar with the other names on the list from Mr. Ramsey. It seemed safe to assume the rest followed the same pattern.

Twelve heirs, unknown to each other and their benefactor unknown to them. The intended heir cut out of the will. The gardener, a witness to the will, removed from questioning. The butler, also a witness, dead.

It was a mess. Pauline couldn't made heads nor tails of it.

She considered asking her friend Lieutenant James Richardson of the Canton Police Department what he thought of it all, but upon reflection, decided to save him as a last resort. Involving James felt more official than the snooping she was doing thus far. He might not be able to help anyway, given the difference in jurisdictions.

Pauline checked her watch. She still had time before meeting Miss Warren for the ride back to Canton. She looked around and took her bearings. The Anderson house was not so far from the Van Camp estate. Pauline found her feet naturally turning in that direction.

She didn't expect to learn anything new at the estate, but she felt compelled to return all the same, to look around once more, undistracted by dead bodies and dismissive policemen. Perhaps there was something there that she had missed before, something that the police, in their insistence on Mr. Gagne's death as accidental, had overlooked as well.

It was worth checking.

Poor Mr. Gagne's body had been removed already, thank goodness. Pauline thought of Miss Warren's wish to do something for the man or his family, how easily she had taken on that responsibility and how quickly she had turned to compassion. Pauline's own instincts tended toward justice; she wasn't sure but that Arabella Warren's way was better.

For better or worse, this was her path. She couldn't change how she was made.

Since the police had declared Mr. Gagne's death accidental, nothing had been done to prevent access to the site. Pauline remembered Mr. Ramsey's words about the hospital wishing strangers to stay away, but she considered this matter more important.

Under normal circumstances, she would never treat legal restrictions so cavalierly, but murder was beyond the normal way of things.

Pauline walked up the long driveway with only the faintest prickling of conscience, catching her breath all over again at the grandeur of the view. The clear, pale blue of the sky came down to meet the darker ribbon of the river, the wooded islands shining with a pale green light in the sun.

Patients who would be fortunate enough to have this as their convalescent home would find their path to recovery aided indeed by such a beautiful spot—so long as Mr. Gagne's ghost did not return to haunt them.

Pauline instinctively avoided the area where she had found the body as she searched the property, stopping and scolding herself for fastidiousness when she realized what she was doing. How could she expect to find anything of use if she wouldn't even examine the spot where he had died?

She told herself over a dozen times that she needed to overcome her folly and inspect the area, and over a dozen times she could not make her feet walk in that direction, exploring everywhere else instead—in vain.

At last, irritated and overheated, she stopped and rested by the shed housing Mr. Gagne's auto. Idly, she wondered what would happen to the vehicle now its owner was dead. At least cars weren't like horses; it could not be expected to miss its master, nor would anyone have to worry about feed or stabling. A roof to protect it from the elements and gasoline when you wanted to go somewhere, that was all an automobile required, as far as Pauline knew.

The black Ford was a handsome vehicle, gleaming darkly even in the shade of the enclosed shed. As she looked more closely, wondering if it was time to update Emma Daring's automobile in her stories, something glinted under the farther front tire, catching a shaft of sunlight slanting in through the open door.

Frowning, she peered more closely. The object, whatever it was, continued to catch the sunlight and reflect it back tantalizingly, but refused to be identified.

Impelled more by curiosity than anything else, Pauline crouched down by the tire and stretched a gloved hand out to the item. It took some scrabbling with her fingers, but at last she had it, hard and smooth and shaped like a small warped oval. She rose and opened her hand to examine her treasure.

Resting on the palm of her hand, nestled on the now rather dirty cream-colored glove, was a blue stone shaped like a teardrop, its facets sparkling like moving water in the weak spring sun.

Pauline knew only slightly more about jewels than she did about automobiles, but she was ready to swear this was a genuine sapphire.

What on earth was it doing here?

It had to be from the Van Camp collection; anything else was too much of a coincidence. But how? And why?

Mrs. Anderson's voice echoed in her ears: *"... left David a pair of sapphire earrings ...came home a few weeks ago ... left just a few days ago to look for more work ..."*

Pauline curled her hand over the sapphire instinctively. No, no, no! Their mysterious Mr. X couldn't be David Anderson. How would he have known about the Van Camp collection? How could he have compelled Mr. Van Camp to change his will? And why would he have only taken one pair of earrings, if so, and then lost one of the jewels?

It wasn't logical. There had to be another explanation.

What if Mr. Gagne was a jewel thief? Perhaps he had stolen the sapphire? But then, why leave the jewelry at all to strangers, and how did he alter the will without the lawyer knowing?

Fragments of memory drifted through her mind. Arabella Warren, confessing her necklace wasn't as thrilling as she'd thought it would be. Jane Casper, insisting her emerald bracelet couldn't possibly be real.

What if Mr. Gagne had replaced the jewels in all the pieces with imitations? What if he had then forged a will, leaving those pieces to people he had come into contact with or heard of (but how?) throughout the region, people he thought unlikely to recognize the difference between a fake jewel and a real one? What if Mr. Van Camp had died without even knowing his will had been changed?

Pauline came up against a snag. The lawyer. Mr. Ramsey had been the one to make up the will for Mr. Van Camp, so he would have known the original bequests. The current will couldn't be a forgery. Besides, now she thought of it, the jewelry had been in his possession as executor before he delivered it to the heirs, and she doubted he would be taken in by imitations.

No, her theory wouldn't hold water. In one way she was relieved.

If Mr. Gagne had been the villain, that would have left them with one obvious question: who killed him?

The answer was just as obvious: the dispossessed true heir, who had discovered the man had cheated his great-uncle and robbed him of his inheritance.

Jonathan Van Camp.

Pauline didn't want to believe the boy could be a killer any more than she'd wanted to believe David Anderson could be. She liked Jonathan, just as she'd pitied and admired Mrs. Anderson for her courage and endurance. Still, she knew that personal opinions held very little weight against logic and evidence. She was just as glad to have her theory fall apart.

None of that answered the burning questions at hand, which were: where had this sapphire come from, and what did it have to do with Mr. Gagne's death and the will?

Slipping the jewel into her handbag until she knew what to do with it, Pauline left the estate to walk back into town to meet Miss Warren.

She would ask the other woman to take her necklace to a jeweler and have it appraised, just in case there had been a switch, and she would phone Mrs. Anderson tomorrow to ask if her husband had contacted her with information about their sapphire earrings.

She would be glad if the small blue gem resting in her bag was the property of the Anderson family, all other questions and problems aside. They needed it even more than Miss Warren needed a neat and tidy solution to her problem.

The Second Murder

It was Arabella Warren who poked the first hole in Pauline's theory, on the drive back to Canton. Pauline had told the older woman her suspicions about the jewels being fake, though not about the sapphire she had found.

"Land's sake!" Miss Warren said. "Now, that's the first thing about this that has made sense. Mr. Van Camp must have switched the jewels himself!"

"Himself?"

"Say he lost money—so many have, you know, since that dreadful crash five years ago—and he needed to sell his jewels. But he didn't want to do without the pieces altogether, so he had them replaced with, oh, what do they call it? Paste, that's it." Her eyes sparkled. "And that's why he didn't leave the jewelry to Jonathan after all! He didn't want his great-nephew to discover he was a poorer man than he made himself out to be, so instead he left them to people who wouldn't notice or care about such things."

It was a logical explanation, and far simpler than the convoluted theories Pauline had concocted. The sapphire tucked in her bag, however, defied such a simple explanation.

"In any case, we should have your necklace checked," Pauline said. "Mr. MacPhee, perhaps?"

The sign on Mr. MacPhee's business on Main Street read "Jeweler and Optometrist," a combination that had always intrigued and amused Pauline, which was why his name stuck in her memory. In the general way of things, she had no need of a jeweler's services.

Miss Warren agreed, and that was all there was time for before she dropped Pauline off at the apartment on Pleasant Street. Pauline felt a pang of guilt for not inviting the woman to stay for dinner, but she could only take so much chatter in a day.

She knew she ought to be more gracious and hospitable, especially in the face of Miss Warren's loneliness, but guilty emotions could not overcome her deep reluctance to give up a peaceful evening.

Back inside, Pauline slipped on a red calico apron to protect her white blouse and navy skirt, and began work on her neglected chores. Sarah had not yet returned, so she had the apartment all to herself. The silence soothed her and helped to settle some of the unease stirred up by the day's events. As she swept, dusted, and washed dishes, Pauline felt the tension loosen from her neck and shoulders, and a mild headache she hadn't even realized was there faded away.

She did not love housework, but the act of bringing order out of chaos helped her feel more calm and regulated in her own mind and emotions. It was too easy to get wrapped up in the griefs and sorrows of other people, and fret over her inability to cure all the world's ills. Better than not caring about the world's ills at all, perhaps, but a type of hubris in its own way. Putting her own small household to rights; that was a good place to begin. Helping others to the extent of her abilities; another good step. Twisting herself into knots because she couldn't do everything; that was arrogance.

The apartment was sparkling and Pauline was standing in front of the cupboard, wondering what to prepare for supper, when Sarah came home.

"Oh, what a day," Sarah groaned, collapsing into her chair at the kitchen table.

A few hours ago, Pauline would have been so wrapped up in her need to solve the case she would have asked Sarah about Miss Nelson without so much as a thought for her friend's own difficult day. Now, she took one look at the weary lines etched into Sarah's face, bit her tongue, and poured her a glass of orange juice cool and sweet from the icebox.

"Recalcitrant patients?" she asked.

"Overbearing doctors and head nurses," Sarah said. She took a long drink. "Thank you. I needed that!"

Pauline freely admitted she wouldn't be able to do Sarah's job. She had neither the patience nor the sensibilities for nursing. She was often ashamed of her own fastidiousness in that way—a nurse was a far nobler profession than journalist or academic—but one thing college had taught her was that there was little point in kicking against the goads. All people were as they were made. God or nature had designed Pauline to be a scholar and a writer, just as Sarah had been designed to take care of sick people.

So long as they both used their gifts to make the world a better place, neither had anything to be ashamed of. All the same, Pauline thought her friend deserved far more accolades than anyone gave her.

"I'm afraid I didn't take the time to visit Miss Nelson," Sarah said now.

Pauline poured a second glass of juice and sat down across from her friend. "Never mind that. Out of all the people I have visited today, the only thing they had in common was having nothing in common. I can't imagine Miss Nelson would be any different."

Sarah sighed. "A fruitless day for you as well, then?"

Pauline thought of the sapphire weighing down her handbag. "Not exactly," she admitted with a wry twist to her mouth. "But that can wait until after supper. Just as soon as I think of what to prepare."

Sarah leaned out from her chair to study the contents of the cupboard past Pauline's figure partially blocking the open door.

"Potato soup," she said. "And while that's cooking, I'll make skillet biscuits and you can tell me what you mean by 'not exactly.' Would you make me wait to hear the answer to that riddle and spoil my meal on top of my dreadful day?"

Pauline laughed. As she awkwardly peeled and chopped potatoes and carrots for the soup, she built up the story of her day, from Miss Casper's sour outlook on life and Brian Nettleton's pleasant bewilderment to Mrs. David Anderson's weariness and fear. Sarah shook her head while she cut the lard into the flour mixture and added just the right amount of buttermilk without measuring

"All very well and good," she said, dropping dough into the cast iron skillet with a practiced hand. "But where's the 'not exactly fruitless' part?"

Pauline realized, as she tipped the vegetables into the pot and added water to cover them, that she was reluctant to tell Sarah about the sapphire. Taking it from the property had been, if not illegal, a reckless and improper move. The correct thing to have done would have been to leave it there and inform the police.

In this case, Pauline didn't think the correct move was the *right* one. But it was difficult to explain that.

"You did *what*?" Sarah said, closing the oven door with a bang. She whirled in a flurry of skirt to stare at her friend and roommate, mouth agape. "You stole a jewel! And brought it back home with you? It's sitting in your handbag by the door—what if we are robbed?"

"Nobody knows I have it, so no one would think to rob us," Pauline said, slightly defensive. "And it isn't stealing! I'm not keeping it for myself. It's a clue."

"Nevertheless, if you had to remove it from the crime scene, you should have taken it directly to Mr. Ramsey," Sarah said severely.

The knowledge that Sarah was right pricked Pauline's conscience, causing her to speak even more defensively than before. "I thought you believed Mr. Ramsey was the villain of the piece!"

"Whether he is or not, there is a way things should be done in a civilized society, and walking off with a jewel that does not belong to you is not that way."

It was the closest the two women had ever come to a true quarrel. They disagreed frequently, but not with the edge of temper that currently trembled beneath their words.

Pauline hated quarrels. She drew a long, steadying breath.

"Perhaps you are right," she forced herself to admit. "I was only thinking of the implications of my discovery, not of the correct procedure."

Sarah smoothed her hands down her skirt front. "I am going to change," she said.

By the time she returned with her face washed, her hair released from its tight bun to curl around her face, and her uniform changed for a pretty flowered house dress, the potatoes tested done to Pauline's fork and the biscuits were ready to be taken out of the oven.

Pauline added salt, a small amount of butter, and a splash of milk, stirred for a few more minutes, and pronounced the soup done.

The carrots were still crunchy and the broth was bland, but overall it wasn't bad, for one of Pauline's meals. Nothing had burnt, which was a pleasant change. The biscuits, of course, were perfect.

By unspoken consent, neither woman mentioned the quarrel or the case during the meal. It made for a fairly silent hour.

Dessert was chicory coffee and fruit cocktail made from canned fruit. Pauline's cooking skills may have been lacking, but nobody could have complained of her coffee making ability. With the first sip, Sarah's face finally relaxed.

"What are you going to do with the sapphire?" she asked.

Pauline accepted the olive branch. "Tomorrow I shall telephone

Mrs. Anderson to inquire if her husband has returned with an answer from the jeweler. After that … I am not certain. It depends on the answer, I suppose."

"I wish all this was happening in Canton instead of Clayton," Sarah said. "Then I could talk you into turning the case over to James."

"I wouldn't require much persuasion," Pauline said. "James would listen to my ideas. The Clayton police patted my head and sent me on my way when I told them my suspicions regarding Mr. Gagne's death. I cannot think they'd listen to me now."

Sarah giggled. "Sorry!" she said. "The image of you having your head patted by a nice stout police officer!"

They shared a burst of merry laughter, the ice between them melting entirely. They took their coffees into the living room and listened to *Bing Crosby Entertains* on the radio before retiring, the evening ending on a far more pleasant note than it had begun.

The next morning Sarah left early for work, saying she might try to stop in and see Miss Nelson after her shift for the sake of completeness. After Pauline cleaned the breakfast detritus, she picked up the telephone and requested the number of the David Anderson family of Clayton, NY. Within a few moments, the line was ringing.

She didn't think anyone was going to answer at first, but as she was on the verge of hanging up, a harsh female voice broke on her ear.

"Who is this?"

Startled, Pauline tried to gather her scattered wits. "Is-is this Mrs. Anderson?" she stammered, then pulled herself together. Really, she hadn't stammered since high school!

"No, it ain't," said the other woman aggressively. "What do you want with her?"

"My name is Pauline Gray, and I hoped—"

"Pauline Gray! I've heard of you. You're that newspaper woman. You vultures, you're all alike. Can't you even let a woman grieve in peace before breaking in with your poking and prying?"

"I don't understand," Pauline said, gripping the receiver hard enough to turn her knuckles white, the familiar nausea of an unexpectedly unpleasant situation churning in her stomach.

The woman snorted, causing Pauline to jump as the sound attacked her ear. "We don't want no reporters here. Good bye!"

She slammed the receiver down, making Pauline jump yet again.

"What," Pauline said aloud as she carefully replaced the receiver on the base, positioning it ever-so-precisely in place, "was that about?"

As if in answer to the conundrum, the telephone rang.

By now Pauline's nerves were too numbed for her to jump again. She simply picked it up and said,

"Hello?"

"Miss Gray?" The voice was eerie in its calmness; it was a voice lacking all emotion or life. So might a dead person speak, Pauline's imagination whispered before she forced it down.

"Yes. Who is this, please?"

"Barbara Anderson … Mrs. David Anderson." The woman stopped and cleared her throat. "I apologize for earlier … my neighbor took your call, she didn't understand … Miss Gray, please, do you know anything about my husband's death?"

"Death?"

Pauline's head spun. "I had no idea," she gasped, reaching out blindly with her free hand for support. Her grasping fingers found the edge of the telephone cabinet and held on for dear life. "I'm so sorry—of course I wouldn't have intruded upon your grief if I'd known."

"Oh." A note of disappointment entered the woman's flat tone. "I thought—I thought maybe you knew something about it. The police insist on treating it as a robbery that got out of hand, but … it doesn't fit. It doesn't make sense, Miss Gray. I thought, since you were here asking questions yesterday, that maybe you had information … knew something the police don't."

"I don't have real information," Pauline said, reason slowly returning. "Not that I'm aware of. But if you wouldn't mind telling me what happened, I might …" She caught her breath at the brazen audacity of what she was saying. How dare she take this on her shoulders, promise anything to this woman, give her false hope?

But if her suspicions were correct, did she dare do nothing? Wasn't that her responsibility—not to promise results, but to at least try? For Mr. Anderson as much as for Mr. Gagne?

Mrs. Anderson took the matter out of her hands. "My husband was murdered," she said, her voice ringing emptily along the line. "Last night or early this morning, as he was returning from his trip downstate. He was robbed and killed—"

Her voice gave out.

"That is dreadful," Pauline said. "I'm so very sorry." She knew she was repeating herself, but what else could one say?

The neighbor's voice came back in response. "That's enough of that!" she said. "Didn't ought to be upsetting her like this, as any decent woman would know. You career women, you've no sense of what's proper."

"I *am* sorry," Pauline said. "Believe it or not, I am trying to help. I am glad you came back on the line—I don't want to ask Mrs. Anderson this. Can you tell me, please, how Mr. Anderson was killed?"

"Not the sort of thing a young woman ought to be asking," snapped the neighbor. "Ghoul!"

"I am not asking for my own curiosity, I assure you," Pauline said.

Muffled noise in the background suggested Mrs. Anderson was requesting her neighbor cooperate.

"Head bashed in with a rock," she finally came back with.

The same method as was used for Mr. Gagne.

"And Mrs. Anderson wants me to tell you that her husband was a God-fearing man who wouldn't have gone into a drinking place, temperance laws done away with or no, much less gotten so tipsy as to brag about them earrings, neither."

"Is that what the police think happened?"

"Seems to be. They found the—him outside one of them devil-places, and it's a shame Prohibition ever ended if you ask me! His pockets were emptied, and they say someone must have heard him talking about his good fortune and decided to take that fortune for their own. But Mrs. Anderson says her husband wouldn't have done that, and not that it's any of your business, but I agree with her. I haven't lived next door to them for ten years without learning something about who they are!"

"Thank you," Pauline said, ignoring the woman's tone and responding instead to the information. "I have only one more question and then I will leave you in peace. I need the name and telephone number of the jeweler Mr. Anderson was going to consult."

The neighbor relayed the request and reeled the information back off to Pauline. Then Mrs. Anderson came back on, her voice showing some signs of life.

"Miss Gray—you believe me."

"I do," Pauline said.

"You do know something about how this happened."

"There's a chance it is connected to a much larger matter, yes," Pauline said cautiously. "I can't say anything for certain."

"I want the culprit found and my husband's reputation restored," the new widow said. "You must find out the truth and publish it, Miss Gray. Please."

There was no answer Pauline could give but, "I will do my best."

After hanging up she dialed the number of the jeweler quickly, before she stopped to think about it. She couldn't fall to pieces now.

It took some persuading for the jeweler to reveal the information to her. She finally had to tell him she was a private detective employed by Mrs. Anderson to discover who had murdered her husband, which wasn't even that much of a stretch of the truth, before he, uttering little cries of shock and horror at the news of Mr. Anderson's death, would share customer information.

The news was as Pauline had expected, but gave her a jolt nonetheless. "The gems in the earrings were paste," the jeweler said. "Well done, but not clever enough to fool an expert even for a moment. Why, I doubt they would have stood up even against the eye of a woman accustomed to jewels, or that of a man buying them for her. I didn't even have to touch them to know the difference."

Pauline was acutely aware of the small blue stone still in her handbag. "What shape were they?"

"Teardrops. Exquisite Classical Revival pieces, you know, designed to resemble the shape of an amphora. What I wouldn't give to see them set with their true stones! A rare and lovely set originally."

"Thank you," Pauline said, and replaced the receiver.

Only then did she allow herself to give in to her shaking legs and sit down.

Another death. Another murder. This proved it. Mr. Gagne's death was no accident. This was no coincidence.

Sarah's question from the previous evening hung before Pauline's eyes as clearly as though the words were printed in the air.

What was she going to do now?

Danger on the Road

The next step, Pauline decided, was finding out if Arabella Warren had taken her necklace to Mr. MacPhee yet. Exerting her will to control the trembling still affecting her hands, she reached for the telephone once again.

Before she could pick up the receiver, someone knocked on the door. This proved to be Miss Warren herself, looking even more flustered than usual.

"Oh good, Miss Gray. Mr. Ramsey's office telephoned, they have some papers they need me to sign and they need the necklace as well. I don't understand why, that clerk mumbles so, and would you mind coming with me? Even when they speak clearly I don't understand all that legal talk, and I'd rather have someone there who could tell me what it is I'm signing."

"Of course," Pauline said, stifling a sigh. Yet another auto ride to Clayton. Like Sarah, though for different reasons, Pauline wished this affair was taking place in Canton. "Have you had a chance to have the necklace evaluated yet?"

"Goodness no, I've far too much to do in the mornings. At least, I don't need to do everything I do—making bread each day is silly when I'm the only one at home, but my neighbors seem to appreciate the extra loaves, and scrubbing my floors sometimes seems futile when nobody ever stops by to visit, but you know how it is, you get into the habit of doing something and you can't seem to stop even when it's no longer necessary."

Pauline didn't understand this at all, but she smiled and nodded before fetching her hat, gloves, and handbag. As a precaution, she transferred the sapphire into an old pillbox and tucked it into the drawer of her nightstand. Not that she expected to be robbed, but it was only sensible to not carry that much wealth on her person, especially when it was also an important clue and didn't belong to her in the first place.

"Lunch in town before we go," Miss Warren declared as they left the apartment, Pauline carefully locking the door behind her. "Mr. Ramsey may want me there as soon as possible, but he will have to accept that we must eat."

She took Pauline to the Hotel Harrington grill, even as Pauline protested it was far too expensive. Canton's only hotel was terribly elegant; Pauline wouldn't have dreamed of eating there on her own.

"Nonsense," Miss Warren said. "Miss Gray, I am not a wealthy woman, although I suppose if the diamonds in my new necklace are real I am now, but I never have been wealthy, and yet I've always had more than enough for one person to live comfortably. I've no children to spend it on, the least I can do is treat a friend once in a while to a nice meal."

Put like that, Pauline could only be ashamed of her reluctance to accept such an expensive treat, and accept with as much grace as possible. She also agreed to the other woman's proposition that they dispense with "Miss" and use each other's given names. It was a step toward intimacy Pauline wasn't entirely comfortable with, but she could not see a way to refuse that wouldn't have sounded snobbish or churlish.

The dining room was an elegant, airy space, lit by electricity, with tables laid with white linen cloths and deft waiters to attend to the diners' every whim. For a few dizzying moment, Pauline was transported to her childhood, when outings like this were common. She had never thought of her family as wealthy—did not her mother complain constantly of not having enough money? After the stock market crash of '29 they had had to tighten their belts along with the rest of the business world, causing Mrs. Gray to moan even more about hard times.

Living in a rural community and supporting herself on her own wages had opened Pauline's eyes considerably. Not only had her family at their poorest had more money than most folks in Canton who were considered well-off, they had led a tremendously sheltered life. Poverty and hard work alike were closed books to Pauline's mother, as to Pauline herself when she had first moved here.

Her own experiences and her friendships with the people of Canton had begun the process of change. She was honest enough to admit she still had a long way to go.

For all that, even with the melancholia that still gripped her at times, Pauline had no regrets about exchanging her former life for this one. She appreciated and enjoyed the luxury of a meal such as the elegant shrimp salad and soft dinner roll now served to her, but as a step outside her everyday life, not as a matter of course.

Even the novels which she could not help but be somewhat ashamed of writing were an honest source of income, not inherited or gotten on the backs of other people. They might not have been the scholarly works she dreamed of someday penning, but she could take pride in them as the work of her own hands.

The meal was prepared to perfection, and both Arabella and Pauline were mellowed as they finally took to the road after finishing with coffee and ices. Arabella was less talkative than usual, and Pauline felt comfortable enough to share some college stories with her.

"This makes me think of the time Katie Holtman borrowed her

father's auto and took several of us on a drive to the river one April," she said. "She forgot to fill it with gasoline so we were stranded by the side of the road for hours until a sympathetic farmer came along and gave us enough to come sheepishly back to campus." She laughed. "We never let Katie live it down, but it became one of my favorite memories, all of the jokes we made and songs we sang while stranded."

"I would have liked to go to college, but my father considered it nonsense. Not because I was a woman, but he said my mind wasn't serious enough. I'm sure he was right, but still I can't help but feel wistful when I think about it. Everyone seems to have such wonderful memories of their time there." Arabella sighed, steering around a gentle bend in the road.

"I think—Oh!" Pauline cried out as Arabella applied the brake suddenly. They were jolted forward in their seats and the auto skidded with a squeal of tires, coming to a halt inches before the brown trunk of an uprooted young ash tree that lay flung across the road.

"Goodness!" Pauline said once she'd caught her breath.

"How on earth did this end up here?" Arabella asked. "There hasn't been any sort of windstorm or rain."

"More importantly, what are we going to do about it?" Pauline said. "I doubt the two of us together are strong enough to remove it."

"Well, we certainly can't do anything by sitting here," Arabella said briskly.

She maneuvered the auto to the side of the road, put it in park, and opened the door to step out. Pauline admired her prompt decision and followed suit, slightly ashamed of her instinct to sit and wait for someone else to take care of the problem.

"If we had some rope, we could try tying one end to the tree and one end to your bumper, and you could drive …" she began, thinking of what Emma Daring, the dauntless heroine of her novels, would do.

Her voice faltered as Arabella shook her head.

"A tractor or a truck would be strong enough for that, but I fear it would only rip my bumper clean off," she said. "Oh," in a different tone, turning her head to look up the road. "Oh, do be careful! Look out!" she called, waving both hands.

The bicyclist approaching at full speed, warned by her cry, slowed to a stop well before hitting the tree. It was Jonathan Van Camp.

"Whew!" he whistled. He swung his leg over the bar of the bicycle, climbed down and leaned the machine against the bank, then walked over to look at the tree trunk. "This is a mess, isn't it? What on earth are you doing here?"

"We are on our way to Mr. Ramsey's office," Pauline answered. "What are you doing?"

He shrugged. "Oh, you know. Here, step back. I can shift this, no sense you two dirtying your gloves."

He flashed a cheeky grin at them before taking hold of the branches at one end and heaving the tree to one side and pushing it off the road.

Pauline wouldn't be distracted. She might not be much use in practical matters, but she knew when someone was evading a question.

"No, I don't know," she said. "What brings you down this road at the precise right time for us?"

A new voice rang out behind them.

"Stop! Hands up!"

Arabella Warren screamed. Pauline spun around.

A masked figure had appeared out of the woods lining the road, an ugly black gun in one hand.

"You—ladies—give me your handbags," he demanded.

A trap! The tree had been put across the road on purpose to stop their car and force them to get out into the open. Pauline exchanged a glance with Arabella.

The diamond necklace was in the other woman's bag. If they let him have it, they would lose their chance to have it identified as paste or real.

But it wasn't worth their lives. Pauline nodded, and turned back to the auto to take out their bags.

"Toss them to him," Jonathan said in a low, urgent voice. "Make him bend down to pick them up."

Pauline grasped the point at once. Of course! It was just what Emma Daring would do. Dangerous and terribly foolhardy, of course, but she trusted Jonathan's reflexes.

She tossed the bags toward the masked figure. They landed with a rattle before his feet, and just as she had hoped, he bent over to reach for them. Jonathan jumped onto the tree trunk and launched himself at the man. It was an unorthodox method, but it worked.

The would-be thief crashed to the ground, dropping his gun as he did, Jonathan on his back and swinging wildly. The boy hit dirt as often as he made contact with any part of the man's anatomy, but his position gave him the advantage. The other man could do nothing but attempt to throw him off.

Arabella screamed again as she watched the two scuffling on the ground, the thief trying to throw Jonathan off, Jonathan trying equally hard to keep the thief down. Pauline's heart was pounding erratically, her lower lip caught tightly between her teeth. She longed to help, but knew she would be more of a liability than an actual asset to Jonathan.

Arabella's third scream took on a more panicked note as the masked man made one final, desperate heave and flung Jonathan off long enough to reclaim his gun and scramble to his feet. He fired wildly into the air, then turned and fled back into the woods.

Uninjured, Jonathan scrambled to his feet and prepared to chase after him. Arabella rushed forward and grabbed his arm.

"Don't you dare! That horrible man will kill you!"

"But he's getting away!" Jonathan protested, tugging at his sleeve to free it.

Pauline scooped the handbags back up. "Let him," she advised. "He didn't get what he came for. This is now a matter for the police. Miss Warren is right, Jonathan. If you chase him, he's bound to shoot you."

The boy stopped struggling. "Very well," he muttered. "But I could have had him."

"You were enough of a hero as it was!" Arabella exclaimed. "Goodness, when I think what would have happened to us if you weren't here. It was positively providential!"

"Er … yes," Jonathan said, eyes shifting.

"We need to get to Clayton to report this as soon as possible," Pauline said. "But first, Jonathan, stop avoiding the matter. It wasn't Providence that brought you here, was it?"

His shoulders sagged. "No," he mumbled. "Got a note—pushed under my landlady's door—not signed. Told me to be here at this time if I wanted to know what really happened with my uncle's will."

Curiouser and curiouser.

They tucked Jonathan and his bicycle somehow into the back of the auto and drove off again, arriving at Mr. Ramsey's office at last.

"But, my dear lady, I never telephoned you! No, nor had George do so," the lawyer protested once he understood their jumbled tale. "Not but what I'm delighted to see you at any time, and Miss Gray as well, but no, I have no papers for you to sign. And I never would have asked you to bring back the necklace! As I told you when I entrusted it to your care, it ought to be in the bank."

He mopped his forehead with a handkerchief held in trembling fingers. "This is dreadful news about the attempted robbery, simply dreadful. George … oh that's right, he's checking the status of his paintings with the post office. He's an amateur artist, you know, and he recently sent three of his best paintings off to be framed, and he wants to be certain the postman understands that when they return they must be delivered here, for safekeeping, not his boarding house, where his landlady has no respect for other people's property … but you aren't interested in that! Eleanor—you all remember Miss Peck, my secretary—we must telephone to the police."

"Of course," the secretary murmured in her dampening way. "I only hope they'll take it seriously."

"Seriously?" Arabella shrilled. "We were nearly killed! If Jonathan hadn't been there we would have been. How could they not take that seriously?"

Miss Peck's smile was a masterwork of condescension. "How fortunate young Mr. Van Camp was there so opportunely, then."

Arabella drew in a breath, but Pauline stepped on her foot. Light had dawned.

Had she and Arabella not delayed to eat luncheon, they would have been on the road much sooner, and Jonathan would have arrived at the tree block after they had already been robbed, placing him in the vicinity of the attack in a highly suspicious position. Would the police have believed his story of an anonymous note? Even if he could produce it, they might have thought he'd faked it himself as an alibi.

No, the more she thought about it, the more convinced she was that the note had been sent to set Jonathan up, to make it appear as though he were the one to rob Arabella in an attempt to steal back his great-uncle's jewels.

How lucky, how very lucky indeed, that Arabella had insisted on a proper meal before setting out! It was, as Miss Warren would have said, providential.

Pauline returned to the present to realize Mr. Ramsey was addressing her.

"Now, I'm sure this is a rare opportunity for you, Miss Gray, eh? Not every day a newspaper woman gets to be the subject of a story instead of the author of it, ha!"

Pauline considered the joke to be in extremely bad taste. "I'm afraid this is outside my purview, sir. I write a regular column. I am not a reporter."

"Oh! Well now, I didn't know it. I don't ever read the papers, myself. At least, not anymore. Too, ah, too busy, yes, far too busy. My dear Eleanor reads them all instead and tells me the bits she knows I'd be interested in. I'd be lost without her, yes indeed I would!"

Miss Peck, now on the telephone with the police, smiled coolly at this paean of praise.

Pauline had never known any man, much less one in the legal profession, who did not read at least one paper. It couldn't be considered a character flaw, but despite herself, her opinion of Mr. Ramsey dropped another notch all the same.

"Make sure she shares with you the tragic story of poor Mr. David Anderson in tomorrow's paper," she couldn't resist saying now. "He was murdered late last night or early this morning, and the sapphire earrings he inherited from Mr. Van Camp were stolen."

Mr. Ramsey's face lost all color. He dropped his handkerchief. "What? No! My dear, you must be mistaken. Why, I saw him myself, yesterday afternoon."

Pauline hadn't realized he'd been out of town. "I'm sorry," she said, softening her tone a trifle. "But it's quite true. Mrs. Anderson told me herself."

"Oh dear, oh dear," the little man moaned. He reached for his forehead, seemed to realize he had no handkerchief, and looked around helplessly for it. Jonathan, who had been standing quietly in the background all this time, picked it up off the floor and handed it to the distraught lawyer.

"We were at a conference for the Bar Association in Utica yesterday, George, Eleanor, and myself, and we bumped into Mr. Anderson at a restaurant during our lunch break. Such a pleasant, well-spoken man. He told us he was having the earrings evaluated, which I thought extremely sensible of him, to get an idea of how much they were worth. And now they are stolen and he is murdered! Dear, oh dear."

Arabella's face was pale as well. "First Mr. Anderson, and today us. Somebody wants very badly to get those jewels."

Miss Peck replaced the receiver and folded her hands together on her desk. "Yes," she agreed quietly. "So it seems."

She looked directly at Jonathan.

"The police are on the way," she added.

Arabella Warren was not a subtle woman, but not even she could miss that implication. She scowled at the secretary. "Those thieves will be sorry when they find out the jewels they are stealing are only paste!"

Pauline would rather have held that information to herself until they had confirmation of the necklace being paste as well as the earrings, but she could not blame Arabella for spilling their suspicion. She hadn't told the other woman to keep it a secret. Now that it was out, she set herself to studying the others' reactions.

Mr. Ramsey's jaw dropped. George-the-clerk chose that moment to return; he tripped on the lintel and nearly fell into the office. Jonathan stared blankly at Arabella. Only Miss Peck remained unmoved by the announcement, raising a supercilious eyebrow.

"That is a very serious accusation, ma'am!" exclaimed Mr. Ramsey. "They most certainly are not paste! Dear, dear, what is the world coming to?"

An Unpleasant Afternoon

"My great-uncle despised paste jewelry!" Jonathan exclaimed. "He would never have sold his jewels, never, no matter how poor he got in other ways. He wasn't poor, not at all, but if he had been, he still would have kept his jewels. The only way the collection could be paste would be if someone here, in this office, stole the real jewels after Great-Uncle Horace died. I knew you were a thief!" he finished up, glaring at Mr. Ramsey.

The little lawyer did not take that well. He insisted that the jewels were real when Mr. Van Camp showed them to him and George at the house, weren't they, George, and they were real when they arrived at his office, because Eleanor's cousin who was a jeweler had stopped in that day to take her to lunch and had commented favorably on their quality, didn't he, Eleanor, and the only way they could be false now was if someone had broken into his office while the will was in probate and swapped them, now what did Jonathan have to say to that?

"If," Jonathan said between his teeth, "you are implying that I did such a thing, I ask where your proof is."

"It makes perfect sense!" the lawyer insisted. "You remember, Eleanor, and you, George, the papers that were disarranged on my desk the day after Mr. Van Camp's death? We finally determined it must have been the breeze from opening the inner door at the same time someone closed the outer door, but now I see it all. You must have come in and broken into the safe, swapped the jewels, and left in the night!"

Pauline had to interrupt at this staggering leap of illogic. "Oh come, Mr. Ramsey. Where would Jonathan learn to break into a safe? Not to mention that such a deed would involve breaking the lock on your front door as well, and yet the only sign left behind was a few mussed papers?"

"Don't tell me about criminals, young lady, I know more about them than a sheltered, gently-brought up young woman like yourself ever could! There are thieves who can break any lock without leaving a trace, and many of them started younger than this fellow here. Isn't that right, George?"

This seemed an odd choice to back him up, as the unfortunate clerk blushed bright red and mumbled something at his shoes.

Arabella gasped. "Mr. Ramsey, you aren't saying your clerk was a thief?"

"Not at all, my dear lady, not at all. Apologies, George. Didn't mean to imply anything. I know it's a sore spot. His brother, ladies. He was a bad egg—no, I'm sorry George, at this point I have to tell them, can't leave them thinking it's you. Had to ship this brother off to Canada before he brought the Norton family name into any more disgrace. And I've seen a look in this young man's eye that reminds me very much indeed of M—"

It was perhaps fortunate that the police entered at this point, or Mr. Ramsey might have been able to charge Jonathan with assault.

Between Arabella Warren's incoherent account, Mr. Ramsey's not-veiled-at-all accusations of Jonathan as a scoundrel and rogue, Jonathan's scornful attitude, and the secretary's usual dampening effect on the room, Pauline's quiet and well-ordered rendering of the tale was lost. After an excruciating half hour, the police left once more, leaving behind the impression that they looked on the entire affair as nothing more than a prank.

"Now then," Mr. Ramsey said the instant the door closed behind the officers, "What exactly makes you think the jewels are paste, Miss Warren? After all, we must look as this in an orderly and logical fashion, mustn't we. Wouldn't do to lose our heads."

Pauline was under the impression that was exactly what had happened, but she was thankful the man was behaving as a member of the legal profession ought, however belated.

"Well, Pauline says that Mr. Anderson's earrings were paste, and she thinks the rest are as well …" Arabella began.

Curiously enough, it was George who responded to that, not Mr. Ramsey. "Miss Gray, that is a highly serious accusation to make based on what seems to be the flimsiest of bases. I trust you have more to go on than women's intuition?"

"Ha!" said Mr. Ramsey. "Well put, George. Yes indeed. Women's intuition, not allowable in the courtroom, is it?"

Pauline's grasp on her temper had been tenuous at best through the interview with the police, and now it slipped entirely. "I learned at my grandfather's knee what was allowable and what was not in a court of law, thank you sir," she said icily. "At this time and in this place, I prefer to keep my conclusions, and the facts that led me to draw them, to myself."

Mr. Ramsey's eyes bulged. "Your grandfather … good grief, Miss Gray, not Judge *Arthur* Gray, surely? Goodness gracious me. Yes indeed. Well, well, well. No wonder you are so familiar with legal procedures, yes indeed. If we'd known, we could have had Miss Gray draw up the will for Mr. Van Camp, eh George? Saved you the effort!" He chortled, seemingly under the impression he had made a statement of great wit.

George's smile was sickly. "Yes sir … sir, it is getting late, and if

Miss Gray refuses to share any more information with us, perhaps we should close for the evening?"

"Oh yes, naturally. Well, Miss Warren—"

"One moment," Pauline said. "Did you say your clerk drew up the will?" She wished Mr. Ramsey had introduced him properly. She still didn't know George's last name, but it would be too insolent to call him "George" as Mr. Ramsey did, leaving her with no option but the awkward "your clerk."

"Standard procedure, young lady, standard procedure! Your grandfather would have told you the same. All perfectly legal and in order. Van Camp had his list of bequests already written out. He handed it to me, I looked at it and saw that everything was in order, and passed it along to George with instructions to put it into the proper form for a will. While he was doing that, Van Camp showed me his jewelry collection along with the paintings he had collected, very fine they were. Then we came back into the room, Van Camp inspected the will, agreed that it was just as he wanted it, and went to the window to call the gardener in as a witness while I went into the hall to fetch the butler. Now, I know what you're going to ask next: don't worry, George covered up the actual bequests of the will so the witnesses wouldn't see it as they were signing."

Miss Peck spoke up again, startling them all with her smooth, spiteful voice. "Perhaps Miss Gray would like to view the will herself, as she seems to think something was improper in its formation?"

Mr. Ramsey drew himself up once more. "Improper!"

"It seems she has taken issue with George," Miss Peck continued. "Perhaps she thinks that because his brother is untrustworthy, he is as well."

"That is a highly regrettable attitude to take, Miss Gray, and not one worthy of your illustrious grandfather," Mr. Ramsey said, his tone indicating more sorrow than anger.

Pauline was too furious to speak. Arabella rescued her.

"Rubbish! Pauline said nothing of the kind. That is a ridiculous accusation. I am sure she never even thought such a thing for a moment. She was merely taking an interest in how it all happened, trying to get a picture of it, as anyone might want to do. For my part, I am honestly disappointed you saw the jewels and are certain they were real before Mr. Van Camp died, Mr. Ramsey, as I had so hoped he had switched them out himself. Then all this would make much more sense and we wouldn't have to have all this fuss. I am sure that was all Pauline was trying to ascertain, isn't that so?"

"Certainly I have no wish to imply impropriety in any of your or your clerk's actions in the writing of the will," Pauline agreed, her voice cold. Much as she loathed physical violence, her palm tingled with the urge to slap Miss Eleanor Peck.

"And now I think we'll leave," Arabella said. "Nothing else is going to get solved today, not with everybody so worked up. Jonathan, I hope you'll come with us."

The young man had been standing in the corner in surly silence ever since the police left. Now he stirred. "I'll need to get food somewhere. My landlady will have stopped serving supper by now."

Arabella patted his arm. "You come home with me, young man. I don't feel safe on the road or in my home without a man around, goodness me, not after that robbery attempt. I can guarantee you that my cooking will be better than a cold supper at your landlady's, even if I say so myself! I do enjoy cooking, but it always seems a waste for only me. It will be a real treat to feed a growing boy."

The quality of Jonathan's stillness changed from that of a boy disgusted by the scene he had been forced to witness, to a wild animal not sure whether or not to flee from an open hand held out to it.

"You want me to come to your home? Have a meal?"

"A meal, a bed … I am asking you if you'd be willing to stay at my house, at least until this matter is cleared up. Only if you want to, of course."

Jonathan licked his lips. "I'll need to let my landlady know," he croaked.

"Of course," Arabella hurried to say. "Pauline and I don't mind stopping by there. I'm sure you'll want to pick up your things, anyway."

A genuine smile broke over Jonathan's face. "Don't have that much to collect."

"Miss Warren—dear lady—do stop and think for a moment," Mr. Ramsey pleaded. "You know nothing of this boy! You could be taking a criminal into your home!"

The smile vanished from Jonathan's face. Arabella placed one hand on his shoulder and faced Mr. Ramsey with eyes flashing.

"That's enough of that nonsense, Mr. Ramsey! This boy saved us from a robbery earlier today, and even if he hadn't, I'm just about tired of accusations without any basis but your own dislike. Jonathan is coming home with me, and that's that. Good evening."

Mr. Ramsey looked as though he wanted to protest further, but Pauline was as fed up as Arabella, in her own way. She stalked to the door with the barest of courtesies to the three remaining. Jonathan leapt in front to open the door for her, and she and Arabella swept through.

"Well!" Arabella said once they were all safely in the auto. "That was a most unpleasant way to spend the afternoon."

Pauline couldn't have agreed more.

Unraveling Tangles

A stranger might have been forgiven for thinking Lieutenant James Richardson of the Canton Police Department was all brawn and no brains, for he was big and sturdy, and kept an easy-going grin on his face most of the time. Pauline knew better. James had a sharp mind and a keen wit, and he was not intimidated by clever women.

At times, his friendship with Pauline had given rise to local gossip, but his recent marriage to a young widow with one son had put an end to those rumors, much to Pauline's relief.

She liked James, no more and no less. She couldn't imagine feeling romantic about him—or about anyone, for that matter. But that was neither here nor there.

More relevant to the matter at hand, he took her seriously when she came into the police station on the first floor of the Opera House the morning after the attempted robbery, sat down in front of his desk, and told him the entire tale, from her first meeting with Arabella—arranged by his own wife—to the exit from Mr. Ramsey's office the previous evening. She set the list of names of the heirs down on his desk, so he could see it for himself rather than trying to keep it all straight in his head.

She even told him about finding the sapphire and taking it home with her, though not without an inward qualm about his reaction toward such lawlessness.

James didn't say anything the entire time aside from the occasional, "mm-hm." His face showed neither skepticism nor acceptance. The neutral expression was cultivated, Pauline knew, and went a long way toward unnerving criminals and subordinates alike.

"Well," he said when she finished. "This is a fine mess, isn't it?"

"That is one way to describe it," Pauline acknowledged with a wry smile. "But what do you make of it all, James?"

He rubbed his square, clean-shaven jaw. "I'm surprised you're asking me at all. I've never known you to rely on a man to tell you what to do."

Prickled, Pauline snapped, "Nonsense! You have been a policeman for several years, and this is only the second criminal matter I've ever investigated. Me coming to you is no different than a student asking a professor for advice on a difficult paper."

He laughed. "I'm sorry, I shouldn't tease you. And in truth, I'm flattered you are including me in this. I'll try to live up to your good opinion of me."

Pauline smoothed her skirts, regretting her outburst. She ought to have known better. James was a good friend, but he did love to tease, especially when it came to women's rights. It never failed to get under her skin.

"It's not my jurisdiction, you know," James said, tapping his fingers on the desk top. "And a good thing for you, or I'd have to report you for taking that sapphire."

"I know I shouldn't have done it," Pauline admitted. "Sarah is quite correctly unhappy with me for it as well. I would say that I don't know what came over me, except I do: I didn't—and still don't—trust anyone else involved to handle this matter properly. Mr. Ramsey is a fool, if I may be blunt, and the Thousand Islands police refuse to believe any of this is connected or significant. Until I know for certain who should have the sapphire, my conscience won't allow me to simply hand it off."

"You and your conscience," James muttered, but he accompanied the words with a faint grin. Pauline gathered he wasn't going to scold her too sharply over her peccadillo.

"I'm not asking you to involve yourself professionally—though I suppose I ought not to have come bothering you with a personal matter while you were on duty. I simply don't know where to go next with this. Miss Warren and Jonathan are taking the necklace to Mr. MacPhee this morning, and I am absolutely certain he will say the diamonds are paste. But even so, what then? What is the next step?"

James tapped his fingers again, noticed what he was doing, and quickly moved his hand off the desk. "It's true there are a lot of pieces that don't add up, and something is clearly amiss here. The trouble it, I don't have any right poking my nose into a case that is so clearly centered in the Thousand Islands, any more than they would be justified in interfering in our affairs here."

"I don't suppose the attempted robbery of two Canton citizens counts?" Pauline asked as a forlorn hope.

"Not for getting involved officially, but I will use that as my excuse if the chief asks me what I'm doing. After all, we can't have you running around getting yourself shot at—nor Miss Warren either."

"Believe me, I will be quite happy if I never in my life see another weapon pointed at me," Pauline said fervently.

"I should hope so."

Pauline waved her hand to dismiss the subject. No sense in dwelling on what had already happened, when they couldn't change the past. "So what do you think?"

"I think your best chance would be to catch your Mr. X in an act so blatant the police have to acknowledge it," James said. "A written confession would be best, obviously."

"Mr. X? Then you don't have one suspect you favor over another?"

Pauline ought to have been glad there wasn't something so obviously pointing to one suspect that only a rank amateur such as herself could have overlooked it, but she was disappointed. It would have been nice to have James see something right away that solved everything. She found herself getting increasingly tired of this case. For very little, she would have handed it over to the police and retired to her desk and typewriter.

"I'm with Sarah, I'd like it to be the lawyer. Unfortunately, I also agree with you that he seems highly unlikely, as he doesn't get anything out of the new will."

"But the paste jewels … what if he stole the real jewels?"

"He still couldn't have altered the will to leave the false jewels to other people," James countered. "His clerk did the actual writing."

"And the clerk couldn't have done it because Mr. Ramsey read the will before and after," Pauline sighed. "Nothing makes sense. It had to have been Mr. Van Camp who wrote the will the way he did, but why? And what does it have to do with the stolen jewels? At first everything seemed to point to one of the beneficiaries. Now we have a jewel thief involved, and no clearer picture of the way the thief managed to stage manage the set. Every time I find another piece of information it makes things more cloudy, not less."

Something tugged at her brain, telling her she'd said something important, that somehow she'd laid her finger on the clue to the entire case … but it was gone before she could focus on it.

"That's often the way it goes," James was saying. "It's like my mother's knitting after I would get into it when I was a little shaver and tangle it. Every time I'd find an end and tug, thinking I could unravel the mess, the knots would get worse. But once Mother would get one knot undone, the rest almost always came loose of their own accord."

Pauline smiled ruefully. "I'm not much of a knitter, unfortunately. Do you have any analogies that are related to writing?"

"Now it's my turn to be sorry. I'm no hand at writing, and not even much of a reader. The papers and the occasional novel Ruby thinks I ought to try, that's it."

The papers … it wasn't the clue she had given herself earlier, but something else clicked in Pauline's brain as she looked again at the list of names on James's desk.

Arabella Warren telling her she had been quoted in the *Watertown Daily Times* for her opinion on the end of Prohibition. David Anderson featured in a piece on the heroic loggers. Jane Casper's prize-winning cabbages mentioned in her local paper. Bertha Nelson's prize-winning quilt photographed for the *North Country Advance*.

"James!"

"What?"

"What old newspapers do you have here?"

"I don't know, why?"

"I think I know how Mr. X chose the heirs, or at least introduced their names to Mr. Van Camp—and it couldn't be Mr. Ramsey. I need all the newspapers for the Thousand Islands region, the *Times*, and, oh, just to prove my point, the *North Country Advance*."

"Mother takes that," James noted absently. "I can have the papers collected for you, but why?"

Pauline was already scribbling in her ubiquitous notepad. "I'll tell you in a minute. I need them for the dates around the time Mr. Van Camp's will was made."

Baffled but agreeable, James sent out for newspaper collection.

"What do you have in mind, Pauline?"

"Look," she said, showing him her notes. "Arabella *Warren*, mentioned in a piece in the *Watertown Daily Times*. Jane *Casper*, lives in Cape Vincent, mentioned in her local paper. Bertha *Nelson* in the

North Country Advance. David *Anderson*, in the *Alexandria Bay News*, among others. And I remember that Arden Jamison was in the *Jefferson County Journal* recently. *Jamison.*"

"I see what you're getting at," James said. "But—why? What's the point of it?"

"I don't know," Pauline said, frustrated. She had been so sure figuring out the origin of the heirs would be the key to solving the puzzle. "Let's confirm the theory first."

It took the rest of the morning, but they were eventually able to find Maria Thompson in the *Thousand Islands Sun* ("They even matched the 'Th,' that's dedication," James said); Richard Bracken in the *Black River Press*; Alan Caruthers in the *Carthage News*; Denis O'Leary in *On the St. Lawrence* ("Surely that should have been a paper starting with 'L'?" James asked, but Pauline insisted it was quite proper); Caroline Swanson in the *Sacketts Harbor Courier*; and Brian Nettleton in the *Northern New York Journal.*

"That's everyone except the Canadian fellow," James said, staring down at the neat list of names atop the scattered mounds of newspaper.

"How odd," Pauline said. "If you are matching surnames to newspaper names, and you are sticking with local papers, why suddenly jump to a Toronto man?"

James shrugged wearily. "Maybe it was a mistake."

"Maybe." Pauline was unconvinced.

"Or it could be that knot we need to undo in order to make everything else come clear," was James's next offering. "At the moment, I can't see which."

Pauline was weary as well, but her mind felt more clear than it had in days. At last they had something concrete. At last logic and scholarly elimination had gotten them somewhere.

"Thank you, James," she said, staggering to her feet—sitting for so long in one position checking the papers had left her horribly cramped.

"I'm not sure I did much," he said. "You're the one who made the connection between the papers and the people."

"I couldn't have done it if you hadn't jogged the idea in my brain."

"What's next for you?"

"Home," she said, savoring the thought. "I'm going to put the entire thing out of my mind for a time and see what else simmers to the surface."

Pauline suited deed to word, walking home in the crisp midday sun and then seating herself at the typewriter once back at Pleasant Street. She spent the rest of the day working on her current Emma Daring novel and typing up a piece on "The Mysterious Van Camp Heirs" to soothe a conscience still uneasy in stretching the truth to so many people in her initial investigation.

Arabella popped in that evening to let Pauline and Sarah know Mr. MacPhee had indeed confirmed the diamonds were paste, and that Jonathan was staying with her, "until we get answers to this riddle and nobody else is in danger."

"Another piece of the puzzle put in place, but the picture overall is still unclear," Pauline said. "Who took the jewels—who made the will—how could anyone do either of those without Mr. Van Camp and Mr. Ramsey knowing?"

"Or are we still looking at Mr. Ramsey as the villain?" Sarah asked hopefully.

"Maybe Mr. Van Camp really did do it all himself, even though Jonathan says it would be entirely out of character," Arabella said, plumping for her choice.

"Which do you think, Pauline? It had to be one of them."

"I think it's someone else entirely, but I don't know who, or how they did it," Pauline said.

"Mr. Gagne could have switched the jewels, and maybe he had a falling-out with his fellow thieves," Sarah mused. "That doesn't explain the will, nor Mr. Anderson's death, nor the attempted robbery. Who else could it be?"

"Who profits?" Pauline said. "That's the question Grandfather would ask, but in this case, it's only the jewel thief, and we've no way of knowing who that is."

"Or why he would go to the lengths of somehow convincing Mr. Van Camp to make a different will," Arabella said. "Wouldn't it have been easier to steal the jewels from Jonathan after he inherited them?"

"What about this Canadian? I want to know more about him," Sarah said. "He's a false note in the rest of this business, and I'd like to get him cleared away."

The three women were sharing a cup of chicory coffee around the kitchen table. Arabella had looked askance at Sarah at first, but was now talking with her as though she had never hesitated a moment.

"Oh!" said Pauline.

The other two looked at her.

"It was right there—everything—the whole solution, right at the back of my mind, and now it's gone. Just like this morning," she said, shaking her head in frustration.

"The important question is, what do we do now?" asked Arabella.

The question Pauline had brought to James at the start of the day. She had no more idea now than she had then.

The Pinkerton Man

The next thing that happened was not of Pauline's doing at all—at least, not directly. She was surprised at her typing the next day by a knock at the front door. She opened the door to reveal a stranger.

He was both tall and broad, straining at the seams of his navy suit, its shining silver buttons looking close to popping open. A bowler hat sat perched on the dark, slicked-back hair atop his head. His face was unshaven, and his small eyes were hard and dangerous. In one gloved hand he held a grimy envelope.

"Are you Pauline Gray?" he demanded as soon as the door opened, without even saying hello.

"I am," she replied. "Who are you?"

"Explain this to me," he said, thrusting the envelope forward and ignoring her question.

Pauline didn't need to look closely to recognize her own script addressing the envelope to Miller Horton, the lone Canadian amongst Mr. Van Camp's heirs. A prickle of undefined fear ran up her spine.

"Who are you?" she repeated.

"Ma'am, you need to tell me about this letter."

Pauline straightened her back and looked the man in the face, letting none of her nervousness show. "Either show me a badge or leave my home," she said quietly.

Heaving a great sigh, as though being asked to do something entirely unreasonable, the man dug into his pocket and flashed a small gold shield, replacing it too quickly for her to read the black lettering.

"Pinkerton's," he said. "Now answer the question."

Pauline frowned. "Why would private detectives be inquiring about a letter mailed to Canada? How did you even get a hold of it?"

"I am the one asking questions here, Miss Gray, and I suggest you start cooperating and answer them!" The man leaned forward, far too close to Pauline for comfort.

She refused to yield to his attempt at physical intimidation, despite the churning in her stomach that presaged an attack of nerves. "Step back, sir! I will answer no questions when they are accompanied by threats."

"What do you have to hide?" the man said, squinting his small eyes at her.

"I am beginning to wonder the same thing about you," Pauline replied. "If you are who you claim to be, and are here for legitimate purposes, you should have no objection to accompanying me to the police station and continuing this discussion there."

"Lady, I don't have time for your nonsense! You answer me right now, or—"

The altercation had drawn the attention of Pauline's landlady, who lived on the first floor of the two-story house. Her kitchen window flew open and she poked her head out and craned her neck to look up.

"Are you all right, Miss Gray? Do you need help? I see Kenny Mulgrew down the street, shall I call to him?" She pointed, and both Pauline and the Pinkerton man instinctively followed the direction of her finger.

Kenny Mulgrew was fourteen years old and the son and grandson of farmers; he already stood over six feet in his stocking feet and could throw feed bags of grain around like they were pillows.

The Pinkerton man snarled wordlessly, then brought himself under control.

"No trouble," he said. "We'll do this at the station. We'll see what your police have to say about you interfering with my duty."

"Thank you, Mrs. Harper," Pauline called down. "I think everything is fine for the moment."

Mrs. Harper continued to watch the detective even as Pauline closed the door in his face in order to put on her coat, hat, and gloves. Pauline's hands shook as she picked up her bag, but she couldn't tell if it was from fear or anger. How *dare* the man threaten her on her own doorstep! Thank heavens for valiant Mrs. Harper and dear Kenny.

Almost to the door, she paused, looking at her bag. She turned back to the bedroom, opened the nightstand drawer, and removed the unassuming pillbox. Something told her she might need its contents before the day was over.

The Pinkerton man had to precede Pauline down the outside staircase, it being too narrow to allow them to descend side-by-side or for him to move aside for her to go first. Once on the ground, he tried to take her arm, but Mrs. Harper cleared her throat from the kitchen window, and Pauline side-stepped him.

"We're going to the station now," she assured her landlady, and stepped out, setting such a brisk pace down the sidewalk that the bulky man was hard-pressed to keep up. Pauline's head was high and two spots of angry color flushed her usually pale cheeks. She was so angry her nausea had passed, though she knew it would return later, once this was over and done with.

The Pinkerton man was huffing and puffing by the time they reached the opera house.

He gaped at the stone building with its gothic windows and the towers on each of the four corners, and the bell tower in front. "This is your police station?" he gasped out, struggling to regain his breath as well as his former menacing mien.

Pauline opened the main door. "This is the Town Hall and Opera Theatre, the heart of our town—police included."

Young Officer Wallace was on duty at the station desk at the back of the opera house. His eyebrows raised nearly into his red hair at the sight of Pauline marching in trailed by a hulking, wheezing, scowling stranger.

"Is Lieutenant Richardson in?" Pauline inquired crisply.

"Y-yes ma'am," young Wallace said. "That way."

"Thank you," she said, walking past him and into James's office without stopping to knock.

That worthy officer of the law was tilted back in his chair behind his desk, studying some papers. At Pauline's entrance, he lost his balance, the chair crashing back down onto all fours, the papers scattering to every corner of the room.

"Tarnation! … Pauline?"

"Lieutenant Richardson," she said formally, still furiously angry, "this man came to my home, demanded I answer his questions without identifying himself or his reason for asking, and threatened me—*in my own home*—if I did not capitulate to his demands."

"What?"

"Now then, miss, no need to be hysterical," the detective butted in. He had recovered enough of his breath and aplomb to step slightly in front of Pauline, forcing her to move aside or be trodden on, and smiled at James in a "we men against these foolish women" manner. "Frank Atkins, Pinkerton's Detective Agency." He handed his shield to James with far more courtesy than he had shown Pauline. "I admit, I was a bit brusque, but I didn't expect the lady to panic the way she did. A bit high-strung, isn't she?" He had the gall to chuckle. "I figured we'd step down here so the little miss felt safer. There was no real need to bother you, but—"

James shot to his feet. His face was dark red, his eyes narrowed and hard as flint. "You come into our town and question our citizens without having the courtesy to inform the police first? You threaten a lady of this town in her own home and then lie to my face about it? I will be telling my chief about this, and if he does not toss you in the lock-up overnight to teach you proper behavior I will be very surprised! This is outrageous!"

Atkins backpedaled rapidly. "No, no, it's all a misunderstanding! It's just a simple question! Nothing to bother the police with, just clearing up loose ends. It's a murder, you see, in Toronto. Last week, a man named Miller Norton. The police found this lady's letter at the scene and thought there was a chance she might have some information that could help them catch his killer, so they contacted us and asked if we could investigate." He scowled. "We used to work for them regularly, until they developed their own investigative department, but they still use us for odd jobs and the like. Hardly worth my time, really."

James and Pauline exchanged a glance.

"The last Van Camp heir?" he asked her.

"The only one who wasn't in a local paper," she confirmed. "The odd man out."

"I'm getting the chief," he said.

"But—" the detective protested.

"This is a larger matter than you realize, as you would have learned had you come to us first," James said. "And we still need to deal with your treatment of Miss Gray."

"She exaggerated!" Atkins said. "She's a woman!"

"If there is one thing I've learned about Miss Gray over the last several years, it is that she never exaggerates," James said. "You, on the other hand, have already shown yourself to be prone to bluster and evasions. Of course I will believe her first. And I fail to see what her being a woman has to do with any of this, except in that it makes your behavior even more egregious."

Atkins shot Pauline a glare of pure hatred as James called into the corridor for someone to fetch the chief, now. Pauline ignored it. He was of no concern to her, not now.

A third murder, the second heir to be killed, and the only one not connected to the papers. If she could, to use James's metaphor, unpick this one knot, she knew she could unravel the rest of it. The pieces were almost all in her hands; she only needed to put them together in the right positions.

Chief Gordon of Canton's Police Department heard James's succinct summation of the case thus far without comment, then withered Atkins with a glare when he heard how the man had come into town to question Pauline without first introducing himself and his needs to the force.

"I think we'd best bring in Miss Warren and the young Van Camp to fill out the details," he said as James wrapped up. "And have someone contact the police in the Thousand Islands. Technically speaking this seems to lie between them and the Toronto police, but since we've been brought into this matter to protect our own citizen from harassment, we'll coordinate matters from here. The letter from Miss Gray will be our justification, should we need it. We've been dragged into this, by gum we're going to see it wrapped up. I also need to contact the Chief Constable of the Toronto Police Department."

"Now look here!" Atkins said. "You can't just—"

"Do not," said Chief Gordon, "tell me what I can and cannot do."

For the next several hours, Pauline sat on a wooden chair in the corner of James's office and watched the activity.

From what Pauline could gather from James's end of the conversation, the police in the Thousand Islands continued to ridicule the notion of a connected conspiracy until he, face red with sheer fury, broke down their stubborn resistance point by point. Chief Gordon then took over James's desk to dictate a telegram to his Toronto counterpart informing him of the link between to cases. The telegram was short, to the point, and unmistakably angry over the breach in protocol by sending a Pinkerton man to Canton without informing the force.

When Arabella and Jonathan arrived, Pauline nodded a greeting to them but did not leave her corner. Arabella had matters well in hand, as her fluttery manner of speaking went away entirely when defending Jonathan Van Camp to the police.

"Thank you, Miss Warren," Chief Gordon said at last. "We don't necessarily suspect young Van Camp here, but we do have to ask these questions. I hope you understand."

"I do, sir," said Jonathan, who hovered as protectively over Arabella as she did him.

"I suppose to have to do your duty," Arabella graciously allowed.

All the while, Pauline mulled over the case, taking each seemingly disparate point and examining it, turning it around in her mind to look at it from a different angle to see if it might fit with the others from another perspective.

"Jonathan," she asked, "how many papers did your great-uncle read?"

"Only the *New York Times*," the young man answered. "He wasn't interested in local news."

Pauline nodded and added that fact to her musings.

"Richardson, where was Anderson killed?" she overheard Chief Gordon ask. "I'd like to know if we need to bring any other forces into this."

James checked the notes from the conversation with the Thousand Islands police. "Where is it, where is it, blast this wretched handwriting of mine, I can't read my own notes—there!" He looked up. "Utica."

Inability to read his own notes … Utica … the lost sapphire …

Light began to glimmer.

"Mr. Atkins," Pauline said, turning to the sulky detective hunched in the opposite corner to hers. "What did you say this Miller's surname was?"

He ignored her.

"Answer the question, if you please," James bit out. "In this place, you will treat Miss Gray with respect."

"Norton," Atkins said, glaring at her. "You spelled in wrong in your letter. Not Horton—*Norton*."

That was it. That had to be it.

"And he was killed last week?"

"I already told you that, didn't you listen?"

"Was his head smashed in?"

"No," he said, pushing the words between his teeth. "He was poisoned."

"A woman's weapon," she said softly. "It all fits."

James looked over at her. "What?"

"I think I know who did it, how, and even why," she said.

"Oh, come now, Miss Gray," began Chief Gordon. "I don't deny you've been tremendously clever to collect all this information, but this is a matter for trained investigators now."

James coughed. "I think we ought to listen to her, sir. She's been right before. You remember the Ferris case last fall?"

"I just need proof," Pauline said. "Mr. Atkins, did Mr. Norton make a will?"

He mulishly clamped his mouth shut.

"Answer the lady's question, Atkins," Chief Gordon said, his mustache bristling with exasperation. However little he regarded Pauline's detective abilities, still less did he care for the Pinkerton man. "You've been warned once."

"Yes," Atkins ground out.

"Was his main beneficiary his brother?"

He stared. "How did you—"

"I need to see a copy of that will," Pauline said. "And I think we need to all take one last trip to Clayton for our final proof. Arabella and Jonathan included, and Sarah as well, for her medical knowledge. Each of them has contributed in one way or another to this case, and they need to be there for the wrapping up of it."

James looked at his chief, who looked at Pauline. She returned his gaze with quiet confidence.

"Very well, have it your way," Chief Gordon said, throwing up his hands in resignation. "Somebody ring them up and tell them to prepare for us."

Truth Revealed

They were all squeezed into the lawyer's office in Clayton—Mr. Atkins holding himself as aloof as possible from the rest; Arabella standing next to Jonathan Van Camp; Sarah in her nurse's uniform, having had no time to change between leaving the hospital and joining the rest of them; Mrs. David Anderson, looking tired but determined, a glimmer of hope at the back of her eyes; James and Chief Gordon with their thumbs hooked in their pockets, waiting for the proof of the murderer's identity; two Thousand Islands police officers scowling at the rest of them; and finally, Mr. Ramsey and his staff.

"Er—I appreciate that you are all here, I suppose, but it is a bit, er, unconventional, isn't it?" Mr. Ramsey said. "Shouldn't you police just arrest the murderer and thief and tell us all about it afterward?" He glared at Jonathan as he said "murderer and thief."

The young man stared defiantly back. "I for one want to have it all out in the open," he said.

"There is such a tangle of information and misinformation in this case that it seems impossible to sort it all and prove the murderer without going through it all step by step, with everyone contributing his or her piece of the puzzle," James said gravely.

Pauline approved the way he phrased it.

"Miss Gray here has assembled most of the framework herself, which is why we will now be turning this over to her," Chief Gordon added. "Miss Gray?"

So many eyes on her, some hostile, some confused, some hopeful, a few confident. Pauline's stomach twisted. If she should be wrong …!

But she wasn't. This was the only thing that made sense.

"The question at the heart of this case has always been: why did Mr. Van Camp make such a strange will? Mr. Ramsey here suggested it was a philanthropic gesture and a way of showing his displeasure with his great-nephew. Others have thought it the quixotic whim of an old man. Miss Warren considered it an act of benevolence toward his great-nephew, once we learned the jewels were fake. I believe it was none of these things. I am convinced that the will we have all accepted as Mr. Van Camp's is a fake."

Mr. Ramsey burst into speech before anyone else. "Now look here, young lady, that is a serious accusation, very serious indeed! How dare you suggest—"

Pauline held up a hand. "Please let me finish." There was a crack of authority in her voice that surprised the lawyer into silence.

"I discovered recently that each heir but one had been chosen based on their name appearing in a newspaper that shared the same first initial—for example, Arabella Warren in the *Watertown Daily Times*. Mr. Van Camp, we have learned, did not read any of the local newspapers.

"The will had been witnessed by two men: Jasper Randolph, the gardener; and Mr. Gagne, the butler-*cum*-valet. Mr. Randolph was gotten out of the country by a mysterious gift he assumed to be from his former employer, and Mr. Gagne was murdered."

"Mr. Gagne's death was declared an accident," spoke up one of the Clayton policemen.

"Yes," said Pauline. "That was a mistake on your part."

He sputtered indignantly, but let her continue.

"The next to die was Miller Norton, a man living in Toronto, Canada, who inherited Mr. Van Camp's small but priceless art collection—the only beneficiary not named in a local newspaper, and the only one to receive art instead of jewelry."

"Horton, you mean," broke in Mr. Ramsey.

"His name was written as Horton on the list you gave Miss Warren, but that was another lie," Pauline said. "Mr. Atkins?"

"It was Norton, sure enough," he growled.

"But that's—" Mr. Ramsey began.

"The next death was that of David Anderson," Pauline said loudly, overriding whatever the lawyer had been going to say. "A good man and loving father, who so questioned the authenticity of the inheritance he received that he asked a jeweler to examine the earrings, and in so doing lost his life. The jewels proved to be as false as the will that directed their disposal."

"Our apologies for the difficult topic, ma'am," said the other Clayton policeman to Mrs. Anderson, shooting a poisonous glare at Pauline.

Mrs. Anderson intercepted the glare and directed it back toward him. "Don't apologize for the topic, apologize for letting this happen! At least Miss Gray is doing something toward catching my husband's murderer."

Pauline coughed, touched and embarrassed by the woman's confidence.

"At first, Sarah—Miss Jones, that is—and I suspected Mr. Ramsey of being our villain. He was the lawyer who made Mr. Van Camp's will; he easily could have altered it. He had the jewelry in his safe, making it simple for him to switch the stones. He was even in Utica at the time Mr. Anderson was murdered. He could have done all of this so he could sell the real jewels and reap his dishonest reward."

"Well, of all the—" spluttered Mr. Ramsey.

"We were wrong," Pauline said.

"I should think so!" exclaimed the lawyer.

"How can you be sure, Pauline?" asked James.

She directed her words toward him while watching the lawyer out of the corner of her eye.

"Because Mr. Ramsey is losing his vision. He can no longer read."

The lawyer's face turned white. His legs gave out, and he clutched at the desk for support.

"I suspect cataracts," she continued. "He mistook my white blouse for yellow the other day, which Miss Jones informs me is a common symptom of cataracts. And while this reception area is a painfully bright white, even to non-diseased eyes, his office is so dimly lit as to make reading anything nearly impossible. Finally, he admitted that he does not read the papers anymore. He passed it off as though he does not have the time, but the excuse rang false from the first. A lawyer who does not enjoy the morning paper over breakfast? Highly implausible.

"Mr. Ramsey claimed he glanced over the list of bequests before handing it over to his clerk to write out properly, but in reality he relied on the clerk to do the reading for him, just as he relies on his secretary to tell him any news of importance in the papers."

Sarah stepped forward to peer at Mr. Ramsey's face. "I do see the beginning of cloudiness," she said. "It's the early stages of cataracts."

He put up a hand to shield his eyes. "How can *you* possibly know that, young woman?"

"I am a nurse," she reminded him. "Why hide it? You can have surgery to remove cataracts. There's no shame in it."

He straightened angrily. "No shame! Who would want a lawyer who is going blind, who has to rely on his clerk and secretary to do all his reading? Nobody would ever trust me again. And don't talk to me about surgery—Eleanor researched all that when my vision first started clouding over and told me that most of the time the surgery leaves the patient worse off than before. No, no surgery for me!" He looked around, his anger turned now to pleading.

"I shouldn't have hidden the truth, I know, but I was too afraid of losing my clients! Eleanor and George said they would act as my eyes, and I thought, well, I would just keep going as long as I could. There's no crime in that!"

"But if he didn't read the list of bequests, or write the will, or even read the newspapers, that means …" Arabella began.

"He couldn't have chosen the heirs," Sarah finished, stepping away from the lawyer with sadness on her face.

"Exactly," Pauline nodded.

"And if the clerk wrote the will, that means—" James said, waiting by the door with a deceptively casual stance.

"Yes," agreed Pauline. "That means our true villains are the pair who kept their employer's secret and used it for their own gain."

George and Miss Peck had been modestly effacing themselves at the back of the office while this was going on. At Pauline's announcement of Mr. Ramsey's eye troubles, they had exchanged uneasy glances and started slithering toward the door.

James and Chief Gordon blocked their way.

"Mr. Ramsey told me of George Norton's unsatisfactory brother who had been shipped off to Canada after he disgraced the family. It's not that much of a stretch to guess his name was Miller. Mr. Ramsey never made the connection between the Miller Horton on the list of heirs and Miller Norton, George's brother, because George never told him the man's first name, only the surname, and that was changed just enough to not ring any bells."

"You can't prove that," George spoke up at last. Everyone had instinctively drawn apart from the pair, leaving a clear space around them. Mrs. Anderson had recoiled almost to the opposite wall, eyes burning in her white face. Pauline couldn't bear to look at her for long.

"Mr. Atkins?" Pauline said.

The Pinkerton man seemed at last to have forgiven her for being a woman and unintimidated by him. The more uncomfortable Mr. Ramsey and his staff became, the more he seemed to be enjoying himself. "Miller Norton in his will left everything of which he was possessed to his brother George Norton."

Pauline broke the silence that filled the room at that pronouncement. "So you see it all starts to come together. George Norton and Eleanor Peck saw their opportunity when Mr. Ramsey was called out to the Van Camp place to make a will. Mr. Van Camp was well-known locally for his jewelry collection and ownership of three Moillon paintings. George of course accompanied Mr. Ramsey, secretly carrying with him a second will form and a pre-written list of names culled from various newspapers. He wrote out the will as Mr. Van Camp intended, and then, while Mr. Van Camp was showing Mr. Ramsey the jewelry, George filled in the second will and changed the bequests intended for Jonathan to the names on his list. Mr. Van Camp saw the will he intended, but the will that was signed and witnessed was the false one. George even had a ready-made excuse, covering up the will for the witnesses to sign as is proper. Mr. Ramsey, unable to read the original will, never knew its contents, and so assumed everything was in order."

Jonathan made a quick movement toward George Norton. "You thieving, lying—"

Arabella grabbed his arm and hauled him back. "Let her finish," she said. "Leave him to the police."

"Worse was to come," Pauline said. "As soon as Mr. Van Camp died and the will passed probate, Miss Peck left for Toronto, where she murdered Mr. Miller Norton so the paintings would come to George."

A cry broke from Mr. Ramsey's throat. "No! Not Eleanor! She

wouldn't betray me like that."

"I'm afraid she did," Pauline said. "In fact, I strongly suspect she was the driving force behind the entire plot. Her lies to you about cataract surgery mean she's been planning something of this sort for a long time."

"Lies?"

"Cataract surgery is dangerous, as is any surgery, Mr. Ramsey, but nowhere near so bad as Miss Peck told you," Sarah said in a gentle voice.

Mr. Ramsey groaned and buried his face in his hands.

Pauline cleared her throat, glancing around the room. Chief Gordon and James were nodding along as she spoke, their attention divided between listening to her and making sure Miss Peck and George didn't make a break for the door. Jonathan continued to glare at George, while Arabella was clearly more concerned with him than with the revelations. Mrs. Anderson—Pauline moved on. Even the Thousand Islands police seemed to believe her now.

"Mr. Ramsey mentioned to me that Miss Peck has a cousin who is a jeweler. I believe she was the one who first thought of switching the jewels; George, the art lover, would likely have been content with adding his brother onto the real will so as to get his hands on the paintings once Miller's debauched lifestyle led to his inevitably early demise."

She had no proof of that, but judging by their personalities she was confident in her assertion. George had struck her all along as weak, whereas Miss Peck was both ruthless and amoral.

George was pale and sweating now, but Miss Peck watched the entire proceeding with aloof disdain, standing somewhat apart from him. Only her fingers, fiddling with the clasp on her handbag, gave away a hint of nerves.

"What about poor old Mr. Gagne?" Jonathan asked.

"I can't be entirely certain, but I suspect he discovered the fraud. Perhaps he saw George changing the bequests, or maybe George dropped the list of names and Mr. Gagne picked it up without realizing at first what it signified. They sent Jasper Randolph away to stop him from gossiping or suspecting anything was amiss, but they couldn't leave the property without a caretaker. When he realized what they were up to, they tried to bribe him with the sapphires taken from Mr. Anderson's earrings. He wouldn't take them, and so George, presumably, lost his temper and hit him over the head with a rock, killing Mr. Gagne and losing one of the sapphires in the process." She stopped and swallowed, the picture she was painting with her words almost too vivid for her own self.

"And my David?" asked Mrs. Anderson, her voice hoarse.

"They didn't want anyone to figure out the jewels were false. Their one hope was for everything to settle down and for nobody to ask too many questions. Arabella Warren was the first to put a spoke in their plans by asking me to investigate. Your husband, Mrs. Anderson, was another complication. They hoped by killing him and taking the earrings they could make it appear he had been murdered for the gems, proving they were valuable. They didn't count on his wife being privy to his plans and seeing the discrepancies in the setup."

"If David Anderson was killed in Utica, how did they do that?" Chief Gordon asked. He kept a wary eye on George Norton, who looked almost ready to bolt despite the officers blocking the doorway.

"You remember I said Mr. Ramsey was in Utica the same night? Miss Peck and George were with him. They even met Mr. Anderson earlier in the day, which is when he told them of his intentions to have the earrings evaluated. After the meeting of the Bar Association finished and Mr. Ramsey retired for the night, George tracked down David Anderson and killed him. I'm sorry, Mrs. Anderson."

The woman nodded, her face tight.

"By now the conspirators were getting extremely nervous. Nothing was going according to plan. The earrings had been evaluated before Mr. Anderson was killed, and the information shared with others. In an attempt to both shift suspicion back onto Mr. Van Camp's great-nephew and persuade people the jewelry was worth something, they attempted to rob Arabella. Not only did the robbery fail, Jonathan stopped George, the would-be-thief, and so simply *could not* have been the robber."

"I should think not!" said Arabella, stretching up to put a protective arm around the boy's shoulders. He gave her a startled glance, and then smiled.

"Now for the final proof," Pauline said. "Mr. Ramsey, you mentioned the other day that George had sent some of his paintings off to be framed and he was expecting them returned any day now. They were coming to the office because he didn't trust such valuable items to be sent to his boarding house. I presume those are them?" She nodded to the brown paper-wrapped rectangles leaning against the wall in the back.

"No!" shouted George, lunging forward.

All was chaos for a few moments as James wrestled George into submission and the Clayton police tore the paper off the parcels, revealing three exquisite Renaissance paintings.

"Those are Great-Uncle Horace's all right," Jonathan said. "He had them hanging in the dining room, where I saw them every week at dinner. I'd recognize them anywhere."

"You still have no proof I was involved in any of this." Miss Peck chose now to speak, casting a disdainful eye at the writhing George. "I have a cousin who is a jeweler and I happened to be out of town at the time George's brother was poisoned. What of it?"

"Oh no," snarled George, still struggling in James's grip. "I'm not going down alone. The entire thing was your plan, from start to finish!

I only thought of defrauding the old man of the paintings and waiting for my brother to die—he drank too much and lived too rough a life, I knew I wouldn't have long to wait. The jewels and the murders were your idea. The whole reason you told Ramsey not to have surgery was so you could use him to cheat people." He stopped struggling and turned his head to look at James. "Van Camp was the first, but she had just been waiting for her chance. I helped, but she was the one behind it. I'll confess everything if it means she gets arrested too!"

Before anyone could move, Eleanor Peck whipped a tiny pistol out of her handbag, pointed it at George Norton, and calmly pulled the trigger. A shot cracked. Arabella and Mrs. Anderson screamed.

James let go of George, stumbled back, and clutched his bleeding arm where the bullet had nicked him. George slumped to the floor, blood flowing copiously from the wound in his chest. Sarah dashed forward to tend him.

Chief Gordon and the other policemen lunged toward Miss Peck, but halted when she turned the pistol on Mr. Ramsey.

"If anyone takes one more step, I will shoot him as well," she said. She smiled contemptuously when everyone froze in place.

"I thought at first I should shoot you, Miss Gray, but you would never have put it all together if Ramsey hadn't talked so much. Oh yes, you're very clever, it took so much effort to put the pieces together with this fool dropping clues right and left, dangling the truth in front of your very nose. I will give you credit at least for figuring out how and why Gagne died. You pieced it together nicely, I admit. It was the list of names he picked up after George dropped them, like a clumsy idiot. And then George had to go and lose his nerve when Gagne refused the bribe, flinging away the sapphire. Hit him over the head with a rock and bolted. I had to go back once he'd told me what he'd done and set the scene to look like an accident, and it took me so long to find the list from where it had blown that I didn't have time to search for the sapphire.

"George was bad enough, but worst of all was you, Alan Ramsey. You never stop talking. Never! After all these years, you never notice George or me as anything more than your cover for your shameful secret and your audience for your endless babbling. We pulled this off right under your nose and you were too busy chattering to see it."

"Put the gun down and let's talk this over," said Chief Gordon in a strained voice. "You've already killed one man, maybe two. You don't want another death on your conscience."

"If I had a conscience, I suppose I wouldn't," said Miss Peck indifferently. "Then again, after two deaths, what's one more? But in fact, I don't particularly care. I am walking out that door, and if anyone tries to stop me, I am shooting Alan Ramsey."

"Oh no you aren't," snarled Jonathan, and he threw himself at Miss Peck. Pauline, body reacting before her brain engaged, swept to the side and pulled Mr. Ramsey with her out of the line of fire.

The gun went off—Arabella cried out again—blood poured from Jonathan's arm but he had his hands on the gun now, wrestling it aside—the police recovered from their stupefaction and moved in to help—it was over. Eleanor Peck was disarmed and in handcuffs.

Her face showed no more emotion than it had at any time Pauline had seen it.

Sarah rose to her feet from her examination of George Norton.

"He'll live," she said. "But he needs to be in a hospital. James, Jonathan, I'll need to look at both your arms and get bandages on them."

"And then," Arabella burst out, the speech pouring forth as though she couldn't hold it in a moment longer, "you're coming home with me for good, Jonathan Van Camp. You and I, we both need a family. I don't care about any diamond necklace, paste or real. I want you to live with me as my son, and you'll never have to worry about a home again. You can even bring your half-sisters to live with us if you think your stepfather will let them go. My house is large enough for you all."

Jonathan had endured the gunshot wound without a whimper, but at that his composure finally cracked. "Oh," he said faintly.

Pauline turned away so she wouldn't have to see his tears.

The police took the two conspirators away, George on a makeshift stretcher with Sarah close beside, checking his pulse. Mr. Atkins followed glumly behind. The case was solved, but he would get no glory from it.

Chief Gordon nodded to Pauline on his way out. "Seems Lieutenant Richardson was right about you. Well done, Miss Gray."

That left Mr. Ramsey and Mrs. Anderson. The lawyer, shaken and defeated, Pauline could do nothing about. In a way, Miss Peck had been right. His deception and self-absorption had allowed this to happen. There was no shame in losing his eyesight, but to lie about it and use others to fulfill his responsibilities, violating his clients' privacy in the process, was appalling. Even if Miss Peck had lied to him and played upon his fears, Pauline could not excuse him entirely.

The actions of his employees were not his fault, but he had to bear the responsibility for his own deeds.

The widow was another matter.

"I wish I could give you a happy ending," Pauline said.

"At least you gave me justice," Mrs. Anderson answered.

"I know this won't restore him, or make up for his being gone, but I have something here that belongs to you," Pauline said.

She hadn't discussed this with Jonathan, but she was confident he would follow her lead. Pauline pulled the blue sapphire out of her handbag. She opened her hand to reveal it to Mrs. Anderson.

The other woman gasped. "That's—the real stone!"

"One of them, anyway."

"But I can't take that. The will was fake."

Pauline glanced over her shoulder. Jonathan had recovered enough from his shock at Arabella's offer to take notice of his surrounding again. He stepped forward.

"It will take the lawyers—proper lawyers," with a glower at poor, broken Mr. Ramsey, "years to figure out who legally gets what, even if they ever manage to recover the rest of the stolen jewels. Miss Warren was right. She and I both need a family more than anything. That's the best legacy my great-uncle could have left me. I think he would have wanted you to have the sapphire, as our family's apology for what was done to you. Please accept it with our respect and sorrow."

Arabella had good instincts. Jonathan Van Camp was proving himself a fine young man already.

"I still feel I ought not," said Mrs. Anderson. "But my children have to eat. Thank you."

She gingerly took the sparkling blue gem from Pauline's hand.

A weight lifted off Pauline's shoulders as the widow closed her fingers around the stone, nodded a farewell to them, and hurried out. It was not enough, but it was something.

Two murderers unmasked, two lonely people given a family, and a widow provided for. It would not bring the dead back to life, nor magically untangle the complications of the falsified will, nor make up Mr. Ramsey's loss. In an imperfect world, justice could never be perfectly accomplished.

Nevertheless, Pauline had done what she could. The rest, she would leave to a higher power.

"Come," she said, looking at her friends. "It's time to go home."

III

SECRETS OF THE PAST

There are no secrets that time does not reveal
-Jean Racine

Old Memories and New Friendships

Pauline Gray gathered together the untidy stack of papers on the kitchen table and smiled at the white-haired woman sitting across from her.

"I think we've done a good bit of work today, Miss Lewis."

Anita Lewis's wrinkled cheeks were flushed a pale pink, as they usually were when she and Pauline finished a writing session. Remembering her past brought back a piece of her youth to the elderly woman. "Indeed yes, Miss Gray. I'm ever so grateful to you for taking the time to come help me. It's been such a pleasure talking to you."

"The pleasure has been mine," Pauline told her sincerely.

When Miss Lewis, a former teacher for both grammar and high school, had asked Pauline to help her write the story of her life, Pauline had agreed from practical purposes more than anything else. Miss Lewis was willing to pay, and Pauline couldn't turn down the chance to fill out her slim purse. In the year 1934, few people could.

As the days and weeks passed, the twice-a-week sessions of Miss Lewis reminiscing and Pauline taking notes shorthand to be typed into a coherent narrative later had become more than a job. Pauline grew deeply interested in the tale of this woman's life, from her idyllic childhood on the family's dairy farm, to a difficult girlhood trying to raise her younger siblings after her mother passed away when she was fifteen, to the winning of her independence with a scholarship to

Elmira College, to the romance cut short when her fiancé died in a tragic accident on his family's farm.

It was an ordinary enough tale, nothing glamorous or particularly exciting, but Miss Lewis had a way of making the past come to life with her words, and Pauline emerged from each session with the feeling she had stepped back in time and herself lived through the occurrences related by the elderly woman.

Today Miss Lewis had reminisced about the difficult years after her fiancé's death, how she struggled to find meaning and purpose to her life, how her father wanted her to return home, but she wanted something more. She had left it there, and Pauline was breathless with anticipation to discover what she did next.

"I think you do it on purpose," she said.

"Do what?" Miss Lewis asked.

"Break off at an exciting part each time. You do it ensure I'll keep coming back, so I can hear the next installment. You don't have to worry, you know. By now wild horses couldn't drag me away."

Miss Lewis laughed in a pleased fashion. "You flatter me, my dear! I can't imagine anything exciting in my life. I still feel it's somewhat presumptuous on my part to even want my story written down, but somehow, I can't bear the thought of no one remembering anything about Mother, or Tom, after I'm gone. My brothers and sisters never had a clear memory of our mother, you know, and Tom was an only child. If I had had children to pass my stories down to, maybe I wouldn't mind so much, but as it is, I take some comfort in knowing their memories will carry on even after I'm gone."

Pauline swallowed a sudden lump in her throat. She had never been interested in marrying, but the older woman's words did convey a sense of the loneliness of a lifetime lived on one's own.

"Enough of this," Miss Lewis said briskly. "How about a cup of tea before you go, dear?"

She said this every time, and every time, Pauline smiled and accepted. She didn't care very much for tea, but she had said "yes" the first time out of politeness, and now it had become something of a ritual.

She enjoyed watching Miss Lewis prepare the brew. First she brought the kettle to a boil while she washed out the flowered china teapot. Then she poured the boiling water into the pot to warm it while setting out the two delicate teacups and adding a cookie from her always-filled tin to each saucer.

Once the pot was warmed, Miss Lewis emptied it, added the fragrant black leaves, filled it once again with boiling water, turned her three-minute hourglass over, set the fine wire mesh tea strainer over the first teacup, and at last, when the three minutes were up, poured the tea.

It was an elaborate process, and it put Pauline in mind of stories she had heard of the Old World, and the ritual that afternoon tea had been in Victorian England. She appreciated this touch of European elegance in her life, and in truth, the flavor of the tea wasn't so bad once one got over wishing it was coffee.

This cookie was molasses, much to Pauline's relief. Some days it was a peanut butter cookie, which took all her grace to eat without grimacing. Those were the days she had to hurry home and eat an apple or drink a glass of milk, anything to rid herself of that cloying taste and feel in her mouth.

Today she was happy to linger over the tea, looking out the kitchen window at Miss Lewis's garden. Mostly vegetables, there were occasional bursts of color and bloom from various types of old-fashioned flowers: sweet peas, peonies, delphiniums, sweet-smelling lavender, and of course roses.

"It is so peaceful here," Pauline said, a trace of wistfulness in her voice.

Miss Lewis smiled gently as she followed Pauline's gaze. "Yes, it is a pleasant home. Small, of course, but I don't need it any larger for myself. I always knew I wanted my home to feel like a haven. I'm glad to hear you feel I've succeeded."

Pauline's thoughts flew to the small apartment she shared with her friend Sarah in town. They had no complaints of it, save for the tiring trek up the outside staircase to get to it on days they were weary, but neither did Pauline think it could be described as a haven. Perhaps there was more to the art of homemaking than she had always thought.

"Tell me, did you buy this house or build it?" she asked, more to make conversation than out of genuine curiosity.

Miss Lewis sat up straighter. "Oh, I'm so glad you asked! I had it built to my exact specifications, oh, fifteen years ago. Until then I'd always lived in other people's houses, and I wanted something that no one else had ever lived in, that was for me and me alone. My brother told me I was a fool to choose a piece of land so close to the County Home, but lands' sake, it's not those folks' fault they ended up in the poorhouse! And I must say I've never had a lick of trouble from any of them, just the occasional escaped chicken that tries to get into my garden."

Pauline laughed along with her hostess, but experienced a twinge of shame. Miss Lewis's house was separated from the County Home, known more colloquially as the poorhouse, by a large field and a row of trees, but even so, Pauline would have thought twice before building so close to society's outcasts. She thought of herself as a thoroughly modern, broad-minded woman, but this elderly retired schoolteacher had far more grace and compassion than she did.

"Yes," Miss Lewis said, still gazing unseeingly out the window. "I've been very happy here, and I'm thankful for it. Would you care for a tour, Miss Gray?"

Pauline set her teacup down carefully on its saucer. "That is most kind, thank you."

Again, she acted out of politeness, to please Miss Lewis, and again she reaped an unexpected reward. Up until this point Pauline had never seen more than the back porch and the kitchen. She had lived long enough in this rural area to know better than to enter by way of the front door! Miss Lewis had offered to conduct the interviews more formally, in the living room, but Pauline had fallen in love with this small, apple-green kitchen dominated by the gleaming, highly polished woodstove, and had firmly stated that she much preferred to sit at the table.

Now she saw how much she had missed in the rest of the house. The kitchen opened into the tiny dining room, which was papered in a soft marbled gold. The air was filled with a sweet scent of the pink roses in an old knobby jug sitting on a lace table runner on the table in the center of the room. The four chairs surrounding it had carved tops and moss green upholstered seats to match the drapes that framed the lace-curtained at the windows. In one corner of the room was a whatnot, its triangular shelves filled with curious objects. Pauline's attention was particularly drawn to the pair of Delftware candlesticks on the top shelf, as well as the green glass perfume bottle overlaid with silver filigree on the next shelf down. The detail of the filigree was exquisite.

"Mementos from my grandfather," Miss Lewis said. "He captained a merchant ship that went up and down the St. Lawrence. He always brought back something special for his children—my mother and her brother. After Mother's death my father wanted to destroy them—grief takes some people that way, you know. They can't bear to have anything left to remind them of their loss. I hid these in the attic until the day I could display them openly in my own home."

Miss Lewis picked up a photograph in a heavy silver frame from the next shelf. "This is a photo of a class picnic from one of my final years teaching," she said, handing it to Pauline.

The small, grainy, sepia faces meant little to Pauline, but she examined them out of politeness. "Very nice," she said.

Miss Lewis pointed to one of the figures. "That's Inez Grant—what a handful she was! And there next to her is Catherine Baker, the quietest and shyest student in her year. That's always the way of it, isn't it? The quiet ones are always drawn to the confident ones."

Pauline looked again. Inez Grant had her head thrown back in a laugh, and her arm was linked with a young man on one side, who looked down at her with obvious adoration. The Baker girl, on her other side, was a heavyset young woman with a scowl on what little of her face was visible through the hanging curtain of hair obscuring her features.

"Endless stories in every individual," she commented, handing the photo back.

She followed her hostess through the arched doorway into the living room, where she beheld an elegant wood-burning fireplace, two cast iron andirons shaped like owls glaring at her out of amber glass eyes from within.

"Charming, aren't they?" Miss Lewis asked with a chuckle, followed Pauline's line of sight. "Those were supposed to be a wedding gift from my Aunt Lillian, but when Tom passed away she gave them to me anyway. Said I should set them up when I had my own home, and so I did!"

Pauline had been startled by them at first, but now that she'd recovered she did have to admit they had a certain puckish charm to them.

The rest of the living room was simply but comfortably furnished with a low sofa and two wingback chairs with matching brocade upholstery. Cut flowers from Miss Lewis's garden sat in crystal vases on the polished wood side tables. A window seat with rose-spattered chintz cushions set into the bow window beckoned Pauline as a good spot to curl up and dream.

"You'll like this next room, Miss Gray," Miss Lewis said as they entered the central hall. She reached for the door handle to the last room on the first floor. "The builders wanted to make it another bedroom, but, goodness, I said, one bedroom for me and one for a guest is all I will ever need. This room is my sanctuary."

She opened the door, and Pauline beheld a vision.

"Mercy," she said once she'd regained her breath. "I've never seen so many books outside a library."

Miss Lewis laughed quietly. "I've been collecting them for a long time."

Aside from windows and the doorway, all four walls featured built-in bookcases filled with books. A wingback chair was placed in one corner, with a small round table next to it holding a reading lamp. A large wooden desk was set beneath the window looking into the back garden, making this the perfect room for reading or for writing.

"I had dreams of writing myself when I was younger," Miss Lewis said, her faded blue eyes going dreamy as her thoughts ranging back over the past. "But I never had the right touch. I can tell a story well enough, but somehow or other it loses all its zest when I write it down. That's why I'm so glad we have been able to collaborate, my dear. You are able to provide the writing skill my little life story requires."

"I must admit, if I had known this room was here I might never have gotten started on writing," Pauline said, eyes roaming over what titles she could see from her vantage point.

Miss Lewis laughed again. "Feel free to take anything home with you that you'd like! My library is open to all. You'd be amazed at how many boys and girls, housewives and farmers, students and workers alike have come out of this room with a book that captured their imagination. All I've asked in return is that if they find a book somewhere in their house that no one is interested in, they bring it to me to fill out my shelves. You'd be surprised at what I've received that way!"

"Wherever did you collect most of these?" Pauline said, taking Miss Lewis at her word and walking into the room to browse the shelves.

"Auctions and estate sales for many of them. Bookshops for others. Former students giving me books as a gift—so thoughtful, all of them. And, as I said, people bringing me their family's unwanted books. I had one farmer bring me a complete set of Dickens, if you can believe it! He said they'd been taking up room in their house for years and it was time they went to someone who would read them. You can imagine my delight.

"Oh yes, books and flowers. I let the neighborhood children pick flowers out of my garden to take home to their mothers, you see. They do the weeding that my arthritic hands can't manage anymore." Miss Lewis looked ruefully at her gnarled fingers. "That's the way to get through life, Miss Gray. Give what you can to others, and allow them to give to you when you have need."

Pauline's motto was more along the lines of "take care of oneself and never be beholden to anyone," but she thought Miss Lewis's way was, perhaps, the better.

After carefully tucking *Barchester Towers* and *Cranford* into her basket alongside a nosegay of roses and campanula, Pauline turned to her hostess, who always accompanied her to the front gate, and said a final thank-you.

Miss Lewis laughed. "Thank you, Miss Gray! I'm delighted to think of you enjoying those books."

As she always did, she opened her mailbox while Pauline mounted her bicycle, and checked to see if Al Denney, the mailman, had left her anything interesting. Today, she pulled out a long, slim white envelope and looked it over with interest.

"Well, I declare. I wonder who this could be? The handwriting doesn't look familiar…" She slipped her spectacles, which she wore on a chain around her neck, onto the bridge of her nose, carefully hooking the arms behind her ears. "Let's see, the return address says Miss Janet Arden. Well now… I wonder…"

Pauline left her still musing over the writer of the letter and began her ride back home. This ride was another source of enjoyment: the river flowed softly on one side of the road and there were only a few scattered houses on the other to interfere with the view of rolling fields and woods.

Pauline passed Miss Lewis's closest neighbor, a large, boxy red brick house with none of the charm and warmth of Miss Lewis's small home, waved courteously to the house's owner standing in her garden peering out into the road, and pondered who could have written Miss Lewis's mystery letter.

An old student? A relative? A relative of her fiancé? A childhood friend, likewise unmarried? The daughter of an old friend?

Not that it mattered in the long run! Pauline simply couldn't help turning over puzzles and attempting to make the pieces fit. At least this mystery was a small, harmless one, unlike some that she had solved.

She dismissed it from her mind until she had more information and set herself to wholly enjoying the ride back home.

Needles and Tongues

Pauline longed to dive into the newly-borrowed books as soon as she reached the small, second-story apartment on Pleasant Street she and her friend Sarah called home, but duty's voice was stronger. Ruby Richardson—who had been Ruby Ferris before her recent marriage to police lieutenant James Richardson—was expecting a baby come winter, and the women of the Episcopal Church were gathering together to help her prepare. Pauline could neither sew nor knit well, and she pitied any baby forced to wear something she had crafted, but friendship meant she ought to at least show up. Perhaps she could hem a blanket or something equally dull.

In truth, Pauline was pleased to have been included in the gathering. She was not a Canton native, having first come there to attend St. Lawrence University and then staying on afterward when she fell in love with the town. Often she felt on the outskirts of things, always the outsider looking in. It was partially her own fault, for she knew her natural reserve and discomfort in society came across as being aloof and disdainful. It bothered her, but—if she was honest—not enough for her to change her ways.

It took her an embarrassingly long time to find her thimble, but at last Pauline stepped back outside the apartment, locking the door carefully behind her, and walked down the creaking wooden steps and down the street toward the towering gray stone church building.

Canton was at its prettiest right now, in early June. Flowers nodded and smiled from every front yard and window box, the trees all wore their daintiest and freshest green and yellow topcoats, and sunlight sifted over everything, turning even the peeling paint on the dingiest clapboards soft and gentle. Pauline walked briskly, enjoying the warmth on her bare arms and uncovered head. She ought to have worn a hat, especially for going to church, but she supposed the omission could be excused as the sewing circle was meeting in the basement.

Pauline took one last deep breath of the faintly-scented wind before entering the church and taking the stairs to the large, dimly-lit basement. She wished they could have met outside, but likely even the staidest and most responsible of matrons would have had a difficult time focusing on her stitches under a clear blue June sky.

"Oh Miss Gray, so glad you could join us," said Mrs. Rev. Hansen. Knowing Pauline's lack of skill from previous gatherings, she handed her a plain baby gown to hem and steered her to a seat closest to a window, with the best light. "We weren't sure you would be able to come."

"Have you been writing anything interesting for your column lately?" inquired one of the other ladies.

Pauline stifled the desire to reply, "No, only dull things," and instead said, "Actually, most recently I've been working on a rather fascinating private project. Miss Anita Lewis has asked me to help her compile her memoirs, so that her stories might not be forgotten after she is gone. For having lived such a quiet life, it certainly has been a full one."

"Oh yes," said Mrs. Hansen. "She did say something about that to me a few weeks ago after the service. Well, I'm glad you are doing that, Miss Gray. Miss Lewis must be full of stories, not just about her family but about all her students. I think most of us in this room were taught by her at one point or another, isn't that right, ladies?"

There was a murmur of agreement as heads nodded over the stitching.

"Were you?" Pauline asked, wondering if their memories of Miss Lewis might make an interesting counterpoint to her memories of them. "We haven't gotten to her teaching days yet. She just finished telling me about the death of her fiancé this morning, and how she looked for meaningful work to fill her life after he passed."

"Oh yes," said one of the older women there. "Tom Martens, poor chap. Mrs. Ingersoll, you live on his farm now, don't you?"

A sharp-faced woman who looked to be in her early forties nodded. "Hank's father bought it at auction and passed it to Hank and me when we married ten years later. It's a good farm: good land, solid house."

"Such a shame Tom died when he did," the older woman continued. "He and Anita were so in love. She seemed to just shrink into herself after he died, and it wasn't until she took up teaching that she came to life again. She poured herself into the children who came through her classroom, every one of them."

"I know I wouldn't have made it past sixth grade without her help in mathematics," agreed Mrs. Hansen. "Mrs. Addison, didn't she help you with one of your subjects as well?"

A quiet, dark-haired woman Pauline hadn't met before now raised her head from the corner where she had been diligently working at trimming a baby bonnet. "Oh yes," she said. "All of them. I was quite the dunce. My parents didn't consider education necessary for women, and so I got no encouragement at home. If it hadn't been for Miss Lewis, I wouldn't even be able to read or write today."

Mrs. Ingersoll clicked her tongue. "Miss Lewis never did approve of ignorance for anyone, no matter what the parents said. Do you remember how she confronted old Dave Billings, who sneered at his boys as sissies whenever he caught them reading?"

A ripple of laughter ran around the room. "Drove her old buggy out to his farm after school and called *him* a few names!" another woman said. "Told him that just because he grew up an ignorant old coot was no reason his sons should suffer the same fate. By the end of it, she had him agreeing to learn to read just so's he could keep up with his sons—and she kept him to that promise. Drove out once a week to check on him, see if he was making progress, bring him fresh materials. Changed his entire life, she did, and his sons' lives as well. Old Dave grew devoted to books, and both his boys went on to college, and the youngest is a professor at a university out west somewhere."

"Oh heavens," Mrs. Hansen added, looking at Pauline, who had long since abandoned the baby gown. "You aren't taking notes on this, Miss Gray?"

Pauline blushed and tucked the notebook and pencil back into her handbag. "Forgive me—it was so interesting I forgot myself. Don't worry, I would never publish anything without permission."

"Goodness, young lady, if you find anything I say worth repeating, do so with my blessing!" said Mrs. Ingersoll. "Nobody's ever cared so much about my ramblings before."

"I begin to think everyone has a wealth of stories hidden away inside them," Pauline said, wincing as she stabbed herself with the needle, trying not to drip blood on the tiny gown.

"I suppose that's true," Mrs. Hansen agreed thoughtfully. "Only some folk would rather theirs stay inside instead of bringing them out into the light of day."

"There are a few things in my past I'd rather others not know," agreed the woman who had told about Dave Billings. "We all have our secrets as well as our stories."

The woman who had called herself a dunce—Mrs. Addison—shook her head. "Not me. My life is an open book. A dull one," she added with a laugh that sounded something like a sigh.

"Now, Mrs. Addison, that's not true!" chided one of the others. "I'm sure you have plenty of stories tucked away, just like the rest of us."

"If Miss Gray is writing Miss Lewis's memoirs, I suppose some of our stories will come out, too," chuckled Mrs. Ingersoll. "I hope none of you ladies have any dark misdeeds in your youth that you want hidden!"

It was a joke, but an awkward silence fell over the room all the same.

"I'm sure Miss Lewis would never betray a trust," Mrs. Hansen said into the silence.

"Isn't that a great deal to ask of anyone, though?" one of the other women said. "I don't know that I'd want to trust any of my secrets—if I had any—to another person, no matter how dependable."

"Best not to have any secrets at all!" Mrs. Ingersoll said with another chuckle. "We should all be so lucky as Cathy here."

Mrs. Addison smiled again, but made no other answer.

"Secrets can be poisonous things," Mrs. Hansen said. "Best to live in such a way that you aren't ashamed to have your past shown up in the light of day."

That may have been good Christian reasoning, but it wasn't the most comforting for everyone, based on the closed expressions on many of the women's faces. Pauline decided it was up to her to give some reassurance. "We can change names if anyone is uncomfortable with any stories told about them. Besides, Miss Lewis seems more interested in sharing her memories of her family and fiancé than in revealing youthful peccadilloes of her students."

"Thank heaven for that!" Mrs. Ingersoll said with an exaggerated sigh of relief, and the tension broke on a general wave of laughter as the conversation turned back to Ruby and James Richardson and speculation as to whether they were going to have a boy or a girl, and what he or she would be named, and how young Jeremy, Ruby's twelve-year-old son from her first marriage, would feel about a much younger sibling.

As the gathering ended, Pauline found herself leaving the building in the company of the dark-haired woman—Mrs. Addison—and Klara Hertz, sister to Heinrich and Margret Berger, who ran a laundry service out of their home.

Miss Hertz—shorter than Pauline and older by ten years or so, with her graying hair braided and wound around her head—smiled cheerfully at the other two. "So enjoyable, to spend an afternoon sewing together for another. It is far better than trying to work in a kitchen full of dripping clothes, listening to Heinrich's old truck rattle and wheeze in and out of the yard as he delivers and collects!"

Pauline laughed with her. "I am afraid my sewing skills mean this poor baby is going to have at least one gown coming apart at the seams, but I agree, it is better than sitting at home by myself."

To her surprise, she meant it. Though it had been difficult to tear herself away from her books and typewriter, this outing had done her good. It was pleasant to be part of a community, and to know that if she were ever in need, these women would come together to help her just as they did for each other.

"I enjoy the chance to escape the kitchen as well," said Mrs. Addison. "And a different sort of sewing than the never-ending mending that comes from three small boys!"

"Ach, you would miss it if it weren't there," said Miss Hertz.

Mrs. Addison smiled. "I suppose I would. We mothers like to grumble, but really, there's nothing I wouldn't do for my boys." A new light shone in her eyes, and for a moment Pauline could almost picture her as a Valkyrie, or Brunhilde.

Pauline's mother had been the sort who continually sighed over how disappointing her children were. Pauline wondered what it would be like to have grown up with a mother ready to take any steps to defend and protect her family instead. On the one hand, it seemed comforting.

On the other, without her mother's all-too-obvious dissatisfaction in her daughter, would Pauline have ever had the impetus to leave home and pursue a life of her own?

Her thoughts were interrupted by a commotion down the street, and she turned to see young Officer Wallace approaching the church with his hand wrapped firmly around the upper arm of a squirming, protesting youngster.

Mrs. Addison let out a heart-rending cry. "Mikey!" She ran forward just as the boy succeeded in pulling away from Officer Wallace and dashing to his mother.

"It wasn't me, Ma, I didn't do it," he whined.

Mrs. Addison wrapped him in a hug, then stood to confront Officer Wallace. Pauline's impression of her as a Valkyrie in defense of her children hadn't been far off—with her arms akimbo and her chin jutting out, she looked ready to tear poor Wallace from limb to limb.

"Officer, what is the meaning of this? How dare you manhandle my poor boy?"

Wallace ran a finger around the inside of his collar, but stood his ground. "He kept trying to run away, ma'am. I was worried he would get run over by an auto or a cyclist or trampled by a horse."

Mrs. Addison cried out again and wrapped one arm around young Mikey's shoulders. "My baby! But what were you doing that made him so frightened of you that he wanted to run away?"

"I caught him throwing mud at the mayor's auto, parked outside the Opera Theatre, ma'am," Wallace said. "When I told him to stop, he tried to run away. I just wanted to get him safely to you so you could handle the matter."

"I didn't do it," Mikey said again, the whine still present in his voice.

Pauline trusted Officer Wallace, but even if she hadn't, she would have doubted Mikey's veracity. For one thing, there was mud all over the sides of his short pants where he had rubbed his hands to clean them. Beside her, Miss Hertz clicked her tongue.

"Those boys!" she said softly. "Always in trouble, and their mother never does a thing to control them."

"I'll thank you to leave my sons alone from now on, Officer, and not make false accusations," Mrs. Addison bit out. "Of course Mikey wouldn't do a thing like that! For shame."

Pauline couldn't stand there and see Wallace made the victim of a false accusation. She started forward, intending to point out the mud on Mikey's clothes, but Miss Hertz placed a hand on her shoulder and stopped her.

"It will do no good," she whispered, shaking her head. "She will only become angry at you as well."

Wallace stepped back. "I'm not making accusations, ma'am, just stating what I saw. The mayor won't be happy about the state of his automobile, but that's your responsibility now. Good day." He tipped his hat with an exaggerated air of politeness, and walked away.

Mrs. Addison looked back, seemingly aware of her audience for the first time. She blushed deeply and hurried off, Mikey's hand in hers, without a word of goodbye.

"Poor Cathy," said Mrs. Ingersoll, joining Miss Hertz and Pauline. "Her own parents were so strict with her, never let her have a moment's peace, always sure that she was doing wrong even when she wasn't. Now she's gone the other way with her lads, and won't hear a word against them, even for ordinary boyish escapades."

"That is not good child-raising," Miss Hertz said. "Either one."

Mrs. Ingersoll nodded. "I always felt so badly for Cathy when we were girls, but she was hard to befriend, always so quiet. Not like me!" She laughed. "I was always in the center of a crowd. Not too good for my grades, but it did make my school years more fun." She winked roguishly at Pauline. "My parents probably ought to have been a little stricter with me! I know they despaired sometimes that I'd ever pick just one of my beaus and settle down." She laughed again. "And now here I am, a staid farmer's wife with a thickening waistline and two sons of my own. My younger self would be horrified!"

Miss Hertz shook her head once more, but she was smiling. "You Americans!"

Mrs. Ingersoll chuckled. "Well, well. I am thankful for Miss Lewis. I could have ended up far wilder in my youth if she hadn't taken a hand. She took Cathy under her wing as well, though in a different way. I think she made Cathy feel… safe. That was her gift, you know. She always saw just what each student needed, and provided it for them."

These words made Pauline look forward even more to the next memoir session with Miss Lewis. Not only for the unfolding story, but for the gentle companionship of the wise and kindly woman who was telling it.

Murder

The next two days passed uneventfully: Pauline typed up her notes from Miss Lewis; forced herself to work further on her current Emma Daring novel; made uninspiring meals for herself; kept the apartment reasonably tidy; and enjoyed her novels from Miss Lewis's library. With Sarah away visiting family in Pennsylvania, Pauline managed to pass both days without speaking with a single soul save Heinrich Berger when he stopped by to collect the linens for his wife to wash. Hence, she was even more eager for company than she had anticipated as she cycled out of the village, following the course of the Grasse River until she reached the white cottage with the rose bushes in front.

But there was an unexpected addition to the front of the house: a black Ford Model T parked by the roses. Pauline skidded to a stop and nearly fell off her bicycle as she recognized the insignia of the Canton Police Department on the side of the car.

What on earth were the police doing at Miss Lewis's?

Through force of will, Pauline ignored the nervous churning in her stomach at this hint of trouble. She carefully leaned the bicycle up against the fence, took off her gloves to wipe her suddenly perspiring palms on her handkerchief, replaced the gloves, and walked around to the back to knock on the kitchen door as usual.

Her path along the garden walkway was interrupted by big, burly, blond-haired Lieutenant James Richardson erupting from the back door to intercept her, bringing with him the scent of freshly-baked bread.

"Pauline!" he exclaimed. "For crying out loud, don't tell me the *Times* has put you onto this just because you're closest? How did they hear about it so quickly, anyway?"

The dread in Pauline's stomach solidified into an icy lump. She had to swallow twice before she could speak. "I am here for my usual appointment with Miss Lewis," she said. "I'm working with her to write her memoirs. Is she all right? Was it a robbery? May I see her?" She hadn't realized just how fond she had become of the elderly woman until there was a promise of danger to her.

James's face grew somber. "That's right, I'd forgotten about that. I'm darned sorry to have to tell you this, Pauline. Miss Lewis was killed last night."

The garden, James, and the back of the cottage all swirled together in front of Pauline's face. She had the vague idea James said something else, but the buzzing in her ears was so loud she couldn't hear him.

Then the nausea grew more intense, and she knew she was going to disgrace herself by being ill.

She barely felt James steadying her, guiding her to sit down on the garden bench and put her head between her knees.

"Deep breaths," she dimly heard him say. "Easy, there. Nice and slow. Breathe."

She focused on her breathing, in and out, slow and steady, and eventually her stomach settled enough for her to dare lifting her head. James was squatting on his heels in front of her, his good-natured face concerned.

"I sent Wallace next door to ask for a glass of water for you," he said. "He should be back at any moment. I'd get you one here, but…" He shrugged helplessly. "It is a crime scene."

"I apologize," Pauline said, embarrassment now mixing with her physical discomfort. "I should not be taking your attention at this time, when you should be free to focus on—on Miss Lewis." She stopped and pressed her lips together, unable to say anything more.

"Gosh, it's not your fault, Pauline," James said. "I shouldn't have broken it to you like that, should've eased into it, had you sit down first or something. You didn't ask for this."

Young Officer Wallace, his red hair a flame against the pale blue sky, hurried back into the garden with a tumbler of water in hand, followed by a short, plump woman, talking busily away.

"…well I knew something was wrong, of course, seeing you all here, and I was worried sick for Miss Lewis, but I never would have guessed it was this bad if you hadn't come over—and I must say I do think her neighbors ought to have been told first, not that it's any of my business, but if there's a madman out there we all ought to know to protect ourselves and—oh, Miss Gray, I'm so sorry, I know how much Miss Lewis was enjoying remembering her past with you—oh, hello, Officer—oh, Lieutenant? I always thought that was military—oh, police as well? Well, Lieutenant, when this young man told me that Miss Gray needed some water because she almost fainted, I knew I had to come right over. You policemen are very good at solving crimes and keeping us safe—though you didn't keep Miss Lewis safe, but I suppose that you can't be everywhere all the time—but you aren't very good at taking care of people. Miss Gray, you come right over to my house and rest on my sofa until you're ready to get yourself home."

Pauline hadn't met this woman before, but she supposed Miss Lewis must have told her neighbor about the memoir and Pauline's role in the project. There was genuine kindness in this woman's face, even if it was tempered by avid curiosity. That was unavoidable, she supposed.

In any case, she couldn't continue to sit here distracting James from his job. She sipped at the cool water, feeling life flush back into her cheeks and down to her hands and feet.

"Thank you, ma'am," she said quietly. "James, will you need to speak to me before I return home?"

"It might be necessary," he said, helping her to her feet and keeping a steadying hand under her elbow. "Once we've finished here I'll come see you at Mrs...?"

"MacNeill, Mrs. Amy MacNeill," that woman supplied.

"Mrs. MacNeill's," James said. "And we'll give you a ride back. Wallace can bring your bicycle."

Pauline would have protested, but common sense told her she would not be fit to ride her bicycle after this—she would be a danger to herself and anyone she met on the road. She nodded. "Very well."

Officer Wallace looked unhappy, but didn't complain.

"We will need to ask you some questions as well, Mrs. MacNeill, about anything you might have heard or seen last night or early this morning," James told the neighbor woman.

"Anything I can do to help," Mrs. MacNeill said. "Poor Miss Lewis!"

She put an arm around Pauline's waist and steered her along the path out of the garden and toward the large white farmhouse on the other side of the fence, talking the entire way.

"Goodness sake, you poor thing, you must just feel dreadful. Did the police officer—that lieutenant—did he say anything about how it happened? That young red-headed one only told me Miss Lewis was killed. Dear, dear… was it a burglar? That lieutenant said they'd be asking me questions, but I didn't hear anything at all last night. Oh dear, you don't think they think I had anything to do with it? That would be dreadful!"

By the time she was seated on the stiff horsehair sofa in Mrs. MacNeill's front room, Pauline's head was throbbing.

"I'm afraid I really don't know anything more than you do, ma'am," she managed to say.

"Oh, of course not, of course you don't. Although I did wonder, since you seem to be on first-name basis with that policeman…" Mrs. MacNeill let the statement trail off suggestively while her eyes went to Pauline's still-gloved hands, rather too obviously searching for the shape of a wedding band.

Pauline held back a groan. Would people ever leave off assuming she and James were romantically inclined toward each other? Of all the nonsense in the world, that which insisted men and women could not simply be friends was the worst.

"Lieutenant Richardson and I are old friends," she said as firmly as she could under the circumstances. "His wife is also a good friend of mine."

"Oh yes, I see. I *thought* Miss Lewis had referred to you as a miss, not a missus," said Mrs. MacNeill, nodding as she seemingly slotted Pauline into her proper place in her mind. What category was that, Pauline wondered: hopeless spinster? Crossed in love? Waiting for the right man?

Bluestocking was the one Pauline heard the most frequently. It fit better than the others, though truly, she did dislike categories.

Mrs. MacNeill plumped herself down in the upholstered chair across from the couch, fanning her face with her hand. Her endless stream of chatter slowed as the reality of the situation seeped in.

"Dear, dear me. You could have knocked me over with a feather, you honestly could have, Miss Gray, when the policeman told me what happened. The milkman's the one who found her, you know, as he was dropping off the milk. I peeked out my window—not that I'm nosy, you know, but one does wonder when the milk is late, and when one sees the truck next door and it doesn't leave and doesn't leave. Well, the next thing I knew the police had showed up, and then I really started to wonder, and then they finally let him go along the rest of his round, and of course I had to ask him what had happened, and he told me he wasn't allowed to talk about it but that something dreadful had happened to Miss Lewis, and then..." She sniffed and dabbed at her eyes with a clean handkerchief. "Then that young policeman came over to ask me for a glass of water for you, and I made him tell me just what had happened, and oh *dear*. She was such a lovely person, and the best neighbor I could have asked for. Oh, it doesn't seem right that she should be killed!"

That was exactly it. It wasn't right; it was all wrong. No one deserved death, but there were some for whom it felt especially wrong, and this was a violent death of some sort. Pauline didn't know how it happened, or who had done it, but a fierce determination swelled in her breast to find justice for Miss Lewis.

"I'm so sorry, Mrs. MacNeill," she said, seeing the other woman as a person for the first time. "I only knew her a little, but you were her friend. As painful as this is for me, it must be worse for you."

Mrs. MacNeill leaned forward and patted her knee. "That's a kind thing to say, Miss Gray."

It was? Perhaps Pauline was getting better at interacting with people.

"Miss Lewis did so enjoy your sessions," Mrs. MacNeill continued. "You brought her youth back to her. She would come over to bring me a bunch of flowers most days, and she always had an extra sparkle in her eyes the days you visited. Even if you weren't able to complete her memoirs, you did a good thing for her, just letting her remember."

Pauline's throat closed. "Thank you," she managed.

Conversation dwindled after that, and it was with relief that both women saw James and Wallace finally leave the Lewis cottage and approach Mrs. MacNeill's front door.

"Of course they would come to the front, rather than to the back like civilized people," Mrs. MacNeill grumbled under her breath as she jumped up to wrestle open the big green door.

James ducked his head as he entered, his hat in his hands. "Ma'am," he said.

Officer Wallace slipped in behind him, an anxious shadow.

"Officer—I mean Lieutenant," Mrs. MacNeill said, "Please, what can you tell me about Miss Lewis's—" she swallowed— "death?"

James shook his head. "I can't release much information yet, ma'am."

Mrs. MacNeill sat back down, frustration and fear evident on her face. Pauline leaned forward. It was her turn to do a kindness for the other woman.

"Lieutenant Richardson, could you at least let Mrs. MacNeill know if she should have someone to stay with her for the next few nights? Is she likely to be in danger?"

Mrs. MacNeill cast her a grateful glance, while James frowned thoughtfully.

"It might be just as well if you did, ma'am," he said at last. "You understand we can't confirm anything, but as of right now, evidence points to this being a burglary gone wrong. You didn't see or hear anything last night?"

Mrs. MacNeill shook her head. "Not that I can remember. What—what time?"

"It would have been before she went to bed, based on, er, based on her clothing," James said. "And that is absolutely all I can say," he added firmly.

It was Pauline's turn to frown. Something about that didn't ring true, but what? She hadn't even seen the scene for herself, so why did it sound wrong?

Mrs. MacNeill thought, then shook her head one more time. "I wish I could say yes, Lieutenant, but I don't remember suspicious—wait! Someone did stop by yesterday evening, but it wasn't a burglar. And he couldn't have been the—the killer, because I heard him say 'goodnight' to Miss Lewis when he left. It must have been her nephew, because he said, 'Good night, Aunt Anita.'" She stopped triumphantly.

James looked at Officer Wallace, and then over at Pauline. She nodded. She'd picked up on the discrepancy as well.

"Did you hear Miss Lewis reply, or see her?" James asked gently.

Mrs. MacNeill considered it. "No, but it wasn't as though I was snooping," she said. "I'm not a nosy neighbor. I was simply out admiring the sunset when he left." She folded her arms across her bosom.

"I see." James pulled out his notepad and pencil and wrote something down. "Thank you, Mrs. MacNeill. I think that's all for right now. Do you have someone you can ask to come stay with you for a night or two?"

"Oh yes, my son will come by, and he'll bring his dog. I'll be perfectly safe, thank you."

"Then we'll say good-bye for now. Pauline, are you ready?"

Pauline rose to her feet and was pleased to find herself perfectly steady. She probably could have cycled home, were it not for the likelihood that James wanted to talk with her.

"Quite, thank you. Mrs. MacNeill, I am so grateful for your kindness."

"Not at all, Miss Gray. I only wish we could have met under better circumstances."

After a few more platitudes, Pauline and James got themselves settled in the police car, and Officer Wallace unhappily mounted the bicycle and wobbled off down the road.

"All right," James said with a sigh, releasing the brake and engaging the motor. "We need to talk."

Too Close to Home

"You think it was the nephew, not a random burglary gone wrong?" Pauline asked.

James kept his eyes on the road as he answered. "It's hard to say. The obvious thought is that someone from the County Home broke in hoping to find something worth stealing. The place was a mess—books strewn everywhere, papers scattered, knick-knacks all over the place, vases overturned and smashed—"

Pauline winced at the thought of the lovely house so torn apart. "I see."

"But," James continued. "Nothing valuable was taken. The silver's all still there, she had a tiny statue still on one shelf that is gilded with real gold, there are good pictures on the walls. So either Miss Lewis interrupted the burglar before he could take anything and he hit her over the head, then panicked and ran when he saw that he'd killed her, or it wasn't a burglary at all." He stopped short. "I shouldn't have told you that detail," he said. "Forget I said it, will you?"

Pauline was only too happy to push the thought of Miss Lewis's death from her mind. "If that's the case, why tear the house apart? Surely a burglar would take the obviously valuable things before ransacking a house, especially if he is so foolish as to come early in the night when his victim is still awake."

"Right," James said. "Not to mention the folks at the County Home are for the most part decent, law-abiding people, just down on their luck."

"Miss Lewis told me she had never had any problems with them as her neighbors," Pauline agreed.

James nodded. "So it looks almost as though the nephew must have done it when he was visiting, then made a mess to make it look like a burglary, and then pretended to be saying good night to his aunt as he left for the benefit of the clearly not-nosy-at-all Mrs. MacNeill."

Pauline had to smile at that description, though it was short-lived. "But why? Why would her nephew want to kill her?" She couldn't imagine why anyone would want to kill Miss Lewis, much less her own family.

James's profile was grim. "I'd say there's a good chance she's left him something substantial in her will. Maybe everything, who knows? That would explain why he didn't actually steal anything valuable, he didn't want to have to hide pieces of his own inheritance."

"That's appalling," Pauline said softly.

James flickered a quick glance at her before returning his attention to the road. "Murder usually is."

"Was that all you wished to discuss?" Pauline asked after a moment or two.

"Oh," said James. "Mostly. It helps to talk through things with another person, and Wallace, much as he's coming along, is far too inclined to blindly respond 'yes sir' to everything I say."

"I see." That was a cheering thought, that James valued her clear thinking enough to want to discuss the case with her.

"I also wanted to warn you to be careful. This is a dangerous person we are working against, and while I know you have had fine successes with a couple of other cases, I would feel much better if you would promise to stay out of this one."

"Ah."

Pauline's first instinct was to prickle up her feathers defensively. So, when James needed to talk through things, she was good enough to be included, but not for anything else? Was this because she had almost fainted? Did he think her too weak? How typically masculine!

Then reason intervened. James was *worried*, the same way she would be if a friend was getting involved in something dangerous. It was what friends did: they cared for each other and worried about each other. He wasn't dismissing her abilities.

"I can't promise that without reservations," Pauline said at last. "I won't be able to help thinking about it and mulling it over and trying to work it through in my mind. But I can promise you that I won't go about actively investigating, at least not without discussing it with you first."

James sighed and smiled at the same time. "I suppose that's the best I could hope for."

He pulled over to the side of the road by the tall, narrow, gray-clapboard building that was home to Pauline, though she had never, in all the years she had lived in the second-story apartment, felt anywhere near as at home there as she had during her few visits to Miss Lewis. She shivered, thinking of all that peace and graciousness, that kindly warmth, wiped out in a moment by someone consumed with greed or anger.

James noted her tremor as he opened the car door for her. "I'd better come up with you, just to make sure you don't lose your balance on the stairs," he said.

Pauline offered him an embarrassed smile. "I'm perfectly recovered now, but thank you. I feel rather a fool for losing my head earlier."

"Nonsense," he said, following her up the narrow wooden staircase that went up the outside of the house. "It would have been a shock for anyone. I shouldn't have dropped it on you so suddenly like that."

Any response Pauline would have made to that died on her lips as she reached her front door. She distinctly recalled locking it behind her as she left that morning. Now, it was slightly open, swinging in the gentle breeze, and there were shiny scratches around the keyhole on the dull metal plate.

"James," she managed to whisper.

He took one look past her shoulder and muttered a word under his breath that would have shocked Pauline any other time. "Get back down the stairs," he hissed, precariously squeezing past her.

Pauline opened her mouth to argue, then closed it again and retreated as told. Much as she would have liked to be able to boldly stride into her own home and confront whoever had broken in, she knew she did not have the physical strength to stand against a man who had already killed once—presuming this was the same person who had killed Miss Lewis, and anything else seemed far too coincidental for Pauline's brain to accept.

She waited at the bottom of the staircase, pulse thundering in her ears, while James slid through the open door and vanished inside her apartment. Almost immediately, she started wondering: how long should she wait for him to come out? What if something happened to him—how would she ever explain it to Ruby? Where was Mrs. Harper, Pauline's landlady and downstairs neighbor? Had anything happened to her?

Before she had time to work herself into a proper panic, James appeared at the door again. His face was grim.

"It's safe," he said. "But I should warn you that it isn't pretty."

Pauline didn't allow herself any more time to think. She ran up the wooden stairs. James stepped back to allow her inside. She set foot in the tiny foyer—and gasped.

It seemed as though all her books and papers had been pulled from their places and scattered across the entire apartment. Her typewriter was overturned; every drawer in her desk had been pulled all the way out and thrown onto the floor; even the newspaper had been torn in two.

"It's like this in the bedrooms as well," James said from behind her. He cleared his throat. "I, uh, I should apologize, I suppose, for going into your private rooms, but I had to make sure the thief was not still here."

"There's no privacy when a crime has been committed," Pauline said through numb lips.

"Nothing else has been touched," James continued after a brief moment. "Your clothing, jewelry, money… it's all been left untouched. The kitchen is fine. Only books and papers. Just like at Miss Lewis's."

Pauline couldn't seem to think. It was as though a heavy woolen blanket had pressed down over her brain. She fought past it. Before James had told her to come up, she had been worried about something. What was it?

She closed her eyes, and a spark of life returned. "James. Could you kindly check in on Mrs. Harper? I want to be sure she was not troubled by thieves as well."

James muttered yet another curse she didn't think she was supposed to have heard, and vanished. Pauline heard his boots on the stairs, thudding quickly from one step to the next.

Pauline forced herself to move further into her home—a safe haven no longer, the violence done here shaking her to her very core. Even if they cleaned it all up, even if they caught the intruder, she wasn't sure she'd ever be able to see this room without seeing this invasion.

Why? What could she have that was so important?

Another spark of life flickered through her brain. The novels she had borrowed from Miss Lewis—what if they were worth more than either woman had realized? What if the murderer had killed Miss Lewis for them, and then come after Pauline when he didn't find them in the house?

She waded through the sea of paper and, after some hunting, her heart hurting with every bent cover or torn page for each book she turned over, she found first *Cranford* and then *Barchester Towers*. Both books were facedown on the floors, their pages crumpled. The intruder hadn't missed them; he simply hadn't bothered about them.

That was one theory gone.

Still, Pauline reasoned that this intrusion had to be connected with Miss Lewis's murder. The similarity of the searches, the timing of it… whoever it was thought she had something that he had looked for and couldn't find at Miss Lewis's house.

She was sorting through papers on the floor, looking for her notes for the memoir, when James returned.

"Mrs. Harper is fine and—darn it, Pauline! You should know better than to interfere with a crime scene! We need to examine everything for fingerprints, hunt for clues, before you start tidying up."

Pauline sat back on her heels. She placed her hands on her flushed cheeks, embarrassed. "Oh dear. I'm sorry, James. I didn't think."

He relented, crossing the room to squat down beside her. "I suppose it's different when it affects you personally."

"Perhaps so, but it shouldn't be. One should always be able to hold to one's principles and keep one's head."

He flashed her a quick grin. "Yes, but one would be hardly human then, and not half so likable."

Some of the ice surrounding Pauline started to thaw at that. She almost managed a smile in return. "Was Mrs. Harper all right?"

"Yes, and I should warn you, she'll be up here shortly. She's not too happy about this, and very upset that I left you alone even to come speak with her. I think she's planning on offering you her guest room tonight, so if you'd rather not sleep with her, think of an excuse quickly."

"Oh," Pauline said. She hadn't even thought of sleeping arrangements.

"You know you're always welcome with us as well," James continued. "Ruby would scold me dreadfully if I told her I left you alone in your apartment after it had been burglarized."

Pauline produced another partial smile. "Thank you, you're very kind. I'll have to think it over, if you don't mind. Right now I can't seem to focus on anything except finding my notes from my sessions with Miss Lewis."

"Ah, so that's what you were doing!"

James examined the floor and sighed. "We'll have to check all these for fingerprints before we do anything else. That's a good thought, though—you put your finger right on the one thing connecting you and Miss Lewis."

"Miss Lewis, me, and paper," Pauline said. "Since it seems to be either paper or books or both that this person is after."

"Doesn't make sense, though," James said. "Surely you wouldn't have anything in your notes that you didn't also hear Miss Lewis say. So why take…" His voice trailed off.

Pauline looked at him curiously.

James swallowed and spoke again. "Actually, Pauline, I think I'd prefer it if you let me take you home to stay with Ruby and me tonight, and every night until we catch the fellow who did this."

It took Pauline's still-sluggish brain a few minutes to work this through. "Oh," she said at last. "Oh, you think there's something she might have told me and I wrote down, and oh." Her voice grew very small. "You think this person might try to kill me too because of what I know."

"It's far-fetched, but I don't like to take the chance," James said. "Unless there's something else she gave you or wrote to you that can make sense of any of this." He waved an arm to encompass the mess.

"Not right now," Pauline sighed. Nothing made sense to her at this moment.

James looked down at the paper nearest him on the floor. "Say, what's this? This looks like part of some story or something. Emma Daring—isn't that the heroine of those adventure novels? What are you doing with—"

Mrs. Harper entered the apartment at that moment, and Pauline had never been so thankful to see her landlady.

Not only had her home been violated and her privacy stripped away, now her greatest secret trembled on the brink of revelation.

Suspicions

Mrs. Harper was voluble in her horror at the damage done to Pauline's property— "And with me in my kitchen the entire time, the wretches! I heard some noises above my head, but I thought it was Miss Gray returned from her outing. If only I'd looked out my window to see that your bicycle wasn't in its usual spot by the fence! Then I would have known something was wrong, and I could have come up and caught them in the act."

"Just as well you didn't," James said gravely. "Whoever it was is a dangerous person, Mrs. Harper. I'm thankful neither you nor Pauline were endangered by him."

That had the effect of silencing Mrs. Harper. Her eyes widened as the implications of James's statement sank in.

"Well," she finally gasped. "You'll sleep in my guest room tonight, dearie, and we'll lock all the doors and windows and put chairs beneath the doorknobs."

"Actually," James interposed, "my wife would like to have Pauline stay with us for a few nights. But locking your doors is a good plan regardless."

Mrs. Harper seemed inclined to bridle at the thought of the Richardsons taking over her lodger, but as Pauline showed no inclination one way or the other her indignation soon fizzled.

"And you didn't see anything helpful, Mrs. Harper?" James asked, escorting her to the door.

"Not a thing. I heard the paperboy earlier, and Mr. Berger delivering laundry—that old truck of his squeaks something awful—but other than that, nothing. My mind was taken up with getting the bread out of the oven and starting the roast for dinner and…"

"Thank you," James said firmly, opening the door.

Mrs. Harper reluctantly left, then popped her head back around. "I'll just bring you a slice of bread and butter and a glass of milk, shall I, Miss Gray? I'm sure you could use it."

Pauline wrenched her mind to the present. "Thank you, Mrs. Harper, I'd appreciate that."

In truth, she didn't think she could ever eat or drink again, but the logical part of her brain told her she would need to take nourishment or she would not be able to function at all.

"All my notes from Miss Lewis are gone," she told James as he closed the door behind her landlady.

"That settles it, then," he said. "The burglar was looking here for whatever he couldn't find at Miss Lewis's house. The question is, did he find it here, or is it still missing?"

"That's not the only question," Pauline said. "The bigger one is, what was it he was looking for?"

James sighed. "And here I was hoping to take Jeremy fishing this weekend. Listen, I need to report back to the Chief. We need someone here to take fingerprints, and I need to see if the doctor has any clearer idea of when Miss Lewis was killed. Once we're done fingerprinting in here and I've had a look around for any clues, you can pack an overnight bag and I'll take you home to Ruby."

Pauline shook her head. "James, I might as well tell you now, I have papers here I don't want anyone else to see. There's nothing wrong in them, but they are—" she hesitated, recalling what she had told him only a short time ago "—private."

"I am sorry," James said. "But you know I can't give you special privilege just because we're friends. The best I can do is promise that anything I see here that seems private, I'll do my best to ignore. It goes without saying that I won't tell anyone your secrets, of course."

Pauline knew that. Still, she hated to concede. There was nothing to be ashamed of in her novels, but she couldn't help it: she *was* ashamed of them. Ashamed that her lofty goals of scholarship when she graduated from St. Lawrence University—however vague they had been—had come down to writing cheap adventure novels without a lick of literary quality to recommend them.

Perhaps it was vanity, but she did not want to see the respect other people held for her diminished by the knowledge she wrote such drivel. Not even from James.

A stirring of anger broke through the numbness that had engulfed her from the moment she saw the desecration of her living space. How dare this person do this to her? It was bad enough he had made her feel unsafe in her own home, now he was continuing to injure her even from a distance.

For the first time, Pauline's desire for justice became personal, rather than an ideal.

She rose to her feet, dusting her hands on her skirt. "So be it," she said. "But I'd rather stay here and clean this place up after you leave. I understand that you don't want me to stay overnight here alone, but I can't leave my home in this condition." She gestured at the area around her. "If nothing else, I have a responsibility to Sarah to make sure nothing of hers was destroyed or damaged."

"We'll be here for quite some time, what with checking for finger-prints and footprints and any other physical evidence," James warned. "And I still don't like the idea of you wandering around town on your own. Someone was frightened enough of information you might or might not have to break into your place in broad daylight and ransack it. Who's to say they won't return, or try to attack you on your way out to our place?"

"Why would they return?" Pauline protested. "They had plenty of time to look for whatever it was they wanted when they were here before. There's no reason for them to come back. As for attacking me, that seems equally unlikely." She hesitated, unable to give a reason for why it would not be likely other than that the very notion sounded ridiculous. How many victims of robbery or murder thought the same, though? "I will telephone you when I am ready to leave so that someone can accompany me to your house."

James visibly wrestled with this for a few moments, then accepted her compromise. "If you insist."

Mrs. Harper returned then with a slice of bread on a delicate plate with roses around the perimeter, clearly the good china rather than her everyday ware. Pauline inhaled the warm, comforting scent, and her hunger rose unexpectedly.

"This looks delicious," she said. "Thank you ever so much."

Mrs. Harper fussed over her until Pauline was seated at the kitchen table, a glass of cold milk accompanying the still-warm bread. As Pauline sank her teeth into the first bite, realization struck her.

"James!"

He hung up the phone, having finished his call to headquarters, and came into the kitchen. "What? What's wrong?"

Pauline chewed and swallowed, eyes wide. Mrs. Harper hovered by the sink, eagerly waiting to hear what she had to say. Discretion sank in belatedly. "Er, nothing, sorry," she said, loathing the lie as it left her lips.

James's eyes flickered between her and Mrs. Harper, and he nodded. "Not to worry," he said casually.

Neither said anything more until Pauline had finished her snack, sincerely thanked her landlady, and that good woman had reluctantly left the apartment once more, this time for good.

Pauline wasted no more time. "James, Miss Lewis couldn't have been killed last night."

"What? What do you mean? Why not?"

"When you opened the back door of her house this morning, I smelled freshly baked bread. In the shock of hearing the news, I didn't pay any attention, and I'd forgotten until just now, when Mrs. Harper brought me a slice of her bread. Miss Lewis had to have been killed this morning, after she'd already taken the bread out of the oven."

James's jaw dropped. "How could I have missed that?"

"Because you are not a housewife," Pauline said. She wasn't, either, but she at least had more experience with housewifery than a man like James did.

"Then it couldn't have been the nephew," James said slowly. "Though we still should call on him to see if he has any insights into his aunt's death. Miss Lewis was alive and well when he left."

"She was in her clothing because she'd already dressed for the day, not because she hadn't gone to bed," Pauline said.

"The doctor should be able to confirm that, but thank you, Pauline, you've saved us going in the wrong direction before getting his report. We'll need to get back to Mrs. MacNeill and ask if she saw or heard anyone there this morning, before the milkman arrived."

A chill settled in the pit of Pauline's stomach. "I doubt it. She would have said something to me if she had. She was talkative enough about the milkman's arrival, and then you and Officer Wallace showing up, and then me."

"Then either someone managed to sneak in without her noticing, which is unlikely, or..."

Pauline finished his sentence. "Or Mrs. MacNeill had something to do with the murder."

They stared at each other in wordless horror.

"And here I thought she was a typical nosy neighbor," James said. "She wanted to know if we were on to her, that's all."

Pauline's brain caught up with their speculation. "Wait, though—she couldn't have burgled this apartment. She was home all morning. I can attest to that, as I was with her."

James nodded. "True, but then, is it likely that she would have been the murderer herself? Far more likely that she has an accomplice who is performing the actual deeds."

"Or she is the accomplice," Pauline said, still having a difficult time accepting that utterly ordinary woman as a master criminal. "But why?"

"Why would anyone care about Miss Lewis's memoirs, enough to kill?" James said. "It made sense when it was the nephew wanting his inheritance early, or at least felt more plausible. But we add in the robbery here, and it's all a muddle again. I don't suppose she did tell you anything worth killing over? No secret treasure hidden somewhere, no deep dark secrets, no horrible scandals?"

Pauline shook her head. "No, nothing like that. If she did know anything of that sort, she took the information to the grave with her."

James scratched his head. "Then how the deuce are we ever going to find the motive?" He sighed and answered his own question. "I guess this is going to be one of those cases where the motive doesn't matter, what matters is the physical evidence. And if we prove that the murderer had to have been at Miss Lewis's house this morning, and that he or she couldn't have been there without Mrs. MacNeill being aware of it, and if she continues to insist she saw nothing and no one, we will have no choice but to arrest her, whether we can come up with a reasonable motive or not."

"We should—or I suppose you should—find out if Mrs. MacNeill has a connection to anyone in Miss Lewis's past." Pauline did not need her notes to remember the names of the individuals Miss Lewis had spoken so fondly of over the past few weeks. "Her fiancé, Tom Martens, died in '81, but he might have some family still living in the area. Or the person who bought the Martens farm after he died might know more. There is a chance her nephew might still be involved, Samuel Crane is his name, her sister's son. Any of her former colleagues might know something. Then there's her former students, any one of them might know something more about her past than what she revealed to me."

James was scribbling all this down. He grimaced at her last suggestion. "She taught half the town over the years, we'd never be able to interview all of them. As it is, there's enough here to keep Wallace busy for a month," he said. "The chief won't like this being dragged out that long."

"Then let me interview some of them," Pauline said.

"Now look here—" James began.

"I can tell them it's to complete her memoirs in her honor," Pauline said. "It's the perfect excuse. I can meet with them in public, so I won't be in danger, and you can even have Officer Wallace or someone else watching me, to make sure I'm safe. It might be the best way to find a connection."

"You want me to use you as bait," James said flatly.

Pauline pushed away from the table and motioned to the mess that was her living room. "Look at this, James! They came into my home and did this! Now you don't even want me to sleep here until they are caught. Yes, I want you to use me as bait. Anything to bring these villains to justice as soon as possible, for Miss Lewis's sake as well as my own."

James walked to the window and looked out. "The chief is here, and Wallace with your bicycle. I'll ask the chief what he thinks, but you must promise me to abide by his decision. If he says no, I don't want you running off into danger on your own to pursue this yourself, no matter how angry you are."

Pauline was angry, but not so much that she had lost all sense. This person had already killed once; she had no desire to follow Miss Lewis into oblivion.

"Very well," she conceded.

If Chief Gordon didn't agree, she would have to come up with another plan that he would agree to. This situation could not be allowed to continue. The murderer must be found and apprehended.

She would accept nothing less.

Moving Forward

The wheels of bureaucracy began to turn, and Pauline found herself on the outside of the affair looking in, though she was in her own home. Chief Gordon wasn't interested in anything she had to say until he had heard it all from James first, nor was she permitted to participate in sorting through any more of the debris scattered throughout the apartment. Her heart sank when she saw Officer Wallace pick up one of her typed pages and glance over it first quickly, then slowly and with more interest as he began to read.

"Say, this is pretty good stuff," he said. "Where's the rest of it?"

Luckily for Pauline's over-strained nerves, James noticed what Wallace was doing and left his report to berate the youngster.

"Never mind that!" he said, taking the paper from the unfortunate young man, who wilted under James's disapproving scowl. "We are not here to snoop through Miss Gray or Miss Jones's belongings, only to look for any clues the thief might have left behind, or any notes from Miss Lewis. Keep your mind on business, not other people's affairs!"

"Sorry," Wallace muttered, his flaming cheeks clashing with his hair.

Despite this intervention, Pauline had a horrible sinking feeling that her secret was out. No matter how discreet the policemen were, once one extra person knew a secret, the information began to spread, and soon everyone would know. Her days of hiding Emma Daring behind a cloak of anonymity were over.

It was almost too much to take in on top of everything else.

One thing for which she could be thankful was that Sarah's possessions remained almost untouched. It appeared the burglar had given her room a cursory search, then left it alone to focus on Pauline's belongings.

"How did he know the difference?" Wallace wondered aloud.

"The nurse's uniforms hanging in Miss Jones's wardrobe would be a good clue," James answered dryly.

It was a good question. However panicked the burglar might have been, he or she was still observant enough to tell the difference between the two women's clothing and belongings, and reasoned enough to not destroy Sarah's things needlessly. It added another layer to the picture Pauline was building of the killer: this was a person who was careful enough to only search where it seemed necessary, yet desperate enough to murder.

Unfortunately, that still wasn't enough for her to put a face or a name to the individual, nor did it do much to ease the humiliation of seeing the policemen examining her undergarments, no matter how respectful they were. It was a relief when the officers finished their search and left with vague promises to keep her informed.

Chief Gordon hadn't committed himself to anything regarding Pauline's suggestion of questioning Miss Lewis's former colleagues and students, stating merely they would have to question Mrs. MacNeill again as well as interview Samuel Crane, Miss Lewis's nephew, before they took any further steps. James reminded Pauline to phone him when she was ready to leave, and then there was nothing but the clatter of boot heels going down the outside steps, and finally, blessed stillness inside the still-disheveled apartment.

Pauline released a long, slow breath, and sank down at the kitchen table, head buried in her hands. It was all too much. Was it really only this morning she had set out so blithely along the road to Miss Lewis's house? It seemed a lifetime ago.

Oh, how her mother would triumph over this. After all of Pauline's insistence on Canton as a calmer, quieter, safer place to live than Albany, now not only to have stumbled into yet another murder investigation, but also to have suffered the indignity of a break-in at her own home! Well, Pauline would not give Mother the satisfaction of crowing over her; she promptly resolved to never tell anyone in her family about this unless she had to.

And for all this to happen while Sarah was away…! Pauline would have to tell her, of course, and what news for her to return home to at the end of the week.

Miss Lewis was *dead*, that kind, gracious woman. Approaching the final years of her life anyway, who could have felt the need to hurry her along into the grave? It was all, all wrong.

On top of everything else, Pauline's identity would soon be revealed to all the world as the author of the Emma Daring novels. How her former classmates would groan or gloat, depending on their disposition, over how far Pauline Gray's lofty ideals had sunk! How her professors would purse their lips in disapproval, that she would waste her talents so. How her neighbors would look at her with scorn, writing trash—harmless trash, but trash nonetheless—to fill her purse.

Pauline remained slumped in her position of despair a few moments longer. Then she lifted her head and set her lips firmly.

No matter. No matter what anyone said or thought, she was done moaning over it. Life was too precious to spend it fretting over things she couldn't change. If there was anything good that had come out of her encounters with murder, it was that realization.

She got up from the table filled with fresh resolve. She would clean this apartment from top to bottom, then go on out to Ruby and James's house, and one way or another, she would find a way to bring justice for herself and Sarah as well as for Miss Lewis.

One step at a time.

The cleaning went better than Pauline could have imagined, thanks solely to Mrs. Harper returning as soon as she heard the thump-thump of Pauline opening the storage closet and pulling out the mop and bucket. That good lady insisted on helping, and did much of the hard labor herself while Pauline smoothed crumpled book pages and organized her papers.

"I doubt we'll ever get the ink stain out of the hearthrug, though," Mrs. Harper said, glowering at the offending blot.

Pauline blushed, hoping Mrs. Harper wouldn't notice that the stain was a few weeks old and therefore couldn't have been caused by the thief.

"And I'd like to put fresh sheets on the beds, but I can't find any spare linens," Mrs. Harper continued.

"Oh, Mr. Berger collected the sheets yesterday," Pauline explained. "He always picks them up on Wednesday and returns them on Friday. But it doesn't matter so much, as I won't be sleeping here tonight, and Sarah won't return until late Saturday."

"Gracious, it will be an uncomfortable homecoming for Miss Jones unless the police have caught the villain before then," Mrs. Harper commented.

It would indeed. That gave Pauline a deadline. Two days—two and a half including the rest of this day—to find and stop a murderer. Could she do it? She would have to.

"Mrs. Harper, did you know Miss Lewis at all?"

"Gracious, dearie, everyone knew her. She must have taught half the town in her time." Mrs. Harper shook her head sadly as her strong hands wrung out the cleaning cloth. "I don't think I've quite taken in the fact that she's passed, poor soul, I've been that upset by what's happened here. I suppose you can't tell me anything more about it than what Lieutenant Richardson did?"

Pauline sat back on her heels, having recovered the very last piece of paper from her desk, hidden under the old wingback chair she and Sarah always offered to James when he stopped by for a visit. "I really can't. He trusts me to be discreet, you know."

"Well, I wouldn't want to encourage you to break that trust, then. It is such a shame, that good woman. I can't imagine who would want to harm her, any more than I can think of someone wanting to break in here. It must be a madman, don't you think?"

Pauline disagreed—there was a chilling sanity to these events, a pattern that didn't make sense to her but surely did to the murderer. Still, she didn't have the energy to contradict Mrs. Harper. "Mmm," she said noncommittally, smoothing the crumpled paper. "I don't suppose there's anything or anyone you can think of from your schooldays who might have held a grudge against her?" She recalled back to the conversation at the sewing bee. "A parent who didn't approve of her teaching methods, or a child who resented her?"

"Nothing like that, goodness me. We all adored her. She was the kindest teacher any of us had! Strict, but we all knew we could trust her with absolutely anything."

Pauline's shoulders sagged. She had known it was a forlorn hope—and she hadn't yet received official permission to investigate at all—but it would have made things so much easier if Mrs. Harper had known right away of someone who had let a grudge fester for years and years until it spilled over into violence, and then tried to hide any evidence pointing to his guilt by making sure Miss Lewis hadn't already told Pauline about him.

A new idea slowly uncurled in her mind. "Mrs. Harper—you said everyone trusted her. You mean that people would have told her their secrets?"

"I never did, but I suppose some probably did. Girls who didn't have friends or parents to talk to found her a safe listener to all their woes, boys who had ambitions everyone else laughed at, that sort of thing."

It all came back to secrets. Something Miss Lewis knew that someone didn't want revealed—and would kill to protect.

Pauline knew whom she had to speak to next, regardless of what James expected of her. The police chief hadn't forbidden her to interfere; she wasn't breaking her promise to abide by his decision if he hadn't made that decision yet.

"Everything looks wonderful, Mrs. Harper," she said, rising to her feet. "Better than it did before. I can't thank you enough."

Her landlady waved off her thanks. "Get along with you. If we can't help each other out once in a while, where does that leave us?" she said. "Are you sure you are up to riding that bicycle all the way to Richardsons, dearie?"

Pauline smiled as she set the lone piece of paper on her desk. "I'll be fine, but thank you. James said he would send someone to accompany me, if not join me himself. Are you going to be all right here by yourself?" she asked, struck by the sudden concern. She didn't think the intruder would return—but then she hadn't expected an intruder in the first place.

"No need to fret, I'll lock my doors and windows," Mrs. Harper promised as she departed for her own quarters.

Collecting her overnight things did not take Pauline long, nor did telephoning to the station. James was just finishing up with his report, he said. Would Pauline be willing to wait for another fifteen or twenty minutes?

She told him to meet her at the vicarage and rang off before he could object.

Pauline hesitated before stepping through the door. It wasn't fear so much as an irrational conviction that leaving would bring about another disaster. The broken lock still dangled from the door, and would until the locksmith James had promised to send arrived. There was no way to keep anyone out… no way to ensure her privacy would not be violated a second time.

Pauline mentally shook herself. This was utter foolishness. There was no reason for the intruder to return. Mrs. Harper was now fully alert downstairs, and her own privacy couldn't be any more degraded than it already was. The household money and the few items of value she and Sarah owned were safely in her valise until the apartment was safe for them—and Pauline—again.

Leaving the apartment wasn't abandoning her home, though it felt like it. Nor was it cowardice. She was doing what was necessary to protect herself and solve the case.

Her fancies firmly tamped down, Pauline forced herself to close the door and walk down the steps to the street, refusing to even turn her head to look back at the upstairs window as she placed her small bag in the bicycle basket and mounted to ride away. She would not give in to sentimental folly.

Luckily Mrs. Hansen was at home in the white clapboard vicarage beside the Episcopal church. Despite the fact that Pauline had never visited before, the vicar's wife didn't look in the least surprised to see that young woman at her door.

"Miss Gray, how splendid," she said, opening the door wide and ushering Pauline inside. "What can I do for you this afternoon?"

Now that she was here, Pauline's stomach knotted. It hadn't occurred to her that in coming to the Reverend Hansen's wife for information about Miss Lewis's students, she would also have to break the news of Miss Lewis's death. James and Chief Gordon would not be pleased with her for that… but in any case, the reverend ought to know.

"I'm afraid I come with bad news," Pauline said, not coming into the house any further than the shabby but clean front hall. "Have you heard that Miss Lewis was killed this morning?"

Mrs. Hansen took a step back, one hand at her throat. "What? Mercy! No, my dear, I hadn't heard. Oh dear, dear, that is tragic. Poor soul. A pillar of the church, and the community. Oh, we shall miss her." She blinked a few times and then focused in again on Pauline. "Did you say killed, Miss Gray? Not an accident or illness? A heart attack, even?"

Pauline shook her head. "I'm afraid not. I don't think the police want the news spread, but it was murder." She hesitated a moment, then plunged ahead with the rest of the tale. "And my apartment was burgled shortly after, which leads me to suspect it had something to do with Miss Lewis's past. I was hoping you might know of someone who would know what that might be."

Mrs. Hansen stared at her. "I think," she said at last, "you had better come in and tell me all of it."

Half an hour later, Pauline left the vicarage with a list of names and a new warmth in her soul. She hadn't expected to be comforted and calmed by this visit, but Mrs. Hansen's genuine warmth and kindness had gone a considerable way toward thawing the ice that had locked her insides ever since seeing James at Miss Lewis's house that morning.

There was evil and hatred in the world, yes, but kindness and compassion as well. Between Mrs. Harper and Mrs. Hansen, and even James's concern for her, Pauline had ample proof of that.

At the Farm

Supper at the Richardson house that evening was an awkward affair. Ruby was genuinely concerned for Pauline and distressed over the case, but was also firm in her rule that one did not discuss such matters at the table. James had a weary crease between his eyebrows that spoke to a long and troublesome afternoon, and he didn't contribute much to the conversation at all. Pauline felt uncomfortable enough about interposing into their family life, not to mention the exhaustion from the day catching up to her. Were it not for young Jeremy, Ruby's son from her previous marriage, chatting excitedly about baseball and fishing, it would have been a silent meal.

Ruby shooed Pauline out of the kitchen, refusing her offer to help with dishes, as soon as the meal was over. Feeling thoroughly worn out, Pauline escaped to the guest bedroom. James caught up with her right before she entered the small but pleasant room.

"We brought Mrs. MacNeill in for questioning this afternoon," he said. "She swears things happened as she said they did, but it was hard to get much sense out of her once she realized we suspected her. Can't tell if her tears and outrage are protective or genuine." He looked tired.

Pauline felt a pang at not sharing the information she had received from Mrs. Hansen with him, but the less he knew about her plans, the less likely he was to try to forbid her from pursuing them. "I still find it hard to imagine her as a killer, lack of motive aside."

"I know," James said. "But when you look at evidence, it's hard to get away from the fact that she must have seen the killer arrive, so she's either shielding him or lying to protect herself."

Pauline frowned. "I feel as though there's something we're missing, something from the apartment that plays a role in this as well…" She shook her head, frustrated. "It's not coming to me."

"You've had a long day," James said sympathetically. "Get some rest. Maybe it will make more sense in the morning."

Pauline managed a smile. "Good advice. Thank you. Good night."

"Good night."

It was too early for sleep, so Pauline pulled the small stack of books she had packed out of her bag and placed them on the nightstand. Her hands closed more tightly around *Cranford*. If she closed her eyes, she could almost imagine herself back at Miss Lewis's, browsing delightedly through her bookshelves, so pleased to find this old friend, one she'd read many times without it ever growing stale. Pauline opened her eyes. For a moment or two, she didn't think she'd be able to read it—not now, not ever again—but she swallowed past the lump in her throat and lectured herself sternly.

"What sort of a tribute to Miss Lewis would that be?" she asked of herself. "To dishonor her final act of generosity to you! You will read this story, and you will enjoy it, just as you always have, and you will think fondly of Miss Lewis when you close its pages. For shame! Will you let her murderer take this away from you as well?"

Her throat aching and her eyes stinging, Pauline sat down in the cane-bottomed chair by the window, and opened the dull red leather-bound cover of the book. It took her longer than she would have liked to lose herself in the story, but by the time she finally did close the pages, her soul was refreshed.

She still wasn't sure she would be able to sleep, but the moment she crawled between the fresh-smelling sheets and pulled the bright patchwork quilt up to her chin, Pauline's eyes closed and she slept soundly, with no dreams that she could remember, until the sun shining through the curtains woke her the next morning.

She was bewildered at first at the strange curtains, the odd placement of the bed, the voices coming from the other rooms… until memory flooded back, and she knew where she was, and why.

Pauline stifled a groan as she climbed out of the comfortable bed. Would that yesterday had only been a dream! She wasn't sure she had the strength to endure this race to the end. Nothing but her sense of propriety made her able to dress, wash her face, and pin up her hair rather than getting back into bed and pulling the cozy quilt over her face.

Perhaps she ought to let the police handle this one… was it really right for her to insist on participating? Or was it cowardice to want to hide from this?

She probably ought to start with breakfast. No sense trying to see the world from a correct perspective on an empty stomach.

"Oh, Pauline!" Ruby said as her guest entered the kitchen, a hint of reproach in her tone. "I was going to prepare a tray for you."

Pauline smiled and took the heavy tea kettle from her friend. "I should be the one waiting on you, Ruby, not the other way around."

Ruby rolled her eyes. "Oh, you sound just like James. I am fit as a fiddle, I do not need any fussing over!"

Pauline couldn't help but laugh even as she worked the pump at the sink to fill the kettle. "Fair enough. I will not coddle you if you do not coddle me."

Ruby's lips curved as she took the filled kettle back and set it on the woodstove. "Agreed." She placed a hand on the small of her back and stretched out the kinks. "James has promised me indoor plumbing just as soon as we can manage it. It won't come a moment too soon for me."

"Your kitchen may be old-fashioned, but it is charming," Pauline said, looking around the light-filled room.

Ruby made a face. "You wouldn't say that if you had to cook and clean in here! Besides," leaning close, "indoor plumbing means *running hot water* for baths and no more outhouse."

Pauline couldn't argue against the appeal of that.

After a light breakfast of fresh biscuits and Ruby's homemade wild strawberry jam, Pauline left the Richardson house with the excuse of wanting to check on the apartment. It wasn't only an excuse—she did want to see how the place had fared overnight, and collect one or two items she had forgotten the previous day—but it was not her only reason for going out. She had her list of people to speak to about Miss Lewis's past, and she was determined to get to as many of them as possible before Chief Gordon remembered to forbid it.

She felt a small amount of guilt over going out unaccompanied, given James's concern for her safety, but she honestly did not think she was in danger. If the murderer was keeping that close a watch on Pauline's movements, they would know that she had already been questioned by the police and told everything she knew. Killing her now would do nothing.

Besides, she had to do *something*. Tempting though it was to leave this particular case to the police, Pauline could not do that. Her conscience wouldn't allow it.

To her relief, nothing about the house on Pleasant Street had changed overnight. Mrs. Harper popped out of her front door as soon as she saw Pauline through the window, and told her nothing had disturbed her sleep in the slightest.

"And Roger Denney from the locksmith is coming by this afternoon to replace the broken lock," she added. "I'll give you a copy of the new key as soon as it's available."

That bit of business taken care of, Pauline set off in search of what once was the Martens farm and now belonged to the Ingersoll family. Mrs. Ingersoll's name was on the list given to Pauline by Mrs. Hansen, and given that they had already met at the sewing bee, she seemed a natural choice for Pauline to question first.

Their farm was outside the village limits, partway up the long, steep slope of Waterman Hill. Pauline was thankful to dismount her bicycle when she reached the split rail fence surrounding their front yard. It was a snug, tidy little farm, with a white house, red barn, and blue silo. Next door was a smaller farm, and the Berger house was across the road. All in all, a pleasant corner of the community. As she stepped onto the pathway leading to the house she saw Mrs. Ingersoll and Mrs. Addison coming around from the backyard carrying an empty laundry basket between them, the wash waving merrily on the line behind their backs.

Mrs. Ingersoll recognized her and waved, setting the basket on the grass and coming forward to greet her guest.

"Good morning, Miss Gray! I thought I might see you soon. Mrs. Hansen telephoned me yesterday and told me about poor Miss Lewis, and said that you wanted to finish her memoirs in her honor and would I be able to help."

Pauline was dazzled at having her path thus smoothed for her. "Yes," she said, meaning every word. "I feel it is the least I can do. Miss Lewis didn't want her loved ones to be forgotten after her passing, and I find I can't bear to think of her being forgotten either, not if I can help it."

"Well, that isn't too likely," said Mrs. Ingersoll. "Not when so many of us have her to thank for our ability to read, write, and figure! But I think it's a splendid thing you're doing for her memory, and I'm proud to help in any way I can."

"Such a dreadful thing," Mrs. Addison agreed, her face pale and somber. "It must have been someone from the County Home, don't you think? They probably tried to break into her house to steal the silver, except she caught them in the act and they turned violent." She shuddered. "I could never bear to live so close to the poorhouse. I'd go in fear of my life and my children's lives every day!"

"Well now, I suppose they can't help being poor," Mrs. Ingersoll said tolerantly. "And I must say Miss Lewis never gave them any reason to want to harm her. Always ready to employ one of them to tend her garden, or mend her fence, or do little jobs around the house. Doesn't seem likely they'd turn on her."

Mrs. Addison shook her head. "Father always said to never trust anyone who ended up in the poorhouse, that they were there for a reason. Miss Lewis should have known better than to encourage them! She even went so far as to allow that Kilpatrick girl to stay with her after her father threw her out of the house for her shame! She said no baby should be born in the poorhouse, no matter what his parents had done. And now look at where it got her."

"I wouldn't have wanted the lass in my house, to be sure," Mrs. Ingersoll agreed. "But there, I have my boys to worry about. Miss Lewis had only herself. I don't think her kindness toward Lucy Kilpatrick and her poor wee son is what caused her death."

Mrs. Addison pinched her lips together, nodded curtly to Pauline, and crossed the yard to her own house. Mrs. Ingersoll watched her go with a faintly superior smile on her face. "Poor Cathy, she always was a mite too narrow-minded for her own good. Well, Miss Gray! I suppose you want to look around the place, see where Miss Lewis would have lived if Tom Martens hadn't died? Poor soul. Well, well, they're together again now."

"Miss Lewis said there was an accident here on the farm, but she didn't give me any more details than that—she didn't want to talk about it," Pauline said. "How did he die?"

It had occurred to her that perhaps Tom had been murdered, and Miss Lewis killed now in order to cover up the past dreadful crime.

Mrs. Ingersoll shattered that suspicion with her response. "Oh, I don't blame her for not wanting to talk about it, even after all these years. I had nightmares after I first learned about it when Hank brought me here to live. Just dreadful. He was out cutting hay, and the scythe slipped…" She must have seen Pauline's face turn slowly green, for she cut short the rest of the details. "Blood poisoning," she finished abruptly.

That certainly did not sound like murder, but no wonder Miss Lewis didn't care to think back to it. Even if Pauline had been interested in marriage, she wouldn't have wanted to marry a farmer. For one, she didn't think she was suited to life as a farmer's wife. For another, she doubted she had the endurance to bear up under the dangers and suffering such a life entailed. Too many things could go wrong with farming.

"But here," continued Mrs. Ingersoll, picking up the empty laundry basket again and moving toward the back door. "After Mrs. Hansen telephoned, I looked out some old letters that had been stashed away in a closet when Hank's father bought the place, and found a couple from Miss Lewis to Tom. They're on the kitchen table, so long as those imps of mine and the Addison youngsters haven't torn them to pieces." She shook her head. "I'm always so glad when school ends for the year, and within a week I'm wishing it would start again! Lucky for me the Addisons live so close, our young'uns can run around together and wear each other out. I keep them here when Mrs. Addison runs errands, and she does the same for me."

"That is fortunate," Pauline said absently, still trying to distract her mind from the image of Tom Martens swinging a scythe and—

"Ah, here they are!" said Mrs. Ingersoll, stepping into the kitchen.

"Right, you lot, out you go. And mind you stay out of my clean linens!" she called as a whirlwind of small boys blew past Pauline to race down to the small brook that flowed out past the clothesline.

"I ought not to complain," she said, handing the yellowed envelopes to Pauline. "Mrs. Addison took them for me yesterday so I could go to town and do the marketing for the week. Well, there you are, my dear. I wish I had thought to look in that closet before, I would have liked to give them to Miss Lewis herself. At least it will help them both be remembered now."

While Pauline cautiously eased the fragile letters out of their envelopes, a light tap came on the kitchen door, followed immediately by a stout woman entering the house.

"Ach, Mrs. Ingersoll, how many times have I told you to let me wash your sheets for you!" exclaimed Margret Berger. "We are only across the road, and it would be my pleasure after all the help you and Mr. Ingersoll have given Heinrich and me when we first moved here."

Mrs. Ingersoll laughed. "I know, Mrs. Berger, but I can't seem to break the habit. Besides, you have enough work to do with paying customers, surely."

Mrs. Berger shook her head severely, then turned to greet Pauline. "Good morning, Miss Gray. We don't often see you out this way."

"No, although the countryside is so pleasant out here I think I must start cycling these roads more often," Pauline said. "I had a lovely conversation with your sister the other day, at the sewing bee for Ruby Richardson."

"Yes, we missed you there, Mrs. Berger," Mrs. Ingersoll broke in.

Mrs. Berger spread work-roughened hands. "Too much work! I am glad Klara went, though. She gets—oh, I do not know the word. Loses interest in things to do."

"Bored?" Pauline suggested diffidently.

"Ah, that is it. Fifteen years in this country and still there are words that slip away from me!" Mrs. Berger said, shaking her head.

"I couldn't learn German if my life depended on it," said Mrs. Ingersoll. "You forget maybe one word every six months, and have barely the hint of an accent. I don't think you need despair! Oh—" looking out the window. "There go my sheets! You boys!"

The guilty parties took one look at the wrathful figure descending on them from the house and scampered away, leaving the mud-streaked sheets tangled on the ground where they had fallen.

"Those rascals!" growled Mrs. Berger, coming out with Pauline behind Mrs. Ingersoll. "They played the nasty trick on my Heinrich yesterday. Mrs. Addison was supposed to be watching them, but ach, she lets them do whatever they please. Oh, Mrs. Ingersoll, now you *must* let me wash them for you!"

Mrs. Ingersoll smiled and sighed and bundled the once-crisp sheets up to pass along to the German woman. "I suppose I must. Thank you, Mrs. Berger. Miss Gray, I'm sorry our chat has been interrupted. Shall we try again? Miss Gray is trying to finish up Miss Lewis's memoirs, as a tribute of sorts," she explained to Mrs. Berger.

"That is good!" exclaimed Mrs. Berger. "She was a gracious lady. She always offered Heinrich a cup of tea when he dropped off the laundry for her, and always asked if we had heard recently from our boy back in the old country. We shall miss her."

And that, Pauline thought ruefully, seemed to be the way everyone felt. How to find who had killed Miss Lewis when everyone who knew her respected and liked her so much? Even those who disapproved of all her kindness, such as Mrs. Addison, couldn't say anything truly bad about her.

The rest of the conversation did not provide any additional insight, though Mrs. Ingersoll did insist that Pauline take the letters with her. It didn't seem likely that they would contain a clue, being merely notes from a young lady to her sweetheart about their future plans, but one never knew. Perhaps a closer study of their contents would help.

Two boys stood by Pauline's bicycle when she returned to it, and she gave them both suspicious looks.

"No tricks here, I hope," she said severely.

The taller of the two laughed. "No, ma'am. We don't do things like that anymore. Besides, it isn't nice to play jokes on a stranger."

"Only on people you know?" Pauline asked, amused despite herself.

"You bet!" the smaller boy piped up. "It's more funny then."

The older boy rolled his eyes.

"I heard you were playing tricks on poor Mr. Berger yesterday," Pauline said.

The boys glanced at each other. "I sure wasn't," the older one said. "I had to help Pa. Were you, Charlie?"

The younger shook his head. "Naw. Me and Bobby were out playing in the woods with Pete and Andy and Mikey. It was swell. Normally Mrs. Addison makes us stay where she can see us, but yesterday we just did what we wanted. Went wading in the brook, climbed trees, and everything!" His eyes were round and he waved his hands in the air as he continued. "She *never* lets us play in the brook, 'cause she can't swim and so she's always afraid we'll drown, even though it's not that deep." His nose wrinkled with childish scorn at the folly of adult fears.

Pauline smiled at his enthusiasm even as she felt sympathy for the poor, overworked mothers, trying to keep such energetic boys out of mischief all the time. No wonder Mrs. Ingersoll had been so pleased by her chance to get away for a short while! Even marketing would seem restful in comparison.

Shaking her head in wonder, she mounted her bicycle and rode on to the next place on her list.

More Suspects

The next person Pauline wanted to question was Samuel Crane, Miss Lewis's nephew. She was sure the police had already done so, but the questions they would have asked him were not necessarily the same ones she wanted to ask. She was quite certain neither James nor Chief Gordon would approve of this course of action. Fortunately, she had an excuse at hand to look Mr. Crane up and offer him her condolences.

As she had suspected, Mr. Crane was at Miss Lewis's house, inventorying the contents and making copious notes. He seemed startled at first when Pauline knocked on the door, but upon her introduction of herself as the person working with Miss Lewis on her memoirs, his face smoothed into a smile.

"Of course, the newspaper woman," he said. "Aunt Anita told me about you. Please, come in. I'm afraid everything is at sixes and sevens. The police just finished up here this morning, and asked me to check to see what, if anything, is missing. What a task, with all Aunt Anita's knick-knacks! Still, I might be able to rustle up a cup of coffee."

Pauline had never considered herself a particularly dense individual, but it only now occurred to her, standing on the back doorstep, that if Mr. Crane *was* the murderer and vandal, she was offering him the perfect opportunity to do away with her as well. And she had been so smugly certain that she would be safe in her investigations, more concerned with avoiding police censure than with her own well-being!

She resisted the urge to take a step back. Surely the worst thing she could do would be to show fear at this point! If he was not the murderer, he would be mortally offended, and if he was the murderer, he would take her fear as a sign of weakness and act accordingly. No, she had been foolish enough to put herself in this position, the only thing to do now was to brazen it out. But oh, wouldn't James scold when he found out!

Pauline cleared her throat. "Would you consider me terribly rude if I preferred to remain outside? You see, it's so soon after—after your aunt's passing. I'm not sure I could bring myself to go in—in where it happened."

A flash of something—was it irritation?—crossed Mr. Crane's face, only to be quickly replaced by his former bland smile. "Of course, of course." He closed the door behind him and motioned around to the side of the house, where a whitewashed wrought iron bench sat amidst the roses.

Pauline seated herself in the middle of the bench, leaving no room for Mr. Crane to join her. His mouth turned down at the corners at that, but once again he said nothing. He leaned against a young cherry tree, the delicate white blossoms of spring replaced now by green fruit waiting to ripen, and waited for her to speak.

"I wished to pass my condolences to you, Mr. Crane, on the loss of your aunt," Pauline began. "I had only known her a short time, but from the stories she told I could see what a rich life she led. Her death will be felt by the entire community." To her horror, her voice thickened on the last words and real tears sprang to her eyes. This was hardly appropriate detective work!

Still, the truth in her words could not be denied, nor would she choose to denigrate Miss Lewis's memory by spouting false platitudes, even if it was to catch her killer.

"That's mighty kind of you, Miss Gray," Mr. Crane said, though he did not go so far as to offer her a handkerchief. "I can't say it's really sunk in yet. Even as I'm sorting through all Aunt Anita's things, I keep expecting her to come around the corner and tell me to stop fussing with it all." He stopped, staring into space. "No, it just doesn't seem real."

Pauline luckily had her own handkerchief in her bag, and was able to dab at her eyes until they stopped watering. "It must be a comfort to you, to be in the house she loved so well."

He crossed his arms in front of his chest. "I suppose. I can't live here, though. My work is in Lisbon, and I can't be trying to get between the two places every day. I guess I'll have to sell it, much as I hate to." He didn't sound very sad about it; in fact, his eyes gleamed as he spoke.

It was not evidence, nor even a sign of bad character—plenty of people these days would be thankful for the chance to put a little extra money in their pocket—but Pauline resented his attitude all the same. How dare he so casually speak of selling Miss Lewis's haven? It was almost sacrilegious.

"Oh? What do you do for work?" she asked, attempting to sound merely politely curious.

"I'm foreman at the plant," he said. At her puzzled expression, he clarified, "The powdered milk plant."

"Ah, yes," Pauline said. Her journalistic instincts got the upper hand, and she said, "That sounds like something my readers would find interesting. I wonder if I might have a tour someday, and an interview?"

She hadn't meant her inquiry to be a sop to the man's vanity, but it worked as one. Before her very eyes he puffed up, seemingly growing taller, and he beamed all over his broad, reddish face. "That's awfully good of you!" he said. "I'd be tickled pink. And speaking of your writing, Miss Gray, I'd like to tell you my aunt was some pleased at working with you on her little project. No doubt the story of an old woman's life was tedious to a journalist like yourself, but it sure did brighten her days."

"Thank you, but I didn't find it tedious at all!" Pauline cried. "Your aunt's life may have been simple, but it was full and rich. In fact, I intend to carry on with her memoirs, as a tribute to her memory. With your permission, of course," she added belatedly.

He blinked his large, pale eyes repeatedly. "Oh," he said. "Er. Well. I suppose… that is, yes, of course. Why not?"

This was all very well and good, but it didn't seem to be getting them any further. Pauline twiddled with the corner of her handkerchief and wondered what to say next. She cast about in her mind, and remembered something just in time to keep the silence from growing too awkward.

"I also wanted to apologize," she said.

"Apologize, Miss Gray?"

"Yes, your aunt had lent me some books, you see, and before I had a chance to return them, someone broke into my apartment, and I'm afraid they took some damage. Pages bent, the spines weakened, that sort of thing. I am certain someone at the university would be able to repair them, but it may take some time." She watched him narrowly, but his face showed no expression save concern when she spoke of the break-in.

"That's terrible! I hope the thieves didn't take anything of value. Don't you worry about those books another moment, Miss Gray. You've got enough on your mind. In fact, why don't you keep them? I'm sure my aunt would like you to have them. I don't have much time for reading, myself."

Pauline managed to repress her wince. "That's kind of you," she said. "Thank you."

There didn't seem to be anything left to say. Pauline rose to her feet and held out one gloved hand. "Thank you for your time, Mr. Crane, and I'm sorry to take you away from your duties here."

"Not at all," he replied, giving her hand a brief shake and then dropping it immediately. "Thank you for coming. Er… you won't forget about that tour?"

Pauline assured him she would not, and made her way back out through the garden and to the sidewalk where she had left her bicycle. She couldn't help but look mournfully at the little white house with the green roof and shutters as she mounted the machine. The next time she saw it, it would likely have new owners, people who cared nothing for the library or the andiron owls or English tea in thin china cups.

It simply wasn't right. But what could she do?

"Miss Gray!"

Pauline turned her head in the direction of the call. A man a few years older than herself stood in front of Mrs. MacNeill's brick house, waving at her. Pauline hesitated. Who was this and why was he calling her?

The man came closer. "You are Miss Gray, aren't you? My mother saw you out the window and said that's who you are."

"I am," Pauline admitted. "Might I inquire who you are?"

"Sorry," he said, mopping his face with a crisp white handkerchief. "Angus MacNeill. I live out toward Hermon, but I am staying with my mother until this mess is cleared up."

"I see," Pauline said, for lack of a better response. What did this have to do with her?

"Miss Gray, I realize this is impolite, me accosting you on the street like this, but I need your help. I've heard that you sometimes assist the police with their cases, and since you were friendly with Miss Lewis and were here right after she was killed…" He stopped and wiped his face again. "Sorry," he repeated. "This is awkward. The police seem to think my mother had something to do with Miss Lewis's death, just because they have some supposed evidence that Miss Lewis was killed in the morning and my mother didn't see anyone coming or going from her house at that time. I don't understand it all, but I know my mother had nothing to do with the murder. It's absurd even to think it! Murder and my mother don't belong in the same sentence."

"I'm afraid I still don't see what this has to do with me," Pauline said, though she had a sinking feeling she did know.

"You have to convince the police to leave my mother alone," Mr. MacNeill said. "Please! Talk to Mother again, and see if you can understand why her story doesn't match what the police say had to have happened. I know she's telling the truth, but I can't make the police believe me. If you can make sense of it, they'll listen to you. It's dreadful of me to just come right out and ask you this, when we've never even met, but I don't know what else to do. My mother needs help, and I can't give it to her."

Pauline couldn't help but hear the sincerity in his voice. No matter what else might or might not be true, Mr. MacNeill was honestly worried for his mother.

The question was, could she believe the rest of his claim? James had said that they didn't think Mrs. MacNeill had done the murder herself, rather that she was covering up for someone else. They hadn't any idea who, though. Now here was her son, who was certainly strong enough from his appearance to murder a frail elderly woman, come out of the blue to defend his mother. What if he wasn't here just to defend her, but to protect himself? What if he had done the killing?

But why—why—why? The question beat at Pauline's mind. Nobody seemed to have a motive in this case, save perhaps Samuel Crane, who inherited a house and its contents and would be able to sell both to line his pockets. In these times, it was a strong motive.

Yet despite an instinctive dislike for the man, Pauline wasn't sure she could see him as a murderer. And as the police had determined, if he were the murderer, how could he have gotten into his aunt's house without Mrs. MacNeill noticing? Into and back out again, for that matter. Perhaps the nosy neighbor might have missed either the entrance or the exit, but surely not both.

Then there was the burglary of Pauline's own apartment. How did that fit in? If Mr. Crane was the murderer, it didn't make sense. Nor had he seemed perturbed by the information that she had two of his aunt's books in her possession.

Mrs. MacNeill had to be lying, no matter how much her son insisted she was telling the truth. And if that was the case, than she could have no reason to lie but to protect someone else. Who better to protect than her son? Perhaps his motive lay deep in the past, as Pauline had speculated. What if Miss Lewis had known something about him, something he was desperate to keep hidden?

If that was the case, then his approaching her like this meant that he was not trying to help his mother, but trying to gauge how much Pauline knew about the case, and her life was in danger. Not that he would try to murder her here, in the street, where Mr. Crane could see everything and any passerby was a potential witness. But if she had thought herself in danger by going into Miss Lewis's house, how much more so into the MacNeill house.

On the other hand, if there was an honest mistake somewhere, and Mrs. MacNeill and her son were both innocent of any wrongdoing, could Pauline live with herself for having turned away from the plea for help?

She wrenched her mind back to the present, where Mr. MacNeill was waiting for her answer. She made up her mind.

"I will speak with your mother," she said. "But I can't do it here. I am staying with the Richardson family temporarily, and she can come and speak to me there this afternoon."

If she had been hoping for Mr. MacNeill to confirm her suspicions by pressing her to come into the house, she was disappointed. He reached for her hand and pumped it up and down enthusiastically.

"Thank you, Miss Gray! Thank you very much! I'll bring Mother over right after lunch. I can't tell you how grateful I am!"

He rushed back into the house and Pauline at last began cycling back to the Richardson house. Whether she had made a mistake, only time would tell, but she hoped not. One way or another, they *had* to get to the bottom of this case.

An Apology Made

James did not often get a chance to come home in the middle of the day, and it was just pure bad luck that this one day, of all days, he was seated at the dining room table waiting to enjoy a hot dinner when Pauline returned to the house. She stopped short, her cheeks flushing with guilt.

"Oh Ruby, I am so sorry," she exclaimed, pressing her hands to her cheeks. "I'm so accustomed to having a light luncheon, it didn't even occur to me that you would make dinner. I should have returned sooner, or at least let you know I would be out. It was so terribly rude of me!"

"Don't fret," Ruby said cheerfully. "We only just sat down. I was going to serve James and Jeremy and wait for you, but as you're here now, we can all eat together."

Pauline removed her hat and gloves, washed her hands, and sat down, wondering how to break the news to James that not only had she defied his wishes by continuing to investigate the case, she had also invited a possible murderer to his house this afternoon. What on earth had possessed her? She picked away at the roast and potatoes until Jeremy spoke up.

"Are you coming down with a fever, Miss Gray? I was just like that with food when I got sick last year. Mother says I've been making up for it ever since." He grinned at her.

"Jeremy," Ruby scolded. "Don't embarrass Miss Gray."

There was nothing for it. Pauline's stomach clenched and her head began to ache, but it was better to speak and get this over with. She set her fork down.

"You're very observant, Jeremy. You'd make a good journalist. I'm not unwell, but I am a little unhappy with myself. Have you ever done something without thinking it through first?"

Jeremy's eyes widened. "Sure! Mother's always telling me to think before I leap. Gosh, you mean grown-ups do that too?"

Pauline glanced at James, whose face had grown suspicious. "Sometimes. And we always feel very foolish afterward."

Jeremy nodded in sympathy. "And then your stomach starts to feel all funny, and you want to tell someone about it but you wish you didn't have to, and you just feel sicker and sicker."

He was astonishingly perceptive for a boy his age. "Exactly."

James cleared his throat. "Jeremy, why don't you run along outside so Miss Gray can talk to your mother and me about what it was she did without thinking?"

Jeremy stood without complaint, even though he hadn't yet had his dessert, and left the table. "No problem, Dad. Don't worry, Miss Gray. Mother and Dad will help you fix whatever your trouble is."

Pauline watched him leave, then turned her gaze to Ruby. "He's a remarkable young man. You should be proud."

Ruby's face creased with pleasure. "I am. Now, tell us what it is that's troubling you. I doubt it's just sorrow over almost making my roast cold."

Pauline drew in as deep a breath as her tight chest would allow, and admitted that she had invited Mrs. MacNeill to come to the house that afternoon.

As she had expected—and, she had to admit, as she richly deserved—James nearly burst from fury.

"Darn it, Pauline! I told you to stay away from this case! I brought you here to be safe, and instead you go ahead and endanger my wife and son as well as yourself! I know you pride yourself on being an independent woman, but this is too much. You have to think of others once in a while instead of only yourself!"

That sounded too much like something her mother might say. Pauline's own temper flared up. "Yes, I made a mistake," she flashed back. "And I am sorry for it. But I *am* thinking of others! I am thinking of Miss Lewis, and of the innocent people who will suffer from being under suspicion if we don't catch the real murderer. I wish I could close my eyes to the situation, but I can't, I simply cannot sit by and do nothing when there is still something I *can* do."

James's eyes were flat and hard. "That still doesn't justify putting Ruby and Jeremy at risk."

Pauline's self-righteous wrath left her in an instant. He was correct. What an arrogant fool she had been! What had she been thinking? She could have asked Mrs. MacNeill to meet her at any public spot, rather than here where there were other innocent people who could be harmed. Her ears buzzed and her breath started coming in gasps.

Ruby coughed.

It was a gentle sound, but it pulled Pauline out of her downward spiral and caused James's gaze to fly to his wife's face. Her expression was unreadable.

"Goodness," she said. "What a tempest in a teapot."

Confusion flashed across James's open face. "What—?"

Ruby continued gently. "You do fuss so, James. Do you honestly think Mr. MacNeill, even if he is a murderer, which I doubt, is going to try to murder three people, two of whom are connected to a police officer investigating this case, as an attempt to hide his guilt in a previous murder? All while his mother stands there and watches? Nonsense!"

"But—" James began.

"Personally, I think Pauline was quite sensible in inviting them here. But as you are so worried, Jeremy can go play baseball with his friends, I will enjoy a pleasant walk in solitude, you can stay here as protection for Pauline, she can talk to Mrs. MacNeill, and hopefully her story will move you one step closer to catching the murderer."

James opened and closed his mouth a few times without sound. Pauline's tense muscles began to ease, and the buzzing in her ears receded. She didn't deserve such graciousness, but she wouldn't compound her error now by protesting that Ruby ought not to be so forgiving. She managed a tight nod.

"Thank you," she said.

James sighed. "Seems you have it all planned out. Who am I to argue?"

Ruby smiled serenely, with a flash of mischief lurking in her eyes. "And, since Jeremy and I ought to leave now to make sure we are both well out of danger's path, that means the two of you will have to clear the table and wash the dishes."

She set her napkin down next to her plate and sailed out of the room triumphantly before either of the other two could gather their wits enough to respond.

James recovered first, breaking into a low, rumbling laugh. "I'd say she got the best of that exchange! What a woman I married." He passed a hand over his smooth head and finally looked Pauline in the eye with his usual frankness. "I'm still mad about this," he admitted, "but what's done is done, and I guess we all do things we afterwards wish we hadn't."

Pauline stood up and began collecting plates to take to the kitchen. "Believe it or not, I was trying to be cautious," she admitted. "I was so proud of myself for not going into the MacNeill house or into Miss Lewis's house when her nephew invited me in. It wasn't until I got back here that I realized I had only succeeded in putting other people in danger as well as myself rather than protecting myself."

James had also started gathering dishes, but at that he stopped short. "Miss Lewis's nephew—gosh darn it, Pauline. I think you'd better tell me exactly what you did while you were out this morning."

She outlined her morning's adventures as they covered the leftovers and put them in the icebox, scraped the plates clean, pumped and heated water, and at last set to washing all the dishes. To his credit, James didn't scold Pauline any more for her escapades. Instead he frowned in concentration as he wiped dry each clean dish she handed him from the sink.

"It's still not much," he said. "But the chief and I haven't had much luck, either. As you found, no one but Crane seems to have a motive, but he has an alibi, and even if he didn't, why would the MacNeill woman protect him?" He scowled blankly at the forks as he set them in their proper drawer. "I don't suppose there was anything useful in the letters Mrs. Ingersoll gave you?"

Pauline shook her head, but stopped as a memory visited her. *The letter...*

"James, have you ever heard of a Miss Janet Arden?"

"Nope," he answered. "Who is she?"

"I don't know, but Miss Lewis received a letter from her the last day I was there. It was in a long white envelope. She didn't seem to recognize the name, either. Did you find the letter or the envelope when you searched the house afterward?"

He paused as he thought, hands stilling on the plate he was drying. "No," he said at last. "I think I would have remembered it. I can double check with the chief, but I'm fairly certain it wasn't there." He resumed wiping. "It doesn't mean much, though. Miss Lewis might have thrown it away herself."

"True," Pauline admitted.

"Still, I'll check in with the police downstate. I don't suppose you noticed the address?"

"I'm afraid not," Pauline had to confess.

"A pity. She could be from anywhere, even another state. No harm in checking, at least. For now, though, it still seems like Mrs. MacNeill is our likeliest lead. I hate to admit it, but maybe it is a good thing you invited her here. She was too flustered and nervous to make any sense when we questioned her. She might feel more comfortable in a home, with another woman."

Something warmed inside Pauline at that, but she couldn't forgive herself quite that easily. She finished with the last knife and turned from the sink to face James as she dried her hands on the rough homespun towel.

"All the same, it was a dreadful thing to have done, and you had every right to be angry with me for potentially endangering Ruby and Jeremy. Sarah has warned me often enough how thoughtless I can be when I am on the trail of something that matters to me, and I see now I should listen better to her. I promise you this: I will never put innocent lives at risk again. Except my own, when I deem it necessary," she couldn't help adding.

James laughed, sighed, shook his head, and put the knife away safely in the wooden block. "I suppose I can live with that. As long as you don't object to me scolding you when that happens. You may be willing to put your life at risk, but your friends aren't as comfortable with the idea."

On that note, a truck rattled into the driveway and stopped, and Angus MacNeill stepped out of the driver's side to open the door for his mother. James's brows pulled together again in a scowl.

"I thought it was just the mother coming!"

"I told you her son was bringing her," Pauline replied. "I doubt she can drive. Besides, this is why you are here, isn't it?"

"I suppose," he grumbled, but he managed to be polite as he opened the door to the two on the step. Mrs. MacNeill seemed inclined to be frightened of the large policeman in his shirt sleeves welcoming them into his house, and Pauline quickly stepped into the breach.

"It's such a lovely day, why don't we sit here on the porch, Mrs. MacNeill? You and I can have a nice chat, and Lieutenant Richardson and Mr. MacNeill can…" She trailed off helplessly. What she wanted to say was that they could sit quietly and not interfere with the conversation, but how to say that and still sound polite?

James came to her rescue, his eyes twinkling despite himself. "Let me show you my garden, MacNeill. It's coming along nicely despite the cool spring. Now if I can just keep the dratted groundhog away from all the tender shoots!"

Angus MacNeill allowed himself to be led away, and Pauline and Mrs. MacNeill sat down on the white wicker rockers on the front porch. The older woman's eyes kept filling with tears that she would resolutely blink away, and her blue-veined hands trembled. Despite her suspicions, Pauline's heart went out to the woman.

"Miss Gray," she said, "can you tell me why the police are so sure I must have some involvement in this awful thing? I thought the world of Miss Lewis—everyone did—I would never want to cause her harm. The chief said something about me not reporting seeing the murderer, but I don't understand. I didn't see anyone, so how could I report what I didn't see?"

Pauline settled on the straightforward truth. In Mrs. MacNeill's voice, she heard the ring of honest bewilderment and grief. As unlikely as her story was, Pauline believed she had to be innocent.

"You see, Mrs. MacNeill, the evidence shows that Miss Lewis was—was killed early that morning, not late the night before, as the police had originally thought. As your house has such a prominent view of hers, it seems impossible that the murderer could have come there without you seeing him that morning."

Mrs. MacNeill shook her head. "No, there was no one! Unless someone walked across the field from the County Home and snuck in through the back. I might not have noticed a single walker coming from that direction. But anyone coming from town, I must have seen."

Pauline wished briefly it were that easy, but all the objections she and James had had initially to the murderer being someone from the poorhouse still stood, and were in fact stronger now that they knew Miss Lewis had been killed in the early morning rather than at night. A desperate person might try to break into a dark house when its occupants were supposed to be sleeping and try to steal something, but only a fool would do so in daylight.

Miss Lewis being the kind of person that she was, she would probably have given any poor soul some money to help with a new life without him having to resort to a threat in the first place.

"I can't see any of those County Home folk hurting Miss Lewis, though," Mrs. MacNeill continued, unconsciously echoing Pauline's thoughts. "Some people don't trust them, say that they wouldn't be in the home if they hadn't done something bad, but Miss Lewis never believed that. Why, I remember once, a few years ago—" She stopped abruptly. "There, I shouldn't share such things with a young woman of your standing."

"Please," Pauline said. "Anything you can remember about Miss Lewis is helpful. I promise, I won't be shocked."

Mrs. MacNeill seemed doubtful, but continued. "Well, it was a young woman who was—well—she was—she was unmarried, you see, and she was—well—"

"With child?" Pauline supplied. The tips of her ears were hot, but more at Mrs. MacNeill's embarrassment than anything on her own account. She was aware of the facts of life, and she rather suspected she had already heard part of this story from Mrs. Ingersoll and Mrs.

Addison.

"Well, yes," Mrs. MacNeill admitted. "Anyway, her dad threw her out of the house, and Miss Lewis took her in so the baby wouldn't have to be born in the poorhouse. There was an awful to-do about it in town. Folk were divided right and left over whether Miss Lewis was encouraging the young woman in her sin or performing an act of Christian charity. Mrs. Hansen was on Miss Lewis's side, wanted the sewing circle to make some baby clothes, but most of the women up and said they would start attending the Presbyterian church if she did any such thing. Old Mr. Baker—he's dead now, dear, you wouldn't have met him—said it was a shame and a disgrace, and that he would write to the bishop. But Miss Lewis didn't give two pins for any of them. She did what she believed to be right and let public opinion go hang."

That sounded like the woman Pauline had come to know over the last few months. "Nothing about this makes sense!" she burst out. "The murder had to have been in the morning because of the bread, but it can't have been in the morning because you didn't see anyone. It looked like a burglary, but nothing was actually taken. Everyone loved Miss Lewis, but someone murdered her." She pressed her hands to her forehead. "Somehow there must be a way to make logic out of this chaos, but I simply cannot see it."

Mrs. MacNeill leaned forward and patted her knee. "There, there, dear. It's good of you to try, but some things are beyond us."

Pauline smiled wanly. She was supposed to be questioning a suspect, not being comforted by one! She cleared her throat and began again.

"Let's start at the beginning of the day, shall we? You were up at what time?"

"Five o'clock," Mrs. MacNeill said promptly. "I like to get a good start to my day, I do. No sense in lazing about half the morning like some folks do! Waste all the best hours of the day."

Pauline would have been happy to sleep until nine o'clock every morning, but she hoped Mrs. MacNeill wouldn't notice her guilty blush.

"I finished off the last of the previous day's milk, like I always do, and had a slice of bread and butter for breakfast," Mrs. MacNeill continued, eyes staring into the distance as she remembered. "Then I got my housecleaning out of the way, again, like I always do. The milkman usually comes around eight-thirty—terrible late for new milk, but he has to get to all the folks in the village first, I suppose—and I like to have my work done and out of the way before he arrives. I'd be ashamed to face him with my floors unswept and the dust still on my furniture!"

More and more, Pauline realized she would never make a proper housewife. She rarely even noticed when there was dust on the furniture, and she only swept because she and Sarah had made an agreement to share the chores evenly, and it wouldn't be fair to inflict her work on her friend.

"And you didn't hear or see anything unusual in all that time?" she asked, brushing aside her inadequacy at keeping a proper house.

"No..." Mrs. MacNeill said, but there was doubt in her voice.

Pauline pounced. "There was something!"

Mrs. MacNeill closed her eyes. "Maybe. But it wasn't terribly unusual. I can hear any traffic that might come down the road, you see, even when I can't see it. So few people come out our way that anyone coming is a distraction. But some of them come so regularly that I don't notice them unless they are there out of their usual time."

"And this was something of that sort?"

"It was... let me think. I was shaking out my curtains and—yes, that's right!" She opened her eyes triumphantly. "I wondered if it was about time for them to be laundered again."

Pauline blinked in confusion. What did that signify?

"And I thought it," Mrs. MacNeill continued, "because Mr. Berger was collecting some of Miss Lewis's laundry. I heard his truck, and was surprised he was there so early." She stopped, her eyes rounding. "Why! How on earth did I forget that? Chief Gordon and that lieutenant there asked me over and over again if I'd seen anyone, but I clean forgot about Mr. Berger."

"Because you didn't see him," Pauline murmured automatically, as her mind frantically turned over this new information. "You only heard him. So your mind didn't make that connection."

"That must be it," Mrs. MacNeill agreed. "And then those two got me so frazzled I didn't know if I was on my head or my tail! Well, now. That's good news, isn't it? Mr. Berger must have seen something that will help you. Should I tell Lieutenant Richardson now?"

James and Mr. MacNeill were walking back toward the porch as she spoke, animatedly discussing proper fertilizer for corn and what to do with that new-fangled zucchini Sal Agosti kept urging everyone to plant.

"Yes indeed," Pauline said.

She didn't say anything else until the MacNeills had left, greatly relieved and blithely unaware of the implications of Mrs. MacNeill's restored memory. Then she and James faced each other, differences aside once more.

"You believe her, I take it," James said, not a question.

"I didn't prompt her," Pauline said in response. "I took her back to the start of her day and she remembered it all on her own from there. But James—I saw Mrs. Berger this morning, and she didn't say a word about her husband being at Miss Lewis's on the day of the murder!" Her eyes were wide with dismay, and her hands began to shake. She liked kindly Mr. Berger and his round, practical wife with her ever-twinkling eyes. Even better did she like Mrs. Berger's sister, Klara, with whom she shared a kindred feeling of enjoying spinsterhood. "He can't possibly have had anything to do with this," she said, arguing with herself as much as anyone. "What would his motive be?"

"Right now if we find someone who was in the right place at the right time, I don't care about their motive," James said grimly. "They could be a homicidal maniac for all I care." He scratched his head. "My father fought in the war, you know, and he always said it was a mistake to let the Bergers come here. Maybe he was right."

"James! For shame!" The Bergers were hardly to blame for the war, and in any case, that had been ages ago.

James had the grace to look ashamed. "Well, I dunno. I've always liked Berger, but he could be a rotten 'un after all. In any case, I have to question him."

"Of course." Pauline recognized that. She just wished Mrs. MacNeill had recalled someone else coming by.

Solving mysteries was never as simple and tidy as it seemed on paper. When real people were involved, heartbreak inevitably ensued. For the first time, Pauline wished she'd never gotten involved.

Unwelcome Confirmation

James left the house immediately afterward to question Mr. Berger. Pauline wandered through the empty rooms and yard for half an hour, trying not to berate herself, before she finally gave up and left for town, making sure to pen a note to Ruby before leaving.

Her feet took her on their accustomed route to her apartment, and Pauline decided she might as well stop by and pick up one or two items she had forgotten to pack the previous day. She only had the pair of gloves she was currently wearing, for one, and they were getting wretchedly dirty, and she wanted fresh stockings as well.

At the house, Pauline was greeted by Al Denney, the postman, just finishing up his rounds for the day.

"Afternoon, Miss Gray," the friendly old man said, tipping his cap. "I was just about to leave your mail with Mrs. Harper, but as you're here now, I can deliver it to you. Any idea how much longer you'll be with James and Ruby? I can start bringing your mail to you there if it's going to be long."

Pauline smiled in gratitude as she took the slim sheaf of letters. A couple of bills, something from her publisher, and an envelope addressed in her mother's distinctive script. Nothing to be ashamed of, but she was just as glad they wouldn't be subjected to Mrs. Harper's scrutiny.

"I hope I shall be returning here very soon," she said. She didn't bother wondering how Mr. Denney knew her current living situation. Not only did news travel fast in a small town, the mailman was usually the one carrying it.

That made her think again about Miss Lewis's letter. If anyone knew the return address, it would be Mr. Denney.

"Mr. Denney, a few days before Miss Lewis was killed, she received a letter from a Janet Arden. You don't happen to remember seeing that letter, do you, and if you do, would you remember the return address?"

"I'm not supposed to talk about post office business with just anyone, Miss Gray," Mr. Denney said, then winked. "But, as I expect you're helping the police solve her murder, just like you did with Bob Ferris, and that business Arabella Warren got mixed up in over in Clayton, you aren't just anybody. And if it helps catch whoever did *that* to Miss Lewis, I'm happy to help." He squinted off into the distance as though looking back through his memories. Pauline help her breath, not wanting to do anything to interfere with his ratiocination.

Mr. Denney slapped his thigh with his cap. "Got it! Don't remember the exact address, but it was from Saratoga Springs."

Pauline let out her breath. It wasn't as much as she had hoped, but at least it would help them narrow the search down.

"Whatever it was, it stirred up Miss Lewis, for certain," Mr. Denney continued. "She had a note all ready to go the next morning when I brought her mail. She wouldn't even put it in the box, handed it to me personally and said it was important it get delivered at once. I put it in my pocket, even, so's I wouldn't lose it in the bag—not that I've ever lost a letter yet, not in my thirty years doing this route, but I wanted to reassure her."

Pauline hardly dared ask this next question, but she had to know. "Do you remember who that note was addressed to?"

"Why, I surely do. I remember because when I got to the Bergers' house I got the letter out, all ready to deliver, and then those Ingersoll and Addison scamps came running out of nowhere and crashed into me, knocking me right over!" Mr. Denney rubbed his back and grimaced. "The eldest Ingersoll lad there at least had the decency to apologize and help me up, but it took ages to get all the mail collected again, and much of it covered in mud and not fit to be seen! I would have given those boys a good hiding if they were mine, but everyone knows Mrs. Addison won't let anyone raise a hand against her boys, and Jim Addison is too soft with her by half to take a firm stand. Those Ingersoll boys aren't half so bad on their own, but put them with the Addison kids and—whew!"

"Yes, but Miss Lewis's letter," Pauline prompted. She didn't much care about poor parenting choices or misbehaving children.

"Yes, Miss, that's what I'm telling you. It was at the Berger house that they knocked it out of my hand."

Mrs. Harper chose that moment to bustle out of the house and join them on the front steps. "I declare, Al Denney, you would get through your mail route twice as fast if you didn't insist on stopping and chatting with every—oh, Miss Gray! I didn't see you there. Have you come back to stay again? The apartment is all ready except the beds. I can't think what is taking Mr. Berger so long with your clean linens."

Pauline's vague dread crystallized in her stomach. "The sheets! Of course!"

Mrs. Harper and Mr. Denney stared at her with near-identical expressions of incomprehension.

"Mrs. Harper, you said you had heard Mr. Berger's truck that morning—the morning the apartment was vandalized—and you thought he was delivering the linens."

"Yes, but obviously he must have been collecting them," Mrs. Harper said.

Pauline shook her head. "He couldn't have been, because he collected them the day before. I remember, because he and I had a little chat about the German language for some, er, research I was doing." Research for her current novel, since Emma Daring's adversary in this one was a former German soldier made bitter by his country's loss in the war, and Pauline had wanted to make sure she got the bits of German interspersed with his English correct.

Mrs. Harper's brow wrinkled as she tried to figure this out. "But if he'd already collected the linens, and he wasn't delivering them, what was he doing here that day?"

That was the question indeed.

A letter from Miss Lewis to the Bergers, one so important the former schoolteacher wanted it delivered by hand. The laundry truck heard both at the murder scene and Pauline's apartment.

Things were not looking good for Heinrich Berger. Yet Pauline still could not believe that kindly man could harm anyone, much less commit murder.

"Thank you, Mrs. Harper, Mr. Denney," she said, hardly knowing what she was saying. "Good day."

The gloves and stockings would have to wait. She needed to know what Mr. Berger had said to James.

Pauline walked the rest of the way to the police station without seeing any of the scenery or even the people she passed. Her mind worked furiously. There had to be a mistake somewhere. The pieces seemed to all fit together... but the picture wasn't right. She simply couldn't put her finger on why it was wrong.

That bothered her almost as much as the thought of Heinrich Berger being a murderer. Pauline solved her puzzles through logic and deduction, not instinct and hunches. So why did she feel so certain things didn't add up here? There had to be a reason, if only she could work her way toward it.

James was in the police station, located in the lower levels of the Opera Theatre, when Pauline arrived. His face was set in lines of weariness and frustration, echoing her own feelings.

"Heinrich Berger says his truck was 'not available for his use' that morning, but he won't say why or in what way," he greeted her abruptly. "His wife says the same, and she also won't give a clear answer. The darn thing about it is I'm tempted to believe them. They seem to be protecting somebody, but who? Mrs. Berger's sister? I can't see them being willing to risk Berger going to jail for anyone less than family, but neither can I see Miss Hertz committing murder."

Pauline's own face felt dragged down by her worry. "It gets worse." She told him her own news from Mrs. Harper and Mr. Denney.

James rubbed his forehead. "So the murderer—whoever it was—drove to Miss Lewis's house in the truck, killed her, ransacked the house for whatever-it-was he was looking for, and when he didn't find it drove over to your house to search there for it, and then calmly drove back to the Bergers' place and… did what? If it was Berger or one of the womenfolk, did they just go back to their normal routine? If it was someone else that they are protecting, where is that person now, and why in tarnation would the Bergers be protecting them?"

"Have you searched the truck?"

James nodded. "We confiscated it. Wallace is going over it with a fine tooth comb now. The chief thinks we ought to arrest Berger now, that there's enough evidence pointing to him as our culprit that motive doesn't matter."

Pauline shook her head mutely, but couldn't think up an argument against it.

"Of course, if what Denney said is true—and it likely is, knowing him—that could give us our motive. Pity we couldn't find that letter, but no doubt the killer destroyed it. Still, I'll have the chief contact the

Saratoga Springs police and we'll find that Janet Arden, and she ought to be able to tell us herself what was in the letter. It's only a matter of time now before the motive comes to light." James rose from his chair, stretched, and reached for his jacket. "For now, let's go home. There's not much more I can do here now."

The trip back to the house was silent. Pauline was still trying to think of a way to explain away everything pointing to Mr. Berger as the killer, and James didn't seem inclined toward conversation, either. As they entered the farmhouse, he at last cleared his throat and spoke again.

"I know you don't like to think of Berger as a murderer, Pauline, but at this point I don't see how we can justify looking for anyone else. The chief wants this settled, and everything points to Berger." He shifted his eyes to avoid Pauline's gaze. "Enough people here remember the war that it won't go overly well with him if it goes to trial. Most folk like the Bergers, but it would be easier to blame a German than to admit one of us could have committed such a violent and senseless murder."

Pauline's lips pressed into a thin line. "And here I thought this was one place that rose above that sort of narrow-minded prejudice. I suppose that means I'm not really 'one of you' either? Not unless our parents and grandparents were born here, is that it?"

"That's not what I meant!" James protested, but he still wouldn't meet Pauline's eyes.

Ruby had entered the foyer by this point, wanting to see what was keeping her husband and their guest. She shook her head and rested a hand on Pauline's sleeve. "That isn't entirely fair, my friend. Yes, we have our share of prejudices here, who doesn't?" She smiled ruefully. "My grandmother had a few stories to tell about the difficulties of being an Iroquois woman married to a white man. My mother had to put up with her share of whispers and snubbing. But I barely ever hear a whisper about my ancestry, and Jeremy's friends think it's 'neat' that his great-grandmother was an honest-to-goodness 'Injun.' Sometimes things do improve." She sighed. "Sometimes they don't. I don't think there's any place or person that lives up to its own ideals. But isn't the important thing that we keep trying?"

Pauline released a breath and her anger at the same time. Ruby was right, of course. She wished she weren't, but there was no place on earth that was perfect. Overall, the good still outweighed the bad here.

"Thank you," she said.

Then she frowned. Something Ruby had said has sparked a vague notion in her brain. What was it?

Unreasonable prejudice… whispers and snubs… the way things used to be…

Nothing hung together yet, but she thought that perhaps somewhere in the murky dimness they had been stumbling through so far a little light was starting to glimmer.

"James, I don't know who it is Mr. Berger is protecting, or why, but I am convinced that he is innocent, as are Mrs. Berger and Miss Hertz."

Before he could answer, yet another figure appeared at the open door, and a new voice joined the conversation.

"I am pleased to hear you say that, Miss Gray. I believe I can give some explanation of my brother-in-law's silence."

New Information

Miss Klara Hertz stood before them, dressed in her Sunday best of a navy suit with a crisp white blouse beneath and a Panama hat covering her hair. She turned her attention to Ruby before anyone could react.

"I apologize for coming in unannounced, Mrs. Richardson, but I am in great distress for my brother-in-law."

Ruby recovered her aplomb. "Of course, Miss Hertz. You have no need to apologize. Please, come in."

She ushered the three of them into the little-used parlor and vanished back into the kitchen, likely to see if her supper could be saved and stretched for an extra guest. Miss Hertz sat on the extreme edge of the horsehair sofa, her back ramrod straight. She didn't do anything so *gauche* as twist a handkerchief in her hands, but by their very stillness as they lay folded in her lap she gave evidence of her distress. Pauline didn't think she'd ever seen Miss Hertz when her hands were still—she was always busy at some task or another, mending or knitting or chopping vegetables or weeding the garden. It seemed wrong for her hands to be so idle.

"My sister and brother believe his truck was borrowed by the Addison and Ingersoll children that morning, and they do not wish to get them in trouble for a harmless prank," she began abruptly.

James whipped out his notepad and pencil and began furiously scribbling. "Hold on a minute there, Miss Hertz. Start at the beginning."

Miss Hertz drew in a deep breath and obliged. "That morning, when Heinrich went to do his usual round, the truck was gone. You know we are neighbors to both the Addisons and the Ingersolls, yes?"

"I do," Pauline put in. "I saw your sister at the Ingersolls this morning when I was out there. And—yes, she *did* say the children had played a nasty trick on her husband the morning of the murder."

James turned his head to look at her. "That would have been helpful for you to remember before," he commented mildly.

"But I didn't know it was in relation to the truck," she protested. "Not until just now. One doesn't tend to associate childish pranks with a stolen truck, murder, and attempted theft."

He acknowledged this with a nod and they both turned their attention back to Miss Hertz.

"Mrs. Addison and Mrs. Ingersoll take it in turns to watch each other's children once a week so the other lady can do her grocery shopping and other such things in peace. The youngsters are always in some sort of mischief when they get together. You know how children are."

James had to smooth away a reminiscent smile as he nodded in agreement, likely recalling some of his own childhood pranks.

"The eldest Ingersoll boy has been driving a tractor since before he was old enough to reach the pedals and see out the front at the same time. He considers himself an expert driver by this point. He 'borrowed' Heinrich's truck once before. His father punished him severely for it, and he said he would never do it again, but when Heinrich went out and saw that the truck was gone, and recalled that it was the day for Mrs. Addison to watch all the children, he believed they must have taken it again. As it was returned later in the day with no scratches or damage, he decided not to say anything. Now he does not wish to put the children under suspicion, so he continues to say nothing."

"But you don't agree," James said.

Miss Hertz's eyes were a very deep, very calm blue. She turned them on James as she answered, "I do not wish to protect anyone at the expense of my brother-in-law's life. He is a good man. But also I do not agree that the children were the ones to take the truck, and so I do not consider that I am endangering them by speaking."

"Who do you think took it, then?" James asked, pencil poised eagerly.

"I do not know. But I did not think it was the children even at the time."

"Why not?" Pauline spoke up, genuinely curious. She didn't either, mostly because the boys had told her they hadn't played any trick on Mr. Berger that day, but she wondered what Miss Hertz's reasoning was. Perhaps it wasn't strictly relevant to the matter at hand, but she wanted to know.

Miss Hertz turned to her. "Because they did it once. They do not like to repeat themselves, those young ones. A trick played once and paid for in full is a trick that is no longer amusing."

Pauline didn't know much about children, but that seemed like sound logic, and it fit with what the lads had told her. From the way James was nodding it appeared he agreed as well.

"Can you tell me anything about when and how the truck was returned?" he asked now.

Miss Hertz shook her head. "It must have been in the middle of luncheon. When we sat down to eat, the truck was not there, and when we left the table, it was. The kitchen is at the back of the house, so we would not have seen or heard anyone bringing it back."

"A pity," James said. "Perhaps the Addisons or Ingersolls might know more—or no, not Mrs. Ingersoll. She would have been out running errands, correct? Mrs. Addison, then."

He stopped speaking abruptly, and his eyes met Pauline's over Miss Hertz's head. She guessed that the same notion that had struck her had also struck him.

Mrs. Ingersoll...?

Pauline's brain shifted into sensational novelist mode. What if the farm didn't properly belong to the Ingersolls? What if Tom Martens had left it to Anita Lewis in his will, and they had obtained it through underhanded means? What if the letter from Janet Arden contained proof of that? Would they kill in order to keep their home?

Farmers all over the country were losing their livelihoods, more and more every day. So far most folk in this region had managed to hang on, but it was getting harder and harder. A person absolutely might kill in order to protect their family's heritage, especially if the victim were an old woman and they could justify it to themselves by saying she was going to die soon anyway.

They might have thought themselves safe for years, until Pauline spoke at the sewing bee about the memoirs. Then Mrs. Ingersoll might have panicked, thinking the truth might be coming out after all these years, and that they had to stop the memoirs from going forward at all costs.

If Mr. Ingersoll was at the farm all day, then Mrs. Ingersoll would have been the one to do it. Deliver the children to her neighbor, steal the truck, drive to Miss Lewis's, hit her over the head, hurriedly search for the letter, leave due to the milkman coming, head to Pauline's on the chance that the letter might have ended up with her, and then back to drop the truck at the Bergers and collect her children in time for lunch.

Could a woman truly do that?

It seemed unfathomable, but Pauline knew that mothers could do almost anything when it came to protecting their children.

But then how could she have been so calm and collected when

Pauline was there earlier? She certainly didn't act like a woman with a guilty conscience. Was she really that talented at dissembling? She had seemed so pleased at the idea of Pauline continuing with Miss Lewis's memoirs. If she was guilty, how could she be so composed?

And good heavens, if she were the murderer, how could they ever prove it?

"Miss Hertz," Pauline said, "did Mr. Denney deliver a note to anyone in your family from Miss Lewis the day before she was killed?"

Miss Hertz shook her head. "No. Had she written to us? Perhaps the letter was lost. The mail had been disrupted and was covered in mud when Mr. Denney did bring it to us."

"What are you thinking, Pauline?" James asked.

"You need to talk to Mr. Denney again," Pauline said. "Our conversation was interrupted by Mrs. Harper. He didn't actually say the note was to the Bergers, only that he had it in his hand when he was knocked into at their house." The garrulous old man enjoyed telling his stories, and could quite easily have been leading up to saying that the note was for Mrs. Ingersoll and he had only gotten ready to hand-deliver it to her at the Bergers.

"And what will you be doing?"

"I need to visit Mr. Crane once more." If the letter was the proof, then Pauline's notes had nothing to do with why her apartment was searched. And if *that* was the case that meant that the killer hadn't found the letter and destroyed it after all. Which meant that either Miss Lewis herself had destroyed it, or else it was still hidden somewhere in her house.

Saratoga Springs was a large city. It could take a long time for the police there to track down Janet Arden, and even then there was no guarantee she would be willing to tell them what was in her letter. Besides, what if she was a visitor to the area, not a resident? If there was any way to get the letter itself, they needed to take it.

James frowned. "You shouldn't be visiting him on your own, even if we are mostly certain he isn't the murderer. You aren't even supposed to be involved in this investigation!"

"I will accompany Miss Gray," announced Miss Hertz, rising to her feet. "If you say your chief wants to wrap this case up quickly even if it means blaming an innocent man, then it will take those of us who are not under his authority to discover the truth."

Pauline couldn't have stated it any better.

"How do I get myself into these sorts of messes?" James muttered with a sigh. "Very well. Just… please, be safe, ladies."

Pauline had cause to be thankful for the long June days as she and Miss Hertz left on their bicycles. She had a headlamp, but she was still nervous about cycling after dark.

Miss Hertz took the lead, and Pauline realized she was an expert on a bicycle. Her legs pumped smoothly and strongly, and she pulled well ahead of Pauline without the slightest appearance of strain. Proof, if any was needed, that she wouldn't have had to use her brother's truck if she'd wanted to get to Miss Lewis's house. She could have managed the bicycle ride with ease.

As she followed the older woman, Pauline's mind was free to range over the case again. The pieces seemed to be fitting together, but something was still not quite right. That idea that had started to emerge earlier, about prejudice and propriety and shunning… what had it been? It had been interrupted by Miss Hertz's arrival and everything seeming to point to Mrs. Ingersoll and the farm, but where had it been leading? Pauline couldn't help but feel somehow they had gotten off track.

There was something else, something about a girl, a girl who had stayed with Miss Lewis after bring thrown out of her family's house. Yes, that was right! Mrs. Addison had spoken about it, as had Mrs. MacNeill. An unwed mother, so Mrs. MacNeill had said and Mrs.

Addison hinted. Shocking and shameful, but Miss Lewis had taken her in out of kindness.

Now, why had she remembered that? What was it about that story that struck her as important? Surely that girl couldn't be connected to this death. So why had it come to mind when Pauline was thinking about secrets and shame? There had been no secret about that girl's child, clearly.

Pauline's thoughts scattered again as Miss Hertz expertly swooped to a stop in front of Miss Lewis's house. Pauline glanced at the big brick MacNeill house as she stopped behind Miss Hertz. Mrs. MacNeill was in her front garden, puttering about. She gave a little wave to Pauline, and didn't even pretend to not be watching them with avid curiosity.

Pauline returned the wave and looked in the other direction, toward the County Home and the few cows grazing on the field between that and Miss Lewis's house. They couldn't be making a mistake, could they? What if everything really was as simple as a man looking to escape the shame of the poorhouse, and willing to commit violence to do so?

There was that word again. *Shame.* Why did it keep sticking in her mind?

No time to dwell on it now—Mr. Crane had come out the front door to greet them.

"Welcome, ladies!" he said, his head tilted to one side a little quizzically. "It seems all of Canton wishes to pay its condolences on behalf of my aunt today. Mrs. Ingersoll and Mrs. Addison are already inside. Won't you join us?"

Mrs. Ingersoll! Pauline's heart jumped. Then the letter *must* be the key. It couldn't be a coincidence that she was here now. She must be attempting to find it before Mr. Crane could.

"Splendid," Miss Hertz said calmly. "Come, Miss Gray."

Pauline never would have imagined herself obeying someone else's command, but to her own astonishment she found herself trailing meekly after Miss Hertz even while her mind raced feverishly to try to concoct a plan for getting that letter before Mrs. Ingersoll could.

She only hoped it wasn't too late already.

Questions Answered

It was with mixed feelings that Pauline found herself walking through the front door of Miss Lewis's house. She had never come in this way before—always through the back, into the kitchen. As Mr. Crane ushered them into the living room, Pauline thought of how pleased Miss Lewis had been to show her this room, and even more so the library beyond it. No doubt Mr. Crane, who had so little time for reading, would dispose of all the books his aunt had collected so painstakingly over the years before he sold the house. What a loss!

To her surprise, Pauline did not feel haunted or squeamish as she walked into the very room where Miss Lewis had met her end. Indeed, the house felt very much as it always had: warm and welcoming, as though its owner was still hovering in it to make her guests comfortable, somewhere just out of sight. Mr. Crane had restored all the items to their former places, save for the flower vases that had been broken or damaged, and the house seemed at peace with itself still.

Insensibly, Pauline felt her mind calm and her nerves steady even as her eyes fell on Mrs. Ingersoll in one of the wingback chairs, with Mrs. Addison tucked into the other. She almost felt Miss Lewis pat her on the shoulder, encouraging her for the task to come.

"It was lucky for all you ladies that you came today," Mr. Crane said, showing Miss Hertz and Pauline to the small sofa. He left the room briefly and returned with a wooden chair from the dining room, sitting on that so as to leave the more comfortable seats for his guests. "I finished my inventory of the house just this morning, and I'll be putting everything up for auction as soon as the police say I may."

An auction! Pauline's heart sank. All of Miss Lewis's precious memories, scattered across the county to people who cared only for their monetary value. She sternly returned her thoughts to the matter at hand.

"You must have found a great many interesting items in your aunt's possessions," Miss Hertz said. "She led such a full life."

"A simple and quiet one, if you ask me," Mr. Crane corrected her. "A few trinkets saved from her parents and grandparents, or given to her by her students, and more books than anyone could ever read in a lifetime. No, I doubt it will bring much at auction, but every little bit helps." He sighed heavily, though none of the women present seemed inclined to share in his self-pity.

How could Pauline bring the conversation around to Miss Lewis's papers without alerting Mrs. Ingersoll? Where would Miss Lewis have been most likely to store the letter?

"I should dearly like to see her books," Miss Hertz continued. "I do not read much, myself—there is always so much work to do!—but sometimes, I do enjoy a good book. In winter, *ja*, when the time has slowed? One cannot knit all the time, after all."

The other women laughed, and Pauline marveled at how well her companion was doing.

"Of course!" said Mr. Crane, springing up and crossing to the library door. "All of you, come in and look, if you like."

"Actually, Mr. Crane, what I would most like to see would be some of Miss Lewis's old photos," said Mrs. Ingersoll. Pauline, about to enter the library, halted abruptly. Old photos...?

Mrs. Ingersoll continued. "Cathy and I were just talking about it on our way here—how Miss Lewis kept so many photographs of all her students, and how we'd like to remember our time with her as our teacher."

Now why would Mrs. Ingersoll want old photographs? Unless that was an excuse, just as the books were for Miss Hertz, and she wanted a chance to rummage around looking for the letter. Or was there another reason?

"Naturally," said Mr. Crane. "Of course you would! Aunt Anita kept most of her photographs in the library as well."

Most of them… but not all. Pauline distinctly remembered Miss Lewis showing her a photo of her former students that she kept in the dining room. She opened her mouth to say so—and then closed it again. What if there really was another reason for wanting an old photograph?

Pauline hung back as the others went into the library, with Mr. Crane leading the way. Mrs. Addison stopped before entering, waving to Pauline to go on ahead of her.

"No, no," Pauline murmured, inclining her head and hoping it would be taken for politeness—the younger woman allowing her elders to go first. "After you, Mrs. Addison."

"No, please," said Mrs. Addison. "You must be terribly fond of books, after all. I'm such a dunce, there's little there to interest me."

The battle of courtesies was broken by Mrs. Ingersoll.

"Oh Cathy, come and look! Here's one from when we were just starting at the high school. Goodness, how scrawny you were! Why do I always remember you as plump?"

Slowly, reluctantly, Mrs. Addison walked into the library to obey Mrs. Ingersoll's imperative summons. Pauline waited only a heartbeat or two more, just long enough to ensure no one was watching her through the open doorway, and then darted into the dining room to look at the whatnot.

Yes, there it was, just as she remembered, a silver-framed photograph of one of Miss Lewis's final classes. Only it wasn't exactly as she remembered—it was crooked in the frame, as though it had been removed and replaced clumsily. Pauline recalled Miss Lewis's comments on her arthritic fingers. What if she had placed something behind the photo in the frame, and had not been able to put the photograph back as neatly as she would have wished?

Moving quickly now, no dithering or doubt hindering her actions, Pauline turned the frame over to remove the back. A thrill zipped through her body as the back came away to reveal a neatly folded piece of stationery. Pauline carefully set the frame down on the whatnot and unfolded the paper. She glanced first at the signature: *Janet Arden.*

She had found the letter.

It had been Pauline's intention to slip the letter into her handbag and turn it over to James without reading it—she recoiled from the idea of reading someone else's private correspondence, and it was the police's business, not hers—but now that it came down to it, she couldn't help herself.

Dear Miss Lewis,

Please forgive a stranger for writing to you like this, but I do not know where else to turn. My mother passed away last month, and left me a letter informing me that I was adopted as a baby, and that you were the woman who arranged the adoption. I would like to find the woman who gave me birth—

Before Pauline had a chance to read any further, a sharp voice interrupted her.

"What are you doing with that? Is that a letter? Where did you get that? Give it to me!"

Pauline looked up to see—not Mrs. Ingersoll, but Mrs. Addison, advancing on her with an outstretched hand and a pinched look on her face as she glanced from the stationery in Pauline right hand to the photograph frame in her left.

"Give me that letter!" she repeated. Pauline clutched the letter close to her chest and backed away, mind spinning.

Mrs. Addison…?

Scraps of conversation and memories began falling into place in her mind. Mrs. Ingersoll commenting on how skinny Cathy Addison was at the start of their high school years, yet her memories of her were always of her being plump… hearing after the sewing bee how strict Mrs. Addison's parents had been… Mrs. Addison blindly defending her son to Officer Wallace… Miss Lewis taking in a young unwed mother despite the scandal of it all… the Ingersoll boys eagerly telling how they and the Addison boys had been allowed to play unsupervised the morning of the murder…

Not Mrs. Ingersoll trying to protect her family's farm. Not any of the Bergers for reasons unknown. Not Mrs. MacNeill or her son, not Samuel Crane.

No, the heart of this crime was Mrs. Addison, protecting a deep and scandalous secret that she could never let out for fear of the damage it would do to her reputation, fear of losing her husband's respect and her sons' love. Even if, as their friends and neighbors claimed, they all loved her blindly and devotedly, her upbringing meant that she could never quite trust that love. So she would do anything, even kill, to keep it, and to keep her upright reputation in town.

While all this was whirling through Pauline's mind, Mrs. Addison had snatched up the poker from the fireplace and was brandishing it at Pauline.

"*Give me the letter,*" she repeated again, her voice low and hard.

For one horrible moment, Pauline almost complied, so urgent was the demand, but her body was moving away before her mind caught up. If this was Miss Lewis's murderer, no matter what her motivation—no,

Pauline could not let her escape justice, no matter what the cost to herself!

Pauline thought she knew now what the rest of the letter said, but she couldn't give it up—it was the only scrap of evidence that existed against Cathy Addison for Miss Lewis's murder. Though the fact that Mrs. Addison was willing to attack her with a poker in front of witnesses might stand as evidence enough, she supposed.

Those witnesses now spilled out of the library to stare at the scene playing out before their eyes: Pauline, breath coming quickly and a mist rising up before her eyes, stumbling over her own feet as she moved backward from the relentlessly advancing Mrs. Addison.

"My dear madam!" blustered Mr. Crane. "What on earth is the matter?"

"Cathy, for heaven's sake!" Mrs. Ingersoll chimed in.

Mrs. Addison paid no attention to either of them. She continued menacing Pauline, who was now backed right up against the wall, letter clutched to her chest, with nowhere else to go.

Miss Hertz wasted neither time nor breath in remonstrating. She took two long strides to reach Mrs. Addison's side, and with her strong hands wrenched the poker away from the other woman. Mrs. Addison whirled on her.

"No!" she shrieked. "I have to have it! No one must read it! No one must know!" She turned back to Pauline, eyes glittering and cheeks bright red, and attacked with only her bare hands, striking indiscriminately as she tried to wrench the paper from Pauline's grasp. "Give it to me, you interfering busybody! Why did you have to come poking your nose into everything?"

Under normal circumstances, Pauline could have fended off the wild attack, but she was hampered by her need to protect the letter from being torn. She hunched in on herself, curling her entire body around the letter she still clutched in her hand, head ducked down in an attempt to escape the worst of the blows. In her dizzied mind was only one thought: justice for Miss Lewis.

"Call the police," she heard Miss Hertz command, and then she was freed from the attack, uncurling to see Miss Hertz holding Mrs. Addison with her arms pinioned at her sides. Even now, Mrs. Addison struggled to free herself, kicking Miss Hertz's shins and attempting to wrench loose. Mr. Crane was nowhere in sight—presumably he had obeyed Miss Hertz's order to telephone the police—and Mrs. Ingersoll stood frozen, hands pressed to her mouth in horror.

"Mrs. Addison," Pauline began, and stopped, helplessly. What could she say?

"I have nothing to say to you," Mrs. Addison snarled. "You have no right to go snooping about in other people's affairs!"

Pauline swallowed and began again. "We all have things we're ashamed of." She was thinking not only of Mrs. Addison's secret then, but her own, but Mrs. Addison reacted before she could say anything more.

"You don't know what you're talking about! How dare you? Be quiet!"

Pauline would have liked to be quiet, but she couldn't. However ugly this was, the truth had to be told. "Miss Anita Lewis knew the secret you were keeping, didn't she? In fact, she was the one who enabled you to keep it a secret. But you couldn't let it rest. The knowledge ate away at you, and it started twisting you up inside. Instead of trusting that your secret was safe with Miss Lewis, you started believing that knowing that secret gave her power over you. You were afraid, afraid that someday she might tell the truth. Perhaps she would even tell it to the journalist who was helping her write her memoirs. Perhaps those memoirs would be published, and then everyone would know the truth. The secret would no longer be safe."

Pauline held up the letter. Mrs. Addison lunged forward again, only to come up short against Miss Hertz's unyielding grip. "That might not have been enough on its own for you to kill her. But then this letter arrived. A letter, I believe, from a daughter looking for the mother who had given her up many years ago. The daughter didn't know who that mother was, but she did know the name of the woman who helped her mother—Miss Lewis. And so she wrote, asking Miss Lewis for her mother's identity. Miss Lewis in turn sent you a note, telling you of the letter and asking to speak with you about it." This last bit was guesswork, but it made sense, and Pauline didn't want to show Mrs. Addison just how shaky the foundation of this reconstruction was. She believed this was how it had to have played out, but if she started asking questions to confirm her belief rather than stating facts, Mrs. Addison still might try to twist out of the truth.

"And so you came, early in the morning, sending your boys out to play with the Ingersoll lads, using Heinrich Berger's truck so no one would know it was you, and you killed Miss Lewis in order to prevent her from ever revealing the truth to your daughter, or anyone else."

"No!" Mrs. Addison said.

"You left our boys unsupervised?" Mrs. Ingersoll demanded, latching onto the least important revelation. "How could you?"

"No," Mrs. Addison repeated. "I was home all morning. I wasn't here!"

"You were not home," Miss Hertz contradicted. "I walked across the road after Heinrich's truck went missing and knocked on your door to ask if you saw who took it, and you were not there."

Mrs. Ingersoll blinked.

"*You?*" Mrs. Ingersoll whispered. "You let our children play together in the woods while you went and—*killed* her? You killed Miss Lewis? Why? For heaven's sake, why?"

Speech poured out of Mrs. Addison all at once like water from a fountain, and she jabbed her chin in Pauline's direction. "It was her fault, not mine! That Miss Gray, always poking her nose in other people's business. All these years, Miss Lewis kept my secret, but she was getting old, her memory was getting shaky, how could I trust that she wouldn't forget how important it was? What if she slipped? Then she sent me that note, telling me about the letter. I couldn't risk it. What if she decided it was her duty to tell? I would have lost everything! I had to do it. I had to. She was old, she would have died soon enough anyway. It's not my fault. None of it has been my fault. I didn't want the baby in the first place. I was just a girl! I didn't understand. I trusted Miss Lewis to make it go away. She helped me hide it from my family and everyone else, had me go stay with a friend of hers downstate for the last few months and the birth. She even found a home for the baby after it was born. I thought I could trust her, I thought it was safe. But I couldn't risk it. I couldn't risk her telling about it. What would everyone think? What would my husband say? What about my boys? I would be shamed forever. I had to do it. I didn't have a choice. It was all her fault." She sneered at Pauline. "Why couldn't you have stayed in Albany where you belong?"

With one brutal twist, she wrenched herself from Miss Hertz's grasp. But this time she didn't come for Pauline—instead she lunged for the front door, pulling it open and racing outside. The other three women tripped over each other in their dash to follow, with Mr. Crane on their heels. They heard a wild wail and the screech of a braking automobile, but only Miss Hertz was close enough to the open door to see what happened.

"Ach, it is the police! They have nearly run her over… no, she escaped, and she is running across the field toward the river. Lieutenant Richardson is chasing her, as is the younger one."

Pauline abruptly turned away. She didn't want to see what she was afraid was about to happen.

"The river?" Mrs. Ingersoll whispered. "But Cathy can't swim…"

Was it Pauline's imagination, or did she hear a splash, as of someone jumping into the water?

"Lieutenant Richardson has jumped in after her," Miss Hertz confirmed. She turned aside and closed the door. "But I do not think he will be able to save her."

Mr. Crane mopped his forehead with his handkerchief. "Bless my soul," he said in a shaking voice. "Bless my soul."

James and Wallace returned to the house a short time later, dripping wet and somber with the news that they could not save Mrs. Addison, and there was no more time for reflection as the story had to be told once more, and the letter, at last, handed over for safekeeping to the police.

"I remember now," Mrs. Ingersoll said in a quiet voice. "I remember that summer. We all thought Cathy had gotten fat as the school year ended, but none of us knew why. Nor did we ever question it when she had slimmed down by the time fall came. She did change after that, though. She'd been full of fun before then, but after that she was quieter, more withdrawn. Why did we never put it all together? And this poor soul—her daughter, you say, Miss Gray?—she only wanted to find her mother, and instead drove her to murder. Oh dear, oh dear."

"If murder was what she was willing to do to protect herself from shame, it would have happened regardless," Miss Hertz said in a hard voice. "No one else is responsible for Mrs. Addison's actions, save she alone."

Pauline couldn't quite agree with that sentiment. Yes, ultimately responsibility rested on Mrs. Addison's shoulders. But the way she was raised must have played a role in her actions, as well as the sure knowledge that she would have been shunned by the community should her deed ever come to light. What was that John Donne quote? 'No man is an island entire of itself.'

In a way, they all had a hand in shaping each other. Miss Lewis's kindness had rippled out and brought peace and comfort to an entire community… and darker deeds brought loss and sorrow to the community as well. Seeds that sprouted and spread in the hotbed of secrecy and untruth.

Before she could think better of it, Pauline opened her mouth and spoke. "I know something of having a secret you wish to protect."

She had thought she would never reveal this to anyone, but Mrs. Hansen had been right when she spoke about secrets at the sewing bee. Secrets were poisonous. It was time to clear away the poison from Pauline's own life, and help all of them recover from the shock and horror of Mrs. Addison's desperate deeds.

"Shortly after my graduation from college, I found myself in a dilemma," she continued. "I had very few job prospects, and my choices seemed to be either find a husband or move back home to be with my parents. I did not want to do either—I loved this town and wanted to stay here, and I was not prepared to take on the responsibilities of being a housewife, even if someone had asked me to marry him, which in any case did not happen."

Mrs. Ingersoll leaned forward and patted her knee. "Give it time, dearie. With a pretty face like yours, you won't have to worry for long about being an old maid!"

Pauline drew in a deep breath and continued, ignoring this mistaken attempt at sympathy. She knew well enough that very few people believed she genuinely did not want a husband. That was not the point of this story. "I applied for a position at the *Watertown Daily Times*, but even if they accepted me, I knew my salary there would not be enough to live on. What I wanted to do more than anything was serious writing, academic writing. I loved to research different topics and then write about them; it was by far my favorite part of college. But it is not so easy to make a living from that, especially not if one is a woman. I was visiting a friend one day and happened to glance at the adventure novel her thirteen-year-old son was reading. 'I could do better than that,' I thought, and the next moment, I decided I would try, at least until something better came along."

Pauline could not believe she was about to do this. The only other person in the world who knew her secret was Sarah, who did not entirely understand why Pauline was so ashamed of her novels but respected her desire to keep them private. She pressed on.

"I dashed off a story in a few weeks and sent it to an editor, never thinking anything might come of it. To my shock, the editor wrote back and said he not only wanted to publish it, he would like to turn it into a series. At first I refused to consider it. I didn't think it was the kind of writing I ought to be doing. Not that there was any harm in it—I wouldn't write anything like that—but it wasn't academic enough. But it paid enough that I could pay rent and buy groceries, and so I signed the contract, but refused to affix my real name to the books. Aside from my roommate, no one else has ever known that I am the author of the Emma Daring books."

James slapped his knee. "Ha! I knew you were hiding something all these years. I'll admit, I never guessed that, though. Well done, Pauline."

Mrs. Ingersoll gasped, but she didn't seem shocked or horrified. "Why, my Charlie loves your books!" she blurted out. "Why wouldn't you tell people?"

"I kept it a secret all this time because I was ashamed," Pauline explained. "I didn't want my former professors and fellow students to know I was writing what all of us would have considered 'tripe.' And the longer I kept it a secret, the more important it became to continue to keep it a secret. That's what secrets do. They take over your life and take on a monumental importance, and eventually you will be willing to do almost anything to keep them buried. Just like Mrs. Addison."

That sobered her listeners, reminding them of the real reason they were all here.

"Willing to murder," James said. "And not only that, but to cast blame on others. Miss Hertz, I believe we owe your brother an apology."

"It was a logical assumption, given everything," the German woman said graciously. "I am not entirely certain of one thing, though—did she burglarize Miss Gray's home to find her memoir notes or look for the letter?"

"Both, I would think," James said. "Since she couldn't find the letter here, she thought she'd check there and make sure there was nothing in the notes that could give away her secret. Well, well, it's a sad story all the way around. Mr. Crane, we'll leave you to your home now."

"Er—yes," Mr. Crane said, still shaken by it all. "Thank you. Goodness me, how will I ever find a buyer now?" he exclaimed, as though struck by the sudden thought. "First Aunt Anita, and then her murderer? It will have a terrible reputation! No one will want to live here!"

In the midst of her weariness and sorrow, it seemed Pauline still had room for grief over that thought. Despite the ugliness that had happened here, she still loved this home—the peace that Miss Lewis had spread from here far outweighed the violence that had happened. Even if Pauline had believed in ghosts, she would have known instinctively that there could be no unhappy ghosts haunting this home.

A thought brushed across her mind. At first she dismissed it as not appropriate for the moment, but it returned, and at last she promised herself she would consider it more carefully once everything was settled. Perhaps this home did not need to be abandoned to decay and loneliness after all.

Outside, James turned to Pauline. "You were both right and wrong about Al Denney. Right in that the note wasn't for the Bergers, but it wasn't for Mrs. Ingersoll, either. It was for Mrs. Addison. I was just about ready to come out here anyway to see if you'd found the letter when Crane telephoned the station. Wallace and I got out here as quick as we could. Not quick enough, as it turned out." He sighed. "Still, I suppose Mrs. Addison preferred it this way. She spared her family the shame of seeing her on trial. And from what you say, I don't think she could have lived with the knowledge that her secret was revealed to the world."

"No," Pauline said softly. "I don't think she could."

"Speaking of secrets…" James said, making a visible effort to shake off his grim mood. "I can't believe you never told any of us that you are a famous author! I did wonder about seeing those papers on your floor, but you were so gol-darned insistent on your privacy I didn't allow myself to speculate. Say, Jeremy is going to be thrilled. He loves those Emma Daring stories. For that matter, I've been known to enjoy one on a Sunday afternoon myself."

"I think they're swell!" blurted Officer Wallace. "In fact, uh…"

"Spit it out, Wallace," James said good-naturedly.

Wallace reached into the backseat of the police car and pulled out a paperback novel, the cover of which featured a young woman in trousers and a motoring coat crossing a deep chasm on a rickety rope bridge while a villain fired a gun at her from behind some boulders on the far side. He held it out to Pauline and blurted,

"Would you mind signing this for me? It's my favorite."

Pauline wasn't sure whether she should laugh or cry. In the end, she did neither. Instead, she pulled her ever-present pen from the bottom of her handbag, and for the first time in her life, gravely signed her name across the front page of an Emma Daring novel.

A New Beginning

Three months passed before Pauline stood in front of Miss Lewis's house again. This time she wasn't alone. Sarah, long since returned from her visit to her family in Philadelphia, stood beside her, and Klara Hertz was on her other side. Behind them was Heinrich Berger's old truck filled with boxes of their possessions and a few small pieces of furniture. Though the roses were long since past, the asters shone like purple stars in the mellow golden light of late summer, and the apples on the tree in the backyard were starting to blush rosily as they moved toward ripeness.

A great deal had happened in the preceding weeks. After long arguments with herself, and even longer discussions with Sarah, Pauline had finally approached the bank about a loan to purchase a house. The revelation of her identity as the author of the Emma Daring novels had, surprisingly, helped her here. With the assurance of the books bringing her in a steady income, even more than her newspaper column, the bank had been happy to loan her the necessary money.

The next step was approaching Samuel Crane. He had been so relieved at the thought of a buyer who wasn't frightened away by the violent death that had happened in the house that he had let it go for a relative song. It seemed his irritation the day Pauline had spoken to him about his aunt's death had been at the prospect of being saddled with a house he couldn't sell because no one would feel comfortable in it.

Next Pauline had contracted a builder to add a small addition to one side of the house, just enough for one more bedroom, this one on the ground floor.

When the builders finally finished, Miss Hertz, Mrs. Berger, and Mrs. MacNeill came in with such an array of buckets, rags, mops, and cleaning solutions that it made Pauline's head spin. Those good women refused to take any payment for their work, saying it was the least they could do to thank Pauline for searching past the obvious and discovering the truth of the murder.

And now, at last, it was ready.

Her very own home.

At first, Pauline had wanted Sarah to co-own the house, but her friend had refused.

"Someday I might want to get married, and then we'd have the bother of having to settle which one of us got the house, and that one buying it from the other," she pointed out. "And frankly, I'm not sure I like the idea of the responsibility of being a homeowner. I'd much rather leave it to my landlord—or landlady—to take care of house repairs and the hundred and one little things that always need taking care of in a house." She grinned at her friend.

Then Pauline had offered to simply let Sarah live there and share in daily expenses, but Sarah would have none of that, either.

"If I stay, I pay my own way, same as I have done here," she said firmly.

Pauline was stubborn, but Sarah was more stubborn yet, and so in the end, Pauline yielded. Sarah had the second upstairs bedroom and paid Pauline for room and board. In truth, the money was welcome, as Pauline was indeed finding that being a homeowner was already putting more strain on her purse than she had anticipated.

The third member of their new trio was the reason for the builders. Pauline was determined to keep this house as lovely as Miss Lewis had made it, and she knew she was not capable of doing so on her own, nor even with Sarah, as both were working women and neither was inclined to give up her leisure hours to housework. Pauline recalled Mrs. Berger speaking of her sister's restlessness in living with them as well as Miss Hertz's own admission that she did not want to live alone even though she found life with her sister and brother-in-law dull, and had tentatively offered Miss Hertz a job as live-in housekeeper and cook.

She had been afraid Miss Hertz would take offense at being offered such menial work by a younger woman, but instead Miss Hertz leapt at the opportunity.

"I like a clean house, a well-tended garden, and good food," she said. "It brings me satisfaction. My sister keeps her own house well, even with the laundry, and I always felt unnecessary there. Here, I can tell you will need me. And—you will let me sit with you sometimes in the evenings, to talk or to listen to the radio together?"

Pauline assured her with perfect truthfulness that she would be more than welcome, and Miss Hertz nodded, her strong features creasing into a wide smile.

"Then I will be very happy. I will have good work to do, and I will not be lonely. What more can a woman ask?"

Pauline couldn't have put it better herself.

Now here they were, ready to move in. Pauline looked down at the key in her hand, marveling. Before she could get too lost in amazement, Sarah nudged her.

"Shall we go in, or do you want to stand out here all day?"

Her tone was teasing but affectionate. Pauline smiled at her, appreciating again what a good friend she was.

"Let's go in," she said.

They walked down the path to the front door, sensing this was one occasion at least where entering by way of the kitchen would be entirely out of place. Pauline inserted the key into the lock, turned it, gripped the doorknob, and opened the door.

Inside, the front hall sparkled, a testimony to the hard work of the three women who had cleaned it. Pauline wandered through the rooms in something of a daze, unable to believe all this was hers now.

The living room with the fireplace, the owl andirons left behind by Mr. Crane at Pauline's request… the perfect place for the three of them to sit in the evenings discussing events large and small, or to enjoy each other's company in silence as they all dreamed their own dreams. The dining room with its old-gold walls… perhaps one day to see friends and family sharing meals around the table, something Pauline never thought she would be able to achieve, or indeed even wish for. The cozy green kitchen… soon to be Miss Hertz's domain, though Pauline anticipated they all would spend a great deal of their time at the table in there. Upstairs, she marveled over the tub and toilet in her very own bathroom, and sighed in satisfaction at the blue and white walls of her bedroom, re-papered at her request by the builders while they were there.

She peeked into Sarah's bedroom, a symphony in yellow and buff, just long enough to assure herself everything was as her friend wanted it, likewise downstairs in Miss Hertz's small white bedroom, and at last allowed herself to open the door into the library.

She had insisted the books remain with the house when she bought it, and Mr. Crane, certain they would bring a mere pittance at auction, had agreed. Pauline trailed one hand along the bookcases as she made a circuit of the room. So many books! Not only for her to read, but for her to continue Miss Lewis's work of loaning out to others who might also take joy in them.

Here she would work, continuing with the Emma Daring novels, no longer her secret shame. They were what had allowed her to purchase this house… she would never hide them again, no matter how trite the writing of them seemed in comparison to the work she had once dreamed of doing. Here she would finish Miss Lewis's memoirs, even if they would never see publication, as a tribute to the woman who had done such good things in her unostentatious way with a life that would seem too small to so many people. Here Pauline would still allow herself to dream of doing greater work, even while she no longer bound her happiness to those dreams.

Sarah poked her head through the doorway. "I thought I'd find you here. We have company."

"What, already?" Pauline said, startled from her musings. "We haven't even unloaded the truck yet!"

Waiting by the front fence was what looked to Pauline's bemused gaze like an entire crowd of people. There were James, Ruby, and Jeremy, dressed in working clothes. There were Mrs. MacNeill and her son Angus, likewise ready to help. There was Mrs. Hansen with a covered basket, likely holding lunch for the workers. There were the Ingersolls, their Charlie already showing signs of wanting to scuffle with Jeremy. There was Iris Ferris, Ruby's sister-in-law from her first marriage. There was Arabella Warren, accompanied by her ward Jonathan, friends who Pauline had helped bring together just this past spring. Young Officer's Wallace's red head shone in the back of the crowd, and Pauline and Sarah's former landlady Mrs. Harper held a basket the twin of Mrs. Hansen's.

Pauline rested her hand on her heart as she fell back a step, stunned.

"You ladies didn't think we'd let you move in by yourself, did you?" James asked with an easy grin.

Pauline had to blink back sudden tears. It seemed she had become part of this community without even realizing it.

"Welcome," she said, after clearing her throat. "Welcome, all of you."

She had indeed come *home*.

ACKNOWLEDGMENTS

Many thanks to my editor and friend A. M. Offenwanger for her tireless work in making these stories the best they could possibly be and her championing of Pauline &co. Thanks are also due to Laura Rizzo and Samantha Johnson, for reading these stories in their earlier stages and helping to make them what they are now; to Carl Ayers for proofreading and continual encouragement, as well as being my driver when exploring all the back roads of Canton in an effort to find the perfect spot for Miss Lewis's house; to Kevin Bates for his support and willingness to answer all my questions no matter how random; to Linda Casserly, the Canton Town and Village Historian, for her help in pointing me toward resources (and for maintaining the wonderful Facebook page with all its old photographs); and to all the people on Twitter and Facebook who said YES when I asked if anyone would read a story about a woman detective in northern New York in the 1930s.

About the Author

Louise Bates is the alter ego of fantasy/sci-fi author E.L. Bates. She lives on the New England coast with her husband and children. When she is not writing she can usually be found reading, knitting, or exploring the nearby woods and shoreline.

You can connect with me on:

🌐 https://www.stardancepress.com

Subscribe to my newsletter:

✉ https://stardancepress.com/how-to-contact